Horizon Crossover Series (Book I)

Horizon Shift

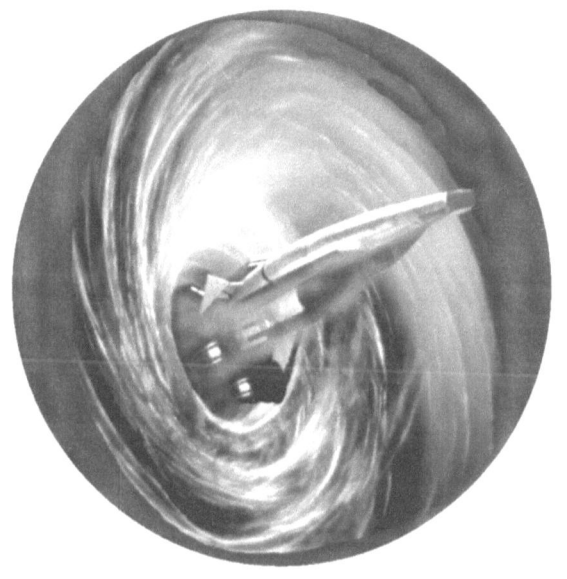

Lyndi Alexander

Science Fiction Novel from
Dragonfly Publishing, Inc.

HORIZON SHIFT
Horizon Crossover Series (Book I)
Science Fiction Novel
Released in 2013

Hardback Edition
EAN 978-1-936381-53-1
ISBN 1-936381-53-2

Paperback Edition
EAN 978-1-936381-54-8
ISBN 1-936381-54-0

eBook Edition
EAN 978-1-936381-55-5
ISBN 1-936381-55-9

Story Text ©2012 Barbara Mountjoy
Cover & Illustrations ©2014 Dragonfly Publishing, Inc.
Dragonfly Logo ©2001 Terri L. Branson

Published in the United States of America by
Dragonfly Publishing, Inc.
Website: www.dragonflypubs.com

Dedication

For Eric, who always wanted to see this story told.

Acknowledgements:

With grateful thanks for everyone who's made this series come to life, including Kellie, Katrina, Eric, Dacie, Luc, Sue and the other member of Maquis Universal who played these characters and helped flesh them out.

Special thanks to my Pennwriters critique crew; Paul, Jean, Gene, Dave, Tom, Jeff, and Todd. Also, to fellow writer Hank Henley for input on my father-son conflict and the rest of the story.

And as always, thanks to Glenda Tudor and Terri Branson for loving the science fiction and fantasy and letting me be part of that publishing world.

Characters and Terms

DOUBTFUL:
Aronka: Bellonan shape-shifting security guard on the *Doubtful*
Brown, Riviera: Second Science Officer on the *Doubtful*
Eddy, Parnell: Ensign on the *Doubtful*
Halian (Hal): Assistant Engineer on the *Doubtful*
Hudson: Security, Gunner on the *Doubtful*
Jamar, Dani (D): Chief Engineer on the *Doubtful*
Jerome, Jerry: Ensign on the *Doubtful*
Montgomery, Heath: Ship's Doctor on the *Doubtful*
Quinn, Benzi: Engineer Assistant on the *Doubtful*
Ramona (Rae): Science Officer on the *Doubtful*
Rogers, Temms: Captain of the *Doubtful*
Rogers, Thomas (Tommy): Chief of Security on the *Doubtful*
Tabio: Bellonan shape-shifting security guard on the *Doubtful*
Tasiq: Communications Officer on the *Doubtful*
Windthorp, Kai: Helm Officer on the *Doubtful*

MARRIEL:
Runyon, Oke: Saloon owner on Marriel
Chen, Liang: Waitress from Marriel
Boro, Okalani: Runaway bride from Marriel

SOL AERIS:
Mosk: Personnel Officer at Sol Aeris
Flan, Gretta: Communications Specialist at Sol Aeris
Williams, Nim: Weapons Master at Sol Aeris

PERPETRA:
Lumina, The: Young girl in training to rule on Perpetra
Arlen, Prince: Grandfather of the Lumina on Perpetra
Rodolphus (Roddi): Liang's former instructor on Perpetra
Benjamin, Captain Stuart: Confederation pilot instructor on Perpetra

TERZA:
Klin, Rabal: minister on Terza
Hace: minor functionary on Terza
Tamala: Olesian liaison on Terza
Boy: Abandoned by the Olesians on Terza

OTHER CHARACTERS:
Burko, Jal: Confederation fleet commander allied with The Agency
Pomeroy, Darien: Captain of the *Victory*
Ankho, Kevan: Liang's former captain on the *Palva*
Rogers, Connie: Ex-wife of Temms Rogers
Alex and Linz: Twins belonging to Temms Rogers
Geoffrey: Okalani's jilted fiancé
Montgomery, Ada: Wife of Dr. Heath Montgomery
Edward, Jowalt: merchant dealer from Roandock

SPECIAL TERMS:
Lok cha: Deadly drug
Sprechan: A deity of sorts
Kiritan: cave dwellers on Lennor, fierce feline predators
Abril: a card game

* * *

Horizon Crossover Series

HORIZON SHIFT
(Book I)

HORIZON STRIFE
(Book II)

HORIZON DYNASTY
(Book III)

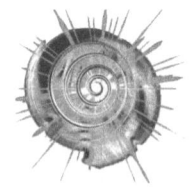

CHAPTER 1

"THEY'RE coming around, Captain! Weapons are locked!" Ramona's voice cracked under the stress of battle. She was the best science officer and partner Temms Rogers had ever commanded, and in a crisis, he trusted her gut. They needed her expertise, and her heart, if they were going to pull through this.

"Recommendations?"

"No choice, Temms. We've got to use the alien tech." Her expression was grim, black hair sweaty on her brow. Her eyes held a hundred worries she might have shared in private, but never here.

"Do it!" Rogers watched the advancing fleet on the monitor, knowing they had minutes, maybe seconds left. "Tactical, return fire!"

Ramona did not wait, her fingers tapping instructions. The ship rocked with incoming fire.

The radio burst into angry chatter. "Rogers, I'll blow you out of the sky! This is a damned act of mutiny against the Confederation!"

Rogers felt his gut twist. He knew it was mutiny. They all did.

They agreed to stop their command from taking this peaceful planet, no matter what it cost. The anxious eyes of his bridge crew flicked away from their boards for just a moment, seeking a response from their captain, seeking the strength he had always given them.

They were a fine crew.

The angry voice roared from the speakers again. "Stand down, Rogers. Save your men!"

Rogers stood, the movement making him feel stronger, more in command, like the captains of the old water vessels. "What you're doing is wrong, Burko! The Confederation is wrong! And we won't allow it!"

He watched the side monitor, where the three remaining Confederation cruisers moved toward his ship and the *Victory*, captained by another rebel. Space around them flashed with bright yellow and white laser fire.

He had lost the lowest deck to a hull breach, some twenty-four crew dead, after a direct hit from the *Talon,* the ship of fleet commander Jal Burko. The ship lurched again.

"Ramona? What's the holdup?"

"Coming on line now, Captain."

The scope's light cast a sickly green reflection on Ramona's face. The alien technology was untested, an archaeological find that Rogers' ship had been assigned to study. Ramona believed it to be some kind of weapon. The rough translation of the relic's hieroglyphics indicated the makers prescribed use of the device "when in a desperate situation." If there was anything more desperate, he could not guess what it might have been.

Rogers prayed it was something against which the *Talon* and the rest of the fleet had no defense, or they were all dead.

Dark skinned helm officer Kai Windthorp helped Ramona program the device with taut determination. The rest of the bridge crew returned to their workstations, their voices a buzz in the background, more immediately concerned with saving their lives than politics.

"We need a miracle, Rae. Make it happen!" Rogers threw himself into his chair, grunting as he hit the hard cushion. "Everyone strap in!" From his seat, positioned in the middle of the back wall of the bridge, he checked each of the other stations. His officers grabbed belts and secured themselves, ready for anything.

Anything was what they were about to get.

"Weapon activated, Captain and positioned toward the fleet. Now!"

With a silent prayer, Rogers clenched his fist and waited to see what would happen.

To his surprise, there was no explosion. Nothing left the ship. A ray of red light seemed to flutter in black space ahead of them for a few moments, and then it coalesced into a cloudy opening. A wormhole.

"May the stars preserve us," Ramona murmured.

The sight on the screen was hypnotizing.

Jolted back to reality as the ship took a devastating hit, Rogers cursed as Ramona's console exploded in a shower of sparks and she went down. Power faded then returned.

He stifled his first instinct to jump to Rae's side. No time for his own tragedy. Blocking the image of his fallen lover from his mind, he barked orders.

"Helm! Kai, take us in! Now!" He did not know where it went, but it had to be better than what they faced: the Confederation fleet poised for a death blow.

"Aye, aye, sir!" Windthorp, face bleeding from flying debris, stumbled into his seat and hit his board. The ship flew ahead into the neon-red glow of the opening as one last powerful volley from the *Talon* seemed to knock them forward.

Jal Burko's enraged voice came over the com system.

"I'll get you for this, Rogers! I'll hunt you down and kill you like the traitorous Gonoran snake you are!" The cloudy violet and red interior of the wormhole pulsed on the screen for a few seconds. Then everything went black.

* * *

ACRID smoke choked the six-seater bridge. Rogers wiped blood from his arm, his face, coughing as he tried to open his eyes.

An alarm blared a critical warning, but the constant thrum of the engines was absent. The midsize vessel *Doubtful* hung, dying, in the black emptiness of the void. He did not know where. Not yet.

With muttered expletives, Rogers used the captain's chair to pull his stocky frame upright, ignoring the scored black cover. Two of the front panels were clearly blown, littering dust and broken chips on the bridge's gray utilitarian carpet.

Five of his officers were down. Rogers clenched his teeth, his bruised muscles screaming in pain, as he climbed over the debris to check each fallen officer. He rolled Ramona over. Her torn, burnt flesh told him she was gone. One lifeless eye stared out at the damaged bridge.

He turned her over again, the sight too painful to contemplate, and crawled to the others.

The exec was dead. So was the navigator. Windthorp groaned when the captain touched him. Rogers helped him up before ordering him to medical.

Rogers knew he could not leave the bridge just yet. As the power shut down, they would lose gravitational control and life support. Steps had to be taken to keep that from happening.

Without Ramona. A wave of sorrow and loss hit his gut like a fist, stealing his very breath away. He deflected it the best he could and tried to concentrate.

Overhead the lights faded. Power sputtered spits of sparks on the control boards. Clamping his emotions down tight, Rogers clicked into emergency protocol mode, trained into him through twenty years of Confederation service. First, secure the ship. Second, secure the crew.

He pulled himself up with a grunt to slap the intercom.

"All decks report!" The smoke sent him into a coughing fit, and he kicked the console that held the ventilation controls, pain radiating all the way up his leg. To his satisfaction, it rattled to life, obviously damaged, but the air began to clear.

That's right, you jump when the captain calls.

There was no answering beep from the intercom. Did he have a crew? He hit the button again. "Anyone hearing this message respond immediately!"

Still no answer.

He sent the message again to each of the three remaining decks. There had been fifty-two souls on deck when they had left base at Gilada.

Could he have lost them all?

He received a crackle of static from mid-deck. Though he could not get anything vocal, he still felt a rush of hope.

"Engineering? Report!"

Frustrated, he limped out to see for himself.

The *Doubtful*, his command for the last three years, had taken a beating under the Confederation guns. In his fifty-two years, he never expected to fire on his own fleet.

As the rebellion spread, friends that had left base on their own ships had been shot and disabled by *Doubtful's* guns. Walking the hallways, he could see the evidence of the damage they had received. Settling dust and bits of walls and ceilings littered the floors.

Rogers wiped dust caked sweat from his face, recalling those on the lowest deck, lost to the breach, some good friends, some who had transferred in just before they left base, all most likely dead. Grief anchored his feet for a moment as the pain threatened to overwhelm him.

Save the ones that are still alive, Temms.

He forced himself to move on. A pile of debris blocked engineering doors at mid-deck. Painfully kicking the debris aside, he found a thick piece of metal and used it to pry the doors apart. Once separated, the mechanism whirred to life and the doors clunked a little wider, until finally grounding into their open position, staying there.

"Dani? Halian? Engineering, report!"

Rogers' pale blue eyes surveyed the room. He stepped over an inert body wearing the maroon and black Confederation uniform, shutting out the bloodless face as he focused on the search for anyone who might be alive.

Engineering, protected by its location in the very center of the ship, seemed to have suffered less damage than the bridge. This was the largest space on the *Doubtful*. The main room measured about twelve meters square in shades of gray with gray lino floors. The left upper deck contained the engineering chief's large tabled workspace, with smaller offices tucked underneath the upper level.

Rogers was pleased to see the percentage of operational consoles. Behind the stations that powered the navigational tools was an exit to a ladder that went below, to the hard tech machinery. The rooms downstairs were double walled, and from the fact there was air here, he guessed that this particular hull area had not been breached below.

Small blessings.

"Anyone here? Front and center!"

A crash of falling wallcrete at the far end of the room revealed a dark hump rising up in response. "Captain?"

"Hal!" Rogers felt a smile creep across his face, as he stumbled around several obstacles to grab the arm of the one who had served with him the longest.

Halian was a large, ugly biped, with light gray fur covering his massive body, and a head resembling nothing so much as a warthog. He did not look like much, but he could coax life from a dead battery and build anything from seemingly nothing. Halian was one of several alien crew members, drawn from the varied planets of the Confederation's territory for their special skills and talents. The Confederation welcomed both human and non-human constituents, more interested in what the individual could give to the organization than what their background might be.

"I should've known you'd make it! Old warriors never die—"

"They just pick up tab longer," Halian quipped in his broken Standard. As he straightened broad muscular shoulders, small pieces of wallcrete shattered into puffs of dust as they hit the floor. He looked pained. The troubled expression did not change as the engineer took a moment to inspect his damaged domain. "Ramona used weapon? Did it work?"

Rogers nodded slowly. "It did something. Just not what we expected."

"What you mean?"

"Ramona was wrong. The artifact wasn't a weapon."

"What it was?"

"That's the big question, my friend."

Rogers shared with Halian the last moments before the blackout. *Doubtful* and the *Victory* running from the remnants of the Confederation force with Burko on their tail. How Ramona activated the device, and Windthorp taking them into the alternating array of light and darkness, punctuated by electric crackle as the ship's struts and welds screamed and whined to their limits. And here they were, half-dead, blind, and deaf.

As Rogers reconstructed the events, the powerful Bricasterian listened thoughtfully. "It was right. If this half of what came at ship, rest would have destroyed us."

"Didn't have much choice. Death versus the unknown. I'll take the unknown any time."

"Where are we?" Halian asked.

Rogers shook his head. "Haven't the faintest. Nav's down. I need it ASAP."

"How many crew left?"

"You and me on our feet, far as I know."

Halian absorbed that news without visible response and lumbered over to the nearest console. "Ship running?" As his yellow gaze flicked over the panels, the lights dimmed.

"Not so much."

"Caffe?" The big engineer leaned over the nearest console and ripped the front panel off, crouching to avoid a shower of sparks.

"Once you get the power on." Rogers gave a slight shrug and then winced as his shoulder muscles pulled, causing pain to shoot along the nerves. "I'll see if I can find any one else alive."

"Good idea." Hal started rearranging pieces of metal and wire, testing the damaged systems.

Rogers knew Halian would continue to work for the next twenty-four hours, if not more, until he improved their situation as best he could. *Wish I had his stamina.* With that thought, and a sinking heart, Rogers left engineering to search for other survivors.

CHAPTER 2

AN hour later, Rogers walked wearily back. He toured the three intact decks. The lowest deck, he thought would be a total loss of personnel, but thankfully the protective seal had locked in, maintaining the integrity of the rest of the ship. Without scanning capabilities, he was not able to tell much. He peered out every port he passed by, but all he saw was space and stars. Medical was in disarray, but at least they had a doctor and emergency power. Rogers found several injured crew members and helped them to medical, although he would not stay himself.

Too much to do. Only eleven alive besides myself and Hal, out of thirty-two.

The ship required a bare minimum complement of eighteen to go into battle. With no idea of their present situation and scanners dark, they had to be ready for anything. Burko could be off the bow, lasers powered up with dead aim for the bridge. His final threat rang in Rogers' ears.

The captain kept walking, ignoring the throbbing, kicking debris out of his path.

Better than being blown to bits.

This time, the door slid open as he approached, just as it was designed to do. To his pleasant surprise, the lights were on and ventilation running full blast. Clanging metallic noise came from behind the engine housing, but it did not hide two voices arguing. "Hal?"

Halian acknowledged the captain through the silver mesh wiring that divided the rest of the room from the engine setting. "Making progress," he boasted.

"I see that." Rogers squinted to see through the lattice. "Who's back there?"

"Just me, sir." Dani Jamar, the chief engineering officer, stood up quickly, spanner in hand.

In her late twenties, fit and compact, just over five feet, the woman was dwarfed by Halian. Close-cropped dark hair was speckled with bits of wallcrete, and the comfortable gray jersey slip on that passed for her uniform wore a crust of some white substance.

"Hal dug me out from under the desk back there." She chewed her lip, as if debating her next words. "We're holding a committee meeting on priorities. I'm guessing life support and sensory devices."

"That would be a good place to start."

Dani hesitated. "How bad is it?"

The captain tightened his jaw, as he thought about all the bodies and the loss of Ramona. "You're looking at about a quarter of the remaining crew."

She paled and turned away. "Damn, we're screwed."

Halian studied Rogers as seconds ticked by. Bricasterians did not react quickly when dealing with the negative. "Third of crew? Cannot fly with only ten, twelve officers."

Tell me what I don't know.

To deflect his sinking spirits, Rogers examined the status board. About two-thirds were alight. He squared his shoulders. "I need bridge power, people."

"Six, maybe seven hours," Dani said.

"Unacceptable. Three, if you can."

Rogers looked over at the mix monitoring panel, unlit and blood covered. Two bodies lay in front, twisted from the impact. He did not have to touch them to know they had not made it. "Hal, old man, let's get these bodies out of here so you can work."

Halian hesitated only a moment to give Dani some suggestions on speeding bridge power-up, and then moved over to the bodies, scooping one into his massive arms.

"We'll put them in the second cargo hold for the time being," Rogers said. "Maybe the doc and I can say some words over them later. Not like we can take them home to their families."

The thought provoked a memory of his own family, left behind now, teen twins Alex and Linz, his ex, Connie, and his pride and joy, Tommy, nineteen years old and enlisted now in the Confederation fleet. The day Tommy graduated from the academy, the young man had angry words for his father. After that they lost touch.

He prayed Tommy wasn't on any of the ships they fought today.

Rogers slid the other body onto a litter improvised from the front panel of a blue metal console. The pain in his back arced down through his hip as he dragged the panel down the gray-carpeted hall to the designated cargo bay.

He distracted himself by going back to priorities. Power was being restored, but he needed more. He also needed to know what was happening outside the ship, and more importantly, where they were. How far had they been displaced?

To find out, the scientific equipment would have to be operational again. With any luck, they were alone and hopefully some place identifiable from the charts in their records.

"Wormhole collapsed? Or open?" Halian asked, showing parallel contemplations.

Rogers shrugged, wincing as the dead weight dragged behind him. "No way to tell. We haven't been hit again. Maybe they couldn't follow or maybe they're right outside, waiting for their power to be restored, too."

"Not good."

The cargo bay entrance balked but opened when Rogers keyed in the code. The lights overhead flickered as they entered with their tragic burdens. The small cargo storage area was half full of crated supplies in black lettered boxes, the air stale with traces of smoke. Rogers stumbled the last few steps and set the end of the litter down, turning it to allow its burden to roll off softly. The thud saddened him.

"No. Not good." He took a deep breath, the pain fading as he studied his companion. "Are you okay?"

The engineer gave the closest approximation of a smirk his porcine face could make. "Dani a smart one. Hide under desk when last rounds fired. *You* should see Doc." The flat statement was punctuated with a firm nod. When the captain turned a hard eye on him, Halian shook his head. "Captain is needed complete and whole again." He shoved Rogers toward the door. "Will handle dead ones with respect."

How could he argue? Halian was the better choice for the job.

"All right. I should check the casualty list anyway. But I want the scanners up ten minutes ago!"

"Will do." Halian nodded and straightened his leather jerkin, now stained with the blood of his former co-worker. "Captain, sorry I am about Ramona. Brave woman, and good to all of us. Her loss will be hard for all."

Rogers' throat closed with unshed tears. He was only able to nod. With exhaustion setting in, he knew he had to keep moving or risk falling flat on his face.

He clapped Halian on his thick shoulder and headed for the medical section. The left flank corridors had thankfully not taken as much damage as the right. Removing the dead was not the only activity that would be exacerbated by short staff.

The situation at medical had improved. Triage was under the control of one of his minor tactical officers, Riviera Brown, a dark skinned woman, easily six feet tall and two-hundred pounds of mostly muscle. Rogers remembered her no nonsense approach to life, especially under fire, but faced with this crisis, she checked the injured with a gentler manner. She looked up with a tired smile, her left arm bandaged. "Everything be under control, Captain. Doc's got four taken care of, working on two more. Find anyone else?"

"Dani turned up in engineering. What does that make now, thirteen? Tas should be here soon."

He looked over those sitting on black folding chairs along the wall. "Any able bodied should help Hal. He's hauling the dead to second cargo. I need him in engineering."

She nodded, kinked hair full around her head, making her look even more imposing. "I think 'bout everyone handled here, sir. I'm available." She stood, pushing her chair in, and then stuck her head inside the medical office. "Hey, Doc, Captain's here."

After a muffled response, Brown volunteered a young freckle faced man waiting with a minor injury and another man Rogers did not recognize offhand for the detail. They left in the direction from which the captain had come.

Rogers took a seat at the main desk in the infirmary. The room was small, by medical standards, five by seven meters, with white walls and a green lino floor. Storage was at a premium, as it was everywhere on the ship. Two walls held floor to ceiling glass door cabinets that kept medical equipment for easy access.

Three medical treatment beds held patients, two men hooked up to life support, covered in bloody sheets and at the third, ship's doctor Heath Montgomery finished sewing up some nasty cuts on helmsman Windthorp. Montgomery's knee length white lab coat was stained, and his normally pale complexion was even sallower than usual.

"On to your room with you, soldier, and stay there until you get a full six hours sleep," the doctor said, dismissing Windthorp.

Windthorp rose from the bed slowly, nodded in greeting. "Captain. Sorry about Ramona and Francis."

The captain studied the young man, hardly old enough to be out of the academy himself. "Thank you for your fast action, Kai. Probably all that saved us. You going to be all right?"

"Yes, sir," he said.

"Go on now, son, get some rest," Montgomery insisted. Windthorp nodded and left for his quarters.

The doctor washed his hands thoroughly at the sink, then folded his long thin legs and took a seat near Rogers, dark eyes examining him from behind silver framed spectacles. "He's going to be all right, Temms."

"Kai? He looked fairly able."

"No. Thomas." The lanky man gestured to the first bed.

"Thomas?" Rogers repeated, confused.

"Your son?"

Horror washed over the captain like a tsunami wave. "Tommy's here?" He shoved himself to his feet, groaning as he pulled his ribs. "When? How?" He stumbled over to the bed and eyed the red-soaked sheets. Under the bandaged forehead, he discovered his son's unconscious face. He reached out and touched the young man's cheek.

"You didn't know he transferred in?" Montgomery pulled out a printed roster. "A week ago. He was below with Brown, made sure she and two others got out before the section sealed off. He's got a broken leg, pretty banged up." He smiled. "Real chip off the old block."

The captain had been so consumed with the details of the conspiracy to save the planet, he let things slip. Like supply lists and new rosters. "Gods above, I had no idea."

Rogers' mind was racing. He wasn't alone. *He wasn't alone!*

"He'll be out another eight hours at least, Temms. I'll let you know when he's awake. Come sit down and let me check you out."

With practiced lean hands he examined Rogers, finding the pulled muscles, as well as a broken rib, muttering something about suspecting another. He wrapped the captain's midsection, and then gave him a shot for the pain. "I know you've got a lot on your mind, Temms, but is anyone going to tell us working folks what's happened here?"

Rogers looked over at Tommy's bed, still stunned by his presence. "Not really sure, Doc. We hit a wormhole. Ended up…somewhere." He shrugged and winced as the doctor adjusted the bandages. "No scanners until bridge power's up."

The doctor looked at him with a weary eye.

"That may fly with the enlisted men, Temms. But my gray hair tells me all this damage didn't come from any wormhole. I heard there were hull breaches below the size of a New Bernia herd-beast. That came from weapons fire, maybe a torpedo?" Quizzical eyebrow raised, he stared Rogers down. "Been with the Confederation for nearly forty three years now and I've seen what's what."

"We're still sorting things out, Heath. I promise I'll let you know as soon as I can." Rogers, feeling the deceit down to his bones, met Montgomery's gaze. "I'm due on the bridge. Keep up the good work,

Doc."

With one final glance at his son, Rogers gave encouragement to the other injured crew members before walking out. What was he doing here? Did he request the transfer? Why didn't Tommy let him know? He must have been hiding below deck, waiting for the right moment.

Only his father's politics had changed everyone's timetable.

Rogers continued, slowly, making his way to the bridge, leaning on the wall as he needed to. Politics returned to his mind. He had lied to Montgomery, and it ate at him.

Montgomery was a solid Confederation Loyalist. He and others below decks had not been part of the discussions Rogers had held with his other officers. The doctor had no idea that the *Doubtful* had turned on their former comrades, or that it was his beloved Confederation that had damaged the ship and killed their crewmates. Rogers wanted to keep it that way as long as he could, because the *Doubtful* needed the doctor desperately.

When Montgomery found out the truth, Rogers hoped he would not have to be terminated.

CHAPTER 3

RECORDING his log in a handheld device did not prove stimulating enough to keep Rogers awake on his silent bridge, nearly forty eight sleepless hours since they had left Persios. He woke to the clang of metal on metal. Heart thumping, he jumped to his feet, digging for a weapon he did not even have. The sudden movement yanked his wrapped ribs and he let out a yelp.

"Who's there?"

Scuffling noise to his left drew his gaze. A sheepish Dani Jamar wrestled a beige panel cover back into place. She wiped it down, taking off the black smoke residue.

"Sorry, Captain. Didn't mean to wake you."

Rogers rubbed his eyes. "I shouldn't have been asleep."

The bodies were gone along with the worst of the rubble. Ramona's station, the console that housed the wormhole technology, had quit smoking, but it was blackened and bent. Three steps down, the lower deck's gray carpet was scorched in several places along the front wall, and stains he recognized with anguish as the blood of his bridge crew.

Damn Jal Burko. Damn him to the flames of the eternal afterlife.

His thoughts flicked to his son, and the mystery of his arrival, but a glance at his personal timepiece let him know that he would not be awake yet.

Get the ship running.

"Status?"

"Everything should be just about—"

She pressed several buttons, chewing her lip, and most of the computer consoles energized in sequence, clicking lower to upper. A few moments later, the full overhead array flickered into light, replacing the dimmed emergency mode.

"Yes!" She grinned and tossed her tool into its blue plastic carton.

The communications board fizzled to life as Burko's voice wavered and faded through a crackle of static. "I'll find you, Temms...think I won't, you low life...snake!"

They blinked at each other in shock, but nothing further came from the speaker.

Rogers shook his head. "Must have been a repeat of their last message. I remember something about a snake." He tried to ignore the icicle that had become his spine.

"We sure he's not here?" She looked around nervously as if the commander himself might appear at any moment.

"Sure? Not at all. We'll figure that out in a minute." Rogers slipped into the navigator's chair on the lower deck. The local scanners operated easily, the slight quiver of the console under his fingers reassuring.

"Nice work, Dani. Take a seat and run a sweep for Burko, or anyone else for that matter. I've got to check astrometrics." Dialing up, he studied the data. "Find out where we are."

Dani complied with her usual resilient attitude, one of her greatest assets, Rogers thought. He had plotted to steal her from another captain who used her as a personal assistant, never realizing how much she loved the feel of greasy metal and the satisfaction that came as an engine part was tuned into the harmony of perfect functioning.

She took the tactical officer's chair and activated the lateral sensor arrays to locate any nearby planets or craft.

Rogers turned on a viewer and set the computer to survey the local planets, compare them against all known star systems. After approximately thirty seconds, white letters on the blue screen announced: *No Common Points of Reference Found.*

"Well, what do you know?"

"Looks like we're clear, Captain, Nothing within firing range." The petite engineer turned to Rogers. "What's the matter?"

"Computer can't tell me where we are." He ran the scan again, framing the question in multiple fashions, but received the same results.

"Huh." She watched him with an even gaze.

He knew she was waiting for him to perform his usual miracle, point out the program error, find the correct code to alter the readings so everything would be right again.

I'd like that myself, just about now.

He guessed a wormhole could send the ship to another part of the Cantrian sector, maybe two systems away. But a whole new sky?

The computer could be malfunctioning. That was more likely than the possibility they had gone beyond measured space. Did he have the technical knowledge to determine which? *If* they had gone somewhere unknown, the crew would have to discover how far they were from home territory, and what it would take to get back. Those were questions for trained personnel to whom he had no access at the moment.

Survival was the immediate issue. The ship's damage required landing the craft to repair, since no Confederation stations were readily detectable.

The question of Jal Burko remained. That message emerging from the newly repaired com-board was more unsettling than he would admit. It was similar to what he heard as they escaped, but something about it jarred his sense of well being. Could they still receive messages from Burko?

Rogers scanned the planetary system in which they arrived. This star had five planets. Four showed levels of population and development. The globe closest to the star was a mid-brown color indicative of barren desert. The next two were more nearly an equal division of land and water, and offered an advanced technological nature, according to the atmospheric emission and pollutant levels. The outer two showed signs of habitation, but much more scattered, less industrialized.

There must be a place with materials compatible with theirs. There had to be. It was the only way to survive.

"We'll need supplies and parts for repairs," he said.

"Captain?" Dani's tentative voice broke into his thoughts. "We're staying?"

He saw emotion boiling in her dark eyes and answered gently. "Don't see as we have much choice at the moment, D. We did what we had to." He indicated the blackened console, one of two which had not regained power under Dani's ministrations. "The artifact may be permanently damaged. We'll have to see when, or if, we can get it operational."

With a brooding look at the empty chair behind the console, he added. "Without Ramona, I'm not sure we'll even be able to decipher it again."

The engineer's face went through a series of expressions, disappointment, anxiety, finally sympathy. "We've lost a lot. Do you think it made a difference, sir? Did it save the Persions?"

"We have to believe it did."

"Then it was worth it." Her quiet words reassured Rogers, and she turned back to the scanners, where reports continued to filter in. She transferred them to the captain's reader.

A small planet with a bucolic population of about fifty million, Persios had a rudimentary technology. Always looking to expand its territory, the Confederation had determined Persios and another planet in its system, Siderian, were suitable to support Confederation rule.

Siderian leaders had eventually 'agreed' to become a protectorate of the Confederation. This meant that the Confederation now patrolled space around the green-blue planet to ward off attackers, or attack uncooperative leaders who resisted the demanded tribute of raw materials and other supplies.

The council on Persios had rejected such an alliance. The Confederation fleet commander, ambitious Jal Burko, decided to make them an example.

"Wipe those ungrateful bastards from the face of the planet!" he had bellowed in the preparatory staff meeting, his commanders seated at the huge wooden conference table on his impressive flagship, the Talon. "Use the neutronic bombs, just clear the people, not the landscape! I want to have my breakfast on that councilor's little ivory terrace."

The *Doubtful's* captain had held the Persion councilor's grandchild on his knee as they compared stories about parenthood. Rogers knew he could not allow the massacre to happen. Rogers' protests found sympathizers in other fleet captains, and the dissenters met, conspired and committed to any and all measures necessary to protect the Persions.

When the dozen ships assembled for the strike against Persios, the *Doubtful* was the lead ship, taking in the others, or so Burko had thought. Just before the fleet penetrated the planetary atmosphere, Rogers' coded signal turned the rebels back to intercept many of their sister ships before defensive capabilities could be brought online. The effort was calculated to shut down the attack, targeting weapons and engines only, not to kill Confederation comrades.

Once Burko's men determined what was happening, of course, the fight was on. Rogers had seen at least two rebel ships destroyed as he studied the monitors, desperately seeking tactical advantage.

He did not know if any escaped through the wormhole with him. It was not likely, but he held out hope.

And the Persions? It would have taken all twelve ships for the takeover to succeed. With four ships in full rebellion and several loyal Confederation ships too damaged to continue the attack, there would not have been enough left to take the planet. Of that he was certain.

Perhaps it had been worth it.

As Rogers began a mental task list, his primary communication tech limped through the bridge doors. Tasiq was humanoid in appearance, tall, thick, with feline characteristics, including deep green eyes with a vertical pupil, which disarmed people meeting him for the first time. His thin russet fur was singed and patchy in several places, and a thick bandage wrapped his right arm.

Tasiq's world circled its radiant star in a course of six-hundred days, an orbit far from its surface. Adapted eyes provided their people with better hunting in the dim light, and the fur kept them warm in the resultant chilly temperatures. Feline hearing contributed to Tasiq's proficiency at communications, as he could detect a wider range of sounds than most humans.

At Rogers' quizzical look, Tasiq bared pointed canine teeth, and spoke in his deep baritone, a rumble from his throat. "Doc Montgomery said I could report for duty." He glanced at the stains on the floor, and back at Rogers.

"Glad to see you, Tas."

Now that he had another bridge officer, he ordered Dani back to engineering, where her skills could be better used.

"Remember, Captain. It was the right thing." She nodded and patted his arm as she passed him.

"Thanks, D."

She stopped even with Tasiq, checking out his injuries. "That's the best you could do? One little bandage?"

Tasiq did not seem in the least ruffled. "Where's the proof of your valor, Jamar? I don't see a mark on you."

She smirked. "Some of us are smart enough to stay out of the line of fire, Cat Man."

"Engineers. Think they know everything. We know they couldn't put a thought together without the instructions."

Dani stared a moment, then laughed and went on her way.

The show of humor bolstered the captain's spirits, and he continued single mindedly. "When that console booted up, we got a message from Burko," he warned. "Sounded like something we'd already received, but it's worth tracking."

Tasiq took the communications post without further question and began a series of diagnostic tests. "Any other orders, Captain?"

"So far astrometrics can't ID where we are. Analysis of local language and cultures within this star system would be helpful. Translator will hopefully handle basic sentence structure and so on." Rogers forwarded the tactical information Dani had provided to Tasiq's monitor.

"Right on it."

Rogers continued to look over his data, wondering how far they could fly. As he received an update from Halian, his outlook darkened.

Not far.

They would have to set down within the next two days to avoid losing air to the breaches on the lower deck, Halian said. The captain glanced back at the readout to see what was within two days' travel.

"Captain?" Tasiq broke into his study. "That message was not a duplicate. Burko is within communication range. Shall I hail the *Talon*?"

That brought Rogers to his feet. "No!" Why had Dani not spotted him? "Where is he?"

"Unknown. Close enough to respond." Tasiq watched him, curiosity twitching both eyebrows.

Rogers shoved himself around the corner of the rail to the tactical board. Intermittent power gave him a few readings, but clearly there was room for error. They had to avoid Burko.

If he was really here.

If they were lucky, communication had simply passed through the wormhole, and Burko was firmly on his side of the crossing. No way was the *Doubtful* battle ready.

"We've got to hit dirt, and now," he muttered as he stalked back to his own chair to read the information there. "This one!" He stabbed at the display, rubbing a hand over his weary face. "I want us down within six hours to restock and repair!"

Tasiq punched up the coordinates, studying the graphic display of the system's planets. "No background data on this planet?"

"I'm sure you'll have some for me soon. And don't use the comm!"

Tasiq's surprise was obvious. Rogers finally had to face the inevitable. He would have to come up with a good story for the crew, especially with the potential of coming nose to nose with Burko.

Most of those who had survived were active participants in the rebellion, Halian, Dani, Brown, Windthorp, and himself. The rest might well be confused and angry if they discovered the truth. The rebels expected to return to Gilada to face court martial. At which point, those not part of the rebellion would have been exonerated, and they would continue on with their careers. The alien artifact changed all that.

Now all their lives had been stolen, with faint hope of return.

"Sorry, Tas. Lot on my mind. We'll have a briefing when we get the fires put out."

The com-tech accepted the explanation and got to work, alternately purring and growling deep in his chest as power drains elsewhere slowed reaction time.

As Rogers continued to study the astronomy of their new home, he found most of the system's planets held atmospheres with sufficient oxygen and nitrogen for them to breathe. At least he and his crew could adapt to life here. If they must.

He was content to remain, having planned to cut his own ties and aspirations when he agreed to mutiny. Life might even be tolerable, as long as he had Tommy with him.

What if this was a peaceful universe, one not driven by the need to conquer? What if all he needed was a ship, a crew willing to travel among these stars, trading with its people and live out the rest of his life without having to fire another shot? He was tired. He had seen too much blood spilled.

What about those who did not want to stay? And now an imminent Burko backlash? How long would repairs take? How would he run the ship with so few crew?

"Captain?" Tasiq's mellow voice broke into his thoughts.

"The planet below seems to be known as Marriel. No dominant races due to the disparity of the land masses. Technology not as advanced as ours, but there are basic space capable vessels." He handed Rogers a printed summary. "Best I could do, working with the translator in this condition."

"Good work, Tas." The report held potential answers about establishment of trade. "Find me a place to put down away from the big cities. We can trade scrap materials and other tech, if we have to. Ask Hal what we can spare."

Unspoken was the thought that in rural areas he was likely to find young men and women looking for adventure beyond their father's farm. He needed at least eight more people if he was going to fly the ship successfully. They would have to come from somewhere.

"Aye, sir."

His need for sleep finally overwhelming him, Rogers got to his feet. "Call a staff meeting for 1600. Have Brown find something for everyone to eat. I'll be in my quarters."

He stumbled off the bridge and made his way to his small suite, one of the few privileges of his rank, three rooms to himself. Hardly noticing as the door closed, the captain littered the floor with his clothing on the way to his bed. He slid face first into the hard mattress and thought of nothing before the darkness overtook him.

CHAPTER 4

"TEMMS. Say Grace." Connie was insistent.

He never dared to deny the woman when she was insistent.

They were at the dinner table in the old house on Gilada. Across from him were Alex and Linz, his freckle faced twins, and at his left, Tommy, his eldest. Everyone held hands and Rogers gave thanks for them being together and for the meal they were to receive from the bountiful gods.

When he was done speaking, there was a grab for the bowls of food. The children chattered about school as Connie corrected their grammar and manners. He watched. He could only watch. He could not move.

Connie said something about the Confederation school and Tommy bragged about how he couldn't wait to become a Confederation officer like his dad.

Temms wanted to tell Tommy he was forbidden to go. He watched as Tommy passed the tray of broiled meat, and small marks appeared on his son's shirt, red marks that got bigger and more liquid as he started to bleed.

Tommy babbled about joining the Confederation corps as he slowly bled out and Connie looked at Temms, accusing him.

"How could you let this happen? How could you?"

He could not move.

Temms woke up with a smothered yell, trembling. The dream had been too real.

He stalked over to the sink and splashed handfuls of cold water on his face until he was sure he was awake. It was not real.

It was not real.

Temms' marriage to Connie had ended five years before, right after Tommy had opted to follow his father into Confederation service. She blamed him. Still did.

The twins were grown. Alex was a transport pilot. Linz moved away and started a family, he had grandchildren he had never seen, would never see now. With a sigh he rinsed his face again, wishing memories washed away as easily.

At one time they had a good life, he, Connie, and the children. Giladan society was ranked by career choice, and military members enjoyed a high standard of living. Connie raised the children and played politics with the other officers' wives. The children were members of all the right junior sports leagues and received good educations.

Tommy starred on his ball team. Temms could remember the scent of fresh cut grass in the air as he spent afternoons in the hot sun cheering Tommy on. They had the luxury of military hops to vacation at beaches or resorts on nearby planets. But that life, and the pain of leaving it, had been over for years.

His crew was his family now.

And Tommy.

Why had he not brought himself to his father's attention? What was he worried about?

Ship's records revealed that Ensign Thomas Rogers had joined the ship at its last port, bottom man of the totem pole in security. After the massacre and the wormhole, he was now top man.

The captain checked the time as he pulled on clean clothes, studying himself in the cracked mirror. His military cut salt and pepper hair was definitely more salt these days. With all these new challenges, he expected to gray even faster.

He probably should not have slept while there were so many unknowns on the table. A couple of hours were enough, he hoped. Ramona always said he was not worth much to anyone without regular sleep. He could hear her in his mind, complaining that he wasn't taking care of himself. By the gods, he missed her! He could not let himself stop to grieve. He did not dare. Not yet.

I didn't even dream about her. He swallowed his guilt, as he checked the time again. It was nearly time for his staff meeting.

Staff? How could fifteen people be a 'staff'? So many that he had come to know and trust were now gone. One thing he was sure of, the event of crossing through the wormhole had been the last moment of rigid job classifications. They all needed to cross train on different systems and equipment and cover extra shifts until they were up to speed again. It was the only way they would survive.

This announcement brought grumbles in the low key discussion that followed the breaking of bread in the conference room. He embellished the wormhole story to include an attack from an unknown enemy that had herded them into it. That was enough to explain the damage to the ship for those who did not know the truth. The rebel crew members did not seem anxious to correct Rogers' presentation. Satisfied, he left it that way.

"How and when can we expect to get back?" asked Dr. Montgomery, participating from medical by holographic projection.

"I can't tell you, Heath. Ramona's console is a mess, worst on the bridge. Frankly I've got higher priorities." Rogers handed out printouts of systems engineering had already begun to patch up. "These first. Anyone else who needs repairs, file requests with Hal."

He studied the group before him. The crew he had left were from various disciplines. Hudson, a gunner, and Tommy were still in medical, both still unconscious. There were two tactical officers, Brown and Windthorp. Tasiq, from communications, the doctor, and two enlisted men who were apprenticed to the deceased weapons master, along with two engineers and some minor officers, and himself.

Hell of a mess.

Rogers looked at the roster the doctor had given to him. "Parnell Eddy, right?" he said, pointing to the taller of the two ensigns, a lanky young man with red hair just curling along the edge of his collar, and freckles.

"Yes, sir!" He snapped to attention.

Rogers shook his head. The ensigns were fresh from the Confederation tech school, not expecting disaster the first time out. *That's what they teach us. When things are foobar, fall back on your training. It gives you purpose.*

"Mr. Eddy, you understand why we're asking you to take on bridge duties, don't you?"

"Yes, sir, I do!"

"We're going to have a tough go of it the next several months. It means we have to think outside the box." Rogers turned to the other man, heavy set and blond, with a round face and misty blue eyes.

"Jerome?"

"Jerry Jerome, sir!" The young man saluted so fast he nearly cracked his hand on the table's edge getting it to his forehead.

"All right, Jerome. Your enthusiasm is appreciated." Rogers grinned at Halian, who returned the amused look.

"Permission to speak freely, sir?" Jerome's jaw set stubbornly, his baby face looking about to tantrum.

"Granted."

"Wormholes, now they're considered theoretical, right? So how can we be sure the instruments aren't wonky? I mean, another *universe?* That's just not possible, is it?"

Rogers nodded. "Normally, I'd agree with you, Jerome. Science wasn't my strong suit at OCS, but I know enough about our star charts to agree there's nothing out there that looks familiar. So we're taking it one step at a time. Safety first."

"Yes, sir." Jerome's confused look remained, but he returned to his seat, apparently satisfied.

The doctor broke in again. "What have we done to get back to command?" he asked. "Jal must have survived, since he always stays safely back in the pack." Montgomery's wry grin poked subtle derision at their fleet commander. "We're planning to rendezvous and regroup?"

Rogers noticed Tasiq's odd gaze fixed on him as he replied. "We're planning to repair and survive right now, Heath."

"But Commander Burko would help us, right, sir?" Jerome persisted. "Haven't we tried to contact him? Have they contacted us? They're the best ship in the fleet! If anyone survived—"

"Com-board still in need of parts and repair," Tasiq interrupted. "Not possible to receive messages yet. Soon maybe." The felinoid nodded to Rogers.

Interesting. Tasiq wasn't one among the conspirators. Why would he lie?

Rogers shuffled his notes a moment, regrouping in light of this puzzle. "All right, thank you, Tas. Eddy, you and Jerome will first be assigned to the bridge, effective immediately. One of you will share duties with Tasiq, the other with the helm officer. You'll need to absorb navigation, tactical, ship's systems, communications. I expect you to be up to the task. Ensign Rogers will follow you when he's up and around."

The two young men twitched as responsibility hit them square in the chest, but they saluted awkwardly. "Aye, aye, sir!" they shouted in unison.

Rogers considered the biographic reviews he had made of his remaining officers before coming to the meeting. "Windthorp, you'll take over at tactical. Brown, you have training in the sciences, don't you?"

"Yes, sir. Undergrad in botany and analysis of ecosystems."

"Perfect. You're the new chief science officer."

Riviera raised an eyebrow. "Sir?"

"It'll be an adventure." Rogers nodded, adding a smile to soften the blow. "Well, that's where we are, people. We're sending a team planet side in eight hours." He consulted his notes. "Brown, D, you'll go with me. Scans indicate straight humanoid population, no sense in sending invading aliens. We'll find supplies, arrange for burial of our dead and hopefully do some recruiting."

He smiled, a trace of hope filtering in for the first time since entering the wormhole. "Any more questions?" He did not meet the eyes of the young men, hoping they would let things be. "No? Finish eating, ladies and gentlemen. No sense letting it go to waste. As you were."

He knew the crew would want to bitch about the new orders and decompress a little, something they could not do with the captain present. With any luck, the rebels would steer the conversation clear of Confederation talk for now. A pointed look at Dani reinforced that wish. Rogers left the room, walking the decks, most cleared, some still ankle deep in debris, taking a few moments to pull his thoughts together.

Clearly, substantial damage had to be repaired once they were on the ground. He just prayed there was compatible material on Marriel. Between the destruction they had suffered and the danger from Confederation forces, if any, he doubted they could make it to the next world.

He continued to the observation port, just a small room four meters by five meters located aft of the bridge section that contained a few skinny chairs and a window that took up the entire rear wall. From there, spectators could look over the aft portion of the ship and into the sky. Marriel hung in space below, jewel bright, landmasses in green and brown, uneven, large bodies of water in sapphire tones. A moon rose over the far horizon.

The stars drew his attention, and he looked out at them, sparkling just as bright as those over Gilada. A strange galaxy. New stars and planets. Novelty did not mean that existence as they knew it was over. Surely, life would not be the same, not with all they had lost, but it was possible to go on.

Rogers took a last look, then returned to the bridge to learn all he could about the planet below before he put himself and his people at risk.

CHAPTER 5

TASIQ scouted the most rural locale he could find with the curious requirements Temms Rogers specified: a graveyard, trading post of sorts and a bar.

Dropping parts as it came out of atmo, the *Doubtful* set down with a creak that rattled the teeth of the ship's inhabitants at a sufficient distance outside town to avoid a stampede of curious town folk.

Windthorp activated what was left of its shield. It would not make them invisible, but would deflect light and most primitive scanning devices. Rogers did not intend to hide from the locals, but until the *Doubtful* was one hundred percent, he wanted to avoid unnecessary confrontation.

Rogers, Dani Jamar and Riviera Brown dressed in clothing that would best match that of the natives, natural fiber fabrics and heavy leather boots. The two women each carried a knapsack full of metal bits they had pried from the ship, uridium and other metals they hoped to sell. A small scanner hidden in their clothing and a weapon gave them protection, if necessary.

Tasiq made an effort to decipher the local tongue with the ship's translation program while monitoring communications, but Rogers expected their implanted universals would handle most anticipated differences in language, both what they heard and as they spoke.

He left Halian in charge of the effort to repair and re-pressurize the lower decks and clear them of debris and the remains of their comrades. Satisfied the rest would carry on without them, he and the two women headed into town on foot.

Since the split from Connie, he had only been off ship for brief periods. Work kept him sane. He applied himself assiduously as captain of his vessel, determined never to degenerate into Burko's kind of man. The tenets the Confederation espoused were his guide and his belief. The people on Persios would never have been in peril under his command. *Never.*

Being on land again, being able to breathe the natural, grass scented air, was energizing. The area reminded him of his grandparent's farm, a place in which he spent a lot of time when he was very young. He remembered the fields, the open skies, the slower pace. Nostalgia slowed his steps as he took in the intense buzz of summer insects, a hum so loud it seemed to penetrate into his bones.

Relaxation settled into his shoulders along with the scent, a little of that earlier freedom running through his mind.

Orphaned at fifteen, his parents killed in a terrorist attack, he lived with his grandparents for several years, free to come and go as he pleased. Temms' friends were free too, and they liked to test the envelope of the law. He had several minor brushes with the correctional end by the time he reached majority. His grandfather had tapped a judge of his acquaintance for a favor, and Temms was accepted to the Confederation officer school. His free days had come to an end.

He stared up for a moment, into the sky, such a peculiar cerulean tint, almost turquoise or azure, not the deep, full blue of the Giladan atmosphere. They were free again. At least until Burko found them.

The reminder ate at his gut with small nibbling teeth. *Keep walking, Temms.*

The countryside was farmed, most fields planted with row crops. The rest held herds of cattle type creatures with three horns. Riviera remarked on the solid amount of meat each provided, shifting her heavy pack full of scrap metals and uridium to the other shoulder.

"Meat? No! They're so cute!" Dani set her pack to the side, trying to coax one of the animals to take grass from her hand. It charged the fence at what seemed impossible speed. The young engineer squealed and jumped aside just in time as the beast hit, one very solid horn impaled into the fence for several minutes until the dull witted creature figured out how to release itself.

"Very cute." Rogers watched, amused.

He had chosen these companions for their indisputable humanity, and their inoffensive appearance, both relaxed and friendly, but more than a pretty face behind either of them.

While Dani had languished at her former captain's beck and call, Riviera Brown's mildly pleasant manner hid a much darker side. The big woman's only life partnership had been devastating. Her husband had tried to control her with verbal jabs, sexual assault and brute force. She finally hurt him. Badly.

Her Confederation superiors had not forced her from the service, but ordered an immediate transfer away from her victim.

Rogers had taken her on. They had one conversation about the incident, during which Rogers was satisfied that it was an isolated occurrence. Since then she had been a model officer and a valuable part of his crew.

"Don't need a man," she had told him. "Never would, uh-uh. Men, they just a part of the journey, just like women, dogs, and furniture. That's all."

As they walked into town, Riviera waxed philosophical. "Nice to breathe the new air, ain't it? Kinda reminds you of the sweetness of life."

Rogers pulled down the front of his short dark jacket, uncomfortable without his uniform, or the bright, flowered shirts that were his off duty favorite.

"Don't think I don't appreciate every minute of it. Especially after the last couple of days." Staring down the road, he shielded his eyes from the bright sun with a hand. "I'm glad you two pulled through. We've seen a lot of action together. I know I can count on you."

"Wouldn't miss it, sir," Riviera said with a grin. "Adventure, that what you said, right?"

"That's what I said." Rogers took a deep breath, his mind, and dark thoughts, clearing.

They kept moving along the dirt road in the direction of town. The twenty minute walk invigorated them, the berm was lush and green with grasses and wild flowers, the air filled with pastoral scents both familiar and strange. The occasional farm worker gave them a friendly wave as they passed.

Finally the team encountered brick and plaster homes, singly and then in pairs. Next they came to a main street, paved in some sort of permatop Rogers had never seen before.

Downtown stretched for six blocks, various mercantile and offices in seeming random order. The women and men on the street wore pants and jackets in non-descript, dusty colors. As the team came into town, the eyes of the locals turned more skeptical, even suspicious.

Rogers noticed Dani inching closer, coming into his personal space as they walked ahead.

The saloon was unmistakable. Tired neon lights flashed in the smoked windows of the squat brick building. The trash receptacle outside was full of empty liquor bottles.

"The locals like their alcohol," Rogers commented.

"Don't look like there's much else to do," Riviera said. She ignored the looks they received as people moved about the business of daily life, occasionally congregating on the front steps of the worn buildings.

Though they seemed unsettled by the strangers, no one moved to take action against them.

Children hustled along in the wakes of their parents, doing what children do. One tow-headed boy cut across their path with an impudent look. His laughing non-apology reminded Rogers of Tommy at that age, back when he was carefree and not trying so hard to prove something to his old man. Montgomery had assured him Tommy was comfortable before he left the ship. He still felt guilty for not waiting by his son's side.

"Seems they must get travelers frequently enough," Dani added. "Good for us."

She ducked out of the way of a speeder type vehicle that floated on some sort of air cushion. It seemed to be the transportation of choice, though powered vehicles, rubber wheeled ones, two or four seaters lumbered along the road, spitting out thick, chemical scented smoke.

"Yes. Good for us." The captain wanted to attract the least amount of attention as possible. In, out, just long enough to get things done. *Until he knew whether they were alone in the sky, best to keep moving.* "All right, you know what to do. Brown, find out about graveyard space. There must be some sort of funeral parlor, or waste reclamation. Whatever's smooth and quiet."

The big woman nodded and handed Dani her pack. "Yes, sir. I got it."

"D, you've got the scrap. Try the trading post first, then the local financial institution. If they don't exchange for trade, they'll direct you, I'm sure." He gave her a confident nod.

"I notice, Captain, you've taken the hazardous duty." Dani Jamar studied the sign over the saloon door that read *Runyon's.* "Are you sure you can handle it alone?"

"I'm the captain. I've got to manage the tough ones." Tongue planted firmly in cheek, he studied them both with sincere concern. "Be careful. Good luck. Meet me back here ASAP." The women strolled away to find their objectives.

The captain hitched up his belt and walked into the bar, on guard for anything. The place was not much different than he expected. Temms Rogers had patronized his share of bars over the years, a lot of them in outlying areas. This was exactly where he wanted to be. No one checked ID, they were looking for easy deals, and often it was the only entertaining place in town. If anyone was itching for action, something to do, likely they would be there. Maybe they would be of a mind to voyage with a space-going vessel.

Men and women lounged at the tables inside, some alone, others engaging in raucous conversation. The rough wooden floor was dusty, and shadowy corners held traces of things that might have been there some time. The air reeked of burnt grease. Behind the polished wooden bar was a row of bottles and beneath the bottles, a row of glasses, mostly clean. At the far end of the room, stairs led up to an open balcony and a narrow hall with several doors in sight.

A burly, rusty haired man with a smudged white apron stood behind the counter, barking orders. Commanded by his pointing finger, a slight girl hastened from table to table, a flash of resentment in her dark, almond shaped eyes.

Rogers took a seat at a table near the bar, at an angle so his back was not to the door. He slouched just enough for his jacket to hang loose, giving him easy access to the pulse weapon in his pocket. It only held stun capability, sufficient enough to stop a potentially deadly situation should one arise. He did not intend to start anything.

At the bartender's growl, the girl came to Rogers' side. "Can I get you something, sir?"

He saw intelligence in the girl's eyes, far more than he would have expected by the way the barman was managing her. Her hand trembled as she held out a menu, but her jaw was set tight. Poor thing was wound like a watch spring. Rogers smiled. "Just bring me whatever's popular. Take your time, honey. I'm in no hurry."

Her chocolate gaze pierced through him, questioning. She seemed about to speak when the barkeep pushed himself around the end of the counter and walked over to them, grabbing the girl's arm. Rogers noticed for the first time a metal wristband, twinkling with small lights on her wrist.

"No time for visiting, missy. Get to work!" The husky man shoved her toward the bar before turning to Rogers. "She'll have that quick as a wink, sar. Don't worry."

Bristling at the barman's rough treatment of the girl, Rogers forced himself not to react. The needs of his ship dictated that he play the games local players expected. He slipped on his best 'good old boy' smirk. "Glad to hear it. Nice little town you have here."

"We like it." The man wiped thick pork chop hands on his apron, and then stuck one in Roger's direction. "Oke Runyon, at your service. You must be passing in?"

"Teddy Roberts." Remembering belatedly he might have someone on his trail, he covered with a false name, and shook the man's hand with contrived, but jovial warmth. "Yes, we had some things to trade...." He let his voice trail off, leaving the possibilities open. "Looking for someone who knows how to get what folks need."

Runyon raised his hands and laughed. "Well, Mr. Roberts, if I don't know where to get it, I know where to find a man who does!"

He stepped aside as the girl hurried over, setting a short, clear glass filled with an amber colored liquid, no ice, on Rogers' table before she flitted away, watching Runyon's raised hand.

"Do tell." Rogers raised his glass to his host before taking an experimental sip. It burned all the way down and brought an almost instant sense of well-being. *No wonder it's a favorite. Addictive as hell, I bet.* He resolved to take the glass very slowly.

As Runyon counted off a list of items that he thought might interest his patron, Temms watched the girl. Men at the other tables tried to get their hands on her whenever she came within reach. She glanced at Runyon, infuriated, but he ignored her. And them.

"Mostways we trade for coin or precious metals, though. No Allied chits, if you get my meaning." Runyon studied the captain like he was a treasure box about to open.

"Chits?" Rogers returned to his broad smile hoping it would deflect consideration of his ignorance, both chit and Allied. "No, we've got metals to trade."

Runyon nodded with satisfaction. "You'll want to see Hoochet at the bank then. You need anything else, you come see me!" He swaggered back behind the bar, wiping it down expansively, his cool gaze on the girl.

Rogers sipped again, hoping Dani had found the bank. When the girl retreated into the back room, he turned his attention to the other patrons, considering potential crew.

Four young men, muscled farm boys from the look of them, played cards, sharing three bottles from which they poured liberal servings. They had no apparent interest in Rogers, bent on their game and tormenting the dark haired girl as she brought them plates of food.

She, in turn, watched Rogers intently when she passed, careful to stay a step ahead of Runyon's quick bellow and heavy hand.

Another pair of men sat at the bar, not far from Rogers, staring into the liquid in their glasses. One, in a worn red wool jacket, was clearly being propositioned by a flashy woman whose giggle seemed incongruent with her age. As her roving gaze caught Rogers', he could see her adding him to her lineup as potential second string material. The captain shut her out of his thoughts and let the amber liquid in his glass touch his lip again, not taking in any this time. Better to keep his wits unsedated.

His mind wandering, he allowed himself a moment of regret that he had rejected his Confederation masters. In his home sky, his injured would have been treated, dead transported, ship repaired, supplies restocked, just for the asking. Now his crew depended on him, alone. For a military man, even a disillusioned one, it was a disarming thought.

No orders.

No facilities.

Just him.

Careful to stay in character, he waved a hand at the girl, and she scurried over. He asked for some sandwiches and more drink.

"Sure, Captain. You're a captain, aren't you?" she whispered.

"Does it show?" Rogers smiled to show the girl he was teasing. She studied him a moment with more than idle curiosity and then went to the back.

What was that about?

The woman and man at the bar apparently came to terms. They went upstairs, him holding her hand as she whispered in his ear. *Saved.*

Dani arrived at the bar a few minutes later. The captain pulled out a chair for her and she slipped into it, face flushed. "I unloaded all the uridium scrap for coin and they wanted more!" she whispered. "There's a whole stack of it on the deck below engineering, where the coils burst. We've got replacements, so we can spare this."

Rogers nodded, noting how the farm boy's attention were now focused on his table. "Well done. Want a drink? I expect the boys will buy you one." He smirked just a bit.

She glanced over at them. "I'm not looking for love, sir."

He chuckled. "I trust you got enough to cover the burial land."

"Depends on the price. Seems to be enough land open, if what we saw is an indication. There shouldn't be a premium."

"Agreed." Dani had piqued Runyon's interest as well. The thick barkeep seemed to be sizing her up. Rogers' hackles rose and a stiff wave moved up his spine. "You'd think they never saw a woman around here."

Dani's fingers traced initials carved long ago in the top of the wooden table. "Time to go?" she asked, without looking up.

He pulled his chair closer and laid a proprietary hand on her shoulder as he spoke. "No, not yet. Don't want to spook them before we get what we came for." *Let's hope these fellows can read body language without translation.*

The girl came from the back with several plates and slapped them on the table. Her eyes had widened at the sight of Dani Jamar and she stumbled a step or two, something unreadable on her face. After a moment's hesitation, she twisted her body until its slight form blocked Runyon's view of her hand, before dropping a small piece of folded paper on the table. She gave the engineer a pointed glare and then moved back to the bar, stacking glasses noisily.

Odd. Rogers and Dani exchanged curious looks.

As if rehearsed, Rogers reached for a sandwich as Dani palmed the paper. Keeping his expression friendly, Rogers finished his drink and took a bite of the sandwich, something with several strips of salty meat, nippy onion-like herbs and slices of a mushy, aromatic, but tart fruit. "That a menu recommendation?"

Making a show of tasting the food, Dani slipped her hand in her lap and scanned the note with her handheld. "It's some kind of code."

"Keep at it."

He tried to relax, but this new mystery kicking his effort into the waste can. Too much he did not know in this strange new universe. His possessive air over Dani seemed to have cooled the interest of the farm lads. Their suitability as crew, however, was not favorable, based on their lack of enthusiasm about anything without breasts, along with their substantial alcohol consumption.

The barkeep, however, still watched her.

A few moments later, Rogers saw comprehension come into his engineer's eyes and then surprise. She sopped up yellow juices on the plate with the bread, breaking into a smile as she tasted it, the tiny size of her first bite almost apprehensive. She finished with a delighted grunt. "I don't know what that is, but it's not bad. Better than the canned crap we've had."

The captain grinned ruefully. "You can say that again. Careful now, the man hasn't taken his eyes off you."

"So I've noticed. Pig." She looked over to the dark haired girl. "When's Riviera due back?"

"Shouldn't be too long."

Dani nodded. "Think the three of us can break that girl out of here?"

CHAPTER 6

THE captain's eyes widened. "Do what?"

"The—uh...." Dani shifted her topic as Runyon came toward their table. "Told him to slough off and I'd tie it up later."

"How's your meal?" Runyon asked, a dark edge to his smile. "This your wife?"

"It's very good," Rogers said smoothly. "And, no."

"I see." He studied Dani again. If her cool gaze had been any sharper, it could have dissected him. "You said you hadn't got money yet? Still trading? And what exactly is it you're intending to trade for your service here?"

The captain covered his defensive reaction with a shrug. "We have some precious metals, like you said. Are you worried about our ability to pay for the meal?" He nodded to Dani, who put several coins on the table surface.

Runyon's obvious disappointment did not slow his hammy hand from scooping up the coins and slipping them into his apron pocket. "If you change your mind, we'd consider other arrangements." The barkeep, scowling, watched the slender waitress across the room. "Last ship that passed in, captain couldn't make his bills. He left the girl as payment. She ain't much for earning her keep."

Rogers avoided Dani's pointed look. "Maybe she'll get better."

The barkeep grunted. "If she wants to live, she will." He fondled the coins in his pocket and strolled over to the table where the card game was wrapping up.

"See? He's going to kill her," Dani whispered.

"So you want us to steal his property when we go? Not a great way to win friends in the new universe, D."

"She's not his property!" Realizing she could be overheard, Dani leaned closer. "She's a trained navigator."

Intrigued, Rogers studied Dani's eager face. "That what the note says?"

Dani nodded.

"And she wants out of here?"

Dani nodded again.

"Wonder how much her contract's worth?"

The petite engineer raised an eyebrow. "You're going to *buy* her?"

"If we're here as business men, then we need to act like it. Maybe we can just pay off her debt." He scrutinized the girl, remembering her soft query about his captaincy. "We could seriously use a navigator. But she can't be more than seventeen, D."

"Maybe she's a kid, but she figured out how to get us a coded note. She understood we might help her. So she's not stupid. Anyone not stupid can be an asset. You said you were looking to take on crew. A navigator who knows the local skies might be real useful."

"I know that."

What he also knew was that the former card players had taken a distinct interest in Rogers' table as they confabbed with the barkeep. "I don't have much inclination to shoot our way out of here, unless we have to. I'd prefer people didn't remember our names, either." He had not shared his knowledge about Burko, and did not intend to just yet. "What damage is done is all right. But let's keep it quiet, if we have a chance."

The door to the street opened and Riviera walked in. Her native "costume" included a wide red striped serape that added to her appearance of height and bulk. As her eyes adjusted to the light, she spied her captain and walked over to sit with Rogers and Jamar. With one look at her, Rogers could see the boys' resolve slipping away.

She laid an estimated bill of sale on the table. "We got a place, Captain. It's out a ways. Hinted it was some sickness that took 'em to avoid questions." She lifted the last sandwich off the plate and took a bite, her wary eye on the farmers. "What's up with those old boys?"

Dani filled her in as Rogers estimated the amount of money they would need by his best determination of the local exchange rate. He showed the figure to Dani and she nodded. "Apparently uridium's scarcer than land."

"Then we're sitting fine." Brown grinned and picked up the captain's second glass, draining it. He tried to warn her, but in the end just stared, amazed as it had no apparent impact. He picked up his own glass and sniffed at it, wondering if it was something different.

The front door opened again, and two men in black suits fidgeted their way inside. Spying Dani, they hurried to her side before they could be intercepted by the barkeep. The taller of the two gave her a quick bow.

"How are you, Miss Stargazer? We were hoping you'd still be

available."

She rose to her feet. "Gentlemen. These are my associates. How can we help you?"

The men exchanged nods. Rogers stayed seated, letting Dani handle it. Riviera had the barkeep pinned with her cool gaze as he retreated behind the bar. Rogers noted the girl staring out from the kitchen door, something akin to anxiety ablaze in her eyes.

"It's the metal you brought to trade, miss. I've found more buyers. Preliminary orders would be eighteen additional cartons." He demonstrated the approximate size in three dimensions over the tabletop, about a cubic meter total. "Payable at twenty sednas each."

Dani tapped a finger on the table, with a sideways glance at her captain. "Eighteen. Well, gentlemen, I've got maybe twelve boxes easily accessible. The others are going to take some work to reclaim. The price? I don't know."

"Price is no object!" the first sputtered, as the other glared at him.

Dani looked at Rogers, who nodded as he parsed the equivalent on his handheld. It was comparable to several hundred credits in the old universe. With any luck, it would be enough for parts for their wounded ship.

Rogers handed her a slip where he calculated a price of thirty-two sedans per box, based on what she had gotten for the earlier samples. She handed the paper to the man. He looked as though he had just eaten a bowl of *jing-sen* soup, his eyes narrowed and his lips puckered. Though he beseeched her, Dani held firm. Finally, the man pocketed the slip with a sigh.

"Very well. Half now, half on delivery." He seemed physically pained as he pulled out a paper, writing the sum on it, and handed it to Dani.

"What's this?" She looked at the paper, brow furrowed. "The other you paid in coin."

A trace of insult heated his voice. "That draft will be honored at the local financial hall."

Rogers cleared his throat. "Mr. Runyon tells us the locals prefer coin. We'd prefer that as well." He glanced over, hoping for Runyon's concord, but instead he saw Runyon had recognized the serving girl's interest in their table. Her look of alarm showed that she did too, and she vanished into the kitchen, door swinging behind her, followed by Runyon.

Mumbling unhappily, the first man elbowed the second, who

produced a purse from his inside pocket, counting out exactly the amount due. "When will we receive the order?"

Dani assured him it would be delivered to their hall within a day. A brusque nod from the two men concluded the deal. They hurried out, brushing the dust off the bar and the crow they were forced to eat from their formal clothes.

Dani eyed the money, pleased. "That should be enough for your dirty dealing, Captain." She slid the cash over to Rogers, with a jerk of her head toward the kitchen door.

"Let's go." They walked over to the bar as a group, Rogers still wary of an ambush. Scuffling and muted grunts came from behind the kitchen door, and then Runyon came out, wiping his hands on his apron.

"Something I can do for you?"

"I was thinking on our conversation. Got a proposition," Rogers said with a lazy grin.

The barkeep studied them with a speculative look. "What is it you need?"

Rogers thought a moment and leaned on the bar. "I need a wife."

Dani's smothered laugh behind him changed into a choked cough before he continued. "You have a girl who's not earning her keep." He shrugged. "Take her off your hands?"

"What about my account? Who's going to pay for that, hmm?" An acquisitive glint entered the barkeep's pig like eyes.

"If you have to dispose of her, it won't get paid anyway. Meantime, she'll eat you out of home." Rogers turned toward the door, one elbow still propped on the bar, trying to look as disinterested as he possibly could.

"You want to trade one of these?"

Rogers hid a grin, thinking what Riviera might say about that. "No, I need them. But I'll pay you for your trouble. What's the damage?" As Rogers could see the barkeep calculating the amount, he beckoned Riviera closer.

She turned a stern eye on Runyon. "The *real* total."

Runyon swallowed hard as he looked up at the woman. "Forty-six sednas and eight golders."

Rogers laid forty seven sednas on the counter. "Keep the change. Send her out here with what belongings she's got. I don't want to have to buy her anything new."

The barkeep grabbed the money and disappeared into the back, yelling for the girl. There was another scuffle, shouting, and a loud crash.

The girl burst through the door, a bruise darkening one cheek.

Runyon came after her, a large welt on his face that had not been there before. "Get her out of here before I have the constabulary haul her away! Ungrateful bitch!"

Dani grabbed the girl's arm. Before Rogers could reply, she and Riviera headed for the door with the girl in tow. Rogers on their heels, they walked with purpose up the road until they were well out of town.

No one followed them.

In the uncomfortable silence, Dani leaned forward to look at the captain, a smirk on her face. "Aren't you going to ask your wife her name, sir?"

CHAPTER 7

DANI'S words galvanized the slight girl, who turned on Rogers. "I will not serve as your wife!" she snapped.

She dropped her small black knapsack on the roadside and looked ready to fight, watching his eyes and his hands. Arms and legs were stiffly poised, a spring hiding in her knees.

"Sweet preservation," Riviera said, turning away. Rogers caught her laugh.

The captain took a step back from their new acquisition, glad they had left the environs of the town. "Now wait just a minute! I had a wife once, and I'll be damned if I'm ready for another one." He glared at Dani for provoking the girl.

"Sir, if you—"

Rogers interrupted. "Young woman, we said what was necessary to get you out of there. Cost us a bit."

"I will repay you every golder." The girl's dark eyes were like obsidian rock. She scrutinized them all as if they were fierce enemies.

"Let me finish, will you?" Rogers crossed his arms in response and eyed the little spitfire. "Better yet, let's start over. Perhaps a 'Thank you, Captain Temms Rogers' might be in order."

She studied him a few moments, unbending. "I will decide if gratitude is warranted once I know what is to be done with me."

The other women waited, idly kicking up a little road dust. Dani started to speak and Rogers held up a hand, cutting her off. "What is to be done? Well. In my culture, normally when someone introduces themselves, the other person reciprocates." He waited a minute, then looked her in the eye. "Hello, my name is Temms Rogers. I'm the captain of the ship *Doubtful*."

The girl struggled for several long moments, the internal battle with her pride clear to the captain. Finally, she brushed her blue-black hair off her bruised face and grudgingly offered her name. "I am called Liang Chao."

"A pleasure to meet you, Liang Chao."

Talking to this girl was like removing a pack of porcupine quills from one's hand. Success, in the immediate moment, seemed even more painful than failure. She would have to ease up, or she would not make it on his ship, even if she was the top navigator this side of the universal rift. He had no time for prima donnas.

"This is Dani Jamar, my chief engineer, and Riviera Brown, our chief science officer. Team, meet Liang Chao."

The women murmured greetings. The girl continued to watch him, her face tight and closed.

What did she want? He could not guarantee a damn thing at the moment, for her or for any member of his crew. She would have to trust him. Had he not proven something by rescuing her? That should have been enough of a first step.

"Now. We have a ship waiting for repair and a shipment of cargo to deliver to the trade hall. So we could stand here on the road and spit at each other, or you could take a hike." He gestured down the road back toward town. "Or we could get to work. Your note seemed to say you wanted work." He eyed her until she nodded slowly. "All right then. Do you need to say farewells? Family in town?"

Liang stared at the ground. "I have no family."

Dani broke in, despite her captain's glare. "You're welcome on our ship. We really need a good navigator!" Her firm, determined jaw condemned Rogers' brusque attitude.

The girl looked at Rogers again, distrust in her eyes. She seemed ready to bolt. The captain waited, noting her unremarkable clothing that may have fit once but was now baggy and the scuffed shoes which she had obviously tried to polish.

Come on, Temms. You know Runyon never treated her the way she ought to be treated. Give her a chance.

"It's true you're a navigator?" Rogers queried.

"It is true." The words were tossed out, defensive.

"You seem very young for that." The captain studied her with skepticism, a hint of challenge in his tone.

"Because I am not an old man like you, this means I cannot have superior skills?" Her cheeks flushed, she eyed him with defiance, echoing his challenge.

"Ouch." Riviera Brown looked away again, clearly amused.

An inner satisfaction sidling up to his annoyance, Rogers began to detect a determination and desire for respect within the girl. He could work with that. "I suppose I could give you a chance."

"Perhaps I will not give *you* one." She stared him down.

Gaining insight on the give and take she wanted, Rogers met her gaze long enough to make sure he had not surrendered. He chuckled. "Very well, Liang. We give each other thirty days. If either of us are unhappy, we part company. If we don't kill each other, maybe we can make a good working relationship. Deal?"

"Accepted."

Liang held out her hand to seal the bargain, and he shook it, feeling calluses on the slender palm. He did not know how long she had been with Runyon, but it could not have been a pleasant existence. Would life aboard his own ship be easier for her? For any of them?

The captain surveyed the road behind them, seeing nothing untoward. At least no one from town was chasing them down. He sent a shortwave to the ship with orders to gather up the scrap ASAP. When he received confirmation, he nodded to the women. "Let's get back."

On the walk, Dani and Riviera shared insights about the people in the town, particularly critical of the bar patrons. They made an effort to include Liang in their conversation but she was reticent, her eyes on the countryside. Rogers noted, however, that she stole frequent glances at her companions, demonstrating a fierce curiosity. Also a good sign. He'd had success with less.

Back at the ship, the captain found everyone healthy enough to be outside taking advantage of the fresh air and warm sun while they pitched in to work on the torn hull. Halian and several men applied themselves to cutting large sheets of ellecium bond, a temporary fix for the huge gaps in the outer layer of the ship.

Rogers surveyed the entire hull, pleased with what Halian and his people had been able to accomplish so far. At least it would hold until it could be properly reinforced with new metal parts. Those they would have to buy with the new wealth from the Marriel bankers. As he finished his tour of the repairs at the open hatch, he met Dani and those hauling the gathered parts and uridium scrap outside.

"I can take these into town if I have some help, Captain," Dani said.

"Just what I was thinking." He indicated the two ensigns, Eddy and Jerome. "You'll need big strong men to fight off the locals, I think."

She eyed him with amusement. "I'll try to keep them entertained, Captain."

As she turned to go inside, the captain cleared his throat. "Whatever you get, pay for the burial ground." He handed her the slip of paper Riviera had brought to Runyon's. "We want to appear responsible to the local community."

"Yes, Captain." She nodded and tucked the paper away safely in her jacket.

Liang stared at the breaches. Rogers could see by her solemn expression she understood what had happened. With a weary smile, he beckoned Riviera to him. "Could you please take our new navigator for a little tour of our ship while I finish getting reports? Save me some explanation."

"Yes, sir." She turned to the slight almond eyed girl. "Come on, honey, let's show you what's what."

Liang shouldered her bag and followed her, moving with purpose.

Rogers walked over to inspect the hole a Confederation torpedo had made in the lower deck of his ship. Burko had killed twenty-four of his people with that little beauty. *And very nearly my son.*

Fury bubbling in him, he stared at it for a long time, the need for revenge percolating through his mind. Letting righteous anger power his weary body, he went inside and down the nearest ladder to the lowest deck to find Halian, now working on the welds from the inside. "Status?" he asked.

"Repair will hold. Need extra internal structural layers for long space flight," Halian said. He indicated several welded spots with a rough hand. "Also many instruments with no replacements."

"Understood. We can still fly?"

"Ship will fly. Short hops, orbital rotations only." Halian peered at him with an intelligent ochre gaze. "No wormhole jumps."

Rogers nodded, knowing that both solved and created problems. "None planned at the moment. I'm hoping to hit a more sophisticated venue next, so get me a list of what you need." He examined the repaired walls. "Good work, Hal."

The Bricasterian beamed. "Yes, Captain." He tossed his tools into a plastic tub and hauled them off to his workspace.

Rogers ran his fingers over the weld, feeling the wound to his ship no less than an injury to his own body. He had struggled to gain his own command and built a team of officers he could count on. Not the most popular, many with black marks on their record, or histories that might be unattractive to a commanding officer, he gave them a chance, brought them along, and they showed their appreciation with fierce loyalty.

Even when that loyalty took them far from home and hearth.

He straightened his shoulders and set his mind back on track. Too many tasks awaited him to be brooding over this. He climbed the ladder to mid-deck, where he found Riviera and Liang finishing their tour.

"Thank you, Brown. I'll take it from here. Get some rest."

"You bet I will, Captain." Riviera smiled and then disappeared down a hallway where the lights had finally stopped flickering.

Liang stood at attention, insight illuminating her face. She seemed subdued. "There is much you did not say."

Rogers nodded, judging her solemnity demonstrated her knowledge of ship mechanics. "We were caught in a firefight and barely escaped with what lives we still have. The ship needs all the help we can get, and so do I." His heart swelled with emotion, but he had no time to deal with it now. "It's a good crew. But I need at least twenty. I have fifteen."

"For this reason you have taken a chance on an unknown entity," Liang stated with a nod. "I trust desperation does not make you believe I am just a body to fill a chair. I am a good navigator, Captain. I shall try to earn your respect." She bowed slightly.

He smiled. "I will be open to giving it. Ask any of the crew, Liang. I'm always ready to be pleasantly surprised. So, do you have any questions?"

The girl hesitated a moment and then looked up, curiosity hot in her eyes. "The name of your ship, Captain. It does not indicate strength, or daring, or military prowess. It is peculiar."

"That it is." Rogers chuckled, the brief memory bringing him a little relief from all the bad news around him. "By Confederation tradition, when first officers receive their own ship, their former captains choose its name."

It still burned him, that name. Rogers recalled late night sessions when the captain would quiz him relentlessly on scenarios. *If a cloaked force came out of a spacial rift, could they take the ship down before you would react? Would a mutiny by the crew leave you stranded on a lonely planet?*

He usually gave the same reply. "Doubtful. This is why…." Then he would go on and explain his thinking. In a tremendous joke understood by all who knew Temms Rogers, the captain christened the newer captain's ship the *Doubtful*. "Good luck, son. You'll need it," the old captain stated.

As Rogers finished the story, the irony of the name in their current state was not lost on him. "She's been the *Doubtful* since."

Liang considered his words before a hint of amusement sparked in her dark eyes. "Your captain respected you a great deal. He realized you would be greater than the name itself."

"Captain Flint was a good man, I learned a lot from him." He juggled a silver lining for a moment, Captain Flint had retired three months before, so he was not in the attack fleet at Persios. Rogers wondered if his rebellion would have held against his former commanding officer.

No time for pointless speculation. He forged ahead. "Let me show you to your quarters." He led her down the corridor to a large room he knew was now vacant, as it had belonged to his security chief. A pile of furnishings gathered in the middle of the room, and pale nets and muslin sheets hung limply on the walls.

"Set it up however you like. We haven't cleared all the crew quarters yet, so if there's a room that's unoccupied, and you see something you need, feel free to grab it."

He turned at the door. "No official meal time for the moment. Everyone just eats and sleeps when they can. We're pulling double shifts during transition. You understand?"

"I do, Captain, Thank you." She stepped inside the space which now belonged to her, not seeming to mind the confusion. "When shall I report for duty?

"Tomorrow morning should be soon enough, unless you're in a rush. Seems like you've earned a break." Rogers gestured to her face, the bruises settling in, dark and purple. "Have Doctor Montgomery see to that."

"Yes, sir." With a little smile, she looked at her hand, rubbing her fingers. "I got the fat man, too."

"Oh, I saw." Rogers chuckled. "I'll remember to stay out of your way."

Without a bit of arrogance, Liang agreed. "It would be wise, sir. I carry two trophy levels in the martial arts and I have an expert marksman classification."

Wondering if the surprises would stop, he merely smiled.

"Make yourself at home, Liang. Welcome aboard."

CHAPTER 8

AFTER he left Liang, the captain went straight for sickbay. Time to deal with Tommy.

He had rehearsed a dozen different approaches. He was not happy with any of them. Was it best to come on strong? More like a commanding officer? More like a father?

Doubtful, and this is why....

Heath Montgomery was not evident as the captain entered. Perhaps he was catching a well deserved nap. Rogers walked straight across to his son, who was awake.

Tommy's face was bruised, but clear blue eyes recognized his father at once, if the anxious shift in his shoulders was any indication. His leg was immobilized by plaster, so he could not escape, at least not easily. He bit his lip, then took a breath and looked into his father's eyes, jaw setting in a very familiar fashion. How many times had he seen Connie's jaw lock in just the same way? Rogers swallowed a sigh. Looked like he was in for a fight.

Go with the commanding officer approach.

"Ensign," he said, standing by the side of the bed, although a chair was in reach.

That got his son's attention. After hurt skittered through Tommy's eyes, he straightened as best he could. "Yes, sir."

"I understand you serve in security. Is that so?"

"I...yes, sir." A tremble now in that not-so-confident voice.

Rogers steeled himself, feeling emotions creeping up through his chest. What he wanted to do was hug the kid silly. Then smack him. Better to stay in commander mode.

"It appears the other men in your unit were killed in the attack, Ensign. That leaves you chief of security." He eyed the boy watching realization sink in. Tommy's eyes widened and his cheeks paled even more.

"Not even Chief Reilly made it?" Disbelief painted the words with a hint of anguish.

"I'm afraid not. I'll need you up and around as soon as possible.

Much to be done." His throat tight, Rogers coughed to loosen it.

"Yes, sir. I understand." Tommy continued to watch him. "Doc said you'd been injured, too." Tears came into the young man's eyes. "Are you okay, Dad?"

That did him in. Rogers could not ignore the burn of his own eyes or the heavy weight in his chest, any longer. "I'm fine, Tom." He leaned forward to embrace his son.

Tommy grabbed on to him, too, and the two clung to each other like drowning swimmers. "Dad, I'm so sorry! I should have told you. I would have, real soon. I just wanted to—"

Rogers shushed him. "If I'd known you were aboard, I'd just have worried about you."

Understatement. If he had known Tommy was there, would it have changed everything? It might have.

"Doc said we're in a new universe? Is that really true?"

"Seems to be."

Rogers extricated himself from his son's grip, straightened his jacket, still wearing what he wore to the planet. He pulled the chair closer to the bed and sat down. "We're still discovering the situation. Security isn't the only department decimated by what happened."

"What about the rest of the fleet? Surely they'd—"

Rogers cut him off. He found himself in a position that made his stomach crawl. Tommy had no idea about the mutiny. He was a loyal, gung-ho Confederation ensign. What would happen when he learned what his father had done?

"We can only depend on ourselves for now, son. I've been to town, we've gotten some local coin to buy parts and make repairs." A firm tone helped straighten his backbone as well as his voice. "One day at a time, Tommy."

The young man looked away. "Any chance we'll see Mom again?"

Not if we're lucky.

He could not bring himself to really say it. "Just another one of the answers I don't have yet, Tom." His burden gaining weight again, he stood up. "I've got a lot of responsibilities that I'm juggling right now, so I'm heading out. Check in with me when Doc says you're able, all right? We'll be in space again soon, and we shouldn't need security so much. You have some time, but not much."

The boyish smile Rogers remembered came back to his son's face, and Tommy managed a smart salute. "Yes, sir!"

Poised to go, Rogers could not help but hug his boy again. "We'll get

through this. You and me, together. We'll get through this." He clapped
the boy on the back gently and ruffled his hair. "I'll stop back and we'll
have dinner together. Let me know if you need anything."

He turned to go, sticking his head into Montgomery's office as he
left, just to let him know Liang would be in to see him. Then he headed
back to his office.

* * *

ONE of the captain's next duties would be to preside over the burial of
the dead. He sighed as he examined Montgomery's final list. Faces
flashed in his mind, memories of past battles, fighting side by side, and
this, the last battle they shared.

He decided on a mass service for those wishing to speak in
remembrance of their lost companions. Their families probably
considered them all lost anyway, as the remaining Confederation fleet
would have notified the home office the *Doubtful* had vanished.

Missing, presumed lost. Marked as traitors all, thanks to what he had
done.

Would Connie even shed a tear? Not for him. If she discovered
Tommy was aboard the *Doubtful*, that would be different. She would
curse Rogers to his grave.

Move on.

He reviewed a memo from engineering with a list of sophisticated
parts they still needed, then forwarded it to Tasiq. He also allowed
himself a personal indulgence and brewed himself a cup of hanafras tea.

One of the pleasant surprises he found when he begun resurrecting
his office was that his collection of exotic herbal leaves for teas remained
intact in their specially sectioned, airtight container made from Tela
wood. He found it under a fallen bookshelf along with a treasure even
more valuable, a hologram of himself with Tommy at his Confederation
graduation. These were the things that made him whole.

The heady scent of the strong red tinged brew inspired his effort to
clear the rest of the debris, and after the better part of an hour, he
achieved acceptable success, brushed off his hands and walked out to the
bridge.

Rogers took his usual chair in the rear row of the bridge, not wanting
to disturb those others who struggled with what they had to do. His data
was limited. He knew they would have better luck in a city rather than
out here in the backwoods. Perhaps it would be even better to deal with a
broker. He had no idea how to find one. He did not trust Oke Runyon as

far as he could pitch him. Perhaps Liang would know.

As Tasiq worked with those newly assigned to the bridge, his growl seemed to indicate the lesson was not going so well. Tasiq sat at the console as the young men stood before him, looking bewildered. "When a partial message is received, what is the best way to restore the signal?"

The yeomen fidgeted and stared blankly. Rogers took pity on them. "Tas, you've got tutorials for them, don't you?"

"Some. Not everything is accessible." Tasiq's gaze was cool, green irises tight and narrow with irritation.

"We're all running a little low on brainpower at the moment. Give them practice runs first. They can use some of the other consoles up here so they get a feel for the place."

He gestured to empty seats, avoiding the gaping emptiness that used to house Ramona's workspace. Someone had torn the twisted, blackened parts out, scavenging whatever was salvageable. *Too bad they hadn't been able to remove his memories of her the same cold way. His heart still ached for her.*

Tasiq acknowledged the order, guiding Eddy and Jerome to new seats, activating a lesson. As the lessons progressed, his ears twitched like dry leaves in the wind, and the captain recognized his irritation.

"Take a break, Tas. I'll babysit."

Tasiq, a seasoned officer, did not wait for a second invitation. "Yes, Captain." He put his station on automatic reception and left the bridge.

As the men worked, gradually catching on to their tasks, Rogers half listened to the buzz of the device monitoring local transmissions, interested in any hint of ships from his own side of the rift. As long as Burko could be alive and in range, they could be in danger if anyone used the communications systems.

Especially those outside the conspiracy.

*   *   *

WHEN the bridge shift was over, Rogers retreated to his office, but continued working until the ship passed over into third turn, beginning at the midpoint of the night. He had reviewed all the damage reports, and found himself actually better off than he would have expected. When someone buzzed for entry, he invited them in, grateful for a break.

"Captain?" Tasiq came in, his felinoid ears laid back, and his nose twitched, telegraphing his deep disturbance.

"Trouble?" Rogers got to his feet. "Let me have it."

Tasiq walked across to the desk and set a data clip on its surface. "I intercepted that message an hour ago."

Most of the playback consisted of garbled static, only an occasional word distinguishable. He recognized the name of his ship, as well as orders to search for it. His eyes narrowed. "Burko?"

"I'm still processing the entire message. But it's Confederation frequency, high level." Tasiq calmed as he waited, as if handing the news over to Rogers would solve everything.

"High level." Rogers considered that. "Coded?"

"No, sir. Confed standard. Not concealing themselves, just deep in space interference."

"On this side of the rift?"

"Unsure. Perhaps the wormhole is the cause of the interference." Tasiq fidgeted and scratched at the bandage still on his arm. "But most likely on this side, yes."

The captain swallowed hard, then asked a question that had been burning inside him. "Tas, why didn't you speak up when the others wanted to know about Burko?"

A twinkle of amusement passed through the other's eyes. "Didn't need to know."

Rogers studied him. "Do you know why I didn't share that information?"

Tasiq nodded and looked him in the eye.

"Captain, I have been your communications officer for five years now. Do you believe anything is sent from or received by this ship that I do not know it? What sort of officer would I be if I allowed that to happen?"

"You knew?" Rogers sat back in his chair, stunned. He thought Ramona had covered their tracks so cleverly. "You said nothing?"

Tasiq continued to pin Rogers in his gaze for several long silent seconds, then he looked down at the desk. "Nor will I. Burko was wrong. Dani said the right of it. What you did had to be done, and was done with courage to protect those who had not the strength."

Overwhelmed, Rogers stared for a moment, then shook his head with a dry laugh. "You could have let me know."

"I could. But if I had committed, then I would have jeopardized my standing with the remaining crew and my counterparts on the other ships. This way, I could facilitate in honesty without outing myself as conspirator."

No question, Tasiq had walked the fence. Perhaps if things had turned out differently, he would have come down on the other side. They would never know.

Better this way. He was in for all the credit now. That's what counted.

"Thanks for looking out for us," Rogers said.

"Of course, Captain. You would do no less for me."

Rogers sat back in his chair, rubbing his temples as if it would help him process faster. Confederation transmission, not coded, high level.

The possibility existed it might be his friend Darien Pomeroy on the *Victory*, the ship closest to his when the wormhole sucked them in. Pomeroy had been a co-conspirator. They worked well together. They could make a future here, the two crews collectively.

But the rebels used code. Always. This transmission was uncoded.

Much more likely that Jal Burko had crossed over with them, now close enough for the *Doubtful* to intercept this, hunting them, intending to make good on his threat.

Blast his greedy carcass to the seventh hell.

"If you get more, let me know ASAP," Rogers said.

Tasiq nodded and stepped out.

The captain considered his priorities, changing as his picture of the new universe changed. He planned to take several days to tend to the burial details, to rebuild the ship. Now it could be dangerous for them to remain here.

He summoned Brown from sleep and sent her with a detail to transport the dead to the burial site before planetary dawn. She looked at him oddly, but complied.

Next, he called Halian, to verify their repair status. The Bricasterian reiterated that they were fit to fly, but not long distances. The ugly biped was less confident of their ability to fight.

"Captain, ship cannot battle Burko. Not yet. But bright side exists."

"Oh, what's that? I could use a silver lining."

"Burko not destroyed us yet. Not found us yet. May be more damaged than *Doubtful*. Perhaps time to get away."

Rogers ran a hand over his close-cut hair. "True enough. All right, we'll have the dead buried and get off planet first thing in the morning. Make sure Riviera has what she needs."

"Will do." With that simple assurance, Halian went back to work and the Captain was alone with his concerns.

The next day, the ship *Doubtful* lifted off from its field, hull intact and departed crew laid to rest. Captain Rogers and Dr. Montgomery shared the mass eulogy as the burials took place. No one remained untouched by the emotion of their loss.

CHAPTER 9

QUIET bell tones caught Liang's attention as she finished zipping the long sleeved maroon and gray jumpsuit she had found in ship's stores, the uniform of the ship's lost Confederation. Temms Rogers' voice came over the hidden speaker.

"Liang, report to the captain's office."

Gathering her black hair, she wound it into a knot and secured it with a half dozen hairpins. Liang studied her thin face in the mirror. Her skin was pale from being locked in Runyon's back room for the last two months.

Bastard. A cruel master, that fat man. Determined to break her. He had come close.

The wristband, she had been unable to remove it. Whenever she neared an exit it shocked her. She despaired escaping her involuntary servitude. Captain Rogers had been her last chance, she was sure of it. Runyon had given up on her. She recalled the last scrimmage in the backroom, as Rogers saved her from Runyon's clutches. It was most satisfying indeed.

Closing her eyes for a moment, she centered, taking four deep breaths. The brief meditation finished, she slipped out the door.

She had been up for hours. In preparation for her shift, she left her quarters and walked the ship to familiarize herself. She knew to choose the right hand corridor toward the bridge. The muted gray hallway arched upward as it reached the bridge level. She hesitated when she arrived, not clear where she might find Rogers, but allowed instinct to dictate her choice, the door just before the one to the bridge. She was correct.

"Reporting as ordered, Captain."

Her almond gaze took in the empty black polished surface of Rogers' desk, one corner cracked as if something heavy had fallen on it. Her first impressions of him had shown a lack of discipline. He spoke as equals with members of his crew. He acted outside the bounds of protocol. She expected to find his space disorganized and cluttered with things to be done. She was happy to be surprised.

Rogers smiled in greeting. "Please, sit down." As she complied, he leaned forward, elbows on his desk. "Liang, I'm in need of information. We're on course for Roandock, our objective to obtain the following supplies." He slid an electronic datapad across the desk to her.

Liang studied the list, recognizing the sort of manufactured parts and devices requested. "Gridmark Industries." She looked over the desk at him. "*If* you intend to pay full price. Others, however, ask less questions, carry used stock and are considerably less expensive." She let the unspoken question hang between them, turning her attention back to the list.

"Comparable quality?"

She nodded. "Because the city is the main source for these items, secondhand parts are plentiful and not used to their limit."

"Then we'll save the money." From his tired smile, she guessed the captain had not slept most of the previous night. "It's hard to tell when we might come into more."

"Perhaps if I understood your intentions, it would be possible to best instruct you. What is the ship's business? How do you earn a living?" She studied him, her face expressionless. Rodolphus's teaching on patience had served her best of all her lessons since she had left school for space eighteen months before. Strength might be developed in the muscles, but the power of one's body came from an internal place, from whence it fed mind and heart. She had devoutly pursued the exercises her mentor had set, keeping her mind and body aligned and clear.

At Rogers' calculating look, Liang wondered if she had overstepped her bounds. She let her gaze fall to the black desktop. "If I am permitted to know."

"The offer is appreciated. At the moment, I'm unclear what the ship's business is going to be. Clearly our previous mission has concluded." An odd smile crossed his face. "We are currently in the business of…survival, I suppose. Other than that, I will share the information as I believe it necessary."

Something in his pale, even gaze reassured Liang that nothing she had done caused the captain's reluctance to speak frankly. "Understood, Captain. Shall I contact suppliers to arrange purchase of these items?"

"See what we can get. Bring me the estimates for approval." He stood in dismissal.

"Yes, Captain." Datapad in hand, she acknowledged his order with an inclination of the head. He walked her to the door, then followed her onto the bridge. Intuitively, she knew which empty seat was that of the navigator and took it, letting her hand slide over the buttons with familiarity. She felt tears sting her eyes, quickly suppressed, at the realization of how much she had missed her place on a ship while relegated to the hell of Oke Runyon's custody. Glancing up, she saw others on the bridge watched her with unbridled curiosity.

Rogers addressed them. "Gentlemen, this is Liang Chao, our new navigator. Liang, this is Tasiq and Parnell Eddy. Tas handles communications and Mr. Eddy is in training to be a bridge officer."

She bowed solemnly. "May fortune smile on you." She studied them as they murmured words of welcome. Tasiq was alien, and this gave her a quiet thrill, as Liang had encountered few who were not human. She took in his feline characteristics, down to the sharpened teeth. He exuded, too, the feline's comfort in his body, his streamlined movements, centered *qi*. Captivated, she hoped there would soon be further opportunity to exchange information about their cultures and backgrounds.

The other one, Eddy, was gawky and nervous, red faced and ill at ease in his chair. She watched as Eddy fumbled through an analytical program, and found it curious that Rogers would allow someone so inexperienced on the bridge. Perhaps he had been another, like herself, chosen simply as a body to fill a vacant seat. The alien seemed to have supervisory powers over the neophyte, however, and monitored his progress. Perhaps his immaturity would not kill them this day. With a last suspicious look at Eddy, she returned her attention to her own console.

Taking several minutes to familiarize herself with the strange mechanical layout, she memorized the location of the crucial functions, and was pleased that most of her knowledge carried over from the *Palva*. Thanks to the doctor's translator chip, she was easily able to understand the markings on her console and the information which appeared on her thin monitor.

A tall, well built man, his skin the color of warm polished mahogany, reported for bridge duty and took the seat next to Liang. He was very handsome, thick hair cut short but curly, large dark eyes like sable pools. Extending his hand, he smiled at her with interest. "Kai Windthorp, tactical officer."

She glanced at his hand and finally gave it a brief squeeze. "Liang Chao."

"Liang is our new navigator. We have every confidence in her," Rogers stated from behind them, as he punched several buttons and studied the results on his monitor.

Liang detected a note of skepticism in the captain's words, making her determined to chase it away. *A positive approach leads to positive results,* her mentor had taught. The captain had saved her from a situation where her life was worthless. She would repay him by making something of the life he saved.

With a slight thaw, she smiled at the muscular Windthorp and turned to the communications officer. "Mr. Tasiq, may I have an open channel to the surface?"

"Channel open."

She acknowledged him and placed her call to Jowalt Edward, a dealer outside of Roandock with whom she had dealt often. After skillfully parrying questions about her absence on the *Palva*, she managed to determine what parts he had in stock, most of what Rogers had requested, with price estimates. Compiling the list into a quick memo, she transferred it to the captain's monitor. She muted the open channel. "It will be quick and dirty, but Jowalt deals straight," she told him.

Liang watched his rugged face for approval. With a nod, he accepted the figures. She placed the order. The final exchange set the time for rendezvous at five bells local time, half a day hence. She shared this information with Rogers and then entered a course specific to the pick up.

Her rushed research on the ship's current status, through the computer's damaged conduits, verified the *Doubtful* had come through a wormhole from another universe, a place called Gilada. The computer library held next to nothing about her universe, and pitiful little on Marriel and its system.

While she had the open link to Roandock, she tapped into the local net, using the *Palva'*s credit codes. Her former captain would not have deleted her permissions from the planetary net. He never thought that far head. Searching the links, she uploaded a full registry of star charts, astrogation routes, cultural data for the sector and physics texts on the universe as taught on Marriel and her own home planet of Tang. A small smile tickled her lips as she finalized the order, charging it to Kevan's account. A small price to trade for the salve to his conscience, knowing he had sold her into slavery.

If he even let it bother him.

Kevan's struggle to keep his ship's business financially solvent had meant a lot of going without, even crew. She had learned everything, devoured knowledge when there was nothing of substance to eat, studied ship's systems and absorbed everything she could from the ship's libraries. She understood several languages, and had a working knowledge of the sector's flora and fauna. She also trained Kevan's security team in the martial arts she knew. In all modesty, she was an extremely valuable person to have on the bridge of an interstellar vessel.

Unfortunately, Kevan's bad business sense had caused several key officers to jump ship at their last stop before Marriel, with most of the *Palva*'s trading cargo in their packs. Kevan had borrowed a stake from Oke Runyon to get new cargo, which he failed to pay back.

She had accompanied Kevan to the saloon, thinking she was simply carrying his rosters, not realizing until Runyon clamped an electronic wristband on her that Kevan had sold her to the bartender in return for his debts.

"Liang, it's just for a few days, a week at most! I swear! I've got a line on cargo on Terza. I'll make it up to you, I promise!" Kevan's unshaven chin did not seem as firm as it did when he was determined.

"After all I've....You bastard!" She struggled with the fat barkeep and received a backhanded slap across the face for her effort. When she got up again, the Palva's captain was gone, and she was a prisoner.

So he could afford to pay for this. She wondered how long it would be before he noticed.

Her conscience pinged as loudly as if hit by a sonar wave. She would do spiritual penance for her underhanded act. But it satisfied her.

Before she could share what she had done, the felinoid behind the console burst out in surprise. "Captain!" The front monitor lit up with chart after chart showing the local sector as Tasiq manipulated the library controls. "It's everything we were searching for, catalogued and at hand." His green eyes narrowed as he watched the data appear in the display.

"Not a coincidence, I expect." Rogers watched a moment, then turned a curious gaze on Liang.

The navigator allowed the ghost of a smile, pleased by their reaction. "This ship would not survive long without such supplemental data. The beginning of my repayment to you, Captain Rogers."

Rogers nodded, his eyes warming. "Accepted. You will let us know if there are any other surprises up your sleeve?"

"None at present, Captain." She felt warmth at the approval in his tone, almost like a father and child. It had been years since someone had plucked her heartstrings. It was rather disturbing and wonderful at the same time. She straightened in the chair, letting a return to business cover her suddenly tight throat. "Orders?"

"Course at best speed to the pick up point."

"Laid in."

Rogers' faint smile that she had anticipated him gave her another shiver of approval. "Execute."

"Yes, Captain." She activated the coordinates and settled in for the ride to Roandock. Engaged in their own activities, the others faded from her conscious perception as she focused on her inner life. Events that had brought her to this navigator's seat crept in around her like several soft leopards, pleasing and colorful on the surface, their power and history contained within.

Liang had been a stellar student in several ways. More than just the stars, she had rabidly pursued the acquisition of information and completed the credits for matriculation a full two years before more ordinary classmates. Captain Kevan Ankho had accepted her application at first glance, despite her mere sixteen birthdays, and she moved her few belongings to the *Palva*. No need for long farewells, she had no true friends at the school. Few were as single minded as she about their work, and her intensity tended to put them off.

Being on her own never troubled her. There was no one for her to leave. She had left her parent's home when she was six and, shortly thereafter, they had died of a contagious fever that had taken half of their colony. The school administrator and teachers were kind enough to allow her to complete her schooling, waiving her tuition fees because of her scholarships. Their confidence inspired her to work even harder to justify their belief in her.

The one person she might have regretted leaving was her philosophy teacher, Rodolphus. A wiry old man with a wry sense of humor and a quick toe kick for the unwary, Roddi had been her surrogate father, mentor and spiritual guide for her years at school. They had spent many hours together, building Liang's discipline and mental strength with exercises that would meld the physical body with the mind.

For most, the graduation ceremony was a moment of triumph, for Liang it was a reminder of what she lacked. Classmates celebrated with their families, while she walked back to her room alone.

Now her path had led her to Rogers, who seemed like an honorable man, despite his deplorable habit of reducing everyone's name to suit himself. Glancing over her shoulder at the captain, she saw a warm twinkle in his eye as he caught her gaze. Pleased, she turned back to the helm. She could make a difference here, she was sure of it.

Their course well set, she helped Tasiq sort out the data libraries she had lifted, selecting certain information bits Rogers might find culturally relevant. *Doubtful* was in orbit of the second planet Marriel. The third planet, Terza, was well populated and industrialized. Perpetra was the next planet out, more mysterious in Liang's experience, as she was never allowed there. Perpetra's air space was thick with security devices. Lennor was farthest from the star that warmed it, but was well within comfort levels and ruled by a pastoral and farming culture. Each had cultural benefits and disadvantages, but Liang was hampered by her lack of information about Rogers' intent.

Tasiq seemed concerned about another ship that faded on and off the scanners. She did not recognize the frequency on which the ship broadcast, nor the signature it gave off. The communications officer tracked the ship, declining Liang's offer to help.

Another mystery to be solved when the time is right.

A short time before the scheduled rendezvous, Jowalt sent up a confirmation message. Liang arranged to set down in a public docking area within five blocks of Jowalt's shop and nodded to Rogers. "Captain, you are expected."

"Tas?" The captain's pale blue gaze was drawn, anxious. "Any uninvited company?"

"Nothing solid, Captain."

Rogers' jaw tightened. "You get a hint of anything, I want to know immediately." He rose from the captain's chair, rolling his shoulders, loosening his neck muscles. "Liang, you're with me. Tas, have Dani meet us in the aft hatchway."

"Yes, Captain." The bridge crew all stared as Liang left the bridge. Surprised, she noted Rogers hesitated before climbing down the ladder to the lower corridor to tuck a compact stunner in his boot.

"Jowalt has not been treacherous in my experience," she said, studying him with curiosity. "I would not think such precautions necessary."

Rogers grinned as they stopped at ship's stores for outerwear. Roandock was on the northern end of the Grian continent, and it was still early in the lunar year, according to the computer. The captain grabbed a thick, lined coat, and he gestured to her to do the same. "Not that I don't trust those dangerous hands of yours, Liang. I just like to be careful. You can never tell, even with someone you trust, isn't that right?"

Wondering if he mocked her, Liang shrugged on a gray jacket that matched the uniform she had chosen earlier. Of course he meant Kevan. A stab of anger went through her. That would never happen to her again. Never. She studied Rogers' back as she followed him to the aft hatchway, speculating whether he could be guilty of such treachery. She did not think so.

But then she never would have suspected Kevan either.

She would remain on her guard. Temms Rogers might seem like a fatherly sort, but they did not yet know each other well. Time would teach them both. They rounded a corner near the aft hatch, where Dani waited with a sleek black case. The two women nodded in warm greeting, and Rogers released the hatch, letting in the chill light and many smells of the city of Roandock.

CHAPTER 10

BACKDOOR dealing was the same in any universe, Rogers concluded, watching where he stepped in the small dim storefront run by Liang's contact Jowalt.

The street outside was a cultural wasteland, devoid of anyone but other 'shoppers' who would not look him in the eyes. Instead they pulled their dirty coats up to hide their faces. The peeling wood frame over Jowalt's door carried no name, just a black scribbled com-frequency on the water stained window.

Though Rogers was careful before setting down, a nagging feeling that Burko was on his tail would not fade. He kept a watch out on the street, looking for Confederation uniforms, while trying to keep his attention on Jowalt Edward.

Jowalt was thin, unshaven, and dark hair hung in his eyes. He wore layers of worn shirts over grease smeared pants that might have once been gray. The man paced himself to Liang's annoyed stride, but Rogers could not hear what he was murmuring to her.

"Come on." Jowalt slumped into the smoky back room through a blue curtain. The *Doubtful* officers took up the grudging invitation, Rogers giving the street outside one last measured look.

Assorted rusty and broken machine parts scattered across the peeling gray surface of a long table that occupied the center of the room. A bright flame burned off one end of a small tank in a rack. Jowalt turned it off as his guests entered. The pervasive odor of burnt fuel penetrated Rogers' head and within a few seconds and he longed for fresh air again. *Maybe that was the explanation. The man was brain dead from chemical inhalation.*

Wall to wall wood shelves held blackened parts. Some Rogers recognized, but others he had no clue about. Dani, on the other hand, was thrilled as she pored avidly through the metal and plasteel parts Jowalt set out for them to inspect.

The dirty man shrugged. "Best I got, but you won't find anything else that reasonable here on the block. Worked off Chao's list." His dark eyes were still fixed on the navigator.

"I think we can make some of this work." Dani sorted through the parts, studying the connections. Her hands were covered in grease. Her eyes shone. "Look at this! Just look at it!" She beamed at the captain.

"Wrap it up, D. Ship's waiting."

As Dani examined the contents of the crates, Jowalt trailed Liang, who fended off questions about her former captain with less and less civility.

Jowalt persisted. "He owes me, Chao, he owes me! Shouldn't even have let you in the door!" The swarthy dealer eyed Rogers. "This deal's cash on the barrelhead, pal. No credit!"

Rogers nodded, using Liang's demeanor as a barometer for his own need to take protective action. Despite the girl's assurances that she could take care of herself, he preferred to look out for his own. "No problem. Dani, show the man our currency."

"Yes, sir." The engineer opened up one side of her case, showing several stacks of bills from the Marriel bankers. Rogers had earlier hidden half the cash in the inside pockets of his jacket. *No need to reveal your hand until it's called.* Jowalt seemed to relax and went back to haranguing Liang.

Quiet but tensed, Liang watched the details of the transaction, marking on her datapad what Dani chose, comparing it against what had been requested. Rogers presumed she knew enough about ship repair to ensure the parts in the crates were those for which she had placed the order. He admired her ability to shut out the yammering dealer, at the same time she watched the doors, ready if action was to be taken.

When Dani completed the inventory, she wandered over to the shelves, interested in the assortment of twisted metal piled there. Rogers did not move from his position in front of the plate glass window, where he had a view of the street outside. "Anything we can use? Get it now while we can."

The engineer smiled. "It's like a museum." She held a meter long, bent hinged metal object in her hands reverently. "But really too outdated for our needs."

Rogers nodded, his eyes on Liang, whose drawn face revealed patience wearing thin. "We can spend time with cultural exhibits later."

"Yes, Captain. This is what we need." She gestured to the several meter squared crates with a last longing look at the scavenged parts on the shelves. As they watched, several small rodents skittered across the top of the metal piece she had just replaced, squeaking mildly.

"Let's go then." Rogers nodded to his navigator, who cut off Jowalt's whining ramble in mid-sentence now that her captain's orders had been fulfilled.

"Enough!" Liang's almond eyes seemed to pierce through the shifty dealer. "I have experienced Kevan's irresponsibility firsthand and I do not care to revisit it with you. Do you wish to trade or don't you?"

Jowalt hastily agreed he wanted to conclude the deal. He pulled a crusty calculating device from his pocket and punched in numbers, holding the result out to first Liang, then Dani. Liang kept an eye on the two until Dani had given him all of the money in the case and some that Rogers had held. Jowalt grudgingly gave her some unpolished change, which she tucked away quickly.

They stepped out the back, Dani giving one last look to the material in the yard when her eyes fell on a used cargo shuttle. "What's this?" She walked over, leaning down to check under it for leaks. "Oh we could use this." She ran her hand over the silver exterior lovingly.

"We've got three slipcraft." Rogers frowned.

"Those are for fighting. Several crew only. These are for cargo. Carrying things. Large things." Dani gestured to the piles outside the door. "Boxes of things."

Liang watched from the doorway. "You do not have such a craft?"

Dani shook her head, pushing the entrance locks a couple of times before it responded. She stepped inside, then came back out quickly, face off color. "What died in there?"

Jowalt shrugged. "Captain had an unfortunate taste for *Lok cha*. Took too much and it pickled his organs. Picked it up, salvage." His eyes lit with a bright arrow of interest. "Want it?"

Rogers stepped gingerly over the numerous and unidentifiable objects in the yard and looked into the shuttle just as his engineer clicked the exhaust fans into gear. A lot of space, and all filled with an indescribable odor. Stepping back, he considered it.

"You wouldn't have to land the ship every time you needed supplies, Captain. We could send the shuttle back and forth." His engineer's face bloomed like a mad petunia with plans for reconstruction and design. She jumped back up into the small ship and a few seconds later, the engine chunked into life.

"Hey! Don't light that up out here! You'll fry the inventory!" Jowalt thumped the side of the shuttle. "Hey!"

The noise from the shuttle coughed into silence. Dani reappeared, stepped lightly down. "It'll get off the ground. At least far enough to rendezvous with the *Doubtful.*"

The dealer leaned against a splintery beam, observing. "Right handy little ship to have. All you got is fighters, huh? A real war ship? What's it called? The *Doubtful?*" He studied the captain, something intelligent and dark flickering in the back of his eyes.

Rogers did not like the sudden interest, did not want to stand out in any way. "No funds for that right now, D. Even if we had the time and staff to fix it up."

"How much is it?" Dani asked Jowalt.

Jowalt lifted his shoulders. "Could part with it for one-fifty."

"One hundred fifty sednas?"

"One hundred fifty *thousand.*" The dealer wiped a grimy hand on his jacket and took a dried leaf from his pocket, slipping it into his mouth and chewing it.

Liang stepped forward and smacked Jowalt in the back of the head, dropping a long string of words in a foreign tongue the translators did not pick up. She continued to the ship, glancing inside, and kept up the invective, stopping on an up note, waiting for Jowalt to reply.

The man hung his head, shifted his weight to the other leg and scratched himself. "Tis used, after all. Fifty thousand. Cash or trade."

Rogers looked to Liang, then Dani. "Not possible. Let's pack up." He started for the door.

"Don't be hasty, Captain. I could give you discount over what the Agency will charge." Jowalt returned to his lazy pose. "Normally they'd charge what, twenty percent, Chao?"

Liang nodded. "If we were in the market."

Rogers glanced up. "Agency?"

The dealer studied him. "You know they keep an eye on major transactions. But we could call it salvage. Maybe they'd overlook it." He shrugged. The captain did not press the issue, not wanting to reveal his ignorance.

The almond eyed girl scowled. "At salvage, we shouldn't pay more than twenty. Parts will cost half that just to get it fully running. Maybe you should pay us to haul the thing off your sorry premises."

"You're killing me, Liang. First Kevan, now this." Jowalt finally succumbed to her ebony gaze and nodded. "All right. Twenty."

Liang looked at the captain. Rogers calculated what he had. Less than half the asking price. He shook his head.

Dani was checking out Jowalt's repair table. "Too bad you don't have a device to extrude your metals and fibers." She picked up the piece he had been working on when they arrived. "You just need several narrow tubes of uridium or plat here."

Jowalt snorted, sure he was being mocked. "Yah? Where would I get something like that, eh?"

Dani turned her smile on the man. "I have one. I could trade it to you for the remaining portion of the price." At Rogers' sudden look of surprise, she shrugged casually.

The captain did not enjoy the prospect of losing anything they had brought with them, as he could be sure those items worked in synch with the ship. On the other hand, he saw the advantages. He eyed his chief engineer. "Off hours only. No assigned work to be neglected."

She nodded, her grin showing she knew she had him. "Yes, Captain!"

"All right. Five minutes. We've got to get those parts back in case we need a hasty exit."

Liang murmured something to Jowalt. With a grunt, he stepped back inside the shop, and Rogers could hear him rummaging around as boxes opened and closed and metals rattled in their containers. A few minutes later he returned with a surprisingly clean contract. Rogers deferred to Liang, who was more familiar with local business practices. After a quick review, she scribbled on the bottom of it and took a copy. Rogers handed her the majority of the money he had in his pocket, and she counted it, then passed it on to the dealer. Jowalt squinted at the paper and handed her a heavy envelope, which she tucked away into her jacket.

Rogers watched a ribbon of pleasure waft over Liang's face before she tamed it into her usual complacent look. *The girl was a born haggler.* Chuckling, he took a last look in the shuttle. "Dani, you had better know what you're doing," he added under his breath. "You sure you can restore this?"

"Absolutely." Her dark eyes shone.

He took a deep breath. "All right. Take it back with your cartons there." The captain pulled his engineer aside, speaking in a low but intense voice. "Tasiq reports another Confed ship in the area. If it's Burko, I don't want to be in one place longer than I have to. Understand?"

Her eyes widened. "Burko? Stars. Understood, Captain, understood."

"Start repairs on our ship as soon as you get aboard. I want these parts installed and intersystem travel available within forty-eight. Have the ensign twins drop off the equipment you're trading. No uniforms. Low key. Got it?"

"Aye, Captain. I'll handle this." She called the ship as Jowalt checked the inside of the cargo shuttle. She could tell Rogers was debating if he should wait for the team to join her, rather than leave her alone. "I'll meet you back at the ship, sir," she said more insistently.

He nodded and turned to find Liang on his heels. With a final troubled look, he left Dani and Jowalt to conclude the deal. Hesitating before he stepped out into the street, he scanned the sidewalks for a familiar uniform or face. He saw nothing specific to alert him of danger. The feeling still crawled up and down his spine. *Burko.*

He caught Liang watching him, and he smiled to reassure her. "I'm a cautious man."

"You are a man looking over your shoulder." She observed. "One who watches behind him expects the hunter on his heels."

Too close to the mark. "Perhaps so. We'll discuss it back at the ship. Any other business on the surface?"

She looked up at him thoughtfully. "You are still short of crew. There is a labor hall not far from here where those between jobs gather."

The captain still needed a dozen men and women to keep the ship even minimally staffed. At the same time, he had other considerations before he chose new officers. Rogers had not yet decided whether his goal should be to return to his own universe. If that was his decision, he could not in all fairness hire on crew unprepared to abandon their homes and their lives for a strange universe, without telling them the whole truth.

Liang was a special case. She had no family, no one to leave behind, if the ship moved on or if they went back. But if the *Doubtful* stayed here….

The matter provoked confrontation with a serious choice he did not want to be forced to make until he studied all his options. As it stood, the ship might not function in either universe. After repairs, he could likely survive here. A return to the Giladan universe would require the repair of the alien device. If that was even possible. The longer he held off the decision, the more options he might have. So he intended to wait as long as he could. As long as Burko would let him.

In the meantime, he needed enough crew to fly. It would not hurt to see what might be available in Roandock. It had to be something better than prostitutes and drunken farm boys. Didn't it?

CHAPTER 11

THE busy thoroughfare was a contrast to the lazy main street in Marriel. Lots of traffic. Lots of people. Lots of noise. A brief open shuttle hop via Roandock public transportation had brought them to the other side of the city. Liang suggested they continue on foot.

She followed him silently, as he filled her in on the personnel needs as he saw them. Reconstruction was a priority, and he only had two engineers. Trained bridge crew and medical staff would be a plus. He would be willing to consider people with assorted skills, any skills, that were willing to train. He was that desperate.

As they walked, he also studied Liang Chao. For someone so young, she seemed to have great depths. The data she provided for the ship's libraries was thorough and vital for *Doubtful's* existence here. Then there was how she handled Jowalt. Despite her talents, she seemed to negate appreciation or recognition. He looked forward to getting to know her better, if only to gauge how much her developing value would repay his meager investment.

They passed through a commercial district blazing with advertisements and brightly lit windows displaying merchandise on dark toned mannequins. Rogers glanced at what was considered fashion on this world, finding little redeeming value in the sparkling pseudo fabrics presented for consumption.

He had never been considered a sharp dresser, much to Connie's dismay, but then he wore his Confederation uniform most of the time. On his off hours, the captain lounged in well worn dungarees and natural fiber shirts in bright clashing colors, an addiction Connie had never been able to cure. "Who would wear that?" he asked his companion, stopping in front of a particularly garish combination of slinky magenta open blouse and slacks.

She gave him an odd look. "It does not seem practical." Dismissing the colorful duo and window shopping in general, her gaze focused instead on passing pedestrians and vehicles.

"Right." He was somehow reassured that she was no more interested in such frippery than he was. "Just as well for what that cost."

Liang nodded. "That would feed a family for two days in the village where I was born. It is an inconceivable waste of resources."

Rogers smiled. *My daughter, Linz would never have considered that rate of exchange. Her main concern would be how her latest beau perceived her new outfit.*

He followed her down the crushed crete sidewalks to a less sophisticated district, no less consumer oriented though the price tags weren't as obvious. Women leaned against painted doorjambs, a seductive light in their eyes. Several taverns blared music on the block where the labor hall was located. Liang never blinked at the open sexuality or the intoxicated people shoving past, but continued with lowered eyes and great attention to their course until they came to the three story brick building which housed the labor union of the Brotherhood.

As Rogers reached for the brass handle, the door burst open and a man came flying out, landing on his back on the potholed street. Stunned for a few moments, the sinewy black haired fellow shook off the impact and weaved upright, turning an intelligent sapphire gaze on Rogers and Liang.

"What you lookin' at, huh?" He brushed off his navy blue shirt and pants, made of some natural fiber and rather obviously worn by work. Noticing the navigator's regard, he smirked. "See something you like, honey?" Before swinging the door open and returning to a large welcoming shout from the men inside.

Liang stiffened beside him, but tightened her jaw and pushed open the heavy wooden door. Rogers expected that most women who spent time space-faring had adjusted to the male oriented culture. The Confederation had implemented rules against gender harassment, but those regs were ordinarily relegated to a dusty shelf with other handy bureaucratic dictates and politely ignored by ship's captains. But seeing how women were treated at Marriel, and not much better here, Rogers mused, a thick skin would be a particularly useful necessity.

Inside, the large paneled hall was smoky and dim, its walls a bland pale beige. The main room had a high ceiling, light fading down over several dozen gray folding chairs scattered in loose rows. Approximately fifty men and women, mostly men, engaged in various activities throughout the room. The vast majority sat in the folding chairs, ones and twos, their faces drawn with anxiety. Some played cards or dice, in waiting mode.

Several heavy wooden desks sat in the front of the hall, each manned by a tough looking foreman with a computer set, several clipboards and a basket of paperwork. Off to the right was a long wooden counter, where applicants wrote on thick yellow paper. Signs printed in black block letters hung on the wall, reading: "Have you paid your Dues?" and "No DUES, No JOB," and "No Spitting, Chewing or Credit Granted." In the rear was a sign that read: "SMOKING ROOM."

Rogers studied the crowd and determined that the men at the head desks interviewed candidates from the waiting pool, and then entered the information into their computers. The applicants would return to their seats, so there must be some way they were notified if their qualifications earned them a shot at a job. The captain considered this and wondered how potential employers registered their needs.

He had never gone through such a process and hoped he never would. The faces he saw reflected desolation, desperation, people down on their luck, uncertain where their next credit would come from. They might wait for the better part of the day, waiting for someone to offer them a hand up to independence. *Maybe one of them is waiting for me.*

Before he could ask Liang how to get the consideration of the union Brotherhood, his attention was drawn by the raised voice of the man they had encountered at the door. He was arguing with another man, better dressed and more tired looking than he was.

The black haired man was unmistakably on the defensive. "C'mon, Cap, you know I'm surely trained for the job!" He took several steps after the man, hands out in supplication. "You ain't gonna find a better engineer this side of Katarr! I rebuilt the bleeding transcoil, for Sprechan's sake!"

The other man was having none of it. "And you know what, Quinn? That's the damn shame of the whole thing. You've got a hell of a set of hands. You've got a brain somewhere inside that damned thick skull—"

"That's what I'm sayin'—"

"That may be, Quinn, but I'm not dealing with you any more! I'm tired of the dirty tricks and the sniping." The captain glared at him. "I've lost three skilled officers I could not spare because of your mouth and your mindset, and I can't keep on this way. I don't care if you could build me a new ship out of rocks and marshmallows. If you can't work *with* us, you're not that valuable." He turned and stalked away. "We're finished! Done!"

"Unbelievable!" The black haired man stared after the captain, looking as if he had opened a long awaited birthday present to find an empty box. "Un-effing believable!" His buddies turned away, and he scowled, then stalked back to the smoking room, muttering.

Do we have rocks and marshmallows?

Rogers squelched the facetious thought. Those who watched the confrontation smirked and snickered, then went back to what they had been doing. Could Quinn really be that bad? He tried to guess how hard it was to get good help. Would the captain have tossed someone with that kind of promise casually aside? Or was the situation really critical?

Worth consideration, though. Not every officer was a fit for every crew. Maybe he just needed a guiding hand.

A moment later, Temms realized his companion was no longer behind him. A quick survey of the room found Liang speaking to a thin, pasty man leaning against a wall that could have used a coat of new paint some years earlier. Listening to conversations around him, but learning nothing useful, he crossed the hall to speak to her. As he neared, Liang nodded to her informant, who smiled a toothless grin as she left him to meet Rogers.

"Tell me you have good news," Rogers said, keeping one eye on the door where the black haired man had disappeared.

Liang lifted her shoulders slightly. "Perhaps. Oster says there's a glut in the market for tech personnel. It is possible you could engage the services of several persons here. However, in recent months the leaders of the Brotherhood have raised their rates for employers to participate. The cost is exorbitant. Two thousand sednas just to register and then for each person hired, a premium of one hundred."

Rogers looked up at the row of desks, where the thick foremen continued to process applications. He had not realized what a bargain he received upon buying Liang's freedom. "No way around it?"

"None."

"Pity. We need personnel and people here need work." He glanced at those waiting and wondering if this would be the day their lives changed.

"Oster said many here have come for weeks without success. The Brotherhood has changed from its early days when its primary function was to help its members find employment. Those in power created complicated circles to keep themselves in power, and this has become the mission of the leadership." She sighed as she glanced around the room. "But the innocents suffer."

Rogers looked at the young woman, thinking how her description paralleled his earlier musings about Jal Burko and the Confederation. "Are they aligned with this 'Agency' that Jowalt was talking about earlier?"

"They pay tribute to the Agency, just as every business organization does." She shrugged and studied his face, seeing his real confusion. "The Agency is not part of the system government, but they work closely, overseeing taxes and collections. As consideration, they are allowed to collect a percentage off the top, so they sample the best technology and cargo from mercenary ships that travel between our planets. They are very powerful. It makes no sense to fight them. We just try to avoid their notice."

Rogers raised an eyebrow. "No one fights them? What about a union of captains or some other group?"

"*No one* fights them." Liang's voice was quiet but firm. "When they get the best tech and weapons, no one has the wherewithal to take them on."

"Huh." Rogers frowned. He noticed two men watching him from across the room. Though their faces were not remarkable, something in the way they stood drew his attention. Their haircuts were sharp and military. That odd sense traveled through his bones again. Could they be from the *Talon*?

"We've got to go," he said quietly, though he was not quite finished. "Don't have money to invest in the labor hall at the moment. We'll have to think of some other way."

Rogers ambled for the door in a path opposite the watchers and past the group where the man they called Quinn had returned to sulk amidst a bunch of cronies. "We won't find anyone here who will be able to tackle our project," he stated, gauging his voice to rise as they passed Quinn. "Looks like the locals don't have the engineering skills we need."

Liang gave him a curious look, but nodded in reply, following him toward the door.

"We shouldn't have expected anyone to want a chief's position." He held the door open for Liang, then stepped out into the street after her, having noticed with satisfaction the black haired man's sudden twist of the head. Waiting just outside the door, Rogers pulled her aside. "Let's see if we caught us a fish."

As the captain had expected, Quinn barreled through the door a few seconds later, looking anxiously up and down the crowded street. "Hey!" Relief evident on his face, Quinn walked up to the captain. "You looking for an engineer?"

Rogers studied him impassively and crossed his arms, trusting that Burko's men would not be in a hurry to follow, if they had pegged him. *If they were Burko's men.* "Could be. Why'd your captain toss you?"

"My cap—" Wide-eyed, Quinn stopped and looked back at the door.

"Oh, you caught that, huh?" Rogers watched the man's face as he struggled for an acceptable explanation, realizing this Quinn was younger than he first appeared. The engineer's face was worn, but his eyes had no crow's feet. "Some of the other crew had it in for me, that's all. Expected special privileges cause they were, you know...." His voice trailed off. "Not like *us*."

"Not like us?" Rogers kept watch on the crowd but the passersby seemed disinterested. The door to the labor hall did not open. Liang was at his elbow, on alert. The captain wondered if Quinn's comment implied something sexist, remembering the man's earlier disrespectful comment to his navigator. "You mean, *men?*"

"No!" The man snorted in disgust. "Sprechan's privates. I mean Not. Like. Us. You know. Alien?"

"Oh, *that* not like us." Rogers nodded, thinking of his crew. *Well, there might be a few surprises for this young man, then.* "I'm the captain of a mid-size ship, and I might be hiring reliable people." From the man's stance and shifty eyes, Rogers guessed there were some things he was not being told. But he had a soft spot for the hard cases. It was what his first captain had done for a troubled, young, Temms Rogers, some thirty years before, when he had barely scraped through the Confederation school. He repaid the debt by doing the same for others.

The black haired man frowned. "How small?"

Rogers raised an eyebrow and described the ship, with its engine capability and full personnel consignment. "We're recovering from a full out battle. Frankly, I'm not sure my people are up to the repairs." This was not true. He knew Dani Jamar and Halian would be able to rig whatever parts they could get to work. But reading this man, he guessed Quinn would use the ego boost to convince himself to accept the position. Besides, this man was familiar with local materials and equipment, which would be valuable in many of the ways having Liang at his side was beneficial.

"So are you contracted with the Brotherhood, Mr—" Rogers jerked his head back toward the door.

The man scuffed a hard booted foot on the crete. "Just got shit-canned. Ain't had a chance to sign on yet for Roandock." His handsome face took on a crafty look and he grinned, revealing slightly crooked but white teeth. "Means no one's gotta fork out payola. You neither."

Rogers nodded. "Exactly. Good for you, good for me." He saw he had the man thinking. *Now the final sell, seal the deal.* He extended his hand. "Captain Temms Rogers."

The man looked at his hand a moment, then shook it warmly. "Benzi Quinn. Future engineering chief of the—"

"The *Doubtful.*"

Quinn blinked. "What kind of name is that for a war ship?"

Rogers caught the flash of amusement in Liang's eyes. "Long story. I'll tell you sometime over some honey ale." The door to the labor hall opened and two men came out. He pulled Liang aside as he ducked carefully next to the wall, behind several taller men waiting to go inside. The men looked both ways down the busy street, turned the other way, and walked away at a quick pace.

Good. Now we get out of here before we find out for sure who those men were.

"We lift off at first light tomorrow." He asked Liang to share the coordinates of their docking unit. "We won't be passing this way again for some time, so I'd say my goodbyes if I were you."

Quinn shrugged again. "Good riddance to this place. Won't hurt me none to never touch down again. See you then, Cap." He winked at Liang. "And you, doll face." He smirked and returned to the hall to share his news and grab his things.

Rogers felt the navigator bristle beside him. He leaned over to her. "Perhaps once he's on board, he will have the opportunity to learn proper manners."

"Perhaps *I* will volunteer to teach him."

Her deadpan delivery did not divert Rogers from her carefully controlled fury. *The boy's got it coming.* He chuckled and led the way back toward the connecting transport for the docks.

CHAPTER 12

UPON his return, the captain was briefed on the positive progress of the repairs and the recovery and return to duty of some of the injured crew, including his son Tommy, who waited for him in his office.

"Doc sprung you?" Rogers said, giving his boy a hug. Upright, Tommy stood as tall as Rogers himself. When had that happened? Tommy left for the Confederation academy before Rogers came home from his last tour. In the two years since they last seen each other, Tommy had grown four inches.

And I've gone nearly gray.

Tommy limped a little as he approached the desk. Braced in a heavy blue splint, his leg extended straight, making his movement awkward. "Yeah. I made him. You need me."

"I do need you." Rogers sat on the front of his polished black desk, torn between his memories of Tommy as a rambunctious child and the young man who stood here, proud, in his Confederation uniform. *Business.* "You and about thirty other bodies."

"Right." Tommy eased himself into one of the chairs at the desk, then shot up again. "May I, sir?"

Rogers waved him back. "At ease, Ensign. It's just us." Amused, he relaxed, too. "Although it's wise to observe protocol when the others are present."

Tommy returned to the seat. "It's going to be strange, isn't it, Dad?"

Probably an understatement. "I'd tend to agree. I never intended for you to be here, Tom." He certainly had not expected to steal his son away to a new universe. He took in a breath and felt his ribs expand, the guilt within inflating to fill every inch of his body. Pushing the breath out of his lungs, however, did not lessen any of his remorse. It only accumulated.

"Guess a lot of things happened we didn't expect." Tommy stared at the floor. "I'm sorry about Ramona, Dad. Everyone says how good she was to you."

Rogers' throat caught. That was the last thing he expected his son to say.

"Thank you, Tommy. I know you kids never...I mean, considering the way your mother felt about her."

It was awkward to be discussing this with him. Connie blamed Ramona for their break up, even though he did not start working with her until three month after he took up residence in the Confederation officers' quarters. Hostility had kept Ramona from family events with him, which hurt him more than it did Ramona. It did not matter any more, for multiple reasons. Tommy and his ship was all that mattered now.

"Are you up to going back to duty?" Rogers asked, studying his son.

"I think so." The young man shifted in his chair, his gaze flickering away, then back to his father.

"It's a big responsibility."

The captain detected a shift in the ship's thrum, considered it, and then let it go as something not of consequence. Refocusing on his son, he considered the security position, not able to let it go quite as smoothly.

Rogers could, perhaps, have ducked making Tommy head of security. His staff choices were limited, but he could have stuck someone else there if he had to. For most of his years, Tommy was a steadfast boy, trustworthy, and he had done well at the Confederation school. Tommy's reckless streak, and an unfortunate tendency to take on more than he could handle, made this appointment less attractive. In their own universe, with a full staff and access to support, he would have felt better about it.

But you lost that option.

His son's face, determined, innocent and honest, seemed to beg for the chance. "I know it is. But Chief Reilly taught me a lot, Dad. I'll do my very best for you."

"I'm counting on it."

His intercom buzzed with a message from Tasiq about the planetary cultural files Liang had sent them. Checking his monitor, Rogers studied the visuals Tasiq found in a sub-archive, images of assorted artifacts with markings much like those the *Doubtful* had used to create the wormhole. "Unbelievable."

"What is it, Dad?"

Rogers looked up. "I've got to analyze this data a bit, Tommy. Why don't you come back this evening, and we'll look at this as a team, all right?"

* * *

"IT can't be an accident that these artifacts exist here," Rogers mused as he mulled over representations he had printed out. He handed them around to his *de facto* command team Liang, Dani, Halian and Tommy, all gathered in his office for a hot cup of spiced tea from Rogers' personal collection and some cookies he had found in stores. He included Liang, intending to blend the two crews, the old and the new, and also because she seemed to have a solid handle on how things worked in this universe. He included Tommy because he did not intend for his son to be out of his sight if he could help it. Even fresh from his sickbed, the young man had an eye for a pretty young girl, and after their introduction, scored the chair next to Liang.

Hiding a grin at his son's perspicacity, Rogers took a moment to express silent thanks to whatever fates had given him this gift, and then returned to the artifact discussion. "This suggests that the Old Ones existed in many universes. Perhaps, they seeded many worlds with their offspring, us in particular, before moving on."

Dani nodded. "Many cultural belief schemes suggest an advanced race that visited more than one world. It's not a huge leap to expand that theory across universal boundaries." She took a sip of tea. "Now that we know there's more than one universe."

"That's right." Rogers turned his monitor to face the others, showing portions of the two sets of artifacts side by side. The characters, faint against the terra cotta rock, had definite similarities. Ramona's relics included more metal than these pictures Tasiq found, but they had to be the same. "The fact that we arrived here would suggest this specific technology be used for traveling between universes, from both sides of the rift."

Halian grunted. "Means if we can gather parts, we can return."

Should they? There was the painful question. An uncomfortable silence ensued while former conspirators Dani, Rogers and Halian traded charged glances. Liang observed the soundless exchange but did not comment.

Tommy sat up tall in his chair. "The sooner, the better."

Rogers cleared his throat. "A discussion for another time, when we have more information."

Tommy stared a moment, questions burning in his eyes, but Rogers gave him the 'you're an officer now' look. That seemed to cool him off. *Blast it all. Walking this line is going to be damned difficult, having to look my boy in the eye and lie every day.*

"It's good to have you here, Tom," Dani interjected.

Distracted, Tommy grinned. "Thanks. I meant for it to be a surprise, and well—"

"That it was," Rogers said.

"You look just like your dad's holo." Dani gestured to the treasured item, back in its honored place of display. "Chip off the old block, hmm?"

Tommy rolled his eyes, then must have realized he was in the company of ranking officers. "Sorry, ma'am," he said.

Hard to be twenty two years old and suddenly head of your department. Rogers lifted his cup in his son's direction. "These after hours talks are informal, Tommy. No need to worry about stepping on toes here."

"Yes, sir. Thank you, sir." A sheepish smile passed across the young man's face. "Dad."

Dani laughed and passed the box of cookies again. Liang refused cookies, adjusting the display so she could study the manifestations. "Who among your crew can decode the language?"

Grateful to change the subject, Rogers thought about his decryption team. Ramona had been team leader, but she and the two others were killed in the attack. "No one who's still alive."

"You've still got the linguistics diagnostic program?" She put her hands in her lap.

"We do, though parts of it are compromised."

She nodded. "We might also seek out people of such training when we interview potential crew members. Assuming we will not always do so on a street corner."

Rogers caught the critical tone as she referred to the acquisition of Benzi Quinn. Tommy bristled but did not say anything. Rogers smiled and reached for his mug. "We find our crew in most unexpected places, wouldn't you agree?"

"Of course, Captain." She stood up. "I have a facility for languages, Captain, I'd like to volunteer."

"Excellent. Any progress is to be reported to me immediately."

"Understood, sir." Liang sat down her empty cup. "I'll begin now, with your permission."

Was the girl a glutton for punishment? "Morning would be soon enough, Liang."

Tommy jumped to his feet. "I'd be glad to help."

Realizing his interest probably had more to do with hormones and less to do with linguistics exercises, Rogers tried not to shake his head.

The boy was likely heading for heartache. Liang had dealt with plenty of infatuated young men, if what he had seen at Runyon's place was any indication. The captain would lay down a years' salary, if he still had one, that she was not going to be interested in the least.

"Go on, then. Liang, remember Tommy just got out of the infirmary, okay? Take it easy on him."

"Yes, sir." With a slight bow, she left the captain's office. Tommy shot him an annoyed look, then left on her heels.

Dani smiled as the door closed behind them. "You weren't sure about Liang, but I knew she'd be a good addition."

The captain agreed. "She's bright. Perhaps brilliant. I like the way she thinks and I appreciate her moral center. I think we haven't scratched her surface yet." He swirled the amber liquid in his cup. "But you know she'll guess what really happened long before Dr. Montgomery and the others do."

Halian grumbled and shifted in his chair, which was built for a smaller, more compact species. "Five, perhaps ten there are who remain unaware of rebellion. Tasiq not a problem. Not care. Doctor more difficult, important man in Confederation politics. Jerome, Eddy both young, excitable. Could be trouble."

Rogers nodded. "I agree. Hudson is still in a coma in medical. Montgomery doesn't expect he'll live." He studied them thoughtfully, and then looked at his monitor. "We can hold off the discussion of repairs to the Ancients' console because we've lost Ramona. Even if Liang is adept with her translation, before we can reconstruct the device, it may take years to find the right collection of parts. *If* they even exist here."

"The logs will be repaired much sooner than that," Dani said quietly.

"Exactly. Then the clever ones will discover we fired on our own ships, and they fired back." He tapped his stylus on the obsidian surface of the desk as he considered his options, then made his decision. He turned to Dani. "I want you to break out the logs of the last three hours before the wormhole appeared. Download them onto hard disks and seal them. Then make it look as if the logs had been permanently damaged. That will keep them from curious eyes."

"Aye, aye, sir." Dani made a note.

"Once we see if we *can* get back, then we'll make the determination if we *will*." He eyed them both. "This whole discussion may be moot if we encounter Burko on this side of the rift."

He explained what Tasiq had shown him, bringing exclamations of surprise as the others realized Tas had been on their side all along. "But the communications aren't all. At the labor hall, I spied a couple of men who might have been *Talon* crew."

Dani frowned. "Sensors haven't picked up their ship. We've done test after test. If Burko's here, he's doing a fine job of concealing himself."

"Sensors, engines, weapons, all have to be one hundred percent ASAP. We may have to cut and run." He rose from his chair to pace, as he considered the unknown quantity of Benzi Quinn. "It's why I picked up Quinn. I'll warn you, he expects to be chief of engineering," Rogers said without apology. "We needed someone local and knowledgeable. So I agreed, despite his issues."

Halian looked somewhat amused, but Dani Jamar bristled at the new man's elevation.

"Chief? He's walking in here as chief? With all due respect—"

Rogers held up a hand. "No. He can call himself chief, king or Grand Center of the Universe, if it makes him do the job. You're still department head. He reports to you, just like the rest of the staff. Once we get to know him and see if he's all mouth, then I'll revisit the issue. But it's not open for discussion."

"Yes, sir." Dani contained her emotions, but the way she would not look at him let him know she was still unhappy. "I'll run him through the drills."

"Thanks, D. I'm counting on you."

Dani looked skeptically at Halian. "He doesn't like aliens, you said?"

"Issues." The captain smirked. "We're giving him some latitude. He'd best do the same."

"Could be amusing." Halian's face twitched in his approximation of a human smile.

"Just don't break him in the first week, all right?" Rogers studied Hal, knowing the unflappable alien would work with anyone. "Call him Chief. He'll like that. We'll get through this." He stretched wearily. "That's all, team. Get some rest."

"Good night, Captain." Dani cleared the rest of the cups as a courtesy and then picked up her datapad from the desk.

"Good night, D."

As Halian groaned to his feet, the captain wondered idly whether the gentle giant had enjoyed a complete four hours' sleep since they had crossed. "Night, Hal."

"Night, sir." Halian plodded out with Dani, both on to a discussion of their next day's work. Hal planned to rebuild the weapons guidance ports. Dani would start on the logs during the third turn, where there would be less eyes to pry.

Rogers stashed his notes in the desk and retired to the observation deck, stepping inside without turning on the lights. He sidled as close to the man sized, floor to ceiling port as he could, immersing himself in the cool, silent darkness of space. Some people felt lost without familiar sights around them, but he experienced this new set of stars as a relief. In letting go of home and all it stood for, he could release the pressure to perform.

As long as I take care of my crew and my ship, here, now, that's enough.

Into the silence slipped echoes of whispers past. He closed his eyes, and could almost feel Ramona's hand on his shoulder, her arm slipping around his waist, as it used to do when they came to this room together. A ghost of breath against his ear, a warm touch, so very close for a moment before reality stole them away.

She was gone. They had left her in a field on Marriel, under the bright sun.

"May the gods bring her peace," he whispered, his throat choked with too much emotion to speak any louder. The remembrance of her in this hour so close to exhaustion tore at his heart, and the grief he had held back spilled over into his hands like a flood of river water, nearly washing him from his feet.

He let the tears come until his anguish faded once again into a dull ache in the background. Like the rest of his crew, he needed to focus on what he had, not what he had lost. A deep breath cleansed the sorrow, for the moment. He returned his regard to the stars before him, tossing out unspoken questions until the lack of answers left him ready for sleep.

* * *

AT daybreak the next morning, Rogers stood at the public docking facility, waiting as last minute cargo, mostly foodstuffs, were loaded and stored in the *Doubtful.* Liang had provided the names of several trade houses, and Riviera Brown had added purser to her set of hats. Using the last of the money Dani received at Marriel, Riviera purchased replacement provisions expected to last the ship for the next month.

The tarmac echoed as carts and small vehicles hurried from point to point, delivering passengers and crates to their destinations. The air held traces of burnt fuel and decaying leaves. The day was clear but cool, reminiscent of his early cadet terms at the Confederation school.

The loading crew came up with the last crate, seeds and plant cuttings for hydroponics. Now Brown could be happy and useful, and we will stop less often for supplies.

No one appeared to take special notice of him or the ship, so he hoped he had lost the men tailing him. *If they had been tailing him.* Only a few more minutes, then the ship would be off planet again, as soon as their recalcitrant bad boy was aboard. In space, once the sensors were up to par, it would be easier to watch for Burko, or anyone else from their side of the rift.

But Benzi Quinn was late.

Disappointed, Rogers checked his chronometer. His attention wandered, caught by activity at the next docking berth. A sleek ship, clearly expensive, was in process of being loaded by several liveried porters. Considering the amount of containers being moved from hovercarts into the ship, he estimated the ship had to be two-thirds cargo space to fit it all.

His real interest was not the cargo, but the striking woman with gently coiffed blonde hair and expensive hat, dressed in white, pacing by herself, gesturing as though conducting an internal argument. Every so often she would grab a package from the porters' hands and set it aside on the tarmac. She accumulated quite a little pile of boxed belongings when she noticed Rogers' observation. She stopped pacing and smiled, revealing a true beauty.

"Did you ever do something because it seemed right at the time and then you realized it was the exact wrong thing?" she called over, clutching at the front edges of her white fur coat. Her voice resonated at a warm, friendly pitch. She balanced perfectly on a pair of white platform sandals, thin straps hardly holding them on her feet.

Why did his face elicit confidences from total strangers? Not like it was the first time. He must just look like a regular kind of guy. "I think we've all done that."

The woman eyed the shiny ship next to her, fingering a ring on her left hand. "But you're never sure, right? I mean, things could turn out. Maybe they could turn out great. As long as you make some people happy. Is your own unhappiness so important?"

Rogers shifted his weight from one foot to the other. He preferred not to hand out advice on personal lives to people he hardly knew. Even pretty ones. Fortunately, she rescued him with a self-deprecating laugh and a vague wave of her other hand.

"Just ignore me. Last minute wedding jitters, right? All the excitement of a new place, leaving everything and everyone you know, that's all. Anyway, my troubles are none of your concern. You're kind to listen." She smiled again and returned to pacing.

One of the porters cried out, nearly dropping his load, blood on the hand he cradled to his chest. The woman's anxiety changed to a professional mode. She dug in the suitcase nearest her and pulled out a medical kit. The deck supervisor stalked over, sharp words spewing from his thick lips, implying the boy had faked his injury.

The woman stood between boy and man, snapping a reply at the supervisor. The captain could not hear what she said, but the supervisor backed away, pale. She returned to bandaging the boy's hand, taking great pains to make sure he had been examined and treated gently and well. When she finished, she spoke softly to him, then let him return to work.

Somehow pleased by the woman's sense of priorities, Rogers checked his chronometer again. Quinn obviously did not intend to impress the captain with his punctuality.

His supplies loaded, Temms turned to walk back up the gangway, but stopped, intrigued, when a large vehicle stopped at the next docking berth. A man in a well tailored black suit, with short clipped black curls and a neatly trimmed mustache, got out, barking orders to the laborers, who rushed to unload several large trunks and assorted boxes from the back of the vehicle. The woman seemed put off at the sheer size of the production. After a few minutes, she approached the tall gentleman, interrupting the process. He just ignored her and ordered the others about more loudly.

She reached for the arm of the boy she had bandaged earlier and pulled him to a stop with a sharp comment. "I said, no!" The others turned to stare, curious.

Face flushed, the man glared at her. "Okalani! We've been through this! I will not tolerate this opposition much longer."

"Geoffrey, I think this is a mistake."

"For the second time, this is the correct ship. You have no reason to doubt my word. Now get aboard." He waved at the porters, who stepped into action again.

The woman shook her head. She slipped off the coat. "No." She waved a hand at the crates still waiting to be loaded. "*This* is a mistake." She tossed the coat at him, retreating toward her little pile. "Geoffrey, I don't want to marry you."

"You have to." He grabbed for the spotless white fur, catching it before it touched the ground, clutching it like a cherished loved one. His frame tensed, and he wagged a finger in her direction. "The contract's been signed!"

Rogers scanned the tarmac for security but saw no one in uniform, or anyone but himself even interested in what was going on. The porters froze, likely unwilling to defy someone who paid their salary. As the man reached for her, Rogers took a step down the gangway, ignoring that small voice in his head warning him not to intercede.

Distraught, the woman glanced at Temms and then back to the gentleman. "It's just a piece of paper!" she cried. "My father can pay the penalty! I'd rather marry the next man who crosses my path!" She turned and started to run, nearly colliding with Rogers.

Why do wives I don't even want keep dropping in my lap? Temms caught her as she tripped in those ridiculous shoes. "Are you all right?" he asked.

"Fine." Her face was hot with embarrassment, and her brown eyes were warm and responsive, and a little desperate. "I'm sorry about all this."

Before Rogers could let her go, the man was on them. "Unhand my wife, you fool!" His right fist sailed toward the captain's chin.

Thanks to his years of military training, Rogers evaded the punch, then shoved the man away, out of reach. "Look, I'm just a disinterested observer. I don't care about marital status. But I don't think you should hurt the lady." He raised his hands, palms open. "Just saying, friend."

Geoffrey's eyes flashed. The tendons in his neck looked tight enough to play like a stringed instrument. Recovering faster than Rogers anticipated, he jumped forward, and caught him square on the right cheek. Eyes crossing, Rogers fell to his knees, a jab of pain running through his jawbone into the back of his head.

"Geoffrey! You're insufferable!" The woman fumbled in her bag for a small spray can, which she proceeded to empty into her former fiancé's face. Acrid fumes filled the air around them, causing everyone's eyes to water. The man stumbled in the direction of the sleek ship, bellowing. Several men ran over, one speaking into a com-unit as the others tended their master.

"What I ever saw in him," the woman muttered. Tossing the empty can aside, she took out her medical kit again. "Hold still. Let me fix that." She knelt down to apply something cool and soothing to Rogers' aching jaw.

"Are you a doctor?" he mumbled. His teeth felt like they had exploded. For a dandy, the man packed some real power. His head spun. *And where's Tommy and my crack security team to protect me, hmm?* He fumbled in his jacket pocket for his com-unit, but she knocked away his hand.

"Sit still a minute!" She reached for his chin, tending to the lump of a bruise he felt already, spray injecting something she took from her kit. "I'm a resident. I have my degree, but I'm not licensed yet." She looked over at the angry man, who seemed prepared to return for round two. "Damn him. If ever I could be anywhere but here."

The last thing Rogers needed was trouble.

The next to last thing he needed was a full crew.

Rogers made a snap judgment based on her kindness to the deck boy, her obvious medical skill, and her current situation. "You wanna job?" he mumbled.

"Job?" She looked up the gangway, reservations clearly written on her face. "With you? On this ship? Where are you going?"

She must have given him something for the pain, because he started to feel better, words passing easier between his rattled teeth. "Our itinerary's not set."

"You don't know where you're going?"

He got to his feet and helped her up. "We're adventuring at the moment. You know, what you said earlier. The excitement of new places, leaving everything you know." He studied her perfectly made up face, and wondered if she might not be too fancy for his little ship. "I'm captain of this vessel, Temms Rogers, apparently at your service." He shared an ironic smile. "You may have other commitments, and I'd surely understand. But we could use someone who travels with a med-kit and knows how to use it."

"Are you kidding?" She repacked her kit, hands trembling a little. "Nothing against you, but you know, the ship. And then Geoffrey." She looked over her shoulder and saw her fiancé conferring with some uniformed men. "I did promise to marry him. For some reason."

Geoffrey saw her glance and jabbed a finger in her direction. "You'll never be a doctor! You'd be too afraid to break a nail! You're nothing, 'Lani, nothing! And you'll never be anything!"

She froze for a long moment, then her jaw set, her eyes hardened, and her spine seemed to snap straight. "You know what, Captain? I think maybe I'm free."

She dashed back to her pile of boxes and bags, and grabbed two small ones and a large one, tucking them under her arm. With the addition of two pieces of matched black luggage, which she strapped on, one on each shoulder, she strode back to extend her right hand to Rogers on the gangway.

"Hello, Captain Rogers. I'm Okalani Boro. I'd like to hire on." She bit her lip, her fingers trembling as her fiancé and several of his men approached, their faces stern. "Now would be a good time."

Rogers shook her hand and gestured to the open hatch. She vanished inside the ship without hesitation. Geoffrey started up after her and Rogers stood firm, blocking his way. "This is my ship. You're trespassing. Remove yourself immediately."

"Not without my property!" he roared.

Rogers eyed the uniformed men. "This man is trespassing," he said. *Better for the locals to handle him. I don't need him dead.*

One of them pulled him aside, spoke into his ear. Geoffrey shoved him away.

"Useless man! I want my property back! Okalani!" he bellowed.

"I gathered she doesn't want you." From where he stood, Rogers could just see the woman hiding inside the hatch. "Isn't that right, miss?"

Her voice came down, though she did not step into sight. "I never want to see him again. He's an obnoxious pig!"

Rogers looked at the officers matter-of-factly. "Clear enough. If you don't remove him, I'll have to dispose of him in my own way." He pointed to the gangway. "He's on *my* property."

The officers nodded and led the protesting suitor to his ship. Rogers held his breath a moment, then called Riviera to have her meet the young woman and find her quarters. Okalani Boro was the third crew member he had added on impulse in the last several day turns. He hoped he would not regret it.

Usually he found his instincts about people to be correct. *Usually.*

He checked the time, found it to be ten minutes after their scheduled departure, and wondered if his first impression of Mr. Quinn had been as true. *His loss.* He started up the ramp.

"Wait!" Running footsteps pounded the tarmac behind him. He turned to see Quinn, long black canvas coat flapping and scarred green duffel slapping him in the back as he reached the gangway. "Hey, Cap." Quinn gave him a dazzling smile.

Did the man really think a ship captain could be won over with an abundance of flashing teeth? No wonder he was having a hard time finding work.

"One more minute and you'd have missed your ride, Mr. Quinn. Let's work on punctuality." Rogers turned and walked up the gangway, giving the order to close the hatch after Quinn, then signaled the bridge for take off.

The captain took Quinn directly to engineering. The captain studied his new man's observation of the floors, walls, and equipment as they walked to mid-deck. Quinn did not seem to miss a detail, appearing curious and interested in everything. He walked like a spaceman, knees just bent enough to absorb the sway of ascent. He wore a cocky grin along with clothing which had not been clean for some time. Temms saw him as a little barnyard bantam, runt of the hatch, all the attitude of a prize fighter inside a body which had not been properly fed or nurtured for years.

When he brought Benzi into engineering, the speculative look on his department head's face as she beheld the scruffy engineer fulfilled her earlier equivocation. Then Quinn got a peek at Halian.

Quinn dropped his duffel bag, his mouth open in shock. "Oh, now wait an effing minute! You didn't say nothin' about no wogs!"

"Wogs?" Rogers' reaction was mild. He had expected much of what he was seeing after the conversation they had in front of the union hall. It was Quinn's first test.

Quinn could not take his eyes off Halian. "Yeah. Wogs. Aliens. I thought this was a human ship."

"Actually the *ship* is made of metals, wires and servos. What we have inside the ship are crew, Quinn. Some are human, some aren't. We all share the same purpose, to work together to serve the ship's cause." *Now drive the point home.* He hardened his expression into that of a stern teacher. "As chief, I'd expect you to show a little maturity and tolerance. I'm sure you will provide an example for the others."

Quinn ran a hand through his black hair, obviously struggling to contain his reactions. "Chief. Right."

"This is Halian. He and I have worked together for nearly twenty years. I think his skills will be readily apparent once you start working together."

Hal looked the new engineer over. "Welcome," he growled.

"How's it goin'?" Quinn shifted uneasily, attention on Halian's hairy non-human face.

Rogers turned to the young woman who had come down from her desk on the open upper level, her dark gaze picking apart her newest crew member. "This is Dani Jamar. She's the department head, so please ask her if you need anything. Team, this is Benzi Quinn." He couldn't hold back a smirk. "If he's half as good as *he* thinks he is, I expect we'll be up to speed in no time."

Under their captain's watchful eye, the three mumbled acknowledgment. They assessed each other even while the hair came up on the back of their necks like frightened cats. "I'm sure systems are still running below capacity, people. Let's get to them."

Better to let them sort things out among themselves. Dani would let him know if there was trouble.

There better not be.

They had plenty of trouble waiting for them as it was.

Letting go of this fight, ready for the next, he left engineering and went to see how his latest acquisition was dealing with the medical unit.

CHAPTER 13

HE arrived as Montgomery pulled a sheet over the head of their former gunner. The lanky doctor looked up, adjusting his glasses, as Rogers walked in. "Sorry, Captain. Hudson's passed. Nothing else I could do."

"Damn it." Though he expected this development, the loss of a man who had depended on him as captain felt like a punch to the gut. Hopefully, this would be the last one. "I know you did everything you could, Doctor."

A staff member in medical whites entered to set up medical trays. What a different picture Okalani presented here in the infirmary: hair tucked tightly into a professional looking twist, pristine uniform, and even sensible shoes. She smiled as Rogers recognized her, seeming comfortable in her new role, but did not interrupt their conversation.

Montgomery followed Rogers' gaze, and his expression brightened. "Very thoughtful of you to recruit an assistant, Temms. Very thoughtful indeed."

The captain debated exactly how hard he had worked at 'recruiting' Okalani, but just smiled. Perhaps she had found him for a reason. He liked to think so. Certainly two people in medical was better than one. "We aim to please, Doctor." His gaze slipped to the bed. "What arrangements do we need to make?"

The doctor cleared his throat. "Hudson wanted his ashes to be sent home to his daughter." He removed his stretchy gloves, discomfort clear in his posture. "I assured him we'd try to get them home."

Ashes would keep, however long it takes. Time enough to confront the issue later. "If we get there, we'll make sure she gets them. Do what you need to do, and see if Brown has some storage space."

"Aye, aye, sir." The doctor tossed his gloves in the recycler. "What about you, Temms?" He grabbed a scanning device and pointed it in Rogers' direction, eyes narrowing to read the LCD numbers. "Ribs seem to be healing."

"No time to be down, Heath. Still have a lot of work to do."

"But I've got you now. Please have a seat and take off your shirt." Under the polite words, the doctor's tone was wrapped in steel. Rogers acquiesced and allowed the doctor to change the wrapping as he considered his next move.

Montgomery's sharp eyes studied him like a lab specimen. "Any news on the artifact repair?"

Stall him. Which lie sounds best? "We're waiting for some of the new crew to catch up. You know we lost Ramona's team before we crossed over. We have to start over and rework all of what we had." What would the doctor hear in onboard scuttlebutt? So much to anticipate. "We did get some data from this planetary system that might help, too. But you know we've got other priorities, Doc. Basics, life support, sensors running."

"Priorities, oh, I'm sure. I know you've got your hands full, Temms. Just making sure I stay in the loop." He finished his ministrations and Rogers put his shirt back on. "I'll want to see your new crew, Captain, make sure they've got all the right stuff, nothing contagious. We'll take good care of medical." Montgomery shooed him toward the door.

Escaping with only a small helping of guilt, Rogers climbed up the vertical ladder passageway one level to the bridge. All in all, they were much better off than they had been. In less than seven days, he and the surviving crew of the *Doubtful* had recovered from near death. The hull was whole, the ship supplied, and power restored approximately eighty percent. He was able to replace several key personnel, though they had yet to judge these individuals' performances.

The next order of business would be to do nothing. No further damage, no further risks, until they had time to process the implications of their situation, now that immediate needs were met. It was unclear if the wormhole was still accessible, or if any 'friendlies' had come through with them. If Burko did follow them through, why had he not taken advantage of their weakness? The crew would be hard pressed to give him answers to all his questions, mostly while their life was in flux. Best to find someplace near their entry point to this universe.

Stepping onto the bridge, he gave the order to find a place to go to ground.

Liang raised a curious eyebrow, but asked no questions. A short time later, she reported a small asteroid very near to the point the ship had entered space over Marriel. In geosynchronous orbit behind the planet, the asteroid was a frozen wasteland. Without an atmosphere, no one would be able to leave the ship without environmental suits. But since most of the outside repairs had been completed, it might not be necessary.

Not wanting to alert the other bridge crew of his suspicions about Burko, Rogers tapped a silent message to Tasiq. *Any indication of Confederation activity?*

The felinoid studied his readouts. *Faint ion trails, deteriorating, but more recent than five days. Definitely Confederation. Unable to verify identity.*

So we play guess who? Rogers analyzed possible scenarios. *But no identifiable ships?*

No ships, Tasiq sent.

Scanners were back on line, they had not registered a ship in close proximity. The faint trail made it quite clear that at least one ship did cross over with them. It could be on the other side of this planet or circling one of the other planets.

He leaned back in his chair, swayed slightly to the left, favoring his bruised ribs, which bothered him more than he let Heath Montgomery know. He had no time for his own recovery. Too much at stake right now. They needed to know who was waiting out there for them. Where were they? How could he find out?

He could broadcast a general coded message, hoping to reach a fellow conspirator. Rogers studied his monitor, thinking what he might say. The longer he thought about it, he realized it would not work.

The problem was that a transmission on any Confederation frequency would stand out like a neon beacon in this new universe where the Confederation did not exist. Revealing the *Doubtful's* whereabouts might bring Burko out into the open. This had advantages and disadvantages. He would be able to confirm the *Talon* followed them. But he was not ready for that confrontation.

Rogers pursed his lips as the ship came in for its landing on the frozen asteroid. When Liang had set down lightly the monitors showed they were on a glacier shelf overlooking a chill body of water that lay like a cake gently iced with fog. He sighed with relief. "All right. Any sign of hostile activity, communication, anything, I want to know immediately."

One thing handled. His thoughts turned to the artifacts again. More secrets, more lies. More information concealed from half the crew regarding the wormhole. He typed a series of questions into his monitor's keypad directed at Liang. Since her seat was on the end, no one else would be able to read the words there.

Current status of decoding alien artifacts? What do ship's archives reveal re: general Confederation knowledge about artifacts? Where to get more information about similar artifacts in this universe? Acquisition of same?

He studied his navigator as she read the transmission silently. As she turned to speak, he pointed to his monitor. She then typed a response. Rogers scanned the answers, deep in thought.

Current status: Developing interface to enable efficient translation. Substantial data recovered from files. No data at present about Confederation level of knowledge.

Search parameter of sector network can track mention of tech within a certain definition. Tasiq can access local network by appropriate query. Once responses come in, then course of action addressing applications can be chosen.

I will update the database and inform you of new finds, potential benefits and risks.

Her bright eyes glanced up at him as he digested the information, and he nodded. With a slight acknowledgement, she turned back to her console and continued her work.

Rogers would not have called himself a religious man, but he was convinced that there was a pattern, a purpose to his life and the paths it took. Liang had obviously been placed in his path to help him, and perhaps so he could help her as well. Fate intended them to interact, for reasons yet unclear.

Glancing over at Liang, he agreed with fate, at least this time. The success of the others remained to be seen.

CHAPTER 14

BENZI Quinn glowered from the safety of his barely padded swivel chair, hiding behind the black metal desk.

Well, well, now I've arrived. Me, Benzi Quinn. Chief engineering officer of the Doubtful. Sure I've got the title of chief, I've got this office…office? Ha! He glared around the three meter square cubicle, its empty gray walls mocking him with lack of commendations or bright décor, before shifting his gaze to the small window through which he could see the others at work. Dani Jamar was supervising the refit of the shielding systems. The others deferred to her, following her orders word for word, even though she was relaxed and joking with them. What kind of management style was that?

After a week on the *Doubtful*, Quinn had mixed feelings about his new position. He tried to assert his authority, convening a marginally successful meeting the first morning he arrived on ship to introduce himself to his minimal staff. Rogers promised they would rebuild to the full eight that were contemplated in the original crew. But how was Benzi expected to run things successfully, prove himself to the captain, with half the people he needed? And with half the authority.

Quinn's eyes pinpointed Dani. The others looked to her for confirmation after every order he gave. She just smirked at his discomfiture and carried on, knowing it ate at him. *Bitch.*

In some sort of twisted irony, the only officer who followed his every directive without question was the blasted warthog.

He was not the only wog on the ship, either. Staring out at the hulking alien, Quinn shook his head. It had been the final screw, Rogers springing Halian on him, part of the grand conspiracy of the universe, making him work with subspecies that simply made his skin crawl. Always trying to get one up on him. He knew it. Even if they did not openly show it. *Never trust a wog. Never.*

Captain Rex on the *Starguide* had been a bleeder, too, an alien sympathizer. "You've got to learn to work with them, Quinn. Skin color doesn't matter. I want results! The Andarian has more training than you, that's why he got the promotion."

Benzi snorted in disgust. *Reason the wog had gotten the promotion was that Rex had wanted to fry Quinn for not kissing up. Well screw, that.* And screw Rogers, if he thought Quinn would tiptoe around this Halian just because he outsized Quinn by quarter of a meter in height and about twenty five kilos. *I'm the chief. By Sprechan's name, I'll make sure everyone knows it.*

On that thought, Quinn swung himself out of his chair and walked out onto the engineering deck. "Report!"

Dani looked up, spanner in hand. "Diagnostics are tracking a phantom short. We're losing connection somewhere." She shrugged. "Can't get better than sixty eight percent efficiency in the cortex."

Quinn frowned and vaulted over the bar to the deck below. "Ain't how it's supposed to be." He crouched down next to the panel. What could cause the malfunction? The dials did not reveal much, the numbers within acceptable limits. He tapped on the glass. "Magnetics?"

Dani crossed her arms. "Checked."

"Calibrations?" Quinn picked up a reader from the tool tray and examined it.

"Checked." The single word was without warmth.

He eyed Dani before he made another suggestion, seeing her closed expression. *She don't think I know what I'm doing.* A glance at the others revealed similar, faintly scornful looks. "All right. I'll handle this. Move on." He grabbed a tool kit and pulled himself deep under the console, peering through the coils and tubes centimeter by centimeter, tracing the conduits.

He imagined the others mocking him while he was out of sight. He just knew in his heart they did not like or trust him. It never occurred to him that what he had done was treat Dani as if she were the one who was a fool. He just knew it was the way life was. *They'll never give me a chance. That's all right. I'll just show 'em. I'll show 'em all!*

Carefully using the blue tinted reflector to check each junction of the circuitry, he let the rest of his mind go on auto-pilot. *Showed my old man, didn't I? Never thought I'd make anything of myself. See me now, Pa? Remember them nights in the old house by the river? Wind howlin' through the window cracks and Pa just sloppin' down them ales to keep himself warm. He come after me one time too many.*

It had been many years since the night he ended up on his own at fifteen. It was the final, vivid scene in a long string of confrontations with his drunken father. He was the last one at home. His older brother and sister left home as soon as they could viably escape and survive. One frozen night his mother, Sierra had left after his father gave her two black eyes and more. Benzi had seen her a few times after that, out in public, her arm through that of a large scaly skinned New Peruvian. She never acknowledged him, though he knew she saw him. She just looked right through him. She would rather have that effing alien.

Benzi and his father lived alone those last couple of years. His father only worked occasionally. No one wanted to hire a drunk, and of course the perception that the world was out to get him only made Pake Quinn drink more, steeping himself in self loathing, a much more bitter brew than the stout he preferred.

That last night, Benzi's father started on him in the kitchen, bullying him for concealing his meager earnings. Didn't matter that he had done nothing wrong, if he was not guilty this time, it probably slipped notice some other time. That was his pa's theory. The older man slammed him into the cook stove, raining punches onto him, while Benzi cowered, trying to protect his head.

"Ungrateful pup!" Pake shoved him through the back door onto the wooden porch that overhung the river. Desperate, Benzi grabbed the railing, the chilled air slicing through him. His feet slid on the two inches of ice formed by the passing boats spray that was blown up from the stinking water.

The elder Quinn stumbled and slid on the ice, grabbing Benzi away from the railing and slammed his wiry son into the doorway before losing his footing and dragging them both to the floor. "Think you're better than your ole man because you got work and I don't? Well, I'll show you." As Benzi clung to the splintering doorframe, his father struggled to get to his feet, slipping and each slip brought him closer to the darkness just beyond the porch edge, where the water rushed cold below.

Benzi watched, darkly fascinated, as his father writhed across the ice from the door to the edge in a clumsy dance of sorts. He felt a lump rise on the back of his neck. Blood trickled where he bit his lip. Mist rose off the putrid water beyond the edge of the porch. The air, cold and damp, penetrated his bones. His father's mumbled curses hung on the air as he finally reached his hand toward Benzi, demanding help.

Instinctively his hand stretched out to his father, but he could not make himself move across the ice to touch the extended fingers. He tried. Knew it was the "right" thing to do. But he could not, even when the old man slipped, grabbed at a rickety chair and disappeared off the edge.

He's not gone. He's not gone! Keep your eyes closed and it won't be true. I didn't mean for him to fall. I just wanted him to stop.

The sound of random gunfire down at the docks minutes later woke the trembling boy from his inner monologue. He crawled across the treacherous span and saw the water had carried Pake Quinn away. Stunned, his hand slipped along the edge of the ice, cold reality setting in.

His mind spinning with possibilities, he crawled back inside, looking at the house that must be his now. Still numb with shock, he reached in the cooler for one of his father's ales. Cracking it open, he prepared to take a drink, and then set it on the table. *No.*

He backed up, the smell nauseating him. *I don't want his life. I don't ever want his life.*

Benzi closed that door in his mind. The more he thought about it, he not only did not want his pa's life, he did not want his house or his things. No ties. He was free. He stuffed a backpack with enough clothes and money to get him by, and left home for good.

And now I'm the chief engineer on a space going ship.

A slightly less congratulatory tone echoed in his mind, the one his father had always used to put him back in his place. *Won't keep that job. Loser. Always been a loser. Even the bitch is smarter than you. Don't sit around and pat yourself on the back. You'll never make it here.*

Benzi shut off that hated voice, focusing on the panel. He worked himself along the entire console without finding flaws in the circuitry. Crawling across to the main panel, feeling Dani's eyes on him as she realigned the power draw, Quinn yanked it open, stepping back as a small brown rodent hissed and jumped at him before it skittered away. One of the techs made a half hearted attempt to stop it. Halian disappeared into the doorway where it had gone.

"Effing voles. Unbelievable." He turned a harsh eye on Dani. "There's your villain."

She nodded. "That would do it." She adjusted the readouts. "More in there?"

Quinn turned back to the open panel, crouching down to peer behind the memory chips and cathodes. "Don't see none. But where there's one—"

"More there are." Halian reappeared, licking his lips. "Will do pest sweep this shift."

Quinn shuddered, realizing what had happened to the rodent. "Yeah, well, whatever works." Pleased with himself for discovering the answer, he turned to Eddy and Jerome, who were assigned to engineering for the day. "Gentlemen. Can I buy you lunch?"

Eddy smiled. "Sure, chief." He elbowed the other, who nodded.

Quinn beamed as they walked out and headed for the galley. It was a figure of speech, of course. Lunch was free for the crew, a step up from his last berth. The rookies praised his detective work, and he pooh-poohed it at the same time he reveled in the attention. Screw the woman and the wog. These were impressionable young guys, the kind that would look up to him, he was sure of it. If nothing else, Benzi Quinn knew the game. He would learned how to pal around with their kind, lose just enough at cards, flirt with the women who were not quite so pretty, be a big man on a small ship.

In the galley, they picked up trays and grabbed a table at the back end of the room. Several of the other crew members he had met but did not know well were breaking for grub at the same time. The doctor picked over some greens, absorbed in a text. He was all right, in Quinn's book. Did not ask too many questions, did not look you in the eye, just did his job. Tasiq, the com-officer? *Wog*.

He watched as the hulking black woman, Riviera Brown, picked up her tray at the galley's open window and walked over to join Okalani and Dani Jamar. The women usually took mess together, fending off any interest from the men.

Not that the men had much energy left for romping after sixteen hour shifts. Shrugging it off as hopefully temporary, he studied the three. Brown he had no use for. She was too big, too lippy and apparently could not stand him either. Dani was prettiest of the three, but also had no use for him. Okalani, though…. He grinned as he caught the blonde's gaze flick in his direction.

"Men. Can't live with 'em, can't live without 'em," she was saying. She blushed as she realized Quinn was watching.

He relaxed and gave her a lazy wink, half listening to some enthusiastic tale the rookies were sharing from cadet life. He knew women were drawn to his rough looks, hair black as the Raplasian coal mines, and sharp blue eyes.

Okalani leaned in and said something to Dani, who glanced over her shoulder at Quinn and then shook her head. Quinn felt his spine stiffen. That mocking inner voice whispered. *Not likely, boyo. You're not good enough for the likes of her.* He forced his attention onward.

Liang read intently, working through her meal, setting a bad example for the rest of them. She thought she was so much better than the rest of 'em, better than *him* for sure. Wasn't enough that she practically spit on him at Roandock, then she had to try to best him in physical fights as well, in these so called matches she set up in the ship's gym. *Maybe she should just go all the way and grow a set of balls and a peter. Then she would be good as a man. Not until.*

"Guess that one would freeze water on her ass, now, don't you think?" Benzi smirked at them. The two, surely knowing they had even less chance than Quinn, roared with laughter. Jerome pounded the table for emphasis, which of course drew everyone's eyes to their table. Liang gave them a withering look and walked out. *Bitch.*

So life was not all bad. Benzi had some mates now, occasional hero worship in their eyes. Wasn't the best billet ever, but it was tolerable. Long as he could avoid the wogs and keep learning about the mechs on this ship until he was the best, he would be all right.

Besides, he had a trump card in his back pocket, one he had told no one about, and he was not going to, either, not until he thought it would play to his best advantage. He was not stupid, he knew that old man Rogers thought Benzi was pretty low on the food chain, and was desperate for a gig. But as it turned out, Rogers has some food chain issues himself.

Right after he agreed to meet the captain at the berth where the Doubtful waited, he went back into the union hall to gloat a bit. Earlier he had noticed two men hanging about the hall. They looked too much like law enforcement to Quinn's way of thinking. He watched them suspiciously as they marched over to him and then offered to buy him a drink across the street.

Benzi Quinn was never one to turn down a free drink, so he grudgingly went along, listened to what they had to say. What would it hurt, right?

"Have you worked with Temms Rogers before?" one asked. He was a little grayer at the temples, but otherwise they were hard to tell apart. Quinn mentally dubbed them Pal-1 and Pal-2.

"Just met the man."

Pal-2 nodded. "He doesn't look like a criminal, does he?" His face smiled, but there was no warmth in it.

"Sure, he don't." Quinn was careful not to show expression, still unsure what these fellows wanted. *No sense in aligning yourself with someone about to be pinched, was there?*

"You just signed up for his crew, right?" Pal-1 took a long drink of his ale, made a face as if he was unfamiliar with the local flavors.

Quinn shrugged in reply.

"Rogers is wanted in another star system for a whole list of crimes," Pal-1 said, with a pointed look at his companion. "We asked around about what kind of man you are. We could make it worth your while to deliver him to us. You know, once you spend some time, learn where he's going to be, what kind of shape his ship is in."

"What is it you want? The man or just information?" Quinn had no loyalty, not yet anyway. He wondered if these pals knew just what amount he would want to make it worth his while. Sizing them up as well, he could see how much they really wanted Rogers. *Then it'll cost you, boyos.*

"Information, first. Then when the time's right...." Pal-2 made a grabbing gesture, then smiled.

Benzi made them hang for his answer, drawing out his moment until it was almost painful. "Sure, I'm your man," he said with his cocky grin. "It'll cost you twenty five big ones. Just to start. Then ten more each time you call me. And I'll let you know how much for the catchnet when you let me know the time's right." His self confidence twinkled and warmed inside him like a firework going off, when he noticed them squirm. *Had he judged them right? Were they as desperate to get someone on Rogers' ship as he thought?*

The men exchanged looks, then Pal-1 reached in his jacket and pulled out a thick wallet, laid the credits on the table. As Quinn reached for them, Pal 1 suddenly laid a hand atop his.

"You're in now, friend. Don't fail us. Because we can get someone else in just as easy. And that one's first order will be to airlock you. Got it?"

Quinn avoided the cold gaze. "Yeah, yeah, pally. I hear you." He raked the credits up and shoved them inside his boot.

Pal-2 dropped a communicating device on the table. "We'll be in touch." He stood up, his companion following suit. When Benzi did not acknowledge them, they walked out. He finished all three drinks. Paid for—might as well.

He hid those credits away carefully when he got aboard and intended to wring all he could out of the desperate men. Maybe he would go all the way. Maybe he would not. Rogers seemed like an okay fellow to him. Hell, he gave him a job when he really needed it.

But Benzi had learned one thing from his father, and that was to look out for himself. He intended to do just that.

CHAPTER 15

FROM the observation deck, Rogers admired the frozen landscape outside the ship.

Jagged white and gray spires rose along the icy edges of a silvery clear pool of liquid. Sciences assured him it was constructed from a poisonous element, though it resembled nothing so much as that pristine cool mountain lake by the cabin he and Connie had rented back on Gilada that first summer, before the children. But this was much more deadly. Any of his people who stepped outside would suffocate in the inhospitable atmosphere in a matter of seconds.

Crazy for us to be here.

That was, of course, the objective. No one would look for the *Doubtful* on this human unfriendly surface. Rogers wanted time to think, and Liang had found him this place. If only his thoughts had the clarity of the chilled air outside his port.

He needed at least eight more people. Over the last two weeks, Eddy and Jerome had progressed, learning to be jacks of all trades. Engineering currently the best staffed, with three experienced crew members. As the crippled systems gradually functioned according to specs once again, they were able to reduce shifts from sixteen hours to ten.

Medical was not critical, those injured in the crossing either healed or dead. Okalani was more than adequate to assist Montgomery in treating everyday cuts and bruises. So far, Dani's efforts to secrete the actual log were successful. At least there was not evidence of anyone trying to access the compromised information. And what about where the doctor's loyalties were?

I'll have to find a way to test him. I need to know where he stands, and what he would do if he discovers the truth.

He was able to have at least one meal each day with Tommy, even if they scarcely cleared their plates before an emergency called one or the other away. Slowly, very slowly, their relationship was being rebuilt. Reminiscing about old times, playing sackball in the back yard with the neighborhood boys, vacations together, remembering how Tommy would tease the twins about their matching freckles, all these things knitted their distance a little closer together.

Rogers' mental checklist moved on. As he stood at parade rest, feet shoulders' width apart, hands tucked at the small of his back, he took in the view, urging his thoughts to fall into neat patterns. Brown had transformed the third cargo bay into a hydroponics unit and it generated fresh produce every day. But that was not enough for long term survival.

Here they lacked the convenience of Confederation protectorates in each system where they were entitled to land and re-provision the ships. If they were to continue in this universe, they needed regular acquisition of supplies, fresh meats, dry goods, as well as tools and other staples. In order to purchase fresh supplies, the *Doubtful* would have to have ready cash in the local currency. Selling bits of scrap metal would only take them so far.

I've got a ship and a cargo hold. I can transport securely. Liang must know of a market.

That left his bridge crew. Kai and Liang worked well in tandem, along with Tasiq. Since Liang had set up search parameters to locate potential artifacts in this universe, Tas coordinated and plotted a search pattern to be instituted once they left the asteroid.

The nearest and potentially most helpful planet was two days' flight, a place called Lennor. Several ships had filed reports onto the interplanetary network that described objects found on Lennor with hieroglyphics very similar to those the *Doubtful* already had. The culture that guarded the relics was called the Lenci, a religious, agrarian society, primitive by choice. Though they selectively traded with passing ships, they preferred their own simple ways.

Tasiq made contact with the Lenci and he was hopeful of a positive response. *The more pieces we have, the more likely it is that we can rebuild the device. If we rebuild the device, we have more options. A captain needs options. I want options.*

The ship's three tone chime signal for the captain broke gently into his rumination. He smiled, a self mocking gesture. *Really, Temms, fifteen minutes to yourself? What were you thinking?* With a last longing look at the peaceful vista before him, he left the observation deck and crossed the narrow corridor to the bridge. "Report."

Liang looked up, her face animated. "The network has recently posted an advertisement from a technical school on Satis Prime. New graduates are looking for entry level openings on ships. Many have qualifications that would serve the *Doubtful*'s needs." She glanced at her monitor again, refreshing her memory. "Because they are being placed from a school, there is no need to go through the Brotherhood or their registry."

Rogers considered the proposal to take on brand new crew with no loyalties. They would be green, but Rogers could train them in his ways and methods. It would be less argument than he was getting from Quinn. "Cost?"

"At the end of their first six months' service, there is a one time rebate to the school of a part of the student's wages for the placement service."

Rogers took his seat. Now there was the irony. Until he was at full complement, he would be hard pressed to run the kind of missions that would pay enough, but until he had a full crew, he was not confident he could staff that kind of mission. *Damn us all to the third hell.* "Do you recommend the quality of the students?"

Liang shrugged, less assured. "It is accredited by the system auditors."

Beggars could not be choosers. A plan came into his mind to kill two birds with one stone. "I'll take the slipcraft to the school this afternoon. Notify Dr. Montgomery I'd like him to accompany me. We can make sure they have no diseases to share with the crew." *And I'll have time alone with the doctor to see how his loyalty will impact the safety of my crew.* "Nice work, Liang."

"Captain?" Tasiq beckoned him to the communications station.

Knees cracking, Rogers got up and walked over. "Problem?"

"Confed transmission." Tasiq ran a graphic representation of a partial audio transmission. "I cannot sort out its origination point. It was sent by top encrypt style as a general message, not to someone in particular."

"Interesting. Encrypted, yet not sent on a narrow band but broadcast generally." The captain's finger tapped a staccato rhythm on the circular monitor where the pattern repeated. But it was not the rebel code, it was Standard. Burko. "Keep working on it. I want the whole message and the coordinates it was transmitted from."

Tas acknowledged the order. "In process."

Rogers was not altogether surprised Burko had not shown himself. Burko's usual *modus operandi* was to allow his smaller ships and less important officers to lead an attack, then he followed when the worst of the fighting was done. He always had a shiny ship and clean uniform to step down on the conquered planet's surface in glory. Rogers glowered at the thought of the cost of that policy, sending the inexperienced ahead to be shot. *It could have been Tommy waiting on the front line.*

"Tas, from now on we limit outgoing transmissions, or scramble them somehow. No sense in being caught stupid."

"Noted, sir." Tasiq pulled Parnell Eddy aside and set him to working on a scramble program.

Eddy looked confused. "Why's the Captain trying to avoid Confed ships? Wouldn't they help us get home?"

"We have our orders!" Tasiq snapped.

"Right." Eddy glanced at Rogers. "I'll get on it." He sat at the designated console and began his work.

The captain heard him and reacted from his gut, last minute inspiration striking. "All right people, this isn't a training simulation! Liang, take her out. We've been hiding long enough. Lay in a course for Satis Prime. Contact that school and set up a meet." His eyes fell on Eddy. "Get that scramble up soonest. Any way to alter our running signature, I'd like that too, as a precaution. It's a good possibility one of the rebel ships has followed us." *That should hold him.* "If anything comes up before we arrive, I'll be in my office."

Seeing them all about their work, he retreated, satisfied, to study up on his personnel needs.

* * *

PULLING away from the ship in the seven-seater slipcraft, Temms Rogers relaxed into his seat. He did not often take the opportunity to sit in the pilot's chair, though he always enjoyed it. He glanced over to the spare figure of the doctor, likewise at ease.

"Feels good to get off the ship," Montgomery said.

"You've been aboard almost every minute since we crossed. Time for you to get some fresh air." Rogers grinned. "How's Okalani working out?"

The doctor chuckled and shook his head. "Talk about your fresh air. That girl has some wild ideas about the relationships between the sexes."

Rogers cocked a brow at the thought of the blonde and the doctor. "She's come on to you?"

"Heavens no! I'm old enough to be her father!" Montgomery brushed some lint off his crisp Confederation uniform. A little smile crossed his lips as he adjusted his black framed glasses. "Doesn't mean I haven't thought about it."

Well, Heath, you dirty dog.

Surprised, yet somehow pleased the doctor had thoughts that strayed beyond the straight and narrow, the captain studied the planet, wide and green beneath them, coming into focus and detail as they got closer. They had awhile before they made planet fall. Liang had arranged the interview before Rogers left the ship, so there was nothing to do but wait. *And talk.*

Trying to find the right opening was difficult. Rogers tested several in his head, but discarded them as too contrived. He and the doctor had known each other for years, served together for the last three, but they had never been close, thanks to the politics of officers' wives.

The doctor's wife, partial to politics, wielded every bit of power she could grab. Rogers' ex-wife Connie had often been on the receiving end, as the fact that her husband commanded Ada Montgomery's husband had rankled the doctor's wife to no end. She assigned Connie to junior projects and less prestigious committees and let her know why. As a consequence, the two men had a professional relationship only, and left their personal lives at the ship's hatch.

As Rogers fumbled with his plan, he felt Montgomery's eyes on him, like piercing dark glass beads. When he looked up, the doctor gave a dry laugh.

"Come on, out with it, Temms. Something's eating at you. You going to spill the beans about the artifacts?"

"Yes, something like that." He shifted in his seat. "We've found pieces of the relics here. Perhaps they could replace those that were damaged. Apparently the artifacts are common to both universes, which says something about the culture which designed them."

"Oh? Somewhere close? Who's got the expertise to install them?" Intently attentive, the doctor straightened.

"No one just yet. Liang is reviewing Ramona's work in the construction of the first console. She has also researched possible replacement pieces in this sector. Hopefully, we'll be able to puzzle out the complete design when she gets more parts."

"And when she does?"

"We'll have to see if we can successfully reproduce the set of circumstances which released the wormhole. It may be possible, it may not."

"You're going to try, aren't you? We have our duty." Montgomery fidgeted in his seat despite his restraining belt. "The rebels may have run us off, but we have to get back, no matter what it takes! I can't understand why we haven't been trying to send messages back in case the anomaly remains open on the other side. Headquarters will want this technology, Temms. Think what worlds we can add to our protectorate if we can channel the ability to cross universal rifts!" His eyes glowed. "We would be invincible."

Rogers nodded slowly, wondering how the doctor knew what messages had or had not been sent from the bridge. "Exactly." *What would less technologically advanced cultures like the Persions do then?* He sighed.

"You miss them, too. Your family." Montgomery nodded with total misunderstanding. "I'm getting short, you know. Retirement in two more years. I've got my little cottage by the lakefront picked out. I'll fish to my heart's content. Maybe get a little rowboat to get around in. I can play the old country doctor if I want, deliver babies, do happy things." He relaxed into the seat, slouching again. "Got a lot waiting for us, Temms. I'm anxious to get back."

"I agree, it's much more comfortable operating in parameters I understand." Rogers let that be the final word on the subject. He understood, all right. He did not begrudge the doctor his plans. Hell, Heath had seen a lot of action in thirty-five years serving the Confederation. He deserved some peace.

How can I avoid Montgomery's blood on my hands?

* * *

AFTER a remainder of the flight spent in small talk, they were greeted on the surface, shipside, by a representative from the Sol Aeris tech school, an officious gentleman in a long navy blue coat trimmed in gold frogs and epaulets. The gentleman announced his name was Mosk, and burbled about the excellent training of the school's graduates as he drove them to the facility in the gilt trimmed transport vehicle.

The campus, a collection of two story tan brick buildings laid out around an attractive greened square, did not impress Rogers. The Confederation school was much the same. The purpose of the buildings was to conglomerate enough young minds together to make stuffing their heads full of technical information cost efficient. The experience also built the groundwork for the camaraderie and teamwork that was the heart of all well functioning ships.

The captain let Montgomery take the lead, asking questions of the obsequious Mosk on the way to the interview rooms, inquiring about accreditation and matriculation, experience, age and health of the recruits. Before taking his first position on an outbound ship, Montgomery had served at the Confederation school medical office, tending to students before sending them off into the cosmos. Under the circumstances, Rogers saw no reason to interfere. Montgomery was clearly in his element.

Seven men and two women were seated in the conference room, and they stood up as the three men entered. Mosk introduced them, handing the captain a small packet of papers, the school records and prospectus for each. Rogers leafed through them as he took a seat.

"Your officer gave us some initial specifications to help narrow your search, Captain Rogers," Mosk said, deference clear in his polished vocal tones.

Not knowing much about the local economy, Rogers had deferred to Liang. She not only drafted job requirements but also a potential pay scale predicated on their anticipated revenues if they went on to become a freelance cargo carrier. The figures did not look generous to him, but she assured him new graduates expected that the kickback to the school at the end of the trial period would come from their pay. *We best be making money by the time that comes due.*

"A fine job," Rogers murmured, looking from papers to individuals. They were so young. He bet none of them truly understood what awaited them in space. Least of all, on a ship like his, where the future was still unsettled, so many variables still in play.

Montgomery leaned close. "Seems like a good crop, if not quite ripe yet." His eyes twinkled.

Rogers warmed up as the man echoed his thought. "Like any good steel, recruits need to be tempered," he replied softly. He sat back, set the papers down, and looked around the table. "I'm Captain Temms Rogers of the ship *Doubtful*, and this is our ship's doctor, Heath Montgomery."

His gaze was met by most of the recruits, all except two, who did not seem interested. He marked them off the list, before giving a brief description of the ship and its capabilities.

To the remaining seven on his list, he shot a rapid fire question session similar to the pop quizzes to which he had been subjected at the Confederation school. *The "What if's" Emergency procedure for Personnel-101? Triage? Allocation of supplies during rationing phase?*

Most responded better than Rogers expected, expanding beyond textbook answers, though none displayed field tested wisdom. He pulled six packets from the stack and set them in front of Montgomery. He wanted the doctor to feel like a valuable part of the administrative team. Let him choose the finalists.

"We need five," he murmured.

The doctor nodded and glanced over the resumes, looking more in depth at the students' backgrounds and written work. Rogers studied those waiting to see if their fates would change, noting a held breath here, an anxious finger tapping there. In this batch were a communications specialist, a science officer with an interest in ancient languages, a weapons master with a high security clearance licensed by system standards, and a tactician cross trained in nav, all specialties he could use. With five more bodies, he would be considerably on the road to making his crew, his space faring family, whole again.

After a few minutes, the doctor pulled one from the pack and laid it back on the second pile in front of Rogers.

"Thank you, Doctor." Rogers took the five remaining and handed them to Mosk, along with the proposed pay scale.

The official reviewed the papers briefly and dismissed those not chosen. "If you would give us a moment, Captain? I will review your offer with my students and let you know if they accept."

"Of course." Rogers, followed closely by Montgomery, left the interview room, getting a drink of water from the fountain in the hallway. The water had a chemical tang, some sort of purifier no doubt. But it tasted better than the recycled liquids they had on the *Doubtful*. The fountain was placed next to a large picture window that opened out onto the commons. The sparse landscaping was green and inviting. Montgomery sighed with such longing, the captain smiled. "Heath, go outside. Feel the sun on you. Doctor's orders."

"You let me be the doctor, young man." Montgomery spoke in mock scolding. "But I'll take that fresh air." He grinned and went for the nearest door, moving a little slowly with his years.

The captain followed him out, wanting a breath of real air, too. What he had at the spaceport had been contaminated with smells off the tarmac. This was so much better. Cool and crisp, a light breeze, a trace of wet, fallen leaves. He let his lungs fill, empty, taking deep breaths to clear out all the traces of his shipboard atmosphere.

The autumnal change of seasons had always been his favorite, associated with the return to classes and a comfortable, safe routine. School had never been easy for him, but Rogers relished the opportunity to stretch his mind, and the competition with other students. Some of his best taught lessons were not from books. He had learned that intellect must be tempered by conscience. He worked at this every day, using mind to drive forward and heart to remind him of what was right.

Which has led you to your current quandary, where conscience led you outside the comfortable, intellectual path.

Shutting off the nagging internal reminder, he returned to the corridor inside with its polished green floors. The door to the conference room opened. A young woman, one of those Rogers had found most promising, gave him a regretful nod and walked away down the hall. Mosk stepped out, the fawning smile returned to his face. "Thank you, Captain, for your patience. Four students are ready to join you."

"I'm pleased to hear it." The captain stepped to the door and studied his newly employed crew. "We're at the Trefer station, Berth-14. We lift in two hours."

"Aye, aye, sir!" came the unanimous response.

Smugly satisfied, Mosk drew him aside to sign the contract guaranteeing the bonus payments to the school. His business completed, Rogers left the building to find Montgomery. Before heading back to the ship, he and the doc could take a stroll about the grounds and stretch their legs.

CHAPTER 16

LIANG sat alone at her galley table, reviewing notes while she ate, when Tasiq brought her news that the Lenci had agreed to meet them.

Her first pleased reaction faded as she read the communication. "Not so simple. We must locate some missing persons before we win the chance to uncover the artifacts."

Accompanying the message was a tantalizing description of a selection of artifacts the Lenci offered. The pieces had been detected by a previous outsider's expedition, scanned in underground catacombs accessible through tunnels in the earth. The scans had surprisingly good detail. From the concentration of hieroglyphics on each, her best guess was that these were crucial pieces.

"I notified the captain." Tasiq shifted uncomfortably. "He, too, was puzzled by the specification that the mission team should consist of only females."

Liang considered what she knew of this culture, which was not much. "If we want a chance at the artifacts, it would seem we must agree. Thank you, Tasiq."

The communications officer left the room. She returned to her reading, but a moment later felt like someone was watching her. Surreptitiously, she took a glance around the galley room and found herself the subject of hot regard by a simmering Benzi Quinn.

Of all the males aboard the *Doubtful*, Quinn was most difficult for her to understand. His outlook was dark as a demon's heart. He seemed to expect the worst at all times, convinced he would not have any measure of good fortune, even though he clearly had received gifts from the universe. Like his strange enlistment onto the crew of this ship. Why would the captain choose someone so obviously a troublemaker and point of distraction?

Instead of being grateful for his rescue, Quinn seemed to take pride in bewailing his situation, begrudging others what they had earned, and almost purposefully setting himself up for failure. His second day aboard ship he propositioned her. She made it clear he had no chance with her. Ever. Since then, he glowered and steamed every minute he was in her presence.

Rodolphus would have said that Quinn was out of harmony with himself, leaving him negative and angry. Quinn's energy vibrations were likewise disharmonious and would resonate with other negative people and events, drawing such situations to him, creating a cycle of destructive experience.

She had attempted to broach the subject with Quinn when he joined her informal martial arts competitions. Most crew members participated, eager for the physical exercise and camaraderie. Male or female, alien or human, she treated them no differently as she led the mental and physical conditioning, grappling, blocking, attack and defense.

The competitions stimulated and extended her abilities, as she dealt with the catlike dance of Tasiq, who nearly always bested her, or Riviera Brown, whose sheer size required a different approach. Most of the others provided an equal number of wins and losses, depending on the day and their attention to the fight.

Quinn sometimes drew Liang as his opponent, the chip nearly visible on his narrow shoulder. He was all fire and jab and strike, coming at her like a boxer in his first prize fight, hungry for the conquest, less interested in the form and the lesson. She easily deflected most of his onslaughts, turning his wiry strength against him because he was all blitz, full out aggression, without the thought and strategy needed to win. When she bested him, though he often called her names or made excuses, the shaded look in his eyes told her he knew he had defeated himself.

Regardless, she had done nothing to merit his burning ire. Surely his energy could be spent better on constructive projects. Feeling his stare, she tried to study her message again. The Lenci also specified what the mission team should wear, but gave no hint what they might expect to encounter. Odd that the Lenci had requested women. But she would be the first to volunteer.

Piqued that Benzi's dark attention had gotten under her skin, she finished the last few bites of her meal and took her tray to the recycler. Gathering her things, she headed for the bridge to complete the arrangements with the Lenci.

The next morning, they arrived at the crystal green planet Lennor. The Lenci leaders provided specified landing coordinates, which the navigator passed to Kai Windthorp for analysis. He studied the results of their sensory readings. "Looks like an open field. No threat within a reasonable distance, Captain."

"Very well. Take her down." Rogers ordered his chosen team, Liang and Riviera Brown, to meet him once they had landed. He gave Tasiq command of the bridge. "Keep an eye on us, Tas. I don't want surprises."

Liang studied the main monitor screen, training the scanners on the open field outside. Surrounded by leafy trees, the grassy clearing was seventy five meters wide. Keeping a respectful distance from the ship awaited five balding Lenci, wearing long pastel robes. They were tall, willowy and ethereal. They stood huddled together in the middle of the green field, amid a patch of yellow flowers. Two carried covered baskets in their hands. The shortest of the Lenci held a bucket, smudging the air around the group with thick blue smoke.

"Liang? You coming?"

Rogers waited at the door to the lift. She tore her gaze from the peaceful scene and joined him. Brown waited below in the heavy leather jacket, dark pants and boots with thick soles that had been recommended by the Lenci. Tommy was also there waiting with a furrowed brow.

"You should take a security detail with you, Captain," he warned.

The captain smirked, letting his eyes fall on Liang before she ducked into the empty cargo bay to change into the suggested gear. She remained in the shadow while she dressed, so she could not be seen, but she could hear them. "We'll be fine, Tom. We're assuming the Lenci know their own situation best. They requested women."

"*You're* not a woman," Tommy remarked dryly.

"I'm not going on the mission. I'm just going as far as that group there." He gestured out the door. "You're welcome to stand here and watch to make sure we're safe."

"How can I do my job if you won't let me?" Tommy growled.

Rogers did not reply, just stared him down. Liang could feel the intensity of that stare as she came back to join them.

"Fine," Tommy said, clearly annoyed. "But I'm staying right here."

"You do that." Rogers clapped him on the arm, then he, Liang and Riviera walked out to meet the Lenci.

They were welcomed with the smell of fresh trod grass and birdsong in the distance. It was an idyllic setting except for the nervous pacing of the Lenci who carried the bucket. As he passed by Liang, her nose wrinkled, tingling inside as she inhaled the spicy pepper like smoke. She analyzed it on her handheld, finding it contained bark from a native tree. Did it have religious significance? The elders seemed to watch him, anxious if he strayed too far away.

Fortunately the Lenci wore different colored robes, or else it would have been difficult to tell them apart. One stepped forward, but he seemed no taller, no thinner and no more sad eyed than the others. He wore a pale blue robe. "Greetings, Captain Rogers. Many blessings on you and your steadfast crew. I am Rez, head of the Council. With me, are Malka, our chief priest, and Zareb, Jonel and Karn, of the Families."

He indicated different individuals in their little clutch of elders as he spoke. Malka was the one carrying the annoying smoke. Riviera stood straight, seeming to be unaffected by it. Liang attempted to do the same. The captain's eyes blinked rapidly as Malka came by, but he kept his expression firm.

"Glad to meet you, sir. With me are my science officer, Riviera Brown and my navigator, Liang Chao." Rogers replied. "Since you requested women."

Rez waved his hand in a gesture Liang interpreted as a warding sign, against evil. The others echoed the gesture. It did not reassure her.

"I am pleased that you have volunteered for this rescue. We greatly fear for our mother priestess, as she has been gone for days."

A priestess? Missing? The Lenci communication had been very sketchy about the rescue mission. Perhaps with intention. If the team could not find the priestess, did that put the acquisition of the relics in danger? Liang bit back the questions that flowed onto her eager tongue. It was not her place to ask.

The captain showed that his thoughts followed the same path. "In return for our assistance, I understand you have agreed that we may retrieve certain items of archaeological interest from your caves."

"Yes, Captain. Because of the danger, we believe this is a generous reward." Rez spoke hurriedly, glancing over his shoulder as Malka passed around them again.

"Very well." Rogers straightened his shoulders. "You're sure you need women?"

Liang bristled, the implication in the captain's voice that women were somehow insufficient. A quick look at Riviera showed a similar reaction.

Rez sighed, and the others twitched and nodded as one. "The males never come back."

"What you mean, they never come back?" Riviera asked quickly.

"Only our women communicate with the Kiritan. If a male goes into the caves, he will not return. None ever has." Again, that gesture of warding off.

The slender Lenci with the bucket circled them several more times, filling the air with the smoke, which started to go to Liang's head. Even traveling into the caves had to be better than being suffocated in the open fresh air.

"Please, tell us what happened," Rogers said.

Rez cleared his throat, recounting the story as if it were already some sort of legendary song to be told around a campfire, the cadence strong and his intonation heroic. "Our women, all women, visit the caves of the Kiritan to gather rocks of healing, to bring them back to the people. They replenish our supply every seven days. Mother priestess, with her acolytes, went to the cave three days ago and should have returned by the fall of daylight. Since then, none of them have been seen. Mother has traveled this path for nearly fifty years. She cannot be lost."

Riviera Brown stepped forward, the Lenci dwarfed by her sheer bulk. Several would not meet her gaze. Her voice was impatient. "So you men won't go get them? What be down there to terrify you so?"

Malka bowed, not looking at their faces. "The Kiritan, mother."

"So you've said, but what is that?" Rogers snapped. "My people need to know what they're facing."

Rez hung his head apologetically. "If I knew, I would tell you, but none of us have seen it, Captain. We dare not go into the caves!"

"What do the women tell you? Surely some of them have said something." Liang asked.

The priest shuddered. "The Kiritan are horrible beasts, large and hairy, with claws like dagger blades. They hide in the tunnels to feast upon the unwary."

Liang took more from the terror barely hidden in the men, than from their words. Fell creatures lived in the caves, yet women armed with no more than incense could survive. This incongruity let her know they would live through the experience. No point in further delay. Facing her first real assignment as an officer on the *Doubtful,* her adrenaline kicked in. She was anxious to begin. "Captain, if they would show us to the place?"

Brown shouldered her pack. "Let's get to it."

The Lenci led them across the clearing to a small rise, which in contrast to the lush emerald field around it, was bare red clay. Behind the crest of the rise was the opening to the cave. The Lenci stopped five meters away and would go no closer. The Lenci priest handed Rogers two sticks of the incense, still burning, from the bucket, his manner very solemn.

"They will need this protection against the Kiritan."

Rogers handed them to Liang.

She studied the dark tunnel, chill mist framing its entrance. The Lenci elders continued to murmur advice, about their boots, how their clothing might protect them against the predators in the tunnels, insisting they needed the contents of the two baskets the Lenci had carried, now at Riviera's feet.

"Questions, Liang?" Rogers asked. His stance was less than firm, a sign Liang had come to equate with his anxiety over a task.

"I would feel more confident if the Lenci would provide us with details about the monsters." She glanced at Rez, who averted his eyes. "We would best serve their missing priestess if they were fully honest."

Rogers shrugged. "So would I, but I guess this is the best we can do. The men don't come back and the women aren't talking. You've got your pistol and a blade, right?" His eyes were troubled. Tension in his jaw twitched counterpoint to his upbeat tone.

She confirmed she did, then extinguished and stashed one of the incense sticks the priest had given them. Each of them picked up one of the baskets. "We shall return as soon as we can, Captain."

"The gods watch over you with blessings," Malka intoned.

Liang allowed a slight smile and nodded to the dark skinned woman beside her. "Let's go." She approached the cave's entry as she would any other unknown place, with a mixture of curiosity and foreboding. This mission had the feel of a mythic journey, entering into the darkness, the subconscious, the depths, and the fears that lurked there. *Whatever waits for us, it is not near the surface, but in the bowels. We will discover it when our fates cross paths.*

The beam from the flashlights shone bright on the brown clay walls, fading into grayness as they were pointed farther into the darkness. The dank air in the cave gobbled the sunlight as they moved inside. The mist grew colder and took on a sulfurous smell.

"Hell's afire!" Riviera said as they walked at a brisk pace on the well worn clay path down the center of the passageway. "None said nothing about freezing to death!"

The dampness swallowed the echo of Riviera's words. Liang looked back over her shoulder at the cave mouth, now the size of a pocket coin, and let slip a small sigh as she wondered whether those they had been sent to rescue might still be alive. "Life signs?"

Brown unclipped the scanner from her thick belt, pointing it from left to right, up and down. "Lot of ghost readings, metals in the walls. Think we best get closer to know for certain."

Liang removed her own scanner from her pack and held it before her, the readout calibrated to that particular resonance which she had discovered in all the genuine artifacts of the Old Ones. Their specific high end frequency read clearly on her device, five distinct pieces, one over a meter in length, larger than any on the ship, located nearly a kilometer below the clay path where the two women currently walked. Ahead she saw only darkness, no clue how this path might reach that underground treasure cache.

Riviera glanced at the small screen in Liang's hand. "Don't suppose there's a lift? Shortest distance between two points and all."

"Highly unlikely." Liang walked ahead, a downward turn in the path removing the sight of the entrance behind them. A torch sweep of the walls showed the shadowy red clay was home to many legged insects, some several centimeters long, which scrambled along the rough surface by the hundreds.

"Several places I know, where these would be fried up for supper." Riviera studied the insects with a scientist's interest, hunching down a couple of times to get a closer look.

Liang redirected her focus. "The Lenci said there were three women, correct?"

"An old priestess and two young girls, acolytes in training." Riviera closed her eyes a moment, recalling the tale shared by the Lenci leader. "Six hours supposed to be gone, he said, but they ain't come back for days."

Liang shook her head, carefully pointing out a wet, slippery spot. "Unlikely they could have survived without food and water."

"Reckon it's so. Got lost, maybe hurt." Riviera shrugged. "What else is down here got 'em, mayhap?" She stopped as they reached a fork in the path. One track went straight ahead into the gloom. The other curved to the left and took a steep descending angle.

Liang took a few steps down each path, slowly scanning. "Logic would dictate that the route leading down would be the rightful one." She hesitated. "But I don't believe that is correct." She could not explain where her instinct came from, something felt, rather than seen. She looked at Riviera's face, impassive in the amber tinged light. "This way."

They walked ahead several steps, Liang still rationalizing her decision, when a drawn out ululation sounded behind them, coming from the slanting path not taken, starting low and guttural and climbing through the range to end in an ear splitting screech. The effect was a chill that penetrated their bones.

Riviera swung around, laser pistol in hand, her pack hitting Liang's right arm, which knocked the light awry, plunging them into darkness for a moment. "Blessed Mother!"

"Wait." Liang, no less affected by the howl, spoke firmly into the blackness, righting their light. She shone it ahead and behind, showing they were, for the present, alone. She reached into her pocket and drew out her laser pistol, checking the charge by habit. "What was in the basket the Lenci gave us?"

"Oh, right." Riviera set down the woven basket she carried and pulled off the cloth that covered it. Inside were several large bones with meat attached, sprinkled liberally with a gray dust like powder. It was clear this offering was meant to satisfy a carnivore. "This just gets better and better."

Liang nodded, her gaze roaming the corridors around them for intruders. "Place some near the fork and we will move on."

Riviera tromped back to the place they left the other hall and tossed a hunk of carcass onto the ground, hurrying back. "Done. Let's git."

The resulting sound of growling and teeth and lips slavering behind them spurred the two to quicken their progress into the cave. Riviera forced a laugh. "I know why men don't come here. Too hard on their nerrrrrr—" Her words turned into a yell as she vanished.

CHAPTER 17

LIANG swung her light left to right, finding herself alone. The faint sound of the botanist's voice came from below. She pointed the light at the floor, discovering a meter wide hole she had not seen before. Had they tripped its appearance somehow?

"Riviera?"

No response. She looked both ways to make sure nothing had crept up on her, then set her basket down to fasten her pack tight. First dropping a basket into the hole, she wrapped her arms tight to her body, took firm hold of her torch and jumped in after her companion.

Liang focused on the air and sound around her. The fall was straight, unobstructed. *Intentional.* The air cooled even further, the smell of sulfur stronger, as she broke out into an open chamber ten meters high. She bent her knees slightly, tucking as the ground came up and rolling to break the fall's impact. The landing jarred her and it took a moment to regain her senses, disoriented.

She wiped the smear of smelly, damp brown clay from her palms as she pushed herself to her feet. Riviera was about three meters away, her boot off. "Are you injured?" Liang asked.

"Twisted my ankle, I think. Not bad, though." She poked at her ankle, prodding the bones and wincing, then slipped her boot back on and buckled it, wiping her hands on her pants. "Look." She pointed ahead.

Liang turned her attention from the jagged, rust colored stalactites hanging overhead to the place Riviera had illuminated, a pile of bones, clearly humanoid, stacked with intention. A chill ran through her. Their enemy was no mindless eating machine, not if it worked so purposefully. *Calm, calm. Keep your wits about you.*

Wanting to look more confident than she felt, she took her scanner from her pocket. The artifact signature was twenty meters ahead, level with them. Glancing to the right, she noted the shadowy wide entrance to another cave. "The artifacts are in that direction."

Riviera got up, still focused on the remains. "I'm more worried about what did that and where it is."

"I understand completely." Liang forced her voice to sound upbeat. "Rescan for life signs. Perhaps the women are on this level as well."

"That would suit me fine." Riviera hung her pack over one shoulder, her weapon in her right hand. She slid her scanner from her jacket pocket, studying it as they started for the darkened hollow. "Sooner we're out of here, the better."

"Agreed." Liang stepped to the side, where she too, could read the scanner. Tracing a cupric marker specific to the Lenci blood cells, she had calibrated Riviera's scanner specifically to find them. A 360-degree sweep revealed six life signs in addition to their own within twenty meters of their location. In the only fortuitous turn of fate so far, the scanner showed the women and the relics were in the same direction.

"There. The women are there. And alive." She gestured toward the next cave. Three Lenci, two of them and three others. *With any luck, they would be able to avoid the other three until they completed the missions.*

She stepped carefully across the damp clay, controlling her light's beam to minimize the chance the predators would visually detect their presence. A faint odor of the Lenci incense remained in the air. The cave walls appeared first red, then brightened to a terra cotta color as faint light increased from below to illuminate the ceiling above. A narrow path curled around the top of the cavern, separated from the lower rooms by a short wall. Liang peered over the wall to find an open space at the bottom of the drop. Three robed figures lay on the ground around a banked fire. Her sharp eyes saw no other life forms.

Riviera inched close behind her and looked down with a sigh of relief. "They asleep?"

"I believe so." Studying the women a moment, she thought she detected faint movement in their brown robes. They were alive, and apparently safe for the moment.

Adjusting the settings on her own scanner, she found the relics were several meters in front of them. Torn for a moment, she glanced down. Rogers counted on her to get the artifacts. She needed to prioritize that confidence. She beckoned Riviera to come with her.

"Shouldn't we get them out?" Riviera asked, looking down at the women.

Liang allowed a small smile. "I am unsure how to return to the level from which we fell." She shrugged gently. "While I solve this puzzle, we can retrieve the artifacts. Then alert the priestess to our presence. Meanwhile, monitor the movement of the Kiritan."

"Got to be a way around. Musta hit something, like a trap door,"

Riviera mused as they inched along the path toward the coordinates. She kept one eye on her scanner, the tiny screen glowing green. "Oh, wait a minute now. What mischief is this?" Riviera showed Liang that the life signs of the Kiritan had shifted, coming closer.

Ahead, Liang could see the bricked in section where the precious artifacts must be stored. She glanced back at the scanner. A second monster was on the move. *I can't risk everyone's safety. I'll do this alone.*

"Go below and wake the women. Lead them out to the main cave. Perhaps they know a safe path to escape. I will meet you there. Be cautious."

"Oh you bet I'll be cautious, hairy teethy monsters sneaking up on me." Riviera grinned wide, handing Liang a stick of incense. "Don't you worry. We'll be fine."

Liang watched as Riviera, moving gracefully for her size, continued around the brim of the path to the place where thick steps led to the cave's floor. Seeing she had safely arrived, Liang moved to the back, quickly scanning to confirm the relics were behind the bricks. That was not all. An opaque force field also protected the artifacts. *How am I going to get through that?*

Focus. Reassuring herself the Kiritan, whatever they were, had not crept up unannounced, she laid a hand on the field to feel out its resonance. It trembled under her palm.

A murmur of female voices rose from below, followed by the sharp scent of the incense. Riviera must have lit her stick. Her com-unit quivered in her pocket as she tried to readjust the scanner to break through the field.

Riviera's alto voice rumbled from the speaker. "Ladies are all fine. Know how to get back up. Want help?"

While she could have used a hand, Liang thought she had a handle on this. Better to make sure both jobs got done. "No. Go to the chamber outside. Watch for the Kiritan."

The vibration of the opaque field had given her a clue. Liang altered her laser settings to pulse at the frequency of the field in an attempt to overload it. The field shuddered, then suddenly released. Dazzled for a moment, she looked at the pieces, copper colored and shiny, unlike the others in the collection held by the *Doubtful*. "Nearly new. Preserved early in their existence."

Aware of time ticking, she quickly removed the relics from the rocky shelves and wrapped the smaller four, tucking them into an auxiliary pack. They were bulky, but surprisingly light for their size. The largest could not fit in the pack. She held it under her arm instead, adjusting the wristband of her torch tighter. She flicked the call button on her com-unit.

"I'm on my way," she said. As she turned to return to the main chamber, she heard a deep throaty growl behind her, very close. A slow chill slid up her spine. Her arms were full. She could not easily reach her weapon. Determined at first to hurry on, at the last moment she could not resist knowing what she faced and looked over her shoulder.

She saw the eyes of the shadowed creature first, electric blue eyes glowing with fierce intensity. It moved sinuously toward her from the shadowed depths of the corridor beyond. The Kiritan studied her as it approached, squared head nearly her waist height, shaggy, built thick and strong, and covered in gray wiry hair. Its odor of unwashed fur threatened to overpower the sulfur in the atmosphere. She thought that was the worst of it, but she was wrong.

Without disturbing its fiery gaze, the beast dropped its jaw and let out a low chilling cry, which echoed around the hollowed earth. A similar howl was repeated farther along the hall behind the beast, and also from the path that led to the open chamber where she had sent Riviera. The sound rattled her very bones with pitch and resonance.

As the beast stepped toward her, the ratchety sound of its claws scraping brown rock drew Liang's torch beam. Easily ten centimeters long, the claws were flat and deadly. She and the creature continued to observe each other for several seconds. Then she took a slow step backward, not releasing her gaze from that of the beast. It growled low in its broad hairy chest and matched her movement.

Liang continued to retreat slowly, swaying from side to side, almost dancing. She regretted leaving the Lenci basket in the other room. The incense was in her pack, but she was reluctant to stop and reach for it now. She had her wits, not much else.

The beast did not attack, but followed her, taking slow measured steps on its four heavy paws, claws dragging on the rock path. The sapphire eyes stared as the navigator inched along, praying she wouldn't trip on an unexpected rock. As she moved toward the main cave, the light from below faded into darkness, making the piercing eyes of the beast more menacing.

I must not let my fear take control.

She took in her environment, the smells of the cave and the feel of the clay under her feet. *Even the strongest oak draws nourishment from the earth and each person does the same. I am enveloped by the earth, it surrounds me, and it will give me what I need.* She bent her knees slightly, letting her center sink. She felt her weight solidly on her feet, hearing Roddi's words echo through her memory. *One must stay grounded to experience stability and strength.*

Studying the Kiritan, she supposed the creature had no abundance of critical thought, acting more from instinct like any wild animal. She would not be able to bluff it. Yet they were both living beings. They shared the air, the water. She reached out with her soul, her heart, reassuring the Kiritan in every non-verbal way that she meant it no harm. Continuing backward, she made sure each step was braced when she set her foot down, in case the beast attacked. Yet the attack did not come. Was the animal toying with her?

She had nearly reached the entrance to the main cave when her com-unit buzzed. A burst of static, and then Riviera's voice.

"Liang! You best—" The rest of the message was masked by weapons fire, which Liang heard both on the unit and in the broad chamber behind her. She turned and bolted for the main chamber, pack on one shoulder and the largest relic under her arm.

The interruption broke the spell for the Kiritan. The unkempt beast howled and rose onto its hind legs, nearly three meters fully standing, claws extended. It lunged, claws raking down the pack and the back of her legs. Pain bright in her consciousness, she dragged herself across the threshold into the next room.

A bright cone of light bobbed up and down mid-chamber as Riviera faced two of the beasts, firing at them, the laser flashes creating eerie shadows along the cave walls. A flick of Liang's torch showed the three Lenci women behind Riviera, the older woman half carried by the younger two through a small hole in the wall on the far side of the chamber.

But she could not let her attention stray. The beast was nearly upon her again. She turned to face it, fumbling for her weapon with her free hand.

"Get down!" Riviera yelled across the cave. Liang obeyed, her leg bending in a sharp burst of pain. A bright stripe of laser fire shot through the space where she had been a second before. The beast screamed and stopped its forward movement, deterred by the blast. It did not fall down, but limped aside, retreating to join its brothers, its coat singed.

"Get on now, ma'am!" Riviera waved the remains of her incense in the air, her other hand holding the laser gun on the beasts.

Liang scrambled to her feet, one leg dragging behind her as she hobbled to the narrow hole in the wall where the last of the three women had disappeared.

The large black woman continued to fire intermittently at the beasts, which had congregated in the center of the chamber, growling, pacing left to right. Liang set the loose artifact gently on the ground outside the duct, then shoved her pack into the passageway, which continued narrow for two meters, then widened out into a regular corridor. Small enough that the beasts cannot get through, Liang realized, hoping Riviera would be able to pass. The Lenci women watched but did not touch the pack as she set it down on the far side, huddling together for strength, the younger two each holding an arm of the priestess.

"Give them the char," the old woman whispered.

One of the girls reached into her pocket and drew out a stick of the incense. "Light this and leave it there." She gestured to the main chamber. "The beasts will be calmed."

Liang nodded and returned to the main chamber, using her laser to light the incense. The sharp scent quickly filled the air as she waved the burning stick. The beasts moved away toward the far wall, gleaming eyes cerulean against the darkness. "Come on!"

"You go," Riviera said quietly, not taking her gaze from the beasts, weapon still ready. "I'm right behind you."

"Very well." Liang tossed the stick toward the beasts and it landed on the ground near them, tip glowing. She picked up the last artifact and pushed it carefully through the opening with a grunt of pain as she maneuvered herself after it.

While they waited for the botanist to join them, she looked at the pack not completely torn through, the relics safe. Her leg was not quite so lucky. The wounds continued to bleed. She took some bandages from the med-kit in her pack and wrapped the blood stained leg right over her uniform, not wanting to delay their escape further. A few moments later, Riviera navigated the narrow tunnel with some difficulty, not as slim and agile as Liang.

The women studied each other in the light from the torches. Riviera checked on the older woman, who was in distress. "Ladies got down here and found this one couldn't get back, some bowel illness. They'd made their final peace, given up on rescue before we arrived," Riviera said. "Last piece of smelly stuff what they gave you."

Liang nodded. "There is a way to the surface through here?"

One of the girls spoke up. "Yes, mistress. It is a protected way. The beasts cannot enter."

Riviera frowned. "So if there be a safe way to enter and leave, how come the men didn't know this? Could have saved you days ago."

The old woman's face crinkled with weary amusement. Her wafer thin voice escaped her dried lips. "We don't tell them."

Liang raised an eyebrow. "Why would you conceal this information? Isn't safety the primary consideration?"

"Women have long struggled to maintain power in the village. The men have taken control of the religion, the economy, even the rearing of the boy children. This is the only ritual they will not touch. We must keep it, hold it as our own." The priestess nodded, fatigue clear in her posture and eyes. "Otherwise the men would reduce us to slaves, to serve them."

Riviera beamed, obviously pleased. "Good! Keep those men in their place!"

A faint growl from the chamber behind them grew louder as the beasts felt less lethargic, time spreading the pungent incense thin. One poked its head into the opening, baring its teeth in a snarl. The sound echoed, as did the scraping of its claws on the rock.

Steeling herself against her own pain, Liang turned to the women. "Can you travel? We should make haste."

"No worries here. I'll handle this." Riviera stepped forward and handed the girls her pack, then lifted the older woman's wasted body. "Let's go."

Liang laid the larger artifact across her shoulder, the added weight almost more than her leg could bear, but the young women seemed afraid of the shiny relics. Instead, she let them light their way up the corridor, armed with the last basket of goodies. Wary of further surprises, Liang concentrated ahead, but listened behind, convinced she could hear the Kiritan's low growl and gnashing of teeth stealing up on her in the dark.

Outside, the light nearly blinded them after the hours below. Riviera took the unconscious priestess to the Lencis' waiting cart. Malka and the others made much of the women, promising celebration as they thanked the team profusely, then left on the path toward their village.

Rogers walked over to meet his two officers, reaching for the large artifact Liang carried. His eyes narrowed as he saw the bloodstains on Liang's bandaged pants.

Liang looked at Riviera and then back to the captain. "Mission accomplished, sir."

When she would have continued to the ship, he took the pack from her as well, slipping it over one shoulder. "What happened?"

Riviera grinned. "She took on the monster to save those pieces there.

But he learnt his lesson. That's what comes of sending a woman to do a man's job." Her eyes twinkled with approval.

Rogers seemed unconvinced. "Can you get back to the ship? I can have medical send a gurney."

"Brown, too, is injured, but we will be well, Captain. No reason to delay."

"Report to medical when we hit the ship. That's an order."

"Yes, Captain."

Rogers turned to Riviera, who shared the dramatic adventure in the caves, leaving certain details shrouded in mystery, as had the Lenci women. Liang limped along beside them, a little farther behind with each step, and half listening, the pain like static in the background, phasing out the conversation. She should be thinking about decoding the hieroglyphics and possible assembly of parts now that they had more of the puzzle. But it was hard to focus.

Tommy burst from the hatch of the ship as they approached, his scowl at the injured team directed squarely at Liang. She looked away from his burning condemnation. The young man might be chief of their security squad, but he had no rank on her. She reported directly to his father. The captain was her father…commander. She shook her head, losing concentration.

Rogers handed off the large piece of the artifacts to Riviera, and the rest to Tommy, cutting off his protests, and ordered them to take the pieces to the science lab. He eyed Liang's pant leg as he waited for her to catch up. "I'm taking you to the infirmary right now."

Liang meant to object, but could not speak over the buzzing in her head. She felt his hand on her shoulder. She was lifted off the ground in his arms.

"You're a fine officer, Liang. I think I'll keep you."

What? Had her status been in question before the mission? Did he mean to let her go? She could not make sense of what he said, because her brain kept running off into dim tunnels. Before she passed out, she made an effort to seize part of his words like a lifeline. They echoed warmly into the darkness that swallowed her.

You're a fine officer, Liang.

CHAPTER 18

IN his office, Rogers spread data plastchips on the desktop before him, as deeply involved in the solution of his own puzzle as Liang and the others were in the resolution of the artifacts.

In the six weeks since they had crossed over, Tasiq had informed him of every trace of Confederation activity on this side of the wormhole. It was now clear that at least one ship from the other side existed here. Planetary contacts revealed that Confederation officers had in fact inquired after Rogers and his ship.

Why hadn't they initiated contact?

Rogers could take the offensive, might do so, once he was assured the ship was up to it. Burko's last salvo had caused damage that took weeks to repair. Rogers would not risk his team, new or old, with a weapons and defense system that was less than ready. Meantime, the ship stayed on the move, using the quick in and out of their planetary transactions as training fodder for the new crew, and for those adjusting to work in a new universe.

For the first time, 'doubtful' was not an acceptable response.

Now a willing conspirator, Tasiq perpetuated the cover story that the other ship was of the rebel persuasion, hunting the *Doubtful* with destructive intent. Working under that theory, every member of the bridge crew took the threat very seriously. Additionally, one of the new tech school recruits, Gretta Flan, had constructed and installed, with the help of Jerome and Eddy, a secondary com-unit tuned to local frequencies. The Confed unit sat silent for the most part, which lessened the chance they would be discovered.

Halian's advice, based on his Confederation record and the fact he lived and breathed these circuits and couplings, was mixed. He told the captain that the *Doubtful* crew was superior to that of the *Talon*. "Even with new crewmen, enthusiasm makes up for inexperience," he said. "Problem is *Talon*'s bells and whistles. Flagship of fleet always better prepared."

Rogers nodded. "A lot will depend on who finds whom."

"Agreed. Weapons in working order, engines at nearly full power. If reasonably alert, *Doubtful* has solid chance at defense," Halian promised. "Not yet ready to attack."

The captain switched to another topic on his mind. "What about Quinn? What sort of chance does he have, you think?"

Halian was silent for several moments, then he shifted in his chair thoughtfully. "Quinn a good man. Means well. Hiding something, deep hurt." The large alien tapped his chest, then bared his teeth in imitation of a human smile. "Dani kick his ass awhile, he do better."

Rogers tended to agree. To his surprise, Quinn provided a bonus amount of information about where to pick up supplies and what ships could be trusted. The 'chief' had helped repair the worst damage to the bridge, and even seemed to make friends with Tasiq, joshing him like they were old friends. The communications officer in turn had schooled Quinn on the bridge systems he needed to learn. It was a very satisfying development.

The new cargo shuttle's refit had occupied the crew's spare time, people from every department contributing and considering it a pet project. Though Dani and Hal were the primary mechanics, even Rogers had joined the effort a few times, though he was not much of an expert with a spanner. They had taken several test runs with the cargo craft and it seemed to be coming along.

Rogers sipped his green tea, a recently acquired passion from Liang, and made some notes. It was hell constantly wondering if each port they approached could hold dangerous surprises. *Was the Talon waiting in orbit?*

He set the cup aside as the door chime sounded. "Enter."

The door slid open and Tasiq entered, pointed ears twitching in a way Rogers knew indicated anxiety. He stepped inside, datapad in his hand, but did not speak until the door closed behind him. Then he walked quickly across to the captain's black desk and set it down.

Rogers did not reach for the datapad. He studied his communications officer. This was something new. *And bad.* "Tas?"

"A new message, sir. I excerpted it immediately." At the captain's nod, the communications officer activated replay. Burko's voice, sharp and tight, tore words from the depths of his own gut.

I'm sure you think you're clever, Temms. I don't know how you pulled the trick, leaping into another time and place, but I'm here to tell you if you think you've escaped from your just punishment, you're wrong.

Rogers felt his hand close tight around the stylus he held, hackles standing up on the back of his neck as he soaked in the bitter hatred of Burko's tone.

I've very little to lose. Half my crew dead, repairs near impossible, but I'm sure you know the feeling. Your ship's damage didn't kill you, either. Snakes and cockroaches seem to live through the worst of times, and you're no better than either.

That's what sustains me, Temms. The thought of wiping that smug look off your face. The determination to mete out the retribution you deserve. Will you face me? Or will you keep running like the coward I believe you to be? Isn't that the true test of a man? Let's end this like warriors.

The poisonous voice hung in the air like toxic smoke. Rogers' hand constricted on the stylus and snapped it. The movement released the tension in the room, and both took a deep breath. Tasiq's body fur looked thicker. The captain realized it must be standing on end. He forced a smile.

"Sounds like he's had a bad day." He tossed the stylus halves into the trash. "I don't need to tell you—"

"Yes, Captain, I'll make sure the others don't catch any more of these."

"Appreciated. Dismissed."

Tasiq moved smoothly for the door, returning to the bridge. Rogers replayed the message, the implications burning him, lighting the wick of his temper. If Burko intended to spur him to rash action by name calling and line drawing, he did not understand Rogers at all. Maybe that was a blessing.

But life went on. Rogers consulted his schedule to find it was nearly time for his meet up with a local commercial concern on the system's third planet, Terza. The Cartesian Consortium was in the market for an independent ship to transport some sensitive cargo, the nature of which had not been disclosed. The gist of the advertisement had been that local captains need not apply for security reasons.

Well we're not local, that's for sure. Rogers smiled a little at the irony.

Payment was described as substantial and the run not so difficult in terms of distance or cargo weight, according to specifications. Security seemed to be the highest priority.

Tommy had put together a good presentation for the consortium, showing it would be near impossible for anyone to hijack or board the *Doubtful.* Between the trained Confederation officers and the newcomers adept in defense arts, Tommy believed they could hold their own against most threats. At least he was prepared to say so.

While on Terza, they also arranged to visit the rural collective at Olesia, to purchase food supplies for an extended space run, a goal now doubly important in light of the Burko transmission. Due to some sort of communications difficulty, the Olesians required a go between to negotiate their transactions. Liang said other traders often passed the collective by, preferring not to deal through a middle man. Rogers found the cost for supplies was reasonable, and the Olesians had even offered a discount, as they were short of buyers.

He buzzed the bridge, summoning his chosen team to meet him at the slipcraft. Reaching for his case, he frowned as the brand new uniform pulled and pinched at him. He had ordered each of the team to be issued a new maroon and gray uniform, knowing they would look graduation sharp, but he ignored the inevitable lack of comfort in a suit that was not well worn. *With the Consortium, though, appearances were important, if Liang was right.* He could suck up a little discomfort if it meant getting a lucrative job. Too many people counted on it.

In his best effort to appear strong and prepared, he and Tommy had chosen Liang and Nim Williams, a weapons master new from the Sol Aeris school. According to Liang's research, aliens did not appear to be a problem at this stop, so he selected Tasiq for his sharp hearing and communications expertise, and Halian for his strength. Tommy insisted on being the last member of the team. As he came into the bay to meet the team, he found them crisp and perfect. Rogers surveyed them with satisfaction.

They filed into the slipcraft and Rogers took a back seat, letting his navigator pilot the small ship to the planet. He glanced out the port as they pulled away from the ship and for just a moment, it chilled him to think how vulnerable this little boat would be if Burko was watching from someplace near. Just one quick shot could blow the slipcraft into molecules.

Tommy leaned close. "If the enemy was this close, the ship would have appeared on our scanners, sir."

Rogers raised an eyebrow. Were his worries so apparent? He did not like the fact he was starting to jump at shadows. Or that his son could read him so well. Maybe he would be reading things he should not know, not yet. Not until Temms could come up with an explanation idealistic young Tommy would accept.

"Thanks for reminding me," he said. His gaze flicked around the small cabin, seeing the others' rapt attention. *The danger is on the minds of more than just the captain.*

Tommy nodded and grinned, satisfied he helped out his old man. Rogers leaned back in the seat, putting on at least the appearance of relaxation. *Mind clear, keep focused.* He turned his attention to the datapad, reading over Tommy's notes.

The slipcraft was directed by the central control tower into a multi level docking platform outside the complex. Tasiq's attempts to scan the complex were jammed. Instead, the team was forced to use line of sight from the small ports in the craft. The complex stretched in all directions, tall and short gray buildings with reflective windows, and also several industrial centers, evidenced by the smoke and activity around them.

Halian's thick brow wrinkled. "If such prosperous base, why need *Doubtful* to move cargo?"

Rogers nodded. "Good question, Hal." He surveyed the team's curious faces as Liang set the craft down, knowing his must have looked the same. "All right, people. We're not here to pry or to argue with their ways. We're here to do the job. Whatever it is they want moved we'll handle it. Once paid, we'll move on."

The Bricasterian rose to his feet, the captain's explanation accepted without question. The others followed, and Rogers led the way into the open air. The sky was bright blue, the Terzan star shining warmly on their ship bound skins. A few delicate pale yellow clouds laced the heavens, leading Rogers to wonder whether some sort of climate control was in place.

Liang took point, Tommy the rear, as the group walked purposefully toward the assigned meeting coordinates. They entered a wide close trimmed square of grass, approximately half a kilometer across, creted with quartz sparkled walkways. The main consortium building, rising five stories tall, stood in its center, no trees or other cover in the square. Strategically located along the edges of the square were metal towers five meters high, a small enclosure at the top of each holding two armed soldiers. Rogers scrutinized the dark liveried guards, noting that guns were not sighted on them, at least not openly. But every move the team made as they crossed the square was being carefully scrutinized. The captain had no doubt that if anything had been out of line, the culprit would be dropped on the spot.

They walked up eight steps to the main building and through revolving glass doors. The air was cool and odorless, as if it had been manufactured or sterilized. Inside they found a sizeable lobby which rose open through the center of the building, bounded in cold glass and steel. Four doors at the far side of the lobby and a glassed in elevator were the only other exits from the marble floored room. Armed men in the lobby and posted on the levels above watched as they crossed the floor to the first security desk, footsteps echoing.

Rogers caught Liang's elbow. "You did mention to them we were coming?"

"I gave them precise identification of all from ship's records, including certified genetic type from medical as they asked, sir. Per your orders to give them whatever they wanted."

Rogers felt a belated red flag of caution wave in the depths of his belly. Perhaps he should have trusted Liang a little less and ascertained a little more about their potential employers. "Genetic type?"

She did not appear concerned or disturbed. "Most sophisticated entities here use this method to guarantee secure transactions."

"New one on me." Would it leave a trail he might not want in the sector? Rogers sighed, keeping his face impassive. *On the other hand, look at the security in this place. Not the sort of people who shared information with just anyone.* He turned to greet the desk officer. "I'm Captain—"

The steely haired guard handed him an electronic clipboard and stylus. "Sign here, sir." When the captain had written his name and ship ID on the list, the officer reached for his hand and pricked his finger in one smooth movement.

"Hey!" Rogers pulled his hand back as the officer handed him a soft wipe.

"Security precaution," the officer said with a polite smile. He studied the testing device, which evidently registered a confirmation. "Welcome, Captain Rogers." He looked at the others, the device in hand. "If you'd all present yourself for testing, please?"

What might have happened if the information was not what was expected? The captain glanced at the guards above them.

Each member of his team was similarly sampled, and apparently passed inspection. The officer directed them to another desk near the entry to the elevator. A guard there scanned their voiceprints. Once those, too, were compared to some data in the computer and approved, they were sent to the transparent lift to ascend to the third level without further instructions.

Tommy sputtered with frustration as the lift doors closed, but Rogers put a hand on his arm. He was more than aware they remained under the watchful eye of the guards as the glass box rose. Certain they remained under auditory as well as visual surveillance, Rogers said nothing derogatory. "Very meticulous security."

Liang nodded, tossing the wipe she had been given into a disposal unit at the back of the lift. "Indeed, Captain. It would be quite difficult for anyone uninvited to enter."

Unconvinced, Rogers simply nodded, still concerned about the possibility of leaving their genetic records to be found by others. While his might not be so remarkable, certainly the aliens' readings would stand out in this universe. All he could do was hope that the Cartesians were as protective about information they acquired as they were of their own.

Whatever they did, Rogers thought, the rich appearance of their surroundings made it clear they were highly successful. If the Consortium reviewed the *Doubtful*'s conduct since its arrival, and he had every reason to believe they had, they would find a universally positive recommendation. If their investigation had been more thorough, it would have found at least half a crew with no previous record at all.

The Consortium seemed like the more thorough type.

But they wanted us anyway.

And that was a mystery worth ferreting out.

When the lift doors opened, the team was met by four guards wearing gold livery with black buttons and trim. The guards led them to a set of heavy wooden doors that opened automatically as they approached, a hiss of air revealing the hydraulic mechanics.

The room was well fitted, framed in a walnut toned wood, decorated in a sparse but classic manner that read 'expensive'. A large tinted two paneled window, took up nearly the entire wall before them, overlooking the Cartesian complex. Three men in dark blue uniforms trimmed in gold sat shadowed in tall hide covered chairs, their backs to the window. None rose in greeting from behind their glass and steel table. The placement of the table before the window must have been another security precaution, allowing those seated a full lit view of whoever entered, while keeping themselves anonymous. *Heavy as they appeared, the backs of those chairs likely held extra padding or even laser-proof panels. These were very cautious people.*

"Captain Rogers." The words came from the seat on the far left. "An interesting selection of personnel. Please, have a seat."

The guards pulled several chairs closer to the glass table, one in front, and the others behind in a row, not enough for everyone. As Rogers took the front seat, he detected a gradient change in the room lighting, which slowly brightened the team's side of the room, illuminating the faces of the three men. All three were mature, the two on the outside silver haired with dark eyes. The man in the center appeared younger, black hair was cut short and perfectly, his left ear pierced with a crystal stoned earring. They watched as Rogers' team sorted out who would have a chair. Tommy stood behind his father, straight as a new cut board. Halian also remained on his feet, not particularly designed to fit in the small seated chairs that matched the classic décor. When the others had taken their seats, the man who had spoken addressed them again.

"I am Rabal Klin, administrator of the Cartesian Consortium. As you are aware, we have a cargo we want transported without incident from here to the fourth planet Perpetra, and it cannot be on one of our own ships. A bit of *human* cargo."

A stiffening of protest slid up the captain's back. Liang had never mentioned the type of delivery. Human cargo implied slavery. *If that's what we're here for, not interested. Not interested at all. No matter how badly we need the funds.*

He glanced to the armed guards, now waiting to the side by a wall of thin leather covered books. Did they dare insult the Consortium by turning down a request? Too many men with guns. Feeling Tommy behind him, practically radiating unease, Rogers tried to keep his face impassive. "I'm listening."

"One of our most influential members has a young daughter who has been here in the complex for an extended visit. She must now return to her grandparents' villa on our fourth planet, Perpetra." Klin delivered the words without emotion, near motionless in his chair as the other two men scrutinized the team. They could have been statues. Perhaps they accompanied Klin only for show.

"Because of declared blood feuds, he fears transporting her himself. Consortium ships might similarly be targeted if the child is suspected to be aboard. Yours, on the other hand, is thoroughly unfamiliar to everyone." A certain sardonic, almost amused, light in Klin's eyes told Rogers that the man knew about the *Doubtful.*

Yet it didn't matter. *Interesting.*

Klin snapped his fingers. The man on his right reached behind him for a black leather case and set it on the table. Klin reached for the case and slid it in front of him, one hand caressing its smooth surface. "Our man has provided a payment of one thousand goldermarks, half to be paid here, and the other half to be paid by his father, Prince Arlen, at Perpetra, upon the safe arrival of the child." He clicked the case open, and then turned it to reveal the gleam of stacks of shiny gold bars.

Rogers glanced at Liang, noting the momentary astonishment on her face. This was a lot of money, then. Perhaps more than she anticipated. Since the explanation seemed to negate his worries about the possibility of human trafficking, perhaps it was time to consider this another bit of luck. He presented Klin with the datapad containing Tommy's security presentation.

Tommy stepped even with Rogers, coming to attention again. "I believe we will be able to meet your requirements, sir. If you'd like me to elaborate—"

The thin man raised a hand to cut him off, and then gave the pad a cursory glance. The others watched, faces like stone. "We are more than aware of your ship's capabilities, Captain. Your weaponry, your shielding, your propulsion source, all are superior to anything in our fleet. For security reasons, we will insist that the ship land to board the Lumina. We will also send a security team to protect the Lumina on your ship. Your only responsibility is to deliver her safely to her grandfather within the three day window."

Transport one little girl from one planet to the next? How much trouble could that be? He looked again at the open case. That was an awful lot of currency. What were they not telling him? The request to bring the *Doubtful* to the surface was not unreasonable, though he felt safer with her in space, in motion. He looked to each of the other members of the team, but none seemed to have any answer he did not have. He went back to what Klin had actually said.

"The…Lumina?"

Klin nodded. "She is the Light of her people. The girl is well born, in training to lead them upon her majority. You will treat her at all times with the respect such a person deserves."

I expect I'll let the child stay in her room and not need to treat her at all. "Of course."

"You will also assure that the remainder of your crew defers to the Lumina, as is her due."

Rogers fought to control the upward creep of his eyebrow. He wanted to remind this bureaucrat that just a few moments before, he had referred to this princess as 'cargo'. And now, she apparently required rarefied air and flower petals strewn on the floor where she walked.

"Master Klin, I assure you the child will travel safely and without incident." He cleared his throat, trying to shake away the annoyance nipping at his sleeve. It was a job. He and the *Doubtful* could handle a job. Preferably without micromanagement. "Perhaps we could meet the Lumina? In case she has any questions?"

Klin's stern expression flickered for the first time. "Meet her?"

"We'll greet her with the ultimate respect," Rogers said, hoping the sense of sarcasm that swirled through his mind did not reach his tongue. He expected the other man to turn him down, in which case they could move on to what needed to get done.

"I'll arrange a meeting," Klin said, the words sounding as if they tasted of something sour and unpleasant. He closed the case and shoved it across the table to Rogers, before dismissing the team, instructing them to wait near the elevator.

In the hallway, Rogers transferred the case to Williams, wanting his hands free. Tommy paced, barely controlled frustration obvious in his muscle tension, right down to clenched fists. Liang watched Tommy, while the others mostly concentrated on the guns of the guards, dotting the levels above and below them.

Well, I asked for it.

After Rogers called the ship to give landing instructions, he, too, took time to examine their surroundings. Every detail seemed designed to project the image of wealth. Expensive trappings, guarded by a host of paid marksmen, the security measures that kept them safe. The Consortium must be powerful, perhaps the moving force of the entire planetary system. Where did they stand vis-à-vis the Agency, the bureaucratic group that dominated the economy on Marriel? Were they competitors? If so, could that be used to his advantage?

"What?" Tommy snapped. His blue eyes practically shot fire in Liang's direction.

The navigator, her hands tucked behind her, stood straight and still. "You should not take it personally. They would have treated anyone the same way."

Tommy crossed the short space between them, easily a head taller than Liang. "My presentation told them anything they needed to know. They shouldn't treat us like—"

"Hired guns? People they've never met before? That's exactly what we are."

Sputtering, Tommy must have felt the collective gaze of the *Doubtful* team on him, and he visibly bit back his response. Rogers studied them, ticking off a mental bonus for himself as he noted Liang's standoffish attitude. That situation had certainly turned out as he expected.

Maybe that's what sparked the confrontation. Young men did not like to be rejected. Her comment about the Consortium could likely apply to his son as well: *You should not take it personally. They would have treated anyone the same way.* With what that young woman had been through, he imagined it would be some time before she was ready to open herself to a relationship.

"I wouldn't worry, Tom. Looks like we're in, if we're going to meet this Light of the world." Rogers checked his chronometer. "Hopefully today sometime."

Shortly afterward, a simpering functionary who introduced himself as Hace appeared. He examined their appearances, clucking at the fit of the aliens' uniforms, but with a deep sigh implying nothing he could do would make them more presentable, he finally walked them down a long hall with many doors, all of them shut.

They found the preteen girl in an office style room at the end of the hall, a slender thing wearing gold Consortium livery, a jacket and slacks, like everyone else they had seen so far. She sat at a delicately carved wooden desk, scribbling on a paper in front of her. Her golden hair was in braids, wrapped in some way Rogers did not understand, but ultimately pinned on the top of her head. Her skin was pale but clear, and her nails were perfectly manicured.

Patrolling the windows were two uniformed guards, one male, one female, both compactly built with olive skin, black hair and yellow eyes. The two were of identical height, the male's shoulders a bit wider than the female's. The guards snapped to attention when Hace came in, similar cold blooded gazes appraising Rogers' team. One guard moved forward, walking around them. Rogers swore he herd a sniffing sound. When the others looked at him, questions in their eyes, he raised a hand to stifle any objection. *What next? Can't we just get through this?*

Hace approached the girl, taking a place directly in front of the desk, waiting until the girl glanced up before he spoke. "Lumina, this humble one is, Captain Temms Rogers of the cargo ship *Doubtful.* He will transport you aboard his vessel." Hace bowed deeply.

The violet eyed child turned a cool gaze on the captain, pencil tapping in staccato rhythm on the desk's surface. "*Your entourage leaves much to be desired.*"

Rogers did not see the girl's lips move, but heard the voice somehow inside his head. Even without sound, the words conveyed a petulant, spoiled tone. He studied her for a moment, allowing himself to adjust to being in the presence of a telepath, then cleared his throat. "This squad will serve your needs. I would not have brought them otherwise."

The girl pointed to Halian. '*That one is ugly. He displeases me. Remove him at once!*"

From the sudden stiffening of his engineer, Rogers guessed the message had been 'heard' by all his team. Ridiculous. The last thing he needed was to be subject to the whims of a brat. He looked into the girl's eyes, seeing a hastily concealed surprise at his reaction. Rogers had no intention of challenging her openly. Klin had been adamant the girl receive the proper respect, and frankly, the *Doubtful* needed that case of gold bars.

Hace paled as if about to be beheaded. He looked to Rogers, a clear appeal on his face.

The captain pondered his options. He was all for proper deference to a future planetary leader, but this child had no reason to question his command decisions. He drew from his past a tone he must have used that time Linz wanted a pony, and there was no way in the seventh hell he intended to buy her one. "I did not bring Halian for his looks, but because he has the strength of three men."

He turned to Halian, who caught the hint and lifted a metal shelf behind him nearly a meter off the floor. The guards moved smoothly between Halian and the girl as he set the piece down with a clang, but did not take action.

"Each of my crew has been chosen with particular skills in mind. *If* I take you aboard my vessel, you'll have to trust my choice of officers."

"Captain!" Hace seemed ready to prostrate himself.

Rogers contemplated Hace a moment, understanding quite well where the girl got her haughty air if all the adults in the complex kowtowed to her like this. "Perhaps there is a misunderstanding. I thought we had been employed by the Consortium for this mission with full acceptance of the notion that I command my team and my ship. If the Lumina chooses not to travel with us, then we'll return to our ship and continue on our way." Rogers turned back to the girl, giving her the final word. "Which is it?"

Her violet eyes met his squarely, then traveled again down the ranks of his team. Her pale face lit with mild amusement at his audacity. "*Your ship is acceptable.*"

"Then your transport awaits." He gave her a deferential nod, echoing her slight smile.

She picked up her small personal bag, waving to Hace to bring her trunk. The functionary scrambled to do her bidding. She dismissed him with a glance, as she started for the door. The two guards flanked her, moving her around the team members as they stepped out into the hall. Tommy followed just behind them, keeping pace, followed by the others. Tasiq received data from Hace, as they walked behind, including passwords for the grandparents' secure facility on Perpetra. Rogers brought up the rear, deciding the girl needed a good spanking, the guards gave him the willies, and he could do with a stiff drink.

The guards took the entourage down an interior corridor into a lift that operated by keyed code only, underground some distance, and then back up a short stairway. Rogers had totally lost his bearings and could only hope this was standard procedure. When they came back out into the light once more, blinking against the brightness, they were at the docking platform. The guards conveyed them up one level to the *Doubtful* without anyone stopping them.

Hace and Tasiq had collaborated to have a suite on the lower deck cleared for the girl and her guards before the ship landed. When they reached the ship, Rogers dismissed everyone but Tommy and Halian, who had taken the trunk from Hace for boarding. The captain led the way to the lower deck.

"Is there anything our security can help you with?" Tommy asked the male guard, as they exited the lift.

The guard did not even look at him. "No."

Tommy bit his lip and his shoulders rippled with tension. Determined, he followed just behind his father, leading the way to the suite, in the front section of the ship.

Rogers opened the door when they arrived, finding the room arranged as a standard crew quarters would have been, a bed, a dresser, a small table, nothing on the gray walls. He had been told the other room was made up for her security detail. "I'm sure it's not what you're used to, but I trust you'll find this adequate for the short journey."

The girl looked around the undecorated room without approval, then flopped down on the bed and took her pad out of her bag, starting to draw. He waited for a response but got none.

Okay, she burns me, too. He gave Tommy a sympathetic nod, excusing him back to the hallway. Setting aside the girl's rudeness, he watched as the guards unpacked the girl's clothing and set out boxes of food prepared for her by the Consortium. He admired their single mindedness and efficiency as he waited by the door, trying to be philosophical. *It's a job. We do it, we get paid, and we move on.*

The male guard opened the door and sniffed the air in the hallway. "We require nothing further," he said, his tone dismissive. When the captain left the room, the guard retreated and sealed the door.

Taken aback once again at the sniffing, the captain stood there facing the door for a moment. "Was that strange, or was it me?"

Tommy growled. "No, it was strange. Ship smells like it always has. Maybe it's not flowery enough for Her Majesty."

"They did it on the planet, too." What could it mean? With all the attention to their genetic identification, was there some odor marker that branded them as well?

"It's not that far to the fourth planet. Let's just get her there."

Rogers grinned. "My thoughts exactly."

"Should I post someone in the corridor?"

The guard had said they did not require anything. It seemed like they brought all the supplies needed for the transit. *Better safe than sorry.* "Why don't you? If they don't need help, I'm sure they'll let us know."

"Yes, sir." Radiating frustration, Tommy stalked off in the direction of the security office. Feeling a bit the same, Rogers moved on down the hall, taking the ladder up to bridge level. When he landed in his chair, he felt a little better.

"Liang, take us out. Best speed for the Olesian collective."

She murmured acknowledgments. He thought again about that case of gold sitting in his ship's safe, and he idly poked some data into the computer, seeking a currency exchange. He accepted Liang's word that the payment would be sufficient, but he discovered the amount promised in full for safe delivery of Lumina, was nearly enough to buy a ship the size of the *Doubtful.* A lot of money. Probably a lot of risk. Maybe they had a big red target painted on the ship now that they had this child.

"Tas, I want an extra eye on the sky. No one tails us, tracks us or gets a lock on. Got it?"

"Yes, sir."

Rogers shook his head, blanking his screen as he thought about the girl and her mysterious companions. *For all that, she was a little girl who will never know a normal life. Never be able to explore alone in the woods or sneak away for a romp at a swimming hole. Hell, even to have a first date without adults carrying guns and dogging her. All that responsibility hanging over her future. Maybe she's entitled to be a little arrogant. All the same, a good spanking might not be out of line.*

With a small chuckle just for himself, he turned to the report Liang had filed for him on the Olesians, preparing for their next encounter.

The ship arrived at the collective within two hours, but waited another hour before the shield over the collective's fields was released so they could land. Rogers conjectured that the proximity to the Consortium must have dictated the extreme security measures, preventing unscrupulous individuals from the opportunity to sneak into Consortium territory. The Olesians surely did not have much anyone would want to steal.

Riviera Brown had orders to oversee the exchange with the Olesians and get the cargo aboard, short and sweet. The cargo manifest had been previewed through the Olesians' intermediary, to allow a quick exchange. No sense in staying any longer than necessary with their valuable cargo. On the other hand, the fact they stopped for supplies instead of shooting straight for Perpetra might tend to discredit the possibility they had the Lumina aboard. All in the eye of the beholder.

During the forty minutes they were on the ground, Rogers spent the time deep in discussion with Tasiq, Liang and their new linguist about the artifact pieces they had obtained on Lennor. The decryption team seemed excited about the possibilities generated by the new batch, and the captain was quickly caught up in their enthusiasm.

As the time scheduled for liftoff came and went with no word, Rogers felt his tolerance meter ticking higher. He nodded to the communications officer. "Find out what's holding us up."

Tasiq buzzed down to the cargo bay. "Brown's supposed to be wrapping things up, Captain. I can't seem to reach her."

"I'll handle it." Rogers stabbed at the intercom. "Brown? Quinn? Report!"

After a delay and a bit of static, Riviera came on the line. "Just a small incident, Captain, we're ready to go now."

Small incident? Now what had Quinn done? "Understood. Tas, take us up."

They lifted off, taking a roundabout route for Perpetra, winging the Lumina to her grandparents' home.

* * *

TOO many things crowding his mind later that night for easy sleep, Rogers retreated to his usual midnight spot on the observation deck, watching the planet as they departed Terzan space. The dark sky was suddenly lit by a sliver of moon that first appeared over the planet's edge, then slowly grew into the bright full gleaming circle of the satellite. Awe filled him as the silent tableau unfolded like a scene in the theater. *No place to see it like the sky.*

The door slid open behind him and a bulky shadow filled the doorway. "Sir?"

He recognized Riviera's silhouette, even before her soft contralto interrupted the invisible protections of the captain's meditation. His personal radar pinged. "Come in."

"Didn't want to bother you, sir, but can't sleep thinkin bout somethin not in my report." She shifted her weight, obviously agitated.

"What is it? Your report seemed very thorough." Rogers took one of the chairs and offered her the other seat. "Don't tell me. Quinn."

She hesitated, then sat down, hands twisting in her lap. She looked out the window, not at the Captain. "It's Quinn. One of the Olesians done somethin' to him, Captain. Stabbed his hand with somethin'. Quinn made out like it were nothing, but he were actin funny, like he was druggie or drunk. I saw his hand afore he hid it down, and it was all purple and nasty. Captain, I think mayhap he got poisoned."

Remembering Quinn's odd response, Rogers felt a flicker of worry prickle through him. "Did he call security? Or medical?"

"He call nobody when I was there. He just kept sayin' as how he was fine. I thought maybe he would see the doc, but I just checked with him. Quinn never showed up there either." The words seemed dragged from her with great reluctance. Ships' officers tended to stick together, Rogers knew this, and it did not seem related to Quinn's crappy attitude. Riviera was genuinely uneasy, and thought whatever had happened was worth violating the unspoken code between officers.

"I'll speak to him about it."

The woman hung her head a moment, then stood up, looking the captain in the eye. "Thank you, sir. Just...." She shrugged. "Quinn's a royal ass. Ain't no skin off me if somethin' happens at him. But he's prideful. I think it stopped him from takin' care of hisself. Without knowin' what they did, it could be somethin' more than just a harm to Quinn. It could be a virus, a bacteria, somethin' that could spread to all us."

"Thank you for your concern. I'll speak to him."

"Yes, sir. Sorry to disturb you." The door shut behind her and he was alone with the stars once again.

Quinn. The man was destined to be a sore spot. Rogers groaned and headed out to find his wayward engineer.

CHAPTER 19

BENZI supervised the loading of cargo with his usual resentment at being assigned to menial tasks. He was chief, after all, not some errand boy. When captain's orders came down from the bridge, he thought about sloughing them off on one of the minor officers to reinforce his small power base. Then he got a look at the thin limbed Olesians waiting at the dock, faint green tinge to their warty skins, and he decided to handle it himself. *Wogs. Might be some entertainment value to it at least.*

Insipid, inoffensive humanoids about two meters tall, Olesians did not speak the common language of the civilized peoples in the sector, but burbled shrilly in their own tongue. Quinn watched with suspicion as teams of four hauled great tan cartons from the dock into the cargo hold, stacking them double deep along the metal walls.

"What's in those?" he demanded. The nearest Olesian looked over and squeaked at him in alarm. "Oh come on. In Galactic, you effing wog!" He scowled. Captain had not recommended the usual translator protocols since the Olesian language structure could not be deciphered by the computer. He heard the Ice Maiden, his new name for Liang, had contacted them through a third party who could converse with both sides fluently. *Another bleedin' wog specialist.*

Riviera Brown eyed Quinn. "Have some respect for those what's bringin' us supplies. Don't matter none do they speak Galac. Food'll taste the same."

Quinn scowled at her and walked over to the wog, determined to assert his authority. He did not dare appear weak in front of Brown. "Hey! I'm talkin' to you, fool!"

He grabbed the Olesian's arm at what passed for its elbow. It let loose a piercing warble, and the others all stopped what they were doing to turn slowly toward Quinn, like a satellite array turning radar dishes to examine a new signal. The room snapped from noisy activity to silence. He stiffened, taking a step backward, feeling the error clear to his gut. "No one told the rest of you to stop what you're doing!"

Glaring, he looked at the one he had been told was in charge, a particularly unattractive sage colored wog named Tamala. "What's the matter now? Get back to work!" A quick look at Riviera was enough to see her hide a smirk before she turned away to discuss something with a security guy. *Bleedin' ulcers. I could smack her too.*

Tamala chirruped at the others. They lost interest in the confrontation and slowly turned their attention to the process of bringing in the tan crates once again. Tamala approached Quinn, who held up his thick papered clipboard at an angle somewhere between a shield and a weapon. Quinn stood as tall as he could, the ugly Olesian topping him by nearly half a meter. "What's the effing problem?"

Tamala reached into a pouch impossibly concealed in its limey hide and drew out something that looked like a thin polished fingernail, as long as Quinn's little finger. Benzi looked from the wog to the nail and scowled. "Look, pal, you're getting paid to work, not waste time."

A crooked grin on his warty face, Tamala reached for Benzi's empty hand, and jabbed the nail into the back of it. He released the engineer and stepped back with a patient air.

Was that acid?

Benzi's hand burned, a stinging fever crawled up his arm and into his shoulder. *I'll kill you, you bastard! What the hell have you done to me?* As his brain raced through filthy epithets, they were trapped inside his mouth, his body frozen in time. Paralyzed, he could only stare at Tamala.

Time seemed to stop inside a deep echoing silence in his head. His gaze moved around the room slowly, so slowly, the way a clock seemed to tick into stagnation when counting down the last three minutes until end of shift. In his heightened state, the layers of perception available to him seemed to triple. He could see detail of each Olesian body, down to the pale mint colored hairs on their skin, and he heard their thick labored breaths. For several moments, dust motes tangoed in the air all around him, stirred by the aliens' passing.

Distracted, Quinn stepped back, trying to regain control of his body. Brown spoke to him in deep sonorous tones, her words drawn out, distorted so he could not understand her. She looked at his hand. He followed her gaze and discovered angry red blistering at the site where Tamala had stuck him.

How could I let my guard down around the wogs? They're out to get you! Always out to get you!

In reflex, trying to conceal from Brown what he had let happen, he forced his hand behind him, the movement taking several long seconds as his awareness continued to skew.

"Quinn?" Brown shook his shoulder. Startled, he glanced up at her, seeing a myriad of colors in the irises of her brown eyes. *I never noticed that, all those tones, gold and black and mahogany. Where did they come from?* "Are you all right?" She glared at Tamala. "What you be about there, sir?"

Benzi fought for control of his tongue. His brain seemed to be moving at lightning speed, jumping from thought to thought as a conscious, defined motion. Time unwound into flashes of moments, hyperawareness of every other living being in the room and every noise, smell and flavor in the air. The floor was awash with textured layers of dirt tracked in by the Olesian crew, a blend of many earth tones. The engines' sound thrummed in the air and entered through his feet like a shadowy intruder sneaking up his bones to rattle in his head.

After what seemed like an eternity, his internal and external worlds started to jibe. Brown's words made more sense. The clipboard slipped from his fingers, clattering on the floor. He bent to pick it up, finding its surface rough, which he had never noticed before with his calloused hands. Brown's anxious inquiries assailed him, echoing through his head. *So loud. So loud....*

He waved her away with the clipboard, the fact he held something between them making their proximity tolerable. "F-f-fine," he said. *Can't show weakness, not now. She'll go to the Cap about it and I'll lose the chief's seat.* "I-I I'm f-fine." His eyes finally fixed on Tamala. Disoriented, he dragged sheer will from his depths to remain upright and calm.

Tamala studied him, large cow like eyes boring into Benzi's consciousness. The Olesian waited several moments, then warbled something high pitched at him. *"There. Now you are civilized and can learn to be respectful."*

Quinn blinked, startled. He stared at the Olesian. *Did the wog just gibber at me and I understood him?* Brown still stood much too close, suspecting, concern written on her face. "Yeah, yeah, what's the holdup? Get back to work!" he blustered needlessly, waving her away with the clipboard as the last cargo boxes came in from the dock. "Brown, check those in!"

Without a protest, the black woman signed for the shipment, then left the room with the manifest, one more troubled look over her shoulder at Quinn. Benzi waited until she was gone and then whirled on Tamala, the movement seeming to continue in a spiral even after his physical body had come to a stop. "What did you do?" he asked, voice tight.

"It won't harm you. You should thank me" The Olesian twisted its bubbled face in what approximated a human smile. It was not a reassuring expression. *"It will take some time before the virus takes full effect—"*

"Virus!" Quinn reached up to yank at the collar of the other's coverall. "You gave me an effing virus? I'll kill you!"

"Mr. Quinn, please calm yourself." Unruffled, Tamala shrilled an order to his workers, who obediently trudged out the open hatch, leaving them alone with a room full of crates.

Quinn was amazed to find he understood everything Tamala said to the others. He had not released the grip he had on Tamala. His heightened senses studied the reedy body, calculating where a vital organ might be found by the susurration of rushing blood in the webby veins.

Once the others had left, Tamala reached for Quinn's wrist, nearly crushing it with a muscled four digit hand, and calmly removed it from his clothing. *"If you would consider this gift I've given you—"*

"Gift! What gift? A virus? How long till my parts start falling off, huh?"

Tamala quivered in amusement. *"You are so closed minded. Examine this from your intellectual center, not your gut. You wanted to communicate. You insisted on discourse with my workers. You could learn our language, or we yours, but it would take weeks, months. Our scientists developed a virus to alter the brain, allowing nearly instantaneous understanding. Something very similar to your translator programs. The benefit—"*

"You never asked my permission, you ass!" Benzi shoved him away and strode around the room, furious. What he really wanted to do was hit something. But his hand hurt too much. "You could have asked me!"

"You would have refused. Therefore I took the efficient route." Tamala shrugged. *"What's done is done. You will see in the weeks to come the extent—"*

"Weeks!" Nausea spilling over him, Benzi stared at the green skinned humanoid. He struggled to keep his hands to himself. *I should kill this bastard right now.* "I'm gonna have this for weeks?"

"You will have it for the rest of your life." The Olesian bowed slightly. *"You are welcome, Benzi Quinn. May the suns smile on your path."* He turned and walked out the hatch, shrilling to the others, who dispersed back to their mudded homes.

The rest of my life? I'm going to be infected the rest of my life? Benzi stood in the center of the room shuddering with revulsion. Wogs. Sprechan-blasted wogs.

In the stunned silence that followed Tamala's departure, the insistent voice of Captain Rogers took several moments to register on Quinn's consciousness. "Quinn? Quinn, report!"

His head still buzzing, Benzi fumbled at the response button of his com-unit. "Yeah, Cap. We're all set." He heard Rogers give the order to close the hatch and the cargo bay went into flight lighting, dimming the scheme to save power.

Quinn counted up the boxes again, his hand aching. He could read the markings on the crates for the first time, too angry to be amazed just yet. Supplies seemed to be right at least. Plastics ones seemed to be hard stock, fresh provisions and food in the crates with planked wood. Thinking he heard movement, Quinn walked over to inspect the wooden crates. "Maybe Brown ordered us up a nice bovine." He grinned, determined to make the best of it. "About time she did something useful. I could use a good hunk of steak."

A cursory examination did not find any, however. He sighed and left the bay, shutting the lights and power to minimal. Walking down the hall, he continued to feel heightened sensations. His feet hitting the worn gray carpet jarred him. Formerly imperceptible details on the wall panels distracted his gaze. The engines echoed in his head as they powered up. *Bleedin' wogs.*

Stopping at one of the brighter juncture of corridors, he studied the large square on the back of his hand, now bruised a violent purple, raised lesions around the round humped black tinged puncture point. Quinn scowled. He was no doctor, but it looked bad, real bad. *Let the effing wog get one over on you, didn't you, champ? Nice work. In front of Brown, too.*

The skin around the puncture pulsed as blood rushed to the injury site. He could feel his blood moving inside his body. It gave him the willies. *Can't go to medical. Be as good as confessing I'm an ass, can't take precautions when dealing with wogs. Doc would have to put that on the record. Then where would I be, huh?*

Left with no choice but to suck it up, Benzi plucked work gloves out of his back pocket, pulling them on despite the pain. At least they would cover the sore, keep it from getting anything in it. It would heal soon, he told himself. *I've had worse. Thousand times. It's nothin'.*

Quinn slung himself around the corner into engineering and slouched to his office to see if there were any new work orders. Finding none, he stepped out onto the overdeck, checking what the others were doing. Dani had her nose in an old paper book, leafing through documents Tasiq had found on the artifacts. Eddy and Halian dissected a flux panel on the main table. Quinn sauntered over to them, preparing to kibitz when something stopped him cold.

Halian muttered to himself in his native tongue, reciting the order of the connections that should be in the panel, from upper to lower. *Benzi understood every word.* Checking the panel, what he had heard was exactly correct. Eddy looked up, an expectant grin on his face, but Quinn just nodded to them and turned away, head buzzing more, the room a blur. *What happened to me? Am I just going crazy?* Whatever had been done to Benzi, it was obviously more than just the ability to understand the Olesians' babbling.

Something very similar to your translator programs, Tamala had said.

Ignoring Eddy's curious look, Benzi retreated to his office, shutting the door behind him, his shock leaving him short of breath, his heart pounding. *What the bleeding hell had happened?* Pacing in the small space, he sunk his mind into the question like a deep sea anchor. Wanting to test his theory, he tapped into the Cyclopedic section of the ship's computer. Purposefully seeking out sections stored in their original alien languages, he paged through several documents. Nothing. All a bunch of nonsense. Maybe it's only auditory. He played the recording of the documents. Still gibberish.

How could he understand Tamala and Hal, but not this?

A virus. What was a virus? A search of the medical database showed him that viruses were parasites that entered living cells and used the host's chemical energy to survive. Benzi's skin crawled thinking about a microscopic parasite squiggling around inside of him, then he caught his breath when he read that a virus would replicate itself. It could copy its own genetic codes onto Quinn's DNA and then it would spread cell by cell in the normal course of things.

Squirming at the thought of little bits taking over every cell in his body, changing it into...what? One of those ugly sage colored bastards? He nearly choked on the bile that rose in his throat. How long would that take? Minutes? Hours?

Stop. Think. This had to make sense, even in some twisted way.

Let's see. The Olesian virus was programmed to interface with the Olesian language. So that one clicked. Hal. Benzi was more familiar with him. He had heard the words before, though he had never understood the guttural talk punctuated with burps and clicks.

Would he have to wait a week, a month, a year? What else would the virus do to him in the long run? Would he evolve into one of those green hairy creatures? Benzi shuddered. He could not face that thought. He would get his sidearm and blow his head off before he degenerated into a wog. *Bet your life, pal. But what if....*

What if the ability to understand other languages expanded? What if he could gradually read, even speak, other languages, all languages? The possibility overwhelmed him.

Looking up, he rubbed his forehead, wondering how long before there were measurable results. The doc might come in handy, testing exactly what the virus was doing. Maybe he could risk talking to the doctor about it. Maybe that blonde. He could snow her easy enough. *Sweet talk her. Yeah.*

Seeing out his small window that the others had not seemed to notice his preoccupation, he was glad. No sense in tipping his hand before he could use it to his best advantage. He would sit on it, just like the information he held over Rogers. Unless....

Benzi's interest suddenly blazed. The artifacts the Captain was so hot to decipher, weren't they were covered with hieroglyphics, all in some other language. Would he be able to read those as well?

A smile crawled over his face. He would have Rogers over a barrel if he thought the engineer could give him his translation. Quinn smirked.

Then we'll show the Ice Maiden who's indispensable.

CHAPTER 20

THE next two days were spent in a walk about pattern through the star's systems.

It seemed to Benzi Quinn that Rogers was doing the best he could not to be *found.* Must be those shady fellows are close on his trail. He debated whether now was the time to play his trump card and give them a quick call, letting them know where to find the *Doubtful.* They had promised to make it worth his while. But somehow he did not quite trust them, either. They thought he was not any brighter than any snitch.

"All the jacks thinkin' they're better than little old Benzi Quinn. Well, let them think it. I got plenty goin' for me now. We'll see how they play once I've got that old relic workin' again." He whistled his way down the hall to his quarters at the end of his shift.

Over the last fourteen years, he had lived in many little rooms in many little ships that all blended together. He did not even pack much any more. The duffel he had brought on board held three changes of clothes, a bottle of alcohol he had snagged on Roandock and some old engineering texts he lifted from a library. His rack lay unmade, several gray blankets twisted from a night of bad dreams. A couple of trays from the galley were stacked on the desk, food congealing on them. Benzi flipped on the light and tossed himself on his jumbled rack, rubbing his forehead. His hand still hurt. He held his hand up to the light, glaring at the purple remains of the bruises as he chucked a silent curse in the direction of Brown, who reported him to Rogers.

It was the middle of the night, when the captain showed up in engineering to interrogate him about the incident. Not ready to share his 'gift' just yet, Quinn acknowledged the confrontation, hard to deny it with the evidence in black, purple and red blisters in front him, but he did not mention its effects.

Sullenly, he had accompanied Rogers to medical where Montgomery did some tests and found nothing harmful in Benzi's system. Doc applied some healing salve and gave him some painkillers. "You have to watch the foreigners, man," Doc said, *sotto voce,* so only Benzi could hear him.

"No shit, Doc." The chief shook his head. "Got somethin' out for us every minute."

The old doctor clapped him on the shoulder. "Good man. Now, back to your post."

Benzi shrugged on his work shirt and went for the door. His suspicious nature made him wait, just out of sight, to see if Montgomery would tattle when he and the captain were alone. What he heard was something else altogether.

The captain cleared his throat. "Heath, how is Okalani working out for you?"

"She's fine, fine. She's a wonderful assistant. Couldn't be better."

"I'm glad to hear it." Rogers paused. "Could she handle more responsibility?"

"What do you mean?" Quinn heard the sound of metal instruments being stacked on a metal tray. As the two men's voices dropped lower, he moved closer to the door wanting to know what was going on. Sprechan's soul, if he had to spy to get enough information to be someone, then he was not too low to stoop there.

"I mean that I'm a little concerned that we've got one doctor. If anything happened to you." A chair scraped on the floor and someone sat down heavily. "I'd like her to be fully capable of dealing with full scale medical emergencies."

Montgomery laughed. "I've survived dead on attacks, chemical warfare and even dinner with my in-laws, Temms. Are you expecting something to happen to me?"

"Not at all. Of course, I didn't expect to be sucked through a wormhole in space. I didn't expect to need to replace half my crew on short notice. It's made me a little leery."

"Does this have something to do with those rebel traces?"

Rogers paused. "I just want to be prepared, that's all," he stated tightly. The chair scraped again. "Think about it, will you?"

Benzi heard the movement and slipped on out the door, suspicious about the request. Rogers had moved women into most of the power positions on the ship. Dani in engineering. Liang on the bridge. Was he trying to move a woman into the lead role in medical too? What was next? Aliens?

Benzi was starting to feel trapped inside this old tin can. Needing to stretch his legs, he took the long way back to his room, through the lowest deck. Trying to get some time on land, he had volunteered to take the mission into the caves at Lennor, but Rogers had chosen Brown instead. He could begin taking workouts in the gym once his hand healed. Not Liang's sissified stilted martial arts matches, either.

Something for real men.

Maybe he would start a little boxing competition. He had been good at that, back when he was a kid, back when his old man cared what happened to him. His Da came to the matches and coached him, cheered him on. Before the booze ate his brain. Benzi shoved away that thought. *No sense in beatin' that dead horse, eh?*

He came around a corner of the quarters section, and a door slid open. Surprised, he approached the entry. These were rooms where the crew had died in the crossover, so he heard. He thought those were empty, left by those who were afraid of ghosties. The door stayed ajar longer than it should without someone triggering it. He reached for the controls, thinking perhaps the proximity sensor was malfunctioning and needed to be repaired.

He felt something push past him, shoving him into the wall. Startled he grabbed for his tool belt, but he did not have any tools to protect himself with. "Who's there?" Even as he spoke, he felt ridiculous. He was obviously alone. *Damned Olesian virus, probably.* He turned to the door again. Something tapped him from behind. He looked over his shoulder to find a rough looking, swarthy man with cold yellow eyes inches from his face. "Yi!" he yelled, jumping back out of arms' reach.

"What are you doing here?" the man asked, a chill hiss under his words.

"I was just walking." Quinn had never seen this man before. Was he part of Rogers' big secret? *If I'd put scary people like this on board, I wouldn't tell no one either.*

A sound came from the open door and Benzi glanced back at the room. A man sized lizard with scaly brown skin and sharp yellow eyes stared at him from the portal. Benzi blinked, dumbfounded. The man behind him hissed. The lizard metamorphosed into an attractive woman of the same coloration as the man, and stepped out into the corridor so Benzi was flanked.

What in Sprechan's name was going on here? Benzi held out his bandaged hand. "H-Hey look now, I'm not causin' trouble to nobody! I'm just on m-my way back from the doc's."

The female stepped closer, sniffing the air. "Best be on your way, spaceman."

"Yes. Move along." The man took a position next to the woman, blocking the open door.

"Right." Quinn inched backwards, not taking his eyes off the two until he found a cross corridor. When the space opened up to his right, he scuttled into it and bolted toward his room, not stopping until he got inside and secured the door, breathing hard. He had never wanted a drink so badly in his whole life.

There was no one in the hall. But they appeared.

And I could swear I saw lizard. I swear I did! But it was a woman. Wasn't it? Hearin' words I don't know, seein' things I can't see. Maybe I'm just goin' mad, eh?

Head spinning, hand throbbing, he wondered what this virus might do before it was done. Popping a couple of pills for the pain, he crawled into his unmade bunk and forced himself to sleep, those frosty golden eyes following him into his dreams.

CHAPTER 21

LIANG, in a form fitting blue leotard, stepped before the mirrored wall in the ship's small gym, prepared for her morning exercises. The ship's timekeeper showed it was two hours before her first turn shift was to begin.

She closed her eyes, gathered her thoughts and looked within to visualize the lighting of a small red candle in her body's center. First concentrating on the base of the candle, her inner gaze moved upward to the flame, seeing the variations in color as it curved from indigo to blue, through orange to the palest yellow at its tip.

As each layer of the flame adds to its heat and light, so does your life force layer through the chakras to reach wholeness.

She could hear Roddi's voice in her head, almost see him standing before the class, a slight figure who could wield the power and presence of a man three times his size. His teachings were the closest to parental words she had received since leaving her mother and father on Tang so many years ago. She could hardly remember their voices, their faces any more.

The crew of the *Doubtful* had now become her family. She treasured her working relationship with the Captain, like that of a father and daughter. He put his faith in her, honoring her by his trust. The bridge crew, strong and capable served each, other, even those that had been so painfully new when she joined the crew. Jerome and Eddy had come along and were developing into good officers.

As the timekeeper gently sounded, she stretched upward gently, letting the familiar movements energize her. Sweeping down in an arc, she extended her arms to the left, then to the right, before gradually coming upright. Opening her eyes to see her reflected form, she froze.

One of the Lumina's guards, the female, stood behind her.

There was no threat in the woman's posture or expression. But how did she come to be here without Liang knowing it? *No one entered through the door. I would have seen them.*

The woman spoke first, intent yellow eyes peering at the navigator, face set in a mask of practiced concern. "I do not mean to frighten you.

Please, put yourself at ease."

Liang, not inclined to simply relax in the face of the unexpected, immediately sorted through reasons the protector might have come here, instead of waiting until she was at her bridge post. "Is there a problem with the Lumina? An emergency?"

"No, the Lumina sleeps." The woman smiled with a hint of sadness. She took several steps, watching her own movements in the mirror. "She is likely dreaming of her great future."

"She will have great responsibility. That is not always a blessing." Liang took a towel from the rack and wiped her face, studying the other. The woman moved like a big cat, solid and powerful, an aura of implacable strength about her. But it was still odd, unnatural, how her olive skin was the exact even tone of her partner's. Among humans, even between people of the same race, there were always variations in skin tone from one to another, from men to women.

"If you want to perform exercise, you have permission to use this facility." She wondered whether the woman wanted to exercise in privacy. "If you desire, I could leave this space—"

The woman crossed to her in a blur of movement. "No, officer Liang Chao, I wished to speak with you. I, we beg you to hear our plea. We know you can help us. You will understand." The woman actually trembled, her eyes downcast. "We seek sanctuary."

Liang raised an eyebrow. The ship was due to rendezvous at Perpetra in six hours, at which time the Lumina and her entourage would leave the ship. Did they intend to prevent the transfer?

"Are you in danger?" she asked. "Will something happen to the child when we arrive?"

"No. Danger is not the issue."

Her answer shed no light on the issue. Did the sentries mean to keep Lumina from her grandparents? "We will not be party to abducting the child," the navigator warned.

The denial was quick and sharp. "That is not our intention. We will perform our duties as required." She smoothly crouched down on her haunches, her expression approximating a smile. "Our motivations are far more selfish, Liang Chao. Let me begin another way. I am Aronka. My partner is Tabio. Our Bellonan species were genetically engineered twenty five years ago to serve the Consortium. Today is our Anniversary."

"The Anniversary of what?"

"We are released from our servitude to the Mayarca family this day after five years. We are free to rejoin the consortium herd." Aronka's enthusiasm faded, and her next words tumbled out uncontrolled. "We know we will be separated for our next assignment. We will not be allowed contact. We will not be allowed to procreate." She looked seriously at Liang. "We do not want to face separation! We are mates now. We will refuse to return to the herd."

Liang imagined what Rogers would say to this complication in what, so far, had been a perfectly smooth mercenary assignment. "What are the consequences for your failure to return?"

"We do not know. We know of no others who have chosen to rebel."

"Where would you go?"

Aronka smiled shyly. "We wish to remain aboard your ship. We have studied your crew and your captain. He is a man of deep honor. He has the vision to see what may be valuable inside an individual if encouraged and allowed to flourish." She stood, her skin flushed with emotion. "We do not come empty handed. We are trained in measures of security, which is always needed on a traveling ship." Aronka cocked her head, as if inwardly debating, then studied the navigator. "There is more you do not know about us." Before Liang could ask, the woman shifted to her feet and then was gone.

Liang stood, startled. Had Aronka moved to the exit? Surely it was a gift to move faster than one could be seen. She went to check the hall, but before she reached it, she was stopped short as the woman faded into view directly in front of her, a calm smile on her face.

Speechless for a moment, the navigator studied her companion. So, not incredible speed, then, but actual invisibility? Considering what appeared to be a miracle in its best light, it was an astounding achievement. "Fascinating. A genetically bred characteristic?"

"One of many." Aronka glanced at the mirror. "Our ability to maintain a human appearance is for the comfort of those we serve." As she watched herself, her skin scaled over with delicate sienna colored bits, her rough facial structure changed to a distinctly reptilian build. Her hair shrank away as her fingernails changed to short claws. "This is our true form."

Caught off guard, Liang could not help but pull back a step. The claws, the long, sharp teeth were very real and dangerous. She could imagine them slashing flesh, opening an arm or leg to the bone. Appearances could indeed be deceiving.

Just as quickly, Aronka reverted to her human form, smoothing her jet black hair back into place. "We are bred as security. In our natural form, we can kill in seconds, with no need for weapons. In our stealth form, we cannot be seen or detected by most devices. In our human form, we are still strong, and deadly." She grabbed a heavy set of weights, lifting the entire rack with one hand, then setting it down with a clunk. "We could be valuable to your captain and ship."

"Understandable. We would have to speak to Captain Rogers." Liang checked the time, it too late to complete the exercise. "I would conduct you to the bridge, if you would wait for me to dress for duty."

"Of course. Tabio awaits my return."

Liang stepped into the small dressing area where her uniform hung. What a curious development. Of course, there were benefits. The Captain wanted a full crew complement, including trained security personnel. This could put his mind at ease.

She also wondered what the *Doubtful* might expect in retaliation from the Perpetrans if the guards did not return as scheduled. If they were free to leave, then they should be allowed to do so. But would Rogers be suspected of doing something to persuade the guards to leave Perpetran service? There was no reason to cause needless trouble for the ship.

As she dressed, the suspicion crept in that the other woman could be watching her, perhaps in arm's reach with those invisible claws. *Nonsense. Without some gain to motivate them, people do not act, whether that gain is selfish or otherwise.* All the same, she dressed as quickly as she could, feeling vulnerable.

When she was ready to report to the bridge, she stepped out to find Aronka, in lizard form, using the space for exercise, her movement thick and fluid as molten metal. The Bellonan completed some planned routine that looked like deadly practice for a real life fight. Liang could not help but hope Rogers would say yes. She could not wait to add the two Bellonans to her training school. What a challenge they would bring!

Knowing Rogers did not like surprises, Liang messaged him that she needed to meet with him on an urgent matter involving a member of the crew. At first, she intended to add an explanation, but she was not sure she could explained in several short words, or even in any manner short of the one Aronka had used. He invited her to join him in his office.

Liang led the way along the carpeted corridor and up the ladder to the bridge level, sensing Aronka's disquiet, which increased as they neared the captain's study. "Captain Rogers has always been fair and generous," she said. "Be of good heart." She waited until the Bellonan was composed beside her, then signaled for entrance.

"Come in."

When Liang and her companion entered, Rogers looked up from a stack of work, consternation blooming on his face at their serious expressions. Liang could almost read his thoughts: *What's gone wrong now?*

"Trouble with the Lumina?" he asked.

Liang shook her head and plunged in. "Captain, Aronka approached me with a request for you. She and her companion Tabio want the opportunity to serve aboard the *Doubtful.* They want asylum."

The captain's eyes widened and he leaned back in his chair, brow furrowed. "Aren't they employed by the Consortium?"

Liang deferred to Aronka for the explanation, which the ebony haired officer provided, in much the same words in which she explained it to Liang. Her expression tinged with fears and desperation, she punctuated her story with momentary demonstrations of her genetic capabilities. Liang watched the captain's face echo her own remembered astonishment as Aronka morphed into a savage reptile and back.

Having a lot to assimilate, Rogers looked thoughtful. He leaned forward and fiddled with the datapad on his desk, then set it aside. "So as you see it, there will be no retribution by the Consortium if you leave its employ?"

The woman stood straight and tall. "By Consortium law, on the Anniversary date, we are free to choose." Her face softened as she hesitated, unsure. "None of my own nestmates have left the herd, but there are stories of those who have gone Outside. They have not returned. We do not know if they survived. What we do know is that if Tabio and I cannot remain together as mates, if we are not given the freedom to choose our lives, even whether to procreate, if we are left alone without each other, then we would not want to survive. The pain of our separation will be too great. We must take the chance."

The emotion in the woman's words swelled Liang's heart. She was no stranger to leaving her past behind to seek her fortune. Frightening enough for a teenaged girl, but at least she had been surrounded by her own kind, capable of both great warmth and treachery.

But for these two, not even human, bred for the single purpose of serving their masters, to take control of the threads of their lives and risk everything for companionship, for love?

She could not imagine the courage this must take. Something beyond the confines of logic or efficiency and into an area of warmth and acceptance and devotion. For this level of emotion to be steaming inside the stiff, regulated exteriors the Bellonans had previously shown to the world was a real surprise.

But at the same time, intriguing. And somehow life affirming.

Rogers swirled a spoon in his cooling tea. "When would you leave your present service?"

"Once we have relinquished the Lumina safely to her caretakers, we may request it of the Prince."

"What if the Prince refuses?"

Aronka hesitated. "Surely he would not violate the law."

Liang watched the decision making process fit itself to Rogers' shoulders. The tension in them grew visibly as he seemingly considered the request. As she herself had already noted, many considerations came together in making such a decision. He was likely also assessing the Bellonans as potential crew, how they would mesh with the rest. In light of their shape shifting capabilities, there would certainly be an adjustment period.

People like Quinn might never adjust. Not that his comfort would be anyone's deciding factor. He had tried to score with her, and she had rejected him. Since then, Quinn kept up a steady stream of hostility that Liang forced herself to ignore. Some of the other young men joined in, including the captain's son. It was becoming more difficult to pretend she did not care. She did. A lot. This shipboard family had grown, and she felt attached to it. For the first time in so long, she wanted not just to excel at her work, but she wanted to belong. She wanted to be part of this ship and its crew for the rest of her life. It was not hard to see why Aronka and Tabio thought the same.

The captain studied Aronka, who waited, her muscles still as stone. "No repercussions? You're sure? These Cartesians seemed like people one would not want to cross."

"It is the law," she repeated, more firmly, as if she were convincing herself. "They must honor it."

"All right. We have six hours until rendezvous. I will give you an answer in four."

"Thank you, Captain Rogers," the golden eyed woman said with a stiff bow.

Liang allowed a small smile to cross her lips. She was pleased to have facilitated this conversation, sure now Rogers would grant the request for sanctuary. It was something in the way he held his shoulders. She had noticed the same thing when he liberated her from Oke Runyon's service. She wondered if he even knew he telegraphed his thoughts in this way.

Rogers stood in dismissal and the two women left his office.

"I must return to my post," Aronka said. "Thank you for your efforts." She hesitated, then awkwardly extended a hand.

Liang took her hand and held it warmly. "I am pleased you asked for my assistance." She let Aronka go, then continued onto the bridge. Activating her monitor, she found a message from the captain.

If we take these two, I'll want a report from you within the first twenty four hours as to their strength, versatility, capabilities and whether they will be in fact a danger to the crew.

Liang raised an eyebrow. Fascinated by the shape shifting abilities Aronka demonstrated, she had not considered potential danger to the crew. Considering the security they provided for the Lumina, surely there was no question whether they could be trusted.

In truth, however, they knew little of the Bellonan species. The teeth and claws Aronka manifested in her reptile form, while not as vicious as the Kiritan, clearly could inflict deadly force. Liang replayed the transformation in her mind and felt a chill along her spine at the sheer power inherent in the woman's body. She was indeed powerful like a leopard or lion, an animal, not a human, no matter how she might appear.

She would wait and see. If the pair successfully negotiated their release from service, she would set up a series of tests to reveal their true skill in each form. With their genetic enhancements, the extent of which she had yet to discover, the Bellonans might surprise all of them with the variety of their gifts. They could well provide service that more than repaid the cost of taking them in.

Liang turned to a report about the status of the artifact reconstruction. The parts recovered from the Lenci cave apparently completed several crucial points in the potential design. Although they had been able to fit the parts together in several different ways suggested by Ramona's earlier notes, they still had not been able to generate a spark of power.

There seemed no 'right' method for construction. All efforts at searching the local Net for a primer, instructions or schematics, failed. Periodic references to artifacts had been found, like those the Lenci held, but no true main source. This continued failure to resurrect the device weighed on Liang's feelings of loyalty and duty.

She owed it to the captain to make every effort to complete the device so he could return to his own universe. He willingly gave her a home, and if she could, she wanted to provide him the same.

And what would she do if he returned to his point of origin?

She had no idea. She did not want to think about it, not yet. *All things in their proper moment*, as Roddi had always taught.

CHAPTER 22

RETURNING the Lumina child to her home proved uneventful, as far as Rogers was concerned. The winding course he chose apparently fooled any potential trackers, as they had no confrontation with any ship during the five days they were en route to the grandparents' compound. Aronka and Tabio had managed the girl, away from the crew. If they moved about the ship to give the girl some exercise, it was always during third turn, when the crew did not occupy the common spaces.

Pleased things had gone so smoothly, upon entry into Perpetran space the captain ordered Tasiq to send the required coded message to allow them to enter. Tabio sent a subsidiary message to verify the identity of the ship and requesting an audience with the Prince before the *Doubtful* left dock.

When they landed at Perpetra, Rogers led the members of his original team, again in dress uniform, to the home where the Lumina was to be delivered, a palace built of black marble in a setting of precisely manicured landscaping, down to the animal topiaries. The girl walked with her guard behind the team, Halian toting her considerable luggage.

Rogers noticed the man and woman as they left the opaque palace door and started down the steps to meet them. The dignified couple was dressed in shades of violet. The three men wearing navy blue uniforms triangulated themselves to the rear and flank of the couple, weapons in hand as their gazes darted left and right in search of potential threats. But knowing what he knew about Tabio and Aronka, Rogers thought the two Bellonans likely provided a greater level of protection than a dozen armed men.

To their surprise, as they approached, the Lumina broke ranks and ran toward the older couple. "Mimi!" she cried, throwing her arms around the gently coiffed woman. The Bellonans faded to invisibility, appearing seconds later on the steps next to the child and her grandparents, where they resumed their human appearance as they continued, like the other guards, to scan the surrounding area.

Surprised by the sudden outburst, Rogers relaxed as the family came together. "It's nice to know she can be a real kid."

"Yeah, who would have guessed?" Tommy muttered. Rogers glanced at him for a moment. Tommy's pride apparently still stung from the attitude of Lumina's personal guards. What would changes would his attitude take once he knows the Bellonans might join their team? *Maybe I should have given him a heads up. I just didn't want to muddy the waters before it was necessary.* If the Cartesians did not release the pair from service, the point would have been moot. And Tommy's pride further dented for nothing.

The older man turned from his granddaughter and walked across the expansive piazza to the *Doubtful* team. His was a patrician face, with even bone structure, worn by time but not wrinkled and dry. The Prince's smile was kindhearted and his violet eyes, so like the child's, were amused at her antics. He was clearly fond of her. He scanned the group and fastened on Rogers. "You're the captain?"

"Yes, sir." Rogers shook out his best company bow. The girl and her grandmother had turned to go into the house, the child animated, talking quickly, gesturing as she spoke.

"On behalf of my wife and myself, I thank you for bringing her safely." The older man reached into his jacket pocket for an envelope, which he handed to the captain. "A personal expression of our gratitude." The older man gestured to one of his men, who stepped forward with a case similar to the one the captain had received at the Consortium's headquarters. Tommy claimed it on Rogers' behalf.

Inside the envelope, Rogers found a letter of reference and a pass of free conduct through Perpetran space and its sphere of influence. This was much more valuable than a cash bonus, no doubt. His heart lit with genuine gratitude. "Thank you for this, Your Honor. It is most appreciated. Our pleasure to be of service."

The prince's detached gaze studied Rogers. "I can also tell you that your enemy is close. Much closer than you think."

Now how did he know about that? The captain stiffened. Panic rose in him, not because this prince knew his business, nor even for the warning about Burko, but that something would be said in front of Tommy. His throat closing for a moment, he scrambled to find a noncommittal response. "We did not intend to endanger this place."

"Nonsense." The prince's eyes danced with amusement, though he never broke his regal stance. "They won't dare to come here. We are under the protection of the Consortium. Your enemy has chosen to align himself with the Agency. He will regret it."

Rogers glanced at Liang. *We never had that conversation about the Agency, after we left Jowalt's place. I'd best get informed on that right away. If Burko's got local backing, then he's even more dangerous. He could be anywhere, represented by any stranger who approaches us.*

Aware that Tommy's expression, no, his whole body, had tightened up with questions, the captain simply acquiesced. "Thank you for sharing what you know. We'll take proper measures for our safe exit, then."

The prince glanced toward his granddaughter. "My patrols will see you safely out of Perpetran air space at least, Captain Rogers. We are in your debt."

Rogers thanked him again and withdrew to a discreet distance from the place where Tabio and Aronka waited on the marble steps, standing at perfect parade rest, appearing at first glance to be more like machines than living beings.

His duty to the *Doubtful* complete, the Prince took leave of the captain and approached the Bellonans, two of his guards standing nearby. The conversation began quietly, but soon became heated. The Prince's face went through a series of emotions, from anger, to confusion, and finally to disappointment. He shot Rogers's waiting team a heated look as he motioned one of his men close and whispered to him, and then sent him running into the house. For a moment the Prince stood still, staring at a distance, before once again crossing the piazza to where Rogers stood.

"I understand from the Bellonans you have invited them to become part of your crew." His tone seemed to indicate he might regret the courtesy he had previously shown.

Detecting a challenge, albeit an unspoken one, the captain shifted his weight and stepped forward. "I was told they had the option to freely join my crew."

The Prince's jaw set in an expression of reluctance. "It *is* the law. On the anniversary date of each contract, they may sever themselves from our service." He glanced at the two, who stood still as rock. "You must not think we are ogres, Captain, even if we regret their choice. They have been with us for many years, and we have treated them well. But we would not hold them against their will. They have been very loyal and good servants."

His aide ran up carrying a small case, and handed it to the prince. The prince took it, then beckoned to the pair, who came to join them. He opened the case and removed several thick packs of paper which he gave to Tabio, a bittersweet smile on his face.

"I do not know of others of your kind who have chosen to live apart in this way. It is a brave choice you make. This payment is a reward for your loyalty, but nothing compared to the rewards you would earn if you remained."

"We are grateful," Tabio said.

The Prince waved a finger in their direction. "You invoke the law, and I must concede you have the right. But remember the law is a double edged sword. If you choose this, you may not return again to the herd. You will never again see others of your kind. If one of you dies, you will be left alone for all time." He looked from one to the other. "Is this understood? This is your choice?"

The implications shook Rogers. Hard enough to leave a universe behind with all its connections, but at least he was surrounded by friends, and others of his species. Would the pair really risk spending the rest of their lives apart from the other shape shifters? The fact they even consider it demonstrated the depth of their love.

Did I ever love Connie that much?

The Bellonans, alike enough to be twins of the same egg, stared into each other's eyes for several long moments, before turning back to face the Prince. "We understand," they replied in unison.

"As you wish. Then I have no alternative but to wish you well." With a curt nod, the Prince turned and walked away, his guards falling into step behind him.

Tabio carefully stored the papers, which Rogers guessed to be some sort of currency, and quite a lot of it, in his jacket. "We are free," he said.

Aronka took his hands, and her face flooded with joy, the first real emotion Rogers had seen on her olive skinned face. "We are free."

Before the team's eyes, the couple vanished.

"What in the fourth hell was that?" Tommy demanded, his face flushed. "And what's that about them being crew? They're security, right? You're putting them in my department?" He gestured wildly at the place where the pair had stood a moment before. "And where did they go?"

Rogers did not have any better answers. "I expect they're keeping their celebration private. And yes, they'll be joining the crew. You'll have the chance to branch out, now that you've got a whole department to command." The captain struggled to come up with an explanation that would prop up Tommy's ego and keep his focus on the benefits to the ship.

I really don't want to be in the 'because I'm your dad and captain and I said so' zone. But I'll go there if I have to.

He studied the expression on the other faces around him, all of them but Liang's, were in some level of shock. At the same time, he was aware of the eyes of the Prince's detail on them. "I can say this development isn't a complete surprise to me. The Bellonans requested asylum, and Liang brought me their request. They're crew now. Not open for discussion. We'll find out more about their capabilities in the weeks to come. Right now, our work here is done."

Your enemy is closer than you think.

Cold nausea washed over him, wiggling its way into the cracks between his bones, and settling into his bowels. He would need Tommy, Aronka and her mate and all the help he could get to deal with Burko. The longer they stayed, the longer they risked being found. "And we need to get a move on."

He started off for the landing port at a brisk walk, letting the others catch up as they would. Liang stayed on his heels, but the others chose a more leisurely gait. A glance over his shoulder showed Tommy had dropped back to walk with Williams, no doubt complaining or at least commiserating. So be it. No need to stifle any opinions. Everyone was entitled to think what he wanted.

But I get the final word.

* * *

PER Rogers' orders, Liang set out to familiarize herself with their newest crew members, particularly their skills. In the first two days, she had already learned a few important facts. In keeping with their reptilian nature, they fed on raw meat, often eating in their cabin, since the sight of them tearing bloody steaks with their teeth alarmed the humans. Preferring nocturnal hours, they prowled the ship late at night, often invisible. Tabio asked that their quarters be kept at a temperature fifteen degrees above that of the rest of the ship to help regulate their body temperatures.

The only space large enough for a full out test of their abilities would be the cargo bay. The boxes and cartons the Olesians had left were still stacked along two walls, but plenty of room remained to practice. Liang brought the training module that had come through the rift with the *Doubtful*, skipping the first half dozen levels when she began the test. She presented herself as a test subject, but Aronka just smiled.

"Better to let us spar with each other. Less chance someone will get hurt."

Her pride definitely pricked, Liang deferred to her new shipmate. She would learn more by observing anyway. "Very well. Begin," she said.

The Bellonans first circled each other, making an occasional swipe before Tabio feinted, then leapt on his mate's shoulders. She growled and engaged. They moved faster and faster, the human shapes flickering, shifting to reptilian as they continued to grapple and score off each other. Liang could scarcely see their movements with her eyes. She moved to the waist high console by the room's entry, the infrared monitors filming the proceedings, keeping better track than she could.

Their blows, powerful and well measured, connected from time to time, scoring torn flesh or clawed face, but each injury seemed to fade, healed, soon after it appeared. Judging by the fierce muscular tension the Bellonans sustained, Liang knew an ordinary human would not have survived.

The fight suddenly stopped, both of the Bellonans sniffing at the air. "Someone is here." Tabio said. He faded from his reptilian appearance back to a more human looking guise. Aronka did the same. In the quiet that followed, Liang heard the rattling noise that quit abruptly as silence set in. She came out from behind the monitoring console as they walked the length of the bay, narrowing the location of the foreign sound.

"There." Tabio sniffed at one box, the lower of two, and then slowly vanished from sight. Aronka stepped out of the way, letting Liang approach the man high square carton, stacked with several others, marked "construction" in scrawled penmarker. Liang gave a three count on her fingers and then grasped the side of the tan box, pulling it open.

Inside, a flurry of activity, dirty gray blankets tossed in the air as a small human burrowed under them in desperation.

"Come out of there," Liang ordered. The heap of blankets quivered. "Come out now." No response.

Tabio pulled the blankets aside, invisible hand closing on the arm of the person to pull him out into the cargo bay light. A moment later, he faded back into view, in human form now, holding what appeared to be a human boy child tightly by the arm.

The child was built small, with intense blue eyes and ragged dirty hair, wearing only a long shirt of some thin cloth which must have been white at one time. He fought and tore at Tabio, trying to bite his hand, but the security officer used his other hand to restrain the feral child so he could not hurt anyone.

Liang hunkered down to meet the boy at eye level. "I am Liang Chao. This is the ship *Doubtful*. What's your name? How did you get here?"

Unspeaking, the boy looked at her blankly, then stared wide eyed at the others.

"No one will hurt you," Liang continued.

Her statement was met with more silence, fear and hostility warring in the boy's eyes. He twisted futilely in Tabio's grip, staring at her without reply.

"How is it the sensors never picked him up?" she wondered. He had to have arrived with the Olesians. Why had they not reported a missing child once the ship had lifted off? Surely they had not intended to abandon the child on the *Doubtful.*

Could they?

Aronka sniffed the air. "His body chemistry is not as yours. There are metals in his system which might block your reading devices."

"That might explain it." While Tabio held the child, she examined him. While he had no identifying marks or jewelry that might give them a clue to his history, she did find fading bruises on his back and arms which were still painful, judging by his reaction. *What animal would beat a child like this?*

Leaning forward, she rummaged through the pile of blankets, the worn acrid smell making her eyes water. She found various bits of food packaging, some heavy paper box bits, a rusty, nicked up spanner, and several small electronic devices in various states of disrepair.

"There's nothing here." She stepped away from the box, brushing off her hands. "We should take him to medical. The doctor should see him."

Tabio pointed the boy in the direction of the door. "Time to go little man."

Released from the steel grip of the security officer, the boy spun and dived back for the blankets. He grabbed the tools and devices, clutching them against the front of his shirt, glaring at the adults as if daring them to take the items. Tabio reached for the child again, but his mate held up a hand to stop him.

Aronka stood back, her posture conveying a lack of threat. She grabbed a small canvas bag lying on top of one of the cartons, and held it out to the boy. "For your things."

He stared at her without understanding.

She held the bag in one hand and pantomimed placing things inside it with the other, then held it out again. The thin child hesitated a moment, before seizing the bag and slipping in his treasures.

Aronka seemed pleased. "You don't need to talk to communicate."

Liang agreed. "It appears so." She called the captain to let him know they had found the stowaway boy. "We're taking him to medical now, sir. He appears to have been mistreated. He refuses to speak."

"I'll meet you there in a few minutes. Rogers out."

The navigator took several steps toward the door to the main corridor, glancing back over her shoulder to see if the child would follow. Tabio and Aronka stood behind the boy, cutting off escape from the rear. The child looked at them, then at Liang, before his shoulders slumped. Clutching his bag and dragging his feet, he reluctantly went with them.

CHAPTER 23

A STOWAWAY? How in hells' blazes?

Halfway out of his chair before he could finish that thought, Rogers was distracted by a flurry of activity at the com-station. He saw Jerome and Eddy scrambling to set a recorder, intently listening to a transmission. "Gentlemen?" he asked.

"It's a Confed trace." Eddy grinned. "But it's no rebel ship. It's the *Talon*, sir!

"All right!" Jerome cheered. "If they figured out how to get here, we can get home!"

Tasiq stiffened and caught Rogers' eye. "Let me review that." He set down the data pad he was reviewing on the artifacts and peered over Eddy's shoulder. "Confirmed, Captain," he added, his voice noncommittal.

He sent the information to Rogers' monitor. A clearly identified Confederation com-signature accompanied the brief transmission: "Olly, Olly, in free."

Rogers carefully froze his facial expression. *Arrogant bastard.* "Secure this message and send it to the monitor in my office."

"Yes, captain." Tasiq canned the message and locked it up as ordered.

His mind wheeling along in high gear, full flight escape mode, Rogers could not help but notice the two young officers' excitement as they returned to their stations. Of course his shipmates might have left more behind at Gilada than he. His own family had fallen apart, his career had lost meaning considering the direction of Confederation politics, but that was not the case for everyone.

Not like I could take them back now, not until we get the artifacts in working order again. That's on our plate. When we get there, we'll have some options.

He hesitated, feeling like he ought to say something. Should he not be happy that their fleet's flagship had come to rescue them? He probably should. But even the thought of his squat adversary choked his throat closed.

"Good catch, Jerome," he mumbled. Then he focused on getting off the bridge with his stalwart mask still in place.

He climbed down the ladder to the next deck, letting his feet land hard. The impact jarred him, and he leaned against the wall for a moment, breathing deeply. Something deep in his thought process reminded him that if the message carried a receptor ping the *Talon* would have been able to detect the delivery of the message. Burko knew it had been picked up. Therefore, Burko knew Rogers knew he was here. That taunting line from the old children's games stung him, too. Was this a game?

Games could be won or lost.

The important thing was to make sure they could keep playing. When he returned to the bridge, he would order the ship back to Marriel, using a 'drunken sailor' heading, similar to the path they had led away from the Consortium's main base. If Burko thought he would freeze in his tracks like a frightened rabbit, Rogers would show him differently.

The walk to medical plagued him with second guesses. Was Burko waiting just beyond the horizon, ready to pounce on the *Doubtful* once he flushed it out? Would they be better off to stay put, since that seemed like the wrong choice? It certainly would not be anticipated. Should they just hunt Burko down and have it out, once and for all? His officers said they were not ready for that. What then?

Scrambling, he fell back on practical lessons from officer's training school. *First choice, best choice.* The gut response was often the correct one. *We go to Marriel.*

Questions about what to tell the loyalists in the crew burned at him. Surely it would not be long before they expected to rejoin Jal Burko, unaware he had become their deadly adversary. *How could he look Tommy in the eye and explain his rebellion, explain that he had lied from the moment Tommy woke up?* He needed a plan.

But first, the stowaway. When the captain entered the medical office, he found chaos.

Benzi Quinn's voice was the loudest. Bloody gauze lay around him on the white sheets of a treatment bed as Okalani tried to corral an arm that jabbed furiously in the direction of the left hand corner of the room. "Get them freaks outta here!" Quinn yelled.

Rogers followed Quinn's gaze to the far bed, where Liang waited with the two Bellonans and a small, nondescript boy, who was being examined with great difficulty by Heath Montgomery. From Quinn's level of agitation, he guessed the invective had continued for some time before his arrival.

Tabio and Aronka bore the verbal attack without open response, although Rogers observed small striations in the tone of their human looking skin. He wondered if that was a precursor to their change in form, He had not seen the process enough to know. What might Benzi think if he knew the whole truth of their shapeshifting capabilities?

"Quinn, put a lid on it!"

The engineer's complaints dwindled to a sullen stream of muttering as Rogers joined the larger group. Rogers smiled at the half clothed, filthy boy, who moaned, holding the canvas bag in front of his face as Rogers greeted him. Not making eye contact with any of them, the boy rocked in place, protectively shielding himself with the bag. Sound came from his throat, an odd dissonant keening, rhythmic, synched with his rocking. His fingers moved over the outside of the canvas as he felt the objects within, their presence seeming to calm him.

The doctor turned the child slightly so the captain could see the fading bruises. Liang had not exaggerated. Did this happened before he arrived here? Did he hide in the box to escape his abusers? Or had the Olesians shoved him in the box and abandoned him on the ship? Rogers considered the condition of the child and wondered whether a rational answer was even possible.

Montgomery muttered something to Okalani about cleaning the boy up. Leaving the uncooperative engineer, she brought a bowl of warm water to the bedside along with a cloth. After several tries at explaining, she finally gave up on persuading the child to allow her to wipe him with the wet cloth, and just started doing it, gently removing what had to be weeks' accumulation of dirt off the child.

The doctor pulled Rogers aside. "I can't get anything out of him, Temms. His heart is running a little fast, but with all the noise. Pipe down there!" he shouted over at Quinn, who had started again. "Seems that the boy doesn't like men much, this is clear. Guessing from his behavior, I'd say he's been the victim of abuse for years. I can't get him to say so, of course. Can't get a good read on his real age. I think he's been starved, too. He's undersized for his age. He needs new clothes, a serious shower, a good feeding and…well, parents."

"Parents. Right. We're a little short of those at the moment." The captain looked around the room. "Have any of you seen this child before today?"

Quinn tore his incensed attention from the Bellonans long enough to share an epiphany. "Kid's got a shirt like those wogs, Tamala and the others that were here unloading cargo the other day." His eyes narrowed as he held out his hand, still a little purple in color.

Rogers raised an eyebrow. "The Olesians?" He glanced at the boy. "I didn't think they were human."

"He's not strictly human, Temms," the doctor said.

"And the Olesians was not human. No way," Quinn insisted. "Hairy little green wogs,"

"You think they brought him aboard? Why wouldn't we notice?" the captain asked.

Montgomery explained the concentration of heavy metals in the boy's system. "It hasn't killed him, but I'm sure it has had some effect on him. Some literature over the years referred to heavy metals as a contaminant, which could cause brain damage, autism, and other disorders. Could explain the boy's behavior."

"What are we going to do with him?" *As if I don't have enough to juggle now.* "Liang, get on the com to the Olesians and see if anyone's missing a child."

Quinn still scowled. "You ain't listening. He ain't theirs, Cap. They was all green and hairy. Not. Like. Us." His spiteful words echoed those he had uttered the first day they met.

This did not make much sense. Rogers glanced over at the boy, now being wooed by Okalani with some sort of candy on a stick. "All right, then. If he didn't belong to the Olesians, how did he get into their cargo container?"

Liang tapped her lip thoughtfully. "The crate contained nothing else but the child and his personal effects. The child did not displace cargo items. The logical conclusion would be that he had been brought here in the crate. Purposefully."

"Nonsense," the doctor said. "Why would they just toss the child on the first ship that came past? Without knowing anything about us?"

Aronka spoke quietly. "Because you were nearly like him. Perhaps they felt he was your kind. They could believe you would know how to care for him, how to heal him."

After a shocked silence, Rogers frowned. "They could have asked."

"Yeah, well they ain't much good for that." Quinn snorted and eyed his bandaged hand.

The captain crossed his arms, annoyed, and then took a step toward the child, wanting to take his measure. When the captain's movement caught the child's eye, the boy stiffened, bobbling the canvas bag, which dropped to the green infirmary floor, spilling its contents.

"Hey! Where'd you get that?" Quinn buckled on his tool belt and slid off his bed. "He's got my Zyger controllers!"

Before the engineer could reach the scattered bits of half-repaired equipment, the boy scrambled down and snatched the pieces, stuffed them back in his bag and backed up against the wall. His rough shirt tore open and he clutched at the edges, as he stared in terror at the adults. A pitiful noise came from deep in his throat.

"Those are mine!" Quinn raised his voice, towering over the boy, his hand out. The boy scrunched down in as small a package as he could manage, dropping the bag and his shirt, cowering, his arms over his head to protect himself as he continued that disturbing keening.

"Quinn!" Rogers barked, prepared to intervene, but Quinn's anger deflated and he backed away, a strange look on his face. Rogers turned to see if the boy was all right, and found that Aronka and Tabio had reacted to the threat by shifting to their reptilian countenance. Even though Rogers had seen it before, it was a shocking transformation.

"I was just—" Benzi protested as his gaze slid over the captain's shoulder to the Bellonans. His eyes grew wide, and his face paled. "Sprechan's privates!"

Montgomery shared the expression of horror on Quinn's face. "What are these, Temms! You didn't tell me we had reptiles on the ship!"

"Enough!" The captain's sharp rebuke brought immediate silence, even from the boy. *Too many people in a small space.* He dismissed Liang as the least necessary. He looked at Aronka next. "Are both of you needed here to control the boy?"

"I believe Tabio is capable, captain," Aronka replied, her skin changing slowly back to its human olive skinned tone. She shot Quinn a look. "We are sorry for alarming your doctor. We perceived danger to the child. It is our nature to—"

"Understood. Please return to your post for now." Rogers waited as they left the room, Okalani following right after them, her immediate work complete.

The boy studied the faces watching him, and inexplicably scampered behind Quinn, his eyes glued to the tool belt Quinn wore. He poked at some of the devices, and Quinn visibly controlled a reaction under Rogers' tense stare.

"Well, Temms? Reptiles?" Montgomery crossed his arms.

Rogers eyed the doctor. "I would have issued a formal report, but we've been a little preoccupied. These two have special capabilities valuable to the security of this crew. As the captain, that's my call."

He turned to Quinn. "And you. I've about had it with this crap about aliens. They do their job, you do yours. End of discussion. *End. Of. Discussion.* Got it?"

Quinn had the grace to look ashamed. The child slipped one of the diagnostic tools off the belt and pushed the buttons with decided purpose. Quinn clearly wanted to grab it back, but the Bellonan was too close. "I hear you, Cap." He would not look at Tabio.

"And what about the boy? He can't just live in a box in the cargo deck!" Montgomery snapped, barely satisfied.

Rogers' tone softened a little. "Of course not." He studied the child, thinking he must have been fairly clever to survive on his own among the Olesians. How long? Seven years, maybe ten? Eating their food, having some sort of conflict that had left him battered and bruised. "What's he doing, Quinn?"

Half turning, Quinn stole a look at the device. "Well, I'll be damned. He's recalibrating the sequencer."

"He's what?" Rogers frowned. "How can he know anything about that?"

"Beats the hell out of me." Quinn held out his uninjured hand, palm up, low down so it was clear he was not trying to hit the boy. "Can I see that, snapper?" The boy glanced up sharply, hesitating, then handed the piece of equipment back to the engineer. Quinn examined it, checked it against one of his other handhelds. "Five percent efficiency increase." As the boy scrutinized him, hands twitching, Benzi put on a smile. "Good job, snapper."

Montgomery crossed his arms thoughtfully. "Intriguing. Seeming incoherence counter posed with mechanical genius. Maybe the autism call wasn't far off."

The savant capacities of the child might be amazing to Rogers, but he was more mystified by the sudden turnaround of Quinn's attitude, surly and loud until he saw the boy cower, and then his hostility had faded. *As long as they're hitting it off, that could provide me with an answer to this problem at least.* "Mr. Quinn, can you keep an eye on the boy for the next few hours until we can determine whether we need to send him home?"

The engineer raised his hands, gesturing helplessly. "Me, Cap? Do I look like some kinda babysitter?"

The captain assessed the boy again, now fussing with one of the devices in his bag. He inched behind Quinn, hiding from Rogers' regard.

"I'd like to spend some time making this child feel at home, but I've got fires that need to be put out," Rogers said. "You seem to be the only one he'll cooperate with without the use of force. I'd like to make his stay here the least traumatic possible."

Seeing Quinn's apprehensive glance at the security guard, Rogers realized he had a final trump card. "Either he's with you, or I've got to send him with Tabio."

Quinn looked at the boy, then to the Bellonan. "Fine, fine. I'll take him. But I'm on shift. He'll have to come with me to engineering."

The captain nodded, inwardly pleased. "Just keep me posted." He turned to Tabio. "I think this relieves you of responsibility for the boy. Thank you for your attention."

"Yes, Captain." Tabio gave a sharp bow and left the medical office.

The doctor's eyes still studied him with hostility. Rogers understood. No one liked to be out of the loop. Especially someone who believed he was pretty high up on the command chain.

"Heath, those two are unusual, but Liang assures me they're safe and have amazing skills. I'll make sure they are available for whatever examinations you think are necessary." From the corner of his eye, he saw that the boy had taken another of Quinn's tools and was turning it this way and that, checking its capabilities. "Something tells me you'll want to keep an eye on that, too."

The doctor's jaw still set, hard as crete, but he must have heard Rogers' determination not to give ground on this point. "You bet I will, Temms. Go on, now. Leave me to some peace and quiet. I need it." The doctor made shooing gestures and walked over to his desk.

When Rogers moved, the child slipped around Quinn, peering out from behind him, his fingers still moving over the dials. "I think he'll be fine down in engineering. Dani'll help you keep an eye." He watched the boy focus on the device. "Who knows, maybe he'll be a helping hand down there?"

Quinn snorted. "Hell, maybe he can be chief."

The boy froze at the negative tone in Quinn's voice, but he did not pull away. He did crouch down. Quinn again softened, and shook his head. "No worries, snapper. You're a good boy." He gave the boy a thumbs up, adding a smile. The boy visibly relaxed and went back to playing with the scanner, the two men fading from his concentration.

Rogers watched the boy a moment. "See, you've got the hang of it already."

"Don't rub it in, Cap. You said a coupla hours. I can manage that."

The captain nodded. "I'll be in touch by end of dayturn. Dismissed, Quinn." Rogers rubbed his forehead as Quinn and the boy left the medical office. One more fire extinguished. Now he needed to concentrate on the bigger issue of Burko and the big lie. Wishing he just had time for a long, long nap, he sighed.

When he looked up, he saw the doctor's gaze intently on him. So Montgomery had not really acquiesced. "What now?"

"The rift in the universes is open? Burko's here?"

The captain barely disguised his surprise. *Someone on the bridge is leaking information.* "We've been tracing some signatures that could be Confed—"

"Could be? Is for sure! That tells me that there's a way through to the other side." The thin doctor stalked over and grabbed Rogers' arm, staring into his face. "Are we looking for the rift? Are we in contact with Burko? If it's him, he can tell us how to get back!"

Rogers looked at the doctor, scrambling for an answer, forcing his voice to sound cold, businesslike, when what rose in him sounded close to fevered panic. "Heath, get hold of yourself!" *Who was it? Who released this information? Do I have traitors on my ship too?* "We're still sorting through the information. We don't want to jump at what…what might be a rebel trick." He focused on his anger and betrayal, let that pour through like hot melted butter onto Montgomery. "When I decide what to do, I'll keep you informed."

"You can't decide for all of us, Temms. You remember that. We have family there. Friends. Lives! We must report to the fleet immediately!"

"I know what protocol dictates." He stepped away from the doctor, his stomach knotting once again. *Bad enough the threat of Burko. But open dissension within the ranks would lead to disastrous consequences, too. Mutiny? More deaths? By the gods, he had lost Ramona. Wasn't that enough punishment?*

He had handled it. Or so he thought. The fabrication about the rebels seemed very plausible. It had always been meant as a stopgap until he and his co-conspirators could generate a permanent story.

Why did it have to be Burko?

The ship to follow him through the rift could have been one of a dozen. If it had been Pomeroy or one of the others who rebelled against their orders, he would have a colleague, someone to bond with, work with. Together they could have patched up their wounds and decided what the next step in their lives would be. But now it was hard to find a path not covered in blood.

The doctor opened his mouth to speak again, and Rogers raised a hand, cutting him off. "Damn it, Heath, leave it alone, will you? I'm handling things the best I can." He turned on his heel and marched from the infirmary, feeling Montgomery's hard stare like knives in his back.

CHAPTER 24

HEADING for his office, Rogers took the long way around the ship, using the time to let his heart race, then slowly return to normal, as the rush in his ears faded and the pounding stopped. Where he passed, he spoke to no one, instead he listened. He listened for revolt, for sedition.

He heard none.

Maybe we're going to be all right.

Finally back in his chair, door closed against intrusive whispers, he brewed a bitter cup of lapsang tea. He would have liked to take it to the observation deck, to commune with the stars, but he did not want to risk another confrontation. Time to get this situation under control.

The issue of Burko, he set aside until the end. He had less influence over that than most any other problem they faced. Instead, he started with his assets. His ship, at last, was well on the way to fully repaired status, properly provisioned and he now had enough personnel to keep them in the sky. That was a lot, considering where they were a few weeks before.

He had new people, as well as aliens, working for him. For now, the mix seemed a hastily made stew, composed of many fragrances and textures, but a dish that would blend together in an appealing way over time. *If they got past Quinn's blasted xenophobia.*

They had collected new artifacts to add to their collection, and Dani's team resurrected some of what he thought was lost in the bridge explosion. Decryption still proved elusive, but each step brought them closer to the option to re-cross the rift.

The thought sent a numbing chill down his back. He had no desire to return to Gilada. His home was here. His family...was here.

Tommy.

But Tommy's family was back on Gilada. His mother, uncle, cousins, sister, brother, and the girlfriend he said he met at the Confederation school. Everyone but his father. Montgomery was right. Rogers had no right to deprive the rest of them of their lives.

Damnation take me! It's not my fault! I didn't mean to bring them all here!

His frustration wound up into a tight ball, then exploded into angry action, as he let his cup fly across the room. It shattered into a sprinkling of glass and a sodden mess on the carpet.

All he had to work with was a hypothesis: that the *Talon* had come across the universal rift simultaneously with Rogers' ship. Ramona had been the only scientist authorized to study and implement the artifacts, that he knew of. She certainly never said otherwise. The most likely explanation was that Burko had followed him in, perhaps sucked in beyond his control.

More likely Burko had followed him in. Now his people were trapped, too, because of what he and his co-conspirators had done.

But they had saved a whole planet from unwarranted domination by force. He agreed with Dani that the effort was worth the cost of a few lives, if that is what it took.

What nagged at him now was the possibility that his worst nightmare might not be Burko. That the danger could come from inside the ship. *Our own could force the issue.*

It was only a matter of time before whoever called Montgomery, or Montgomery himself, with all good intentions, managed to arrange contact with their enemy. The truth would be revealed. Then the shooting would start in earnest.

With a silent curse, Rogers wondered again who the culprit could have been. *Who would have done this?*

Disappointed, Rogers stalked out onto the bridge, glaring at each officer in turn. The furrow in his brow must have been fierce, for Liang rose to her feet.

"Captain? Is there a problem?"

He waved her to silence. Windthorp, Tasiq, Liang: none of these would have reason to be in league with the Confederation. *Who was missing?*

Jerome was not at his post.

Rogers remembered Jerome's excitement at the discovery. He sighed. *Jerome. Of course. Who could blame him? Any young man with his life, his pre-planned, ordinary life, ahead of him would be thrilled to be on his way home again.* Feeling twenty years older than he had that morning, he tossed orders at Liang. "Notify me when we hit Marriel."

"Yes, Captain."

Doing his best to ignore their mystified looks, Rogers left the bridge, returning to his office. He needed help with this and he needed it now. Once back in the safety of his office, he summoned Dani and Halian to meet with him immediately.

* * *

THE small group was grim as he shared the news with his fellow rebels. "Despite our best efforts, it's come down to the truth."

"What are we going to do, Captain?" Dani asked.

"Good question. I'd like to wring the boy's neck." Rogers frowned. "At the same time, I understand his excitement. We all left family and friends back at Gilada. To find that someone from home was here, perhaps offering the return trip? As far as he knew, this was the answer we'd been looking for." He shrugged.

"Rift still open?" Halian grumbled.

Rogers shook his head. "Nothing has shown on the scanners. But who knows? We never expected it when it appeared the first time. The only thing we're sure of is that Burko is close, and raring for a fight. We'll be back at Marriel soon, and can take some time to reconnoiter, see if there's evidence of an active wormhole."

He turned to his engineering department head. "What about it, D? You want the one way ticket back?"

Dani held her teacup close, fingers wrapped around the warm blue ceramic. "With the mess the artifacts are in, I'd figured it wasn't something we'd have to face for awhile." Brow furrowed in consternation, she thought out loud. "I'd sure hate to have Burko drag us back in shameful triumph."

"Agreed."

She looked at him, dark eyes troubled. "And if so, what if they took Persios anyway? It would break my heart to know all we sacrificed was for nothing."

Halian straightened in his chair and dropped flat words on the air. "Not go back. My lot with captain. One for all, all for one." He looked at Rogers, a smirk curling his porcine lips.

Dani leaned forward, elbows on the edge of the desk. "Exactly. I knew that from the time we joined the *Victory*'s plan." She set her cup down. "The bridges are burned. I sent my mother a message explaining myself. I'm dead to her now. Best to leave it that way."

Rogers cleared his throat, emotion getting the better of him as his people stood beside him, committed to their cause. "Then we have to figure a way to survive a confrontation with the *Talon* and remain in this universe."

"Easy to say, not to do." Halian shifted in the hard black leather chair. "*Talon* flagship of fleet. Much power. Many weapons." He turned to Dani. "Maybe not damaged."

"But if they followed us in undamaged, they would have blasted us," Rogers insisted. "Burko said he had lost half of his crew after he was hit. Maybe he was telling the truth."

"Even so, Captain, it would be tough to take them one on one. We've got the ship held together with wire and plaster. Hell, half the parts aren't even original issue, just the bits that Liang found. Burko could tear us apart like a kid going through wrapping paper at holiday."

Rogers leaned back in his leather chair, a contemplative look on his face. "Then we can't fight him openly."

Dani scoffed. "How are you going to avoid that? Invite him to tea?"

Standing and stretching, Halian agreed. "Cannot avoid him. Must take him on. May have to destroy him to my thinking."

"If he came on our tail, and the rift closed, maybe that's the end of it. We're all stuck here, and we'll make the best of it. But what if the Confederation has more alien tech, more artifacts, and now they know what the pieces will do, in the right configuration? Will they send someone after him? And someone else?" Tension also drove Rogers to his feet.

"I can't imagine that would be cost effective," Dani said. "Especially until someone learns how to cross the other way."

"When did you ever know an acquisitive government that was cost effective, D? What if they think they can conquer a whole new universe if they can just get over here?"

"No! They couldn't!" But Dani's expression admitted the possibility many times over.

"Burko's our most immediate problem. He's apparently got the backing of this Agency group. That will help him with local resources we're only now developing." He shared with them the conversation he had with the Prince on Perpetra. "If we can't beat him, do we play cat and mouse for the next how many years? Want to talk about whether that's cost efficient? It's doubtful." He shook his head. "I don't want any more loss of life, if there's any way to avoid it. If we can find a way to get those back across who want to go, we should take advantage of it. I can't imagine our new crew wants to leave this universe, and at least the three of us don't want to go, either. We're clear on that." He looked from one to the other. "So?"

Dani rubbed her forehead as if she felt an explosion coming and could circumvent it. "So. We still have more questions than answers, Captain."

"We sure do." Rogers moved back to his desk, and set his hands square against its surface, feeling how solid it was. He would start from that unyielding point in space and move forward. "We need options. We've got limited time to come up with them. I want answers before we get to Marriel. Twelve hours." He straightened. "Dismissed."

They acknowledged his order with a few mumbled words and left his office. Rogers considered what he had accomplished, and decided he had one more meeting to conduct if he intended to safely get where he was going. He sent for Aronka and Tabio.

CHAPTER 25

WITH the boy following him close as a shadow, small fingers rubbing the canvas bag and his precious metal pieces inside it, Benzi Quinn left medical and headed to the supply room to find something more suitable for the kid to wear. It took some time going through the cadet blue metal lockers to find anything that even approached what would fit a small boy. Discouraged, Benzi finally chose a two piece maroon uniform in the smallest female size and gave the boy a belt. "There you are, snapper. Good as new."

The boy looked up at him, dark puppy dog eyes troubled with confusion. He touched the uniform hesitantly and drew his hand back. Benzi ran rough fingers through his own hair, dragging it out of his eyes, his arm faintly aching and pulling at his bandage.

He could not read the expression in the boy's face now, but he had felt it loud and clear back in sickbay. When Benzi tried to get his tool back, the boy had been terrified. Benzi was instantly sent back to his own past, all those nights hiding, trying to avoid his father's rage. When he had seen that look in the boy's eyes it had stopped him cold.

I don't want my father's life. Even some wog-raised, dirty little foreigner don't deserve that.

The boy had been through some rough treatment, the doc had said so, and Benzi felt for him. A little spooky because he did not talk. Maybe he did not hear either. But maybe it was just because of what happened to him. Give him a week or two of being safe, and he might snap right back to how he was supposed to be, right?

"C'mon, snapper, let's get dressed." He held out the uniform to the child. The boy just stared at the clothing, then at him. "Take off that dress and put on man's wear!" Frowning, he mimed taking off his own clothes and putting on the uniform as the boy watched, wide eyed. With a deep sigh, he reached for the child, who scurried out of reach.

Frustration drenched him like an exploded water balloon. Benzi scowled. His instincts screamed to haul off and smack the boy into compliance. He was determined not to. There had to be another way. *Most guys you can bribe into something, Benzi. What's this one want?*

After a few moments, he turned back to his kit with a grin. With the child fixated on his every move, he mimed getting dressed, putting on his belt, and then attaching tools to the belt. He pointed to the child's clothing and the belt he had picked out, then held out a couple of clip on tools. "You'll have to put the clothes on to get these, friend."

The boy's eyes lit up when he saw the tools. He caught on quick enough after that, shimmying out of the torn wreckage of the Olesian robe and into the uniform, working the belt perfectly to closure. Like a young cocker spaniel performing tricks, he awaited his reward. Benzi laughed and hung the tools on his belt. "You're a pistol, snapper. No joke. Now let's get me back to work, hmm?"

Benzi tried to figure what he could have the kid do to stay out of trouble once he got back to engineering. *Like Rogers said, I'll get Dani to take him off my hands. She's a woman, she's got mum hormones. She'll take one look and, bingo bango, there we be.*

It was a gallant plan, anyway.

Once Benzi checked in with Dani he expected, somehow, that she would just take over, especially once he explained the boy was abandoned. Thinking he was set, he studied a list of the day's scheduled work as Dani cajoled the boy, trying to get him to sit at her desk on the upper deck. But the boy refused to leave Benzi's side. He ignored friendly advances by any other staff, hiding behind the chief.

"Unbelievable." Benzi looked down at him. "I've got to get some work done. I told the Cap I didn't have time to mess with you."

"What's he got in the bag?" Dani asked.

"Stuff he'd cadged from round the cargo bay, I guess. And my Zyger controllers. Musta left them down there when I was babysittin' them Olesians the other day." He grinned, remembering something. "And lookit this." He took the tool off his belt that the boy had adjusted in medical. "Little devil upgraded this sequencer. Check the efficiency rating!"

Dani, with Halian watching over her shoulder, scanned the nearest console and looked at the results. "The boy did this?"

Benzi nodded. "Right little genius, apparently. But he don't talk. Or hear. Or...." He looked down at the small face that was studying each expression on theirs. Oddly, the kid did not seem to be frightened of Halian. With grudging admission, Benzi considered that. *No reason for him to be, I guess. Hal's good enough, for a wog. No meanness to him. Seen humans be much worse to each other than anything Hal had given out.*

The chief looked back at the datapad. "But I've got to get some of this done." With a sudden inspiration, Benzi picked up broken parts of things that had been lying about and set them on the table next to his own workspace along with a handful of diagnostic tools. The boy watched him with large, dark, curious eyes. "Go ahead. Show me what you can do, snapper."

The boy's eyes widened in surprise, as if he could not believe he had been given such a gift. He looked at Benzi, then at the tools, his fingers twitching in anticipation. Benzi laughed and shook his head, gesturing to the open table. "G'on with you."

He and the others moved a few steps away. Seeing him hesitate still, Benzi started on the stack of work on his own meter square table, cracking the cover off the ratchet gear assembly to peer inside. He kept a watch on the boy from the corner of his eye at first, before getting wrapped up in his work and his dark thoughts about the ship's current situation.

He held tight to the information he had on Rogers' criminal history. Jerome and Eddy spilled the beans to him about the message the other ship had sent. One guy to another, he was tempted to tell them what he knew, or what he thought he knew. The men from the union hall had not contacted him, as promised. Perhaps they had communication issues?

The two junior officers told a tale of narrow escape, crazed rebels after them, and how anxious they were to reunite with their fleet. Quinn listened and compared the bits of glory against what he knew of Captain Temms Rogers and that of the story from the men at the union hall. One thing was clear, something did not add up. Maybe Rogers was on the run. Maybe Pal-1 and Pal-2 were traitors and liars. Meantime, he had their money. With any luck, he would get more.

Some time later, the silence around him gradually tickled his senses. Benzi discovered the whole department watching the gray topped table next to his. Ready to bark, he looked over to see what trouble the boy had gotten into. To his surprise, the child had disassembled two of the broken units Benzi had casually tossed there and was studying them, reconstructing them, building them into a single unit, without a manual. He watched, as much in awe as the others, as the kid worked steadily, picking up pieces as if by instinct and fastening them in the proper place. He was oblivious to the watchers, who stared in disbelief.

Dani inched closer to Benzi, not wanting to disturb what was happening. "Where did you say they found this kid?"

"Guess the wogs left him in the cargo bay the other day."

"But he's human."

Benzi remembered the doc saying the boy was not really human, but looking at him, he did not want to believe that it was true. *But then those effing lizards look human too, when they want to.* He shuddered. He preferred to think of the kid as something close to human, just with a few differences. The metal thing, whatever the doc had been yappin' about. The boy was fine. He was fine. "He's human, all right."

As long as the boy was occupied in something non-destructive, as unproductive as it might be, Benzi knew he had other things to do. "I've got to read up on the manual for these upgrades." He indicated the datapad. "You sure the weps need more power so soon?"

"Captain's orders," Dani said idly, her attention on the boy.

That certainly echoed of what Jerome had said. "Something ahead?"

"Captain's orders," she repeated firmly.

"Right." Benzi studied her a moment, seeing she was not going to yield on this one. "If the boy's okay here, I'll be in my office."

The engineer's attention returned to the boy. "I'll look after him."

Benzi smirked. *Bet she's thinking of putting him to work on that beat up shuttle already.* He had done several hours' work on the crate himself, and in all actuality, he knew they had done several test flights. Just some minor tech work on the inside and they would be finished. But the kid had some mighty hands. "I'll be back in a few."

Leaving the child hard at work and not likely to cause trouble under so many watchful eyes, Benzi went into his office. He activated his reading monitor and glanced over data on engine calibration and capacity he had earlier uploaded for perusal from the system Net. Calling up the first one, he made it halfway through before he even noticed it was not in standard Galac. Surprised, he skimmed it again, and went on to the next ones, finding the material encompassed tracts in several languages. Three he had never seen before, but now understood perfectly. "Well, damn my eyes." He grinned, fascinated, looking eagerly for more entries, surprised as anyone might be who knew how badly his school career had gone.

Benzi had never been much of a student. Most of the time he had been in school, at least after he was twelve, his father made him work for his food and shelter. Late nights at the docks or the stores had left him without enough sleep to focus well in day classes. He would cut up, try to be class clown, just to make the whole school experience appealing, or more often, to keep himself awake. At fourteen, he had just blown it off. There had not seemed to be much point to it. The teachers never taught him anything he really wanted to learn anyway.

But this? This was information he was driven to read. He devoured it, page after page, educating himself with a joy and elation he had not believed possible from learning, until the boy burst through the door, face alight, to hand Benzi a piece of equipment. Benzi took the device and studied it a moment, activating it, testing it. "Holy Sprechan's gonads, ain't you somethin'." Best he could tell, the child had in fact rebuilt one complete unit, in working order, from the parts he had available.

He looked up and saw the boy hungrily watching his face for approval. "That's a boy." He smiled wide and the boy's eyes lit up. The child held his hand out for the mechanical object, and Benzi handed it back. The boy pushed buttons, delighted as the device crackled and beeped.

Dani watched them from the door. "The boy's got a gift," she said.

"Aye, that he does." Benzi felt a little sense of pride. *Stop it now, you sound like he's your own kin, Benz.* "Hey, snapper, you hungry?" At the boy's blank look, Benzi took the scanner from him, and set it down on the desk. He raised his hand to his mouth, making eating gestures. "Eat?"

The boy glanced back to the device, then to Benzi.

"What? Hungry? Yes? No?"

The boy stepped back, stiffened, as the irritation in Benzi's voice registered.

Dani watched, concerned. "You said he's deaf?"

"I know he can hear me." Benzi frowned with frustration. He tried speaking more clearly, louder, but the child did not respond.

"Maybe if you—"

Benzi's frustration broke. *Shortest distance between two points.* "Hell with it. C'mon, kid. Time for chow." He took the boy's hand and pulled him into the hall, taking him along to the galley.

The boy hung back, cowering from the changing scenery. Once they reached their destination, he stared wide eyed at the room and the unfamiliar equipment. An immediate buzz of interest rose from the handful of people in the room, none of whom had seen the boy before.

Fending off questions, Benzi crossed to the galley window and asked for assorted food items he thought maybe a small boy would like, drawing on his own history as example. The boy trailed after him, staring at the floor. Benzi got two trays and took a table apart from the others, not sitting with his usual crowd of young men.

"What's up with you, Benz? Babysitting duty?" Parnell Eddy called across the room. He sprawled on his chair, leaning back, elbows cocked, hands behind his head.

"Yeah. Don't they have a nurse to mind the young'uns?" Jerry Jerome added, digging into his meal with great enthusiasm.

Benzi gave him a dirty look as he seated the child and pushed in his chair. "Mind your business, boyo. This here's a special project from the Cap." He set dishes on the table in front of the boy, some fruits, a creamy pale pudding, and poultry parts. "Now that's a fine feast, snapper. Enjoy." He put a spoon and fork next to the food and sat down across from the boy.

The child never moved from the position Benzi put him in. He looked at the food with such craving, Benzi wondered how long it had been since he had a real meal. Finally he glanced up at Benzi, on the cusp of a cringe.

"Well, go on, snapper, eat up." Benzi frowned, wondering what the problem was. Maybe he had never used utensils. Benzi picked up his own fork and demonstrated slowly. "Mmmm," he said as he chewed his food. The boy just stared, starting to tremble. Benzi put his fork down, perturbed. Anger clawed at his gut, but before he lashed out at the child, he heard another voice in his head. *What's the matter, boy? My food's not good enough for you? Workin' man's food not as good as yer mum's?*

Then a flashback hit of a little game his old man had played when he was being particularly sadistic. He would wait until Benzi was viciously hungry and set plates of food on the table. When the ravenous boy would grab food from them, his father would take off his belt and beat him for eating without permission.

Who knew what this kid had been through? With sudden inspiration, Benzi reached for a piece of fruit and placed it in the boy's quivering hand. "For you," Benzi said. "Eat." He took a piece of shiny crimson fruit for himself, taking a big bite out of it, acting out his pleasure in the sweet treat.

The boy watched Benzi's hands, then his face, waiting for a reaction, then pulled back out of arms' reach and devoured the red fruit, juices streaming down his chin. When that was gone, he looked at the others on the plate and Benzi nodded, shoving the other plates closer as well. Brief glances from the corner of his eye showed him the boy's shyness had faded, and he was eating like he had been starved.

Eddy and Jerome gave up taunting him for the moment, maybe worried he would get mad at them, and they would lose his companionship. They did not have a lot of friends, being new on the ship before this cruise, but Benzi was newer. That gave them some leverage. Riviera Brown watched with open interest, but said nothing to interfere, chewing her food thoroughly like a contented herd animal. Kai Windthorp ate his salad without much attention to anything but the ticking datapad in his hand.

Assured his young charge was tended to, Benzi studied the two young officers, hot in conversation on some topic that had Windthorp glancing over at them every so often. The helmsman finally got up and walked over to them, speaking under his breath with a look around the rest of the room. The two looked chastened. Windthorp tossed his tray into the recycler and walked out soon after, followed by Brown.

Jerome looked after the tall dark skinned helmsman with some rancor. "Who does he think he is, huh? Telling us to keep a lid on things. Like everything's not going to be hopping before too long."

Benzi lounged in his hard chair, gulping his coffee, which had retained much more of the bitterness than the warmth it first had. "Hopping, is it? What's up?"

Jerome glanced at the door, then got his tray and walked over to stand behind Benzi, wary of the boy who had frozen as he approached. "We're about to be rescued! Told you the commander was here with us. He's practically outside the hatch!" He grinned from ear to ear. "Before too long, we'll be on our way back through the rift. Just in time for my birthday party. All my Confed-mates will throw me the biggest blast ever!"

"So we're taking this ship back to your home place?"

Benzi had overheard Liang and Dani's conversation about the possibility of crossing over using the reconstructed artifacts, but he always assumed it was some kind of theoretical horse manure. *You didn't hop from one universe to another. It just wasn't natural.* But if Jerome was right, they would all be taking the return trip to the *Doubtful*'s point of origin. He was not sure he liked that idea.

"Well, sure. Now that the commander's here, everything will fall back into place," Jerome replied.

Benzi was not so sure that was true. Besides, the facts still did not add up. *If we're all friends, then....* "Then how come we're still working to upgrade the weapons?" This he knew was true, because the engineering staff had refitted most of the components, as well as the constant work on the translation of the relics.

Jerome grinned with enthusiasm. "Cause when we get back, Captain'll take on the damned Persions. Teach 'em a lesson for what they did to us."

"Well, we'll see. Cap's not always so predictable." Quinn leaned down and looked under the table. *Like presenting me with this little fellow.* The boy huddled next to the gray metal bench behind him, his eyes wide open, watching every move of Benzi's hands and feet. The engineer shook his head and pushed his chair back from the table, hunkering down to beckon the boy forward.

"What's the kid doing here, Quinn?" Jerome studied the boy. "Where's his folks?"

"Damned if I know. Some wogs left him here the other day. Cap thought I didn't have enough to do, I guess. Stuck me with him." Benzi continued to beckon the child, realizing that it was not all the captain's doing that the child was 'stuck' with him. The child sensed a common bond somehow, something beyond the boundaries of language and communication, that they had been treated very much alike.

"We're so desperate for new crew, we're going to take in orphans now?" Jerome scoffed. "And what's with those new security people?"

Quinn held up a hand, remembering the cold wash up his spine when he had seen the two go lizard. "Don't get me started on those two. They're a whole new category."

"Yeah? Spooked me for sure, those yellow eyes, no feeling to them."

"You don't know the half of it." Benzi pushed Jerome back a meter, in case his presence was alienating the boy. His nerves were jangled by the number of plates his life's juggler had spinning in the air at the moment. What with the chief slot and this new 'gift' he had received from Tamala. Then there were too many questions about what was going on and now the mute boy. *Got to get something under control. Just…something.* "C'mon, snapper, we've got to go back and play with the tools." He mimed repairing something.

The boy's eyes lit up and he moved cautiously out from the shadow of the table and stood up, shooting Jerome a nervous look before snatching the last fruit from the plate and shoving it in his pocket. Benzi chuckled. "Catch you guys later." He headed out to return to his post, the boy trailing after him.

CHAPTER 26

IF we're being Effing 'rescued', how come so much of this looks like preparing for battle? Don't make no sense.

The boy poked around into various cabinets and consoles while Benzi puzzled over the captain's orders. Upgrade all weapons systems. Update on the artifact reconstruction. Engine to be up to full speed capability before next dayturn. Benzi considered the systems and their interrelation and came to a conclusion.

Cap wants to be able to shoot.

And run.

The revelation ringing around the inside of his brain like a shiny ball in an arcade game, Benzi absently remembered the kid was loose. The boy was not readily visible, so he went looking. He found the child in the rear workspace of the lower deck, where the artifacts lay on a large open surface made by three worktables shoved together. The two dozen brown and black pieces, assorted sizes from two centimeters to a meter and a half in length, lay in a single layer on the tan surface. Liang had arranged them in an order that seemed to follow continuity in the characters inscribed on the chunks. The boy stood in front of the tables with his eyes closed, hands out straight in front of him, waving them slowly over the relics as if he were conducting a huge silent orchestra.

"Snapper, what is it?" Benzi's eyes narrowed as he watched the movements, baffled. He knew Dani and Liang had spent the better part of the last week trying to add in the pieces obtained from the Lenci. They still did not function. But they fit. Benzi did not intend for the unpredictable boy to disrupt what had been completed. He spoke more sharply. "Snapper!"

The boy twitched back to reality, opening his eyes. His hands jerked, then reached for the items on the table.

"No!" Benzi stepped in and pulled him back. "No." He let the boy go as soon as he was out of arm's reach of the table to show he was not going to punish him. "Anything else in here but that." He waved a hand around at the other consoles and nodded, then pointed to the table and made his face stern. "No."

He expected the child to cower, but the message was apparently clear that Benzi was not upset. The boy retreated to the table he had been working at earlier, toying with the remaining wires, gears and left over transmitters, quickly absorbed and oblivious to the room once again.

No question, the little street rat had some innate skills. More than Benzi had himself. That was saying something. Even as a teenager, Benzi had always been quick with his hands. Though he did not have much formal training, he lucked into a couple of jobs when he was younger. His predilection for constructing electronics was fed, sometimes inadvertently. He experienced such *flow* while his hands were wrapped around the tubes and servos. The same feeling he read on the boy's face now. *When things were coming together, it felt like magic.*

Benzi stepped into his office to retrieve the datapads Tasiq had downloaded from the local Net on the history of the artifacts, then returned to sit next to the child to read them. The first several lines were in an unfamiliar language, but by the time he assimilated the script of the first paragraph, he found the rest came to him. Some scholar had studied the distribution and hieroglyphics of the relics and hypothesized that in order to determine the meaning, it would first be necessary to construct a working device.

Benzi read to the end, but felt his attention wander as the material became drier. *Well, no shit, Mr. Answer Man. Question is, how do you make the effing thing work?*

Dani and Halian returned, their worried faces broadcasting their low spirits. Benzi watched them, holding his tongue. *Yep, something big is up, and it ain't no friggin' rescue.* Hal went right to the weapons console, beginning some work Benzi could not decipher from where he sat. Dani came over and sat down with Benzi and the boy.

"So, does he have a name?" Dani asked, visibly trying to put a more pleasant face over her troubles.

Benzi shrugged. "Beats the hell out of me. S'pose we should give him one so's we don't have to keep callin' him 'Hey You'."

The petite engineer smiled. "Better than what you call most people."

A sheepish feeling crawled into Benzi's gut at her gentle criticism. "Yeah, maybe." He fiddled with the gear box as he pondered how to con Dani out of information on the status of affairs. As he thought, Jerome came in, very disgruntled.

"Guess I'm assigned down here now," he said, stalking up to Dani and Quinn. "Liang dismissed me from the bridge. No explanation. Something's going on."

Dani rose to her feet, her expression clouded. After a moment, she nodded, her smile coming slowly, like an old woman to the breakfast table. "We can use the help. Quinn, have you got the engine recalibration started?"

"Next on the list. If you'd watch him...." He let his words trail off. Here might be just the opportunity to learn what was what. Jerome was one to spout off when he was angry and it seemed to be one of those opportune moments. "I can take Jerome below to get started."

"Do it. I'll keep an eye on the kiddo." Brow furrowed, Dani glanced over to the counter where the artifacts were spread.

Benzi bent down to pick up spare parts that were lying on the floor under his workstation, tossing those in front of the boy as well. The child's dark eyes lit up as he touched the new additions, turning them in his hands to admire them. "I'm going below, snapper. I'll be back."

Entranced with his fresh materials, the boy went back to his tinkering without a response. Benzi shook his head. "Effing mad genius, he is." Muttering, he grabbed his tool case and followed Jerome to the open deckway behind the power consoles. Holding the ladder just right so his feet did not catch on the rungs as he passed, he slid down to the lower level. He jumped off just before he hit bottom and looked around. "Come on, Jet. We got work to do."

Jerome followed, climbing down in the traditional way. "Hey, I'm all for boosting the weps, don't get me wrong. If those Persion farmers think they're gonna run us off this easy, we got to show them a thing or two."

Benzi studied his companion as they lifted the panel cover off the wall to get at the calibrators. "You think he's boostin' the engines to go after farmers, do you?"

"They were shootin' at us! Nearly blew us to bits! We lost half the blasted crew! Captain's been holding everyone up saying the artifacts aren't working, but don't you see? Now it doesn't matter, because someone else has figured it out! We don't need the artifacts!"

"So how's Burko done it?" Benzi's mind raced as the pieces were fed in. Sure, it all could have happened the way Jerome said.

"Burko's got the sweetest ship, flagship of the fleet, the *Talon*. The man's a legend. He's taken four dozen worlds for the Confederation. If anyone could have gotten through, it would have been him." Jerome's attention went to the energy channels now exposed under the panel and for a time he worked, instead of talking. "Me and Eddy both applied to get on the *Talon* out of the Confederation school. But you gotta pay your dues to get there."

Benzi nodded, understanding how that worked. "So as soon as it was clear this other ship was here, the captain got right on the horn and hailed them? Started plannin' strategy?" He leaned down for a diagnostic device, checking the charge.

Jerome shook his head, questions written in the scrunched flesh of his brow. "No way. He acted like he didn't even want to know. Made it all hush hush. That's what Windthorp had his panties wrapped about in the galley." He shrugged. "But I told the doc. He's a Confed man through and through, he wants to get back and see his new grandson. I mean, Captain shoulda reported in, huh. ASAP. You'd think he would have been happy to see the *Talon*, comrades in arms and all." He stopped, spanner in midair. "Unless...."

Quinn nodded. "Unless." What could Rogers have been doing when he hit the wormhole? And just who had he been running from?

"Oh, man, I've got to talk to the doc about this. He'll know what to do. I can't believe the Captain is...." He stared at Quinn, stunned.

"How's it coming down there?" Dani called from above.

"Slick as goose guano, woman. Leave us be!" Satisfied that he had gotten what he expected, Benzi grinned at Jerome. "We men are talking about the important matters of the universe," he stated as he continued working.

Jerome's face remained pale, his expression shocked. "Someone's got to do something. It's an officer's duty to report. If the Captain's not following his duty, then he's a...traitor." Eyes wide, he stared at Quinn.

Benzi just smiled and tuned the energy coil, pleased as it lighted in his hand. Somehow, he suddenly liked and respected old Temms Rogers a hundred percent more. Somewhere inside that head was a free spirit. That, Benzi could respect. *Sounded like old Pal-1 and Pal-2 might end up being disappointed if they expected Benzi to tell tales about his captain.*

CHAPTER 27

TENSION floated in the corridors of the ship. Liang could almost taste it, a bitter mix of fear and distrust.

Two days after they received the message from the Confederation ship, the captain had changed his orders for Marriel, opting instead to return to the frozen asteroid. The sensors would easily find any other ship that followed them in.

The captain had placed the crew on high alert without explanation. Rogers reassigned Jerome from the bridge to engineering. Jerome's angry reaction at his dismissal from the bridge made her wonder what was really behind it. Rogers asked her to his office before her shift began, leaving the subject matter a mystery.

Halian rose as Liang entered. "Will stand by," he grunted, with a brief greeting for Liang before he left the office. Dani sat in a chair pulled up to the desk, where she poured two cups of tea. Liang read the sharing of tea as a gesture that the Captain wanted at least the appearance of a social occasion. Aronka stood like a statue to one side, without a cup, though. *Was she participant or a sentry?*

"Please sit down," Rogers said with a warm smile. She studied his face and saw the captain looked well rested for the first time in weeks. The strain that lived in the creases of his face had faded. His blue eyes were as pale and clear as a worn stained glass window panel. He had given up on the uniform, wearing a defiant floral print shirt in bright blue and green with yellow sea birds emblazoned across the back. Liang recognized the signs. *He's come to some decision.*

Dani smiled and pushed a cup across the black surface to Liang. The navigator studied the petite engineer and saw that she, on the other hand, appeared not to have slept at all judging by the dark circles under her eyes. Liang thanked her and sat, straight backed, her silent analysis held gently in her lap like ripening peaches, waiting for whatever news the captain intended to give her.

Rogers took a deep breath. "You know when we arrived at Marriel that we had recently come to this universe after a battle, having sustained substantial damage?" Liang nodded. "What you weren't told, though you may have suspected it, was that the damage to the *Doubtful* was something we had earned."

Rogers' words rang with truth, and she nodded. The crossing of a universal rift was a momentous occasion, it would not be something that happened without due cause. She reached for her cup and took a sip, intending to set the captain at ease. "Please go on, sir."

The captain explained the circumstances which had brought them to the skies over Marriel before Liang and the *Doubtful* had met. She listened silently, sorting the details of the story into categories for analysis, some to be digested now, some to be chewed after much rumination.

When he paused, waiting for her response, she sat down her cup. "You believe Jal Burko may have found you, his intention is your destruction as punishment for your rebellion." She looked at Dani, then Rogers. "Is he able to return to your universe?"

The captain shook his head. "Not that we can tell. We haven't been able to detect an open rift near those coordinates. We don't know what Burko is capable of at this time."

"We *do* know what he was capable of," Dani muttered darkly.

"In terms of a crossover." Rogers glanced at his engineer with a sad smile before turning back to Liang. "New information has come to light which makes time of the essence in determining our response." He nodded to Aronka.

The Bellonan stepped forward, her uniform spotless. "As you asked us to do, Captain, Tabio and I patrolled the ship while invisible to the human eye. We uncovered a conspiracy to take over the ship between the doctor and two ensigns who have worked on the bridge, Eddy and Jerome. As we listened, the doctor placed a subspace message to the other ship and spoke with someone personally. We were unable to determine the recipient of the message."

Liang dropped her eyes as she considered this information. After the two, clearly untrained, had been trusted with the importance of a bridge post, they would turn on the man who had given them such a chance? Unthinkable.

Aronka continued, her voice a monotone. "During this conversation, the officer on the contacted ship informed the doctor of the events which the captain has just revealed. The doctor immediately put in motion a plan to re-establish contact with the Confederation ship in six hours, to notify them of our whereabouts at that time, intending to have secured this ship by placing the officers responsible for the rebellion under arrest."

Liang admired Rogers' ability to remain calm. "I see. However, you are still at your desk," she stated with a hint of ironic amusement.

Rogers chuckled. "Your powers of observation are not in error, Liang. Tabio monitors that situation as we speak. I want to hold off a showdown with the doctor as long as possible, so Burko does not know we have discovered their secret communication. The lockers for hand weapons have been secured with a new code only known to people in this room." He slid a datapad across the black surface. She glanced at it, seeing a list of numbers and letters. "The com-channels have been restricted, and are being monitored by Tasiq."

Liang noted the restrictions, but had no need to memorize the codes. For now, she was content to send her messages through Tasiq. The whole situation presented itself as irregular. Rogers' son, for all his arrogance and young self confidence, had proven to her that he could handle the job, especially with the Bellonans backing him up. But the fact he was excluded from this meeting, while Aronka was here, indicated to Liang that something still remained to be disclosed. "Captain, it seems odd that the chief of security seems to remain uncommitted to either side."

Rogers exchanged a look with Dani. A sad smile came to his face, and the pain in his eyes warned Liang the circumstances were worse than previously set forth.

"Ah, yes. Tommy. Now that's something we'll have to deal with."

"I don't understand." Perhaps this was above her clearance level? With everything as touchy as it seemed to be, she did not want to upset the captain further.

Rogers took a deep breath in, held it a moment, then blew it out between his lips, almost making a whistling sound. "I had no idea Tommy was aboard when we carried out our rebellion. He doesn't know the truth about what we did. Frankly, considering how long it took to rebuild our relationship, I'm not sure how to tell him." He glanced at Aronka. "Have you overheard anything that would reveal his standing in this matter?"

Aronka's intent gaze flicked away for a moment.

The captain's muscles tightened. His eyes narrowed. "What haven't you told me?"

The Bellonan straightened, looking across the room over the captain's head. "He has not met with the doctor and the others. He is, however, a confidant of the other young men. Apparently they shared time at the Confederation school. He likely knows what they do."

Liang watched the captain assimilate the information, clearly something distasteful to him. Words came to her heart, words of comfort, an urge to volunteer to intervene, somehow to protect the captain from further pain. But, in all honesty, this was not her task. He would have to come to terms with his son in his own way.

"So, we are preparing for a confrontation with Commander Burko?" Her mind leaped ahead to bigger questions. *Could this ship survive an open battle? Would other members of the crew defect? Would Rogers escape retribution by returning to his own universe?* It did not seem likely.

"Indeed we are." Distracted, Rogers cleared his throat and reached for his own cup. "In light of the news that Burko may be allied with the Agency, I need more facts. You and I know someone on Marriel who deals in the business of information."

The name nearly stuck in her teeth on its way to her lips. "Runyon."

The captain nodded. "If there's anything I know about the Confederation, it's that they play by the book. Wherever we've touched down, we've left someone who remembers us. Your friend Jowalt is one. Probably someone at the labor hall. The Consortium certainly knows about us but they did not release information, if I read them right."

"Confederation protocol," he continued, "would lead Burko to begin with the planet nearest the rift, then move on. Because of you, I'm sure Oke Runyon remembers me. If he was asked, particularly if a reward was promised, I'd believe our friend would be interested in talking."

Liang recalled the barkeep's face the day she left, his cheek bearing a bruise she had given him. *Oh yes, he would remember. That avaricious fat fool would go out of his way to spite both her and Rogers, given the chance.*

Rogers leaned forward, elbows firm on his desk. He glanced at Dani. "I need to know if Burko is at Marriel." He looked to Liang expectantly.

She juggled her floating analyses to feed her thought process. "If you went to the surface yourself, you or any of the crew who crossed with you would be too easily recognized." As the captain nodded, she continued. "The same would be true of your small ships as well. They would be shot down before they landed." With sudden realization, she looked at Dani. "The cargo shuttle."

Dani's tired grin confirmed her hypothesis. "Exactly. The *Phoenix* is space ready, all tested and systems go. It's of this universe. We can send it down and it won't trigger any recognition by the Confeds."

Liang saw her opportunity to help. "I volunteer to perform reconnaissance."

"I hoped you would." Rogers' smile was warm, though Liang saw the muscles of his face tense. He apparently was not convinced of the mission's success. "Aronka will accompany you to the surface." He handed Liang a second datapad. "This will provide you with reference information for Burko and other members of his elite staff, including picture ID."

The navigator glanced at the pictures, picking out the one who must be Burko by his frozen eyes.

"Once you confirm or deny Confederation presence on the planet, you are to return immediately." Rogers included Aronka in these orders by his glance. "You are not to engage the enemy, except in extreme conditions, and only in self defense. Their weapons are more powerful than what you'll have and the people on Marriel are not at all prepared for the kind of onslaught Burko can lay down. He won't care who's in the way. If it comes to a showdown, I want it to be just us, one on one in the sky. We must leave innocents out of it."

Aronka gave a sharp nod. "I understand. I am authorized to proceed invisibly?"

"Absolutely. In fact, it might be preferable. Liang by herself doesn't look like much of a threat."

Liang felt a prickly bristle rise inside at the captain's casual dismissal, but appreciated that she was easily underestimated. That could be an asset. "Immediately, Captain?"

Rogers' desk unit buzzed, and he hit the button. "Yes, Tas?"

"Captain, I think you'd better see this."

He looked at the women, with a clear expression of 'now what?' before heading to the bridge, closely followed by the others. Tasiq gestured to the front monitor screen. "Five ships have just entered airspace above us, Captain, on a heading for Marriel."

Liang studied the screen, taking a few steps forward to get a better look. Rogers immediately ordered the ship to stealth mode. The largest ship, a substantial cruiser with delta wings, was sleek, black, and ran with few lights. The other four were clearly subordinate, somewhat larger than the *Doubtful*'s slipcraft. She knew they would carry a crew of six or eight and a full array of particle beam weaponry. Each bore a registry code beginning with a symbol of a clenched fist inside a red diamond and concluding with seven letters and numbers in blood red. "The Agency," she said in a hushed tone.

Aronka confirmed her statement with an icy assessment. "A full detachment, led by a Commodore class vessel. They must have discovered something extraordinary."

Rogers turned to Tasiq. "Who are they talking to?"

Tasiq manipulated his controls for a few moments. "Unknown, Captain. Their frequencies are encrypted."

"What would they want here? Anything besides the obvious?" Rogers slipped into his command chair and punched in a data request.

Liang leaned on the rail, wondering the same thing. The Agency limited their play to high stakes games. The organization operated throughout the entire star system, skimming ten percent charge off most business transactions of any consequence and twenty percent off those of particular profit. Over the years, the Agency accumulated a vast array of technology by appropriation. If they found something more powerful than what they had, they would try to purchase if at a favorable price. If they could not, they would confiscate it. Armed with the best, the Agency struck fear into even little back street dealers like Jowalt. Everyone complied with their directives. *Or else.*

Rogers read up on the Agency, while Aronka read over his shoulder and filled him in on other details. "The Consortium has long opposed the rule of the Agency," she said. "They have successfully resisted its demands for the last two generations. After a few bloody incidents, the Agency has conceded the Consortium's business is its own."

Rogers was skeptical. "Despite the superior technology?"

Aronka smiled darkly. "There are many forms of technology. For example, the Agency does not have genetic breeders such as ourselves."

Liang crossed her arms, feeling a chill rise through her. "That does not explain why they are here, now."

"Most likely they have discovered something they want."

"There is nothing on this planet anyone could want," the navigator replied, scorn sifting through her words.

"Or there wasn't until now." Rogers frowned. "If they're after new tech, any Confederation ship will have weapons and shielding they've never seen before."

"Your association with the Consortium has likely provided your ship some protection," the Bellonan speculated.

Rogers shifted uncomfortably in his chair. Liang's glance flashed around the bridge, noting that the young men suspected in the conspiracy were noticeably absent. When he spoke again, though, it was in a hushed tone, as though he expected to be overheard.

And for all they knew, he would be. It was a wise choice.

"You believe they are here to back up Burko, as the Prince suggested?"

"That is most likely. They are likely also interested in the new technology," Aronka answered. "The commander may have promised them the *Doubtful*, with its technology, as reward for their assistance. They'll take what they can, from whomever they can, Captain. Great caution is advised."

"So the game has changed. New players, new possibilities." Rogers rubbed his chin, deep in thought. "Tas, Kai, any readings below? Can you detect the *Talon*?"

Both studied their consoles, then replied in the negative. "Definitely Confederation transmissions on the planet, Captain," Tasiq added. "Someone's down there. But the ship itself is not in immediate airspace."

"Liang, can you read the Agency transmissions?"

She shook her head. "They're known for their highly secretive codes, Captain. No one's broken them."

After a few moments of hesitation, his gaze fixed on the dark armada, the captain turned to Liang. "We're not going to learn anything from just watching them. I don't see any other choice. We've got to go with the plan. You're our best candidate. You know your way around down there." He sighed. "But be careful. Report every half hour. I only want you there long enough to tell me who's there and what they're doing. Got it?"

Pleased she could serve the ship and her shipmates and ignoring the dangers involved, Liang confirmed the order. "Yes, Captain." Nothing left to be said, she went for the door, Aronka falling into step behind her. Her mind focused ahead, on the coming confrontation with Oke Runyon. The fat man would have a few surprises coming, some of them visible, and others totally unexpected. *Which is how we want to keep things.*

CHAPTER 28

ROGERS contemplated the oncoming Agency force as long as he could stand it, then retreated to his office, with strict warning to Tasiq to let him know the moment anything changed. Consumed by the thought that men on his ship had broken the chain of command to go behind his back, to endanger the rest of their comrades, he paced in his office, trying to come up with a solution.

It wasn't their fault. He had started this chain of events.

Although he knew this intellectually, it still burned him that they were prepared to betray him after all he had gone through to save them, to rebuild the ship and the crew.

What could he do? He could contact Burko himself. He could arrange to transfer the men who wanted to return to the Giladan universe back to Burko's ship and let them go home. He would stay. He, Dani, and Hal and together they would pull their new crew together and explore this new universe.

And if you believe that, let me tell you the one about imaginary magical beings that sprinkle glittering confetti on their friends and make life happily ever after.

Because Burko would never let that happen.

So how was Rogers going to keep all his soldiers safe?

His door flew open, not even a knock to announce someone's intent to enter. About to snap at the intruder, he saw it was Tommy. And his son was a bristling ball of sharp anger.

The young man fumbled with the words that wanted to come out of his mouth, stopped up like a crowd trying to exit a door that was too small. Flushed with exertion, his face held blue eyes that accused his father. His fingers clenched tight into fists. Clearly, he had heard. It was time.

"Come have a seat, son."

Tommy shook his head. "I'll stand."

So it was going to be that way, was it?

"Suit yourself." Rogers steeled his resolve, forcing himself to sit in the chair behind the table, placing the distance of command, between him and Tommy. He could dictate a course of action, even a misguided one, as his son's captain. What he really wanted was to share the truth with him, have him understand as his father's son. "You have something you want to say?" he asked.

His son moved closer to the table, a moment or two passing before adrenaline released the flood of words that followed. "Is it true? Is Commander Burko here to help us and you're running from him? What's happened, Dad? Where are these rebels you briefed us about? How come we're not hunting them down, working with the Commander? Why are we in hiding? Why haven't we joined up with him again, Dad?"

Rogers' throat closed on a reply. *So easy to explain, so hard to make him understand.* Tommy's eyes slowly widened in horror.

"It *is* true," he gasped. "You're a traitor!"

"Tommy," the captain said. "I know this seems hard to you—"

"Shut up!" Tommy turned his back on his father for a few moments, hand covering his mouth. He started to speak several times, but no real words came out.

"You want the truth? I can—"

"I said, shut up!" Tommy reached for the sidearm holstered at his waist, his badge of office. He pulled it out, holding it tight against his thigh, not pointing it at his father. "I've got to think."

Rogers took a deep breath. *Now that would be pretty ironic. I escape retribution from Jal Burko only to be shot by my patriotic, if somewhat misguided, son?*

"Sit down, soldier!"

As expected, something in Tommy responded to the commanding tone. He dropped into a chair across from Rogers. The captain held out his hand. "Give me the weapon."

Tommy looked down at the firearm as if he were surprised to find it in his hand. "I—"

"Now!" The young man slapped the weapon onto his father's hand. Relieved, Rogers stashed the gun in a shelf under the table. *Damn. I locked up all the guns and forgot the security chief could have as many as he wanted. Hope he doesn't have another one tucked away somewhere.*

"Tommy, I'm going to be straight with you—"

"Now that you're caught!" A bitter response.

"Now that we can sit down like two men and talk about this openly."

"You think you can talk your way out of treason?"

"I think you're a smart boy and you can use your brain, that's what I think." Rogers leaned back in his chair and studied his son. "You're just out of school, so you believe you know all about the universe and the state of affairs in it. The Confederation has the answer to all problems, and if you just follow orders, all will be right with the worlds."

Tommy's nostrils flared. Heat flashed in his eyes. Rogers cut him off by a raised finger, before he loosed his rebellious retorts. "Tom, I know because I've been there, in those exact shoes. When my career began, just out of school, I was going to change the universe, bring all the planets in it fresh justice and a great way of life." He detected a note of sarcasm in his voice and did what he could to bury it. If he was going to reach his son, he would have to overcome more than just the rift that might have developed between them over the years. *I've got to let him know how important this is. To all of us.*

Feeling a tremble in his fingers, he folded his hands on the black surface in front of him. "If all the men and women in the universe had only good motives in their hearts, maybe we could actually have that world, the one we expect the first day we become officers. But they don't. Once people begin to gather power to themselves, once they believe they have the rights to control other people, then they make decisions to bring themselves more power."

"You're a liar!" Tommy sprung up out of his seat.

"What I'm telling you now is the gods' own truth." Rogers pushed himself out of his chair, needing to keep his son's attention. "People like Burko, they've perverted the mission of the Confederation. We're not officers so we can take over planets, to force other populations to submit to us. We're officers to help other civilizations realize their potential and become what they were meant to be."

"But sometimes people don't want to cooperate," Tommy sputtered, "We're authorized to take measures to—"

"At the cost of their lives, Tom? That's what was happening here. Burko and the fleet were ordered to take this planet, Persios. Take it. At any cost. Even if it meant killing the entire planetary government to force them to submit!" He glared at his son. "*Cooperation* was not the issue. The Confederation meant to make an example of these people for daring to stand up for themselves. That's not our mission."

"But you had orders. You disobeyed."

Rogers stood straight, letting the words hang in the empty space between them. A part of his brain tugged at his attention, reminding him of the Agency ships outside, the mission on which he dispatched Liang and Aronka, but he knew he had to concentrate on this. If he lost this battle, he might as well lose the whole war. "I did. *We* did."

Tommy's face was suddenly suspicious. "Who else?"

"Does it really matter who? People you've respected on this ship. Good officers. Fine officers, on this ship and half a dozen other ships, who agreed to do this. Together. We stood up for what was right. Despite the orders."

"But the Confederation trusts the Commander with their best ship. He wouldn't use it to do what you said. He wouldn't." The stubborn set to his jaw echoed Rogers' own. "That still doesn't explain what we're doing here. Was that all a lie, too?"

Rogers considered what he had previously shared with the crew. "No. We used a piece of alien technology to save ourselves from Burko's attack. It punched a rift into this universe and we came through it. We had no idea at the time that the *Talon* followed us. We didn't know what ship it might have been until Burko confirmed it."

Tommy looked confused a moment. "And now you can't communicate with him because you know he'll crucify you for what you did."

Rogers nodded slowly. He held his breath, praying to any gods who still believed in him that Tommy would see things the way they really were.

"You know Eddy and Parnell got the doctor to message the Commander."

"I do."

Tommy rocked on the ball of his right foot for a moment, staring at the floor. "You took all of us away from our homes, our families...." He trailed off and gave Rogers a look that left no doubt exactly which family he was talking about. "Maybe this was your plan all along. It wasn't enough you broke up your marriage to Mom. You wanted to punish her, to punish all of us for your failure as a husband. As a *man*." Tommy caught his breathe, his jaw trembled for a moment.

"You're wrong, Tom."

A shudder ran through Rogers as he watched the changing expressions on his son's face. Damn it, he could not fall apart now. He had lives in his hands. He had responsibilities. But he had to explain. "I loved your mother. She loved me. We both loved you and your brother and your sister." The pain of all those years of separation lanced through him. He had always thought he was doing his best, serving the Confederation, making the worlds safe for his family. *All that time, I was serving a false master.*

"Being in the service of the Confederation means being away from home, away from everything you love. When I started out, I didn't understand what that meant. What it *really* meant. Missing years of your lives, first steps, school events, ball games. Connie...." His throat closed, and he had to fight to get the words out.

How long had it been since he thought of those days, all those nights on missions, when he and Connie had barely been able to exchange a few words over a tenuous long distance connection before he was out of range again. The ache of those brief conversations, the crazy longing for each other, both faded as the missions continued and the years passed. "I...It wasn't anyone's fault, Tommy. We just grew apart."

Tommy had recovered his equilibrium, even as Rogers was losing his own. "Funny, that's not how it felt to those of us you abandoned." He took a deep breath in, and blew it out, the action seeming to straighten his backbone. "Good thing we don't have to depend on you. Commander Burko will rescue us. He'll take us home." His eyes shone with unshed tears. "If I never see you again, I won't lose one damned night of sleep. Not one."

Rogers' chest ached. He could argue, but Tommy's attitude made it pretty clear it would not change his mind. *By the hells, it took me twenty years to realize the truth. Why would he believe me in one day?*

He had come so far with Tommy since they had crossed over. He thought the wounds that had separated them after the divorce was nearly healed. Watching his son now, seeing the walls come down before his eyes, all the progress he thought they had achieved slipped away like a suck of dirty water down the drain. He was alone again.

Rogers cleared his throat, forbidding the tears that tore at him from making their appearance. "So how's it going to be, Tommy? Are you going to be able to do your job? Can I count on you as security chief?"

Tommy's eyes narrowed with scorn. "You really expect me to go along with you? After you stick me with those lizards, without so much as asking my opinion? After you lie to me? After you show your lack of respect for every bit of authority you've ever been subject to?"

"I'm deep in a course of action now, Tom. You know we've been working on the artifacts, to see if we can send anyone back. I'd send anyone who wanted to go with Burko, if he'd take them. I'm not bent on depriving you boys of your futures, not at all. But I can't fight Burko on the outside and you on the inside. I won't." Feeling the ground slipping from beneath his feet, he eyed his defiant son. "Last chance."

"Go to hell."

The pain of Tommy's rejection turned like a knife in his midsection. Rogers nodded. "All right. Take him."

"Take—Hey!" Tommy's confused look changed to one of dismay as Tabio appeared from nothingness to grab his arm. "See? This is why I hate you!"

"Hate me if you have to, Tom. I mean to save your life. One way or another." He waved a hand at Tabio. "Lock him up. No one's to talk to him. Leave Eddy and Jerome alone for now. I don't want them to know I know, not yet. We'll see what else we find out when Liang gets back."

Tabio dragged an ice cold Tommy out of the room, leaving the captain drowning in a sea of loneliness and disappointment as he returned to his desk, his work cut out for him. All his adult life he had sacrificed for his family, his children, his career. *The sacrifices aren't done yet, my friend. Not by a long shot.*

CHAPTER 29

THE *Phoenix* handled easily on the voyage to the surface.

In an abundance of caution, Liang plotted a course that doubled back on her trail once, in case the rehabilitated shuttle was being tracked. As they approached the town, she looked for somewhere to set down, her first instinct to hide the shuttle. "Perhaps in the fields."

Aronka's golden eyes studied the sensor map. "No doubt the Confederation has discovered the ship's previous landing spot." She cocked her head. "Why do you not land where the other public vehicles land? Wouldn't it be more suspicious to try to conceal the ship?"

She had no specific orders on this point. The navigator considered her options. It was a better idea to have the ship at hand if they had to escape quickly. "Agreed."

Making course adjustments, she brought the shuttle to a designated landing area, where several other ships rested, most unremarkable in any way. No slipcrafts similar to those in the *Doubtful*'s small hangar area or any ships with Confederation markings awaited them. Nor were there Agency ships. Perhaps they had overreacted to the presence of the Agency at Marriel. It did not have to be due to Rogers being in the area.

May it be so.

Liang secured the shuttle, buckled on a laser pistol over the old clothing she had worn, not the uniform of the Confederation. "Remember what the Captain said. In and out."

The security woman looked back with no change of expression except perhaps a slight warming of those amber eyes. "That was understood." She faded from view.

Closing her eyes for a moment, Liang was barely able to determine Aronka's whereabouts in the gathering silence as the shuttle powered down. Working with the Bellonans, she had learned to sense their life force, their field of energy, even when invisible. That would not help her when Aronka was hidden from view. She would not be able to communicate without revealing herself. Liang knew that she would be, for the most part, on her own.

She stepped out the aft hatch into the street. Puddles of water lay in the unpaved areas, reflecting skies gray with dark underpinnings of storm. A heavy odor of burnt wood permeated the damp air. Orienting herself to the town, she set off walking along the crete sidewalk toward the main street. The sound of men shouting came from ahead, around the corner. Liang took a deep breath and kept her hand near her weapon.

She sensed Aronka move ahead of her as they approached the corner of the first building set along the street. Liang stopped just before the turn, then peered out cautiously. The sound came from at least another block over. "That is not usual," she said quietly.

"I will investigate." The whisper thin voice floated on the air like a gentle fog in the rising sun.

The navigator moved on toward the saloon. When she had come to Marriel, the town had bustled, speeders weaving through the many pedestrians, transactions occurring mid-lane. Now the street was empty. *Something was definitely not right.* She continued to the doors of Runyon's saloon.

Inside were uniforms, six of them, Confederation maroon and gray, on men at the bar. In the corner, two black jacketed men watched the door. *Agency.* Her first instinct was to retreat, already in possession of the information she was sent to gather. But it was too late, she had been noticed.

They could have some other reason for being there. But she doubted it.

Yanking her self control in, close reined, she marched to the bar, shoved her way between the uniforms and grabbed the nearest empty mug, banging it on the hollow counter. "Runyon, I'm here for my pay!" Heart pounding in her ears, she tried to remember to breathe as the fat man came out of the back. "You owe me money and I want it now," she snapped.

Eyes burning with interest, Oke Runyon ran a hand through his thinning hair. Grease streaked across his once white apron. "Well, well. I didn't think I'd see you here again." He looked her up and down. "You seem well fed, *misha.* You still with Rogers? Or did he toss you for a lousy attitude like I did?"

Liang shrugged. "Men are pigs. He's no better." She turned to spit on the wooden floor. "I just want my money." As she turned, she let her awareness float, hypersensitive to those within her strike zone.

The uniformed men had started at the mention of Rogers' name. Their respiration quickened, and they surreptitiously checked on their weapons. The Agents perked up, too. Her hopes faded. The team clearly waited for Rogers.

Risky to challenge them openly, her mission had been to confirm their presence. She had done that much faster than expected. Now she had to survive to take that information back to the ship.

Runyon laughed. "I don't owe you, girlie. Except a good clip for my black eye!" He made a fist and shook it at her.

One of the Confederation men laughed. "This little bit nailed you?"

"She's a wildcat. Bet she took your Rogers apart. You probably won't be able to find hide nor hair of him." Runyon smirked, then froze pale under the cold gaze of the Agency men.

The uniformed Agent closest to the door studied Liang, then got up, crossing the room, placing himself between her and the exit. "So what did happen to Captain Rogers? When's the last time you saw him?"

She stepped away from the bar, out of reach of the Confed men, wanting the Agent to think, she moved to face him, her stance bold and straight. "Six weeks ago. He dropped me at Roandock when I failed to perform wifely duties." Her almond eyes stared into his.

The man glanced at his nearest companion. "You file breach of contract papers?"

"No, I wouldn't give him the satisfaction." She spit on the floor again, using the half turn to check the men at the bar. Two now on their feet, the tension level in the room crept upward.

"I think the little native girl needs to be taught some manners," one of them said. Liang thought it might have been the tall one with the hangdog expression. There was a round of low laughter. The speaker then moved to grab her shoulder.

She spun away, whirled so her back was to the wall and she faced them all. Runyon started to issue a warning, but they cut him off with a dark look. He shrugged at Liang, a smirk playing on his lips as he wiped his hands with a grimy white towel, before leaning back against the counter, arms crossed.

The Confederation men moved toward her in a semi-circle, all taller than she, obviously thinking they could handle this 'little bit' handily. She could see it in their eyes. *One against six. Is that better or worse odds than sparring with Tasiq? With Halian? Or perhaps the under handed Mr. Quinn?* Inner speculation continued in some small disconnected part of her brain. She watched their shoulders for betrayal of their movement. Their eyes reflected the darkness of Quinn. That gave her the first indication of what to do.

If she could get to the kitchen, she could escape.

She ducked behind a free standing table, tossing a chair directly at the two on the far left. One ducked, but the other got tangled in deflecting the chair. The Agents moved to block the door completely. Liang tucked and rolled, making it nearly to the bar before one of the Confederation men got a hand on her. She had her weapon in his face and pulled the trigger before he could grab tight. The blast hit him in the shoulder and he fell backward, knocking over another one of his companions.

"Take cover!" one of them shouted in the mad scramble that ensued.

She ducked behind the end of the bar, flashing her weapon at Runyon when he moved toward her. "I'll do you, fat man. Back off!" The hatred in her voice startled her. It must have done the same for Runyon, because he moved to the far end of the bar. The others hung back, waiting for her to make a move.

An explosion in the street shattered the tavern's front windows. Screams and smoke filled the space out front. The Agents rushed out the door. Three of the remaining Confederation men followed them, joining the shouting.

Liang peeked out from the end of the wooden bar just long enough to see the other two had not moved from behind the table they had pulled over on its side. She glanced back at the kitchen door. She would never clear it before they could take her out.

The front door flew open, and then shut as the commotion continued. After a brief moment, and a deep growl, the two officers jerked aside, their expressions astounded to discover angry red blood spurting from their chests. Aronka faded into visibility, in lizard form, her amber eyes on Runyon.

The bartender just stared. He needed a change of pants, Liang noted. *Good. That's how it feels, you bastard.* Pleased for him to be terrorized as she had been in his custody, Liang found it difficult to focus on their orders. But she knew she had to.

"Leave him. He's nothing," she said, gesturing with her head at the kitchen door.

Aronka growled at the fat man, pinning him in her cold gaze for several moments. Runyon did not move even one lax muscle. The noise out front grew louder. "We have only a brief window," Aronka warned.

Liang nodded and shoved her way into the filthy kitchen, the smoky air choking them. Once they were out of the room, Runyon yelled for help and started after them.

As Liang ran, she knocked boxes and cartons aside, leaving them in his path. He crashed into one of the obstacles and cursed her, making her feel like she had accomplished two missions for the expense of one. Aronka, just behind Liang, shoved her through the door into the back alley as weapons fire seared into the wood above her head.

They blocked the door with a large garbage container before sprinting down the alley to their shuttle. Liang used her remote access control to open the hatch as they approached the lot, feet hitting the puddles with small splashes.

A shout came from the street mouth off the alley. Half a dozen uniformed men fired down the passage at the fleeing women. Aronka faded from sight, and Liang concentrated on traversing the space in an evasive pattern. Brick bits flew from the walls around them and stung her face. Just when she thought the heavy boots were on her heels, something grabbed her wrist and yanked her forward into the opening hatch of the shuttle. Her weapon left its holster and seemed to shoot of its own accord, mowing down the soldiers who had gotten too close.

"Get us in the air!" hissed a voice from the empty air.

She was propelled forward, and stumbled to the pilot's seat. Blood trickled down her face from multiple wounds. She smacked the control to close the back hatch and fired up the engines, lifting off as soon as she was able. Aronka faded into human appearance beside her, strapping herself into the co pilot's seat.

"Rocket launcher," the Bellonan warned.

"Taking evasive action." Continuing their steep upward climb, Liang made a wide circle to get a good look at the situation. A burning speeder sat in the lot across from Runyon's. "That was the distraction."

"Yes." Aronka's voice was disapproving as she directed Liang's attention to an open field past the bar. Several cadres of uniformed soldiers looked up, curious, as the shuttle pulled away and up. "They have many men here."

On the ground at the far end of the field, Liang saw two of the Agency's smaller ships as well as two Confederation slipcrafts. They had not been there before. One was preparing to launch.

The encounter alarm went off. "Incoming fire!" Liang swirled wide, using evasive tactics, dropping heat generating counter measure devices Halian had built for the shuttle, since it had no defensive system yet. Dani intended to install at least simple weapons, but that was put on the hold when the deciphering of the artifacts was moved to top priority.

This was supposed to be a simple mission. Simple.

Aronka monitored the counter measures. "They've taken out what we've sent so far. But they're still coming."

"Hold on." Liang executed Dani's pet upgrade, the powerburst, taking them almost straight upward. The G-forces crushed them into the seats. The shuttle rattled and strained, but when they leveled out, there was nothing on their tail. Once she was sure they were clear, she scaled it back to remove the strain.

Aronka hailed the ship, her voice devoid of emotion. "*Doubtful*, this is the *Phoenix*, with hostiles in pursuit. Have medical standing by for injured personnel." She received a curt confirmation and settled in as the shuttle took them safely home.

CHAPTER 30

ROGERS leaned back in his chair, grim thoughts filling his head as Okalani effected repairs to Liang's bleeding face.

Dani had brought the resident to his office to meet the wounded girl, leaving Montgomery out of the loop in light of the potential mutiny. She assured them both that Liang would have no lasting effects from the injuries, once the bits of stone were thoroughly flushed to speed healing.

Rogers studied the navigator's notes, able to identify all the Confederation men at the saloon as officers from Burko's personal ops team. The Agents remained nameless, but no less fearsome. Aronka had been debriefed and waited silently, standing at attention by the wall.

"Well, if we'd wanted to grab Burko's attention, we couldn't have chosen a better way."

Liang sat stiffly in the chair across from Rogers, her eyes on the desk's surface. "We were not left with much choice."

"I'm not upset with you, Liang." The girl had already apologized. He knew she felt responsible. Rogers leaned forward and gave her a reassuring smile. "We knew going in could be dangerous. You had to defend yourself. At least we know where we stand."

He shuffled through some papers on his desk, all of which carried depictions of the hieroglyphics on the artifacts. "What we really need is to get this figured out. It's the only variable in our control. Burko has us out powered, out classed, and out gunned. He has spies on this ship. He has powerful allies. We might have some advantage in that we are more familiar with this system, perhaps. He's been here longer than we believed." He tapped a finger on the stack of papers. "Regardless. The device saved us once before and it may do so again. Whether it creates a wormhole to a new place, or even something that just gives us a small jump, a fighting chance, we *have* to make it work. I'm putting this at highest priority. Everyone who can work on it does, as long as it takes."

Liang rose to her feet. "I will begin immediately."

Dani did the same. "I've cleared another counter space. Even Quinn's been on it for about eight hours. You can hardly tear him away. And the boy, too. They're both almost hypnotized by the relics. But he needs a rest. I could use Tasiq—"

"Pull him. I'll get Brown on the com," Rogers said. He glanced at Aronka. "Are you in need of rest?"

The Bellonan shook her head. "We are capable of remaining alert for three of your days. If you need me, I can continue."

"Why don't you tell Tabio to follow Dani to her office?" He stood up, a thoughtful look on his face. "I want him posted just inside the doors of engineering, unseen. I've got Jerome off the bridge, but if I move him again, he'll be suspicious. All of you will have to watch him. He must not sabotage the artifact reconstruction. I've got a plan in mind for our malcontents."

"And Eddy?" Liang asked.

"He's on a detail in the medical office. Easier to keep track of. Aronka can go watch him and the doctor. Dismissed, everyone. Good luck."

* * *

DANI, Liang and Aronka left the ready room and went to their assigned tasks. Sometime between the upper floor and lower level, Tabio joined them, fading from view before they reached the door. In engineering, they found Quinn and Halian studying the layout of all the artifacts, including several more pieces from the wrecked console on the bridge, which lay separately on Benzi's personal workspace. Most were blackened, seemingly ruined. No one held much hope that they would be able to function again.

All the same, they had once been a working model. The expectation was that if the crew could rehabilitate them somehow, they would be again.

Liang approached the two, studying the parts as Dani went to generate a stimulant beverage. "Where is Mr. Jerome?" she asked.

Quinn shrugged. "Ain't showed up yet after lunch." He walked around the table to get another view, hitching up his pants. He poked one of the long thin pieces into place.

The navigator deliberated over changes in the artifact layout since she had last been in engineering. Satisfied she had no questions, she nodded to Quinn and Halian. "You are relieved."

"Yes, ma'am," Quinn said without hesitation, before ducking into his office.

Halian trudged off.

Taking a deep breath before she began, Liang found Dani's attention focused behind her. The wild boy stood at Benzi's workstation, handling the burnt relics. Alarmed, she started to correct him, but Dani grabbed her arm.

"No, wait. Watch what he's doing."

Liang hesitated, but as she watched, the boy gently, reverently cleaned the sections with a stained white cloth, then studied them, turning them in his hands, letting his fingers rub, almost cherish the surfaces, taking in the essence of the object itself, his eyes closed.

With a start, Liang recognized the technique. It was the Seeing, an exercise Rodolphus had taught early in her education. One took an inanimate object in one's hands, feeling it, both physically and internally, understanding its characteristics, becoming the object. She had experienced this on many occasions and attempted in fact to understand the relics in the same way, but the gateway had not opened for her.

It has for this child.

The twisted bit the boy held began to resonate with a deep hum, the metal skin of it seeming to lighten by several color tones, the characters inscribed on it shading dark. Quinn left his office, datapad in hand, and started to reprimand the boy, but he stopped, staring in wonder.

"Sprechan's effing foot," he said. "What's the boy gone and done?"

Dani grinned, raising her cup to him. "Not sure, but I say we let him keep doing it! You're right, he's a genius."

Liang agreed. The captain wanted fast results. No one else had made this kind of progress. "Has he had access to the main table?"

Quinn shook his head. "I wouldn't let him, thought he might break something." He shrugged. "Not like one of the regular consoles, ya know. No replacement parts, and so on." He took a deep breath. "But there was this odd thing." He told them about the little scene he had discovered as the child was examining the artifacts on the table, eyes closed, much as he was now. "Can't imagine he knows the big picture."

Liang looked Quinn in the eye. "Can *you* make it work?"

The engineer's ego bristled, but he finally looked away. "Ain't been able to yet."

"Then we will see what this child can do. Simply because he approaches the puzzle from a different direction does not demean his inner map," Liang said.

"Yeah. The snapper here's got a way with mechanics." He smiled. "If you don't mind, ma'am, I think I'll take my break here. Don't want to miss anything, if you get my meaning." Quinn was uncharacteristically respectful, and Liang did not fail to notice it, as well as the hint of real affection in his voice when he was speaking about the child. He rubbed his forehead, then settled into the chair in his office, where he could see them through the windows. A few minutes later, Liang noticed that he had dozed off in his chair.

Liang declined Dani's offer of a hot drink, finding stimulation instead in watching the child at work as she joined him to study the artifacts on the main table. The young face was smooth and relaxed. He seemed to be in awe of each piece on the table, cleaning every one reverentially in sequence and setting it at a peculiar angle when he was finished.

"We'd never tried that," Dani said, watching from another console as she checked the engine upgrades. "Look how he's found a fourth edge to them, the way he's set them down."

Liang leaned closer to see them. "Fascinating."

A loud voice echoed as the door opened. Jerry Jerome walked in, yelling to someone passing in the hall. All eyes went to him, including those of the boy, who nearly dropped the piece with which he had been communing. Irritated at the interruption, Liang bit her lip. Somewhere in the room, she knew Tabio waited silently, observing, protecting.

Jerome balked at all the attention. "What?"

Dani pulled him aside, directing him to the life support console a level below. "Captain wants a diagnostic run on oxygen maintenance," she explained.

As Jerome was handled, taking a toolkit below, Liang studied the pieces before her. She turned them, examining to see if they could be angled as the ones the boy had handled. From the corner of her eye, she watched the table where the boy had set the newly polished pieces, studying his layout, and tried to set the pieces as he had. Once she turned them, however, the tentative design they had earlier come up with failed. The table became a pile of worn sections of foreign metals.

There must be some rhyme, some reason.

She walked around the tables, dimmed the light level. In shadow, the hieroglyphics stood out against their metal hosts.

Some moments later, she felt a presence at her elbow. The boy held several of the cleaned pieces in his hands. He set them on the edge of the table. Hands out in front of him, he stepped aside and closed his eyes. As he waved his hands over the pieces, they changed color. Liang could feel waves of heat coming off them.

The door slid open and Tasiq walked in. He glanced first to the table and the boy, then over to a point near Dani's upper level office. Liang saw nothing there, and realized Tasiq's feline senses were sharper than her own.

That must be where Tabio watches.

Liang beckoned the communications officer closer to see the boy at work. After several seconds, the boy suddenly opened his eyes. He reached out several times, very tentatively, as if he could not stop himself, but withdrew, becoming distressed. Mewling, he ran to his table, and then scampered into Quinn's office. He pulled on the sleeping engineer's sleeve until the man came out of the office, rubbing the sleep from his face.

"Ship on fire, snapper? What's up?" Quinn blinked at Liang quizzically. The boy grabbed his arm, pulling him toward the main artifact table. He stumbled along as the child seemed powered by something superhuman. "Somethin' goin' on?"

"I don't know. He was studying these pieces. Then he suddenly stopped what he was doing and went to find you." Liang watched, curious, as the boy pulled Quinn to the edge of the table and then waited. He pointed to the table and looked to Quinn, several times.

Half asleep yet, Quinn stared blankly at the child. "Speak up, snapper, will you?"

Fretting, the boy continued to point at the table, careful not to cross the plane of its edge with his hand while Quinn was standing there.

Dani looked down from above. "He told the kid not to touch any of that."

"Huh? Oh. Aye, I did." Quinn hitched his pants up, stepping over to his work table for a heavy work shirt, which he pulled over his shoulders. "D'you want to be responsible for anything he does to 'em?"

The desperation on the boy's face answered for her. "The captain said whatever it took. We'll try it."

"All right. It's your ass." Quinn shrugged and looked at the boy, gesturing at the table with an exaggerated nod, showing approval. "Go for it, snap." He stepped back, with an inviting hand pointed to the artifacts.

The boy heaved a sigh of relief that seemed to shake him to the core. He collected several pieces, a selection of those acquired by the team and those scavenged from the bridge console. He rearranged them on the table, three long and narrow, one short and angular, turning each to rest on the opposite edge from the one on which they had been laid. In proximity, their markings changed, the relics almost glowing from inside, as had the ones the child touched earlier. The three adults watched, spellbound, as the task they had tried to accomplish for weeks started coming together. Dani came down from the deck above, as fascinated as the others.

Focused on the action at the table, they did not see Jerome come up from the lower level, sneaking along the wall panels.

He grabbed for the edge of the workstation table and the boy. "You think by activating this, you will defeat Burko? He will kill all—"

Before any of them could react, a dark blur jumped over the upper level rail and knocked the young man to the floor. Quinn stepped in front of the boy, who had snatched up a large piece of metal, holding it in front of him. Tasiq pushed Liang aside as Tabio's reptile form faded into view, crouched over Jerome, a deep growl in his throat, claws at his chin.

"You will come peacefully with me, remaining alive only by what choices you make and your actions," Tabio said. Jerome's eyes widened. He gasped several times and then fainted. As he became sure the man was no threat, the Bellonan allowed his appearance to become human again. "Good choice," he said, coming to his feet.

Liang frowned. "Take him to confinement."

Tabio nodded once and tossed the unconscious man over his shoulder, walking out with him.

Liang returned her attention to the boy. "You are safe now." He blinked but did not respond. He looked up at Quinn.

Quinn held the last piece the boy had touched, running his fingers over the characters carved in it, as if he were reading materials marked for the blind. "Go back," he said. "Don't stop." When the boy just stared, he took the child's hand and physically put it on the pieces. "More. More!"

A little twitchy now, the boy tentatively continued his rearrangement of the artifacts, constantly glancing up, as if expecting intruders. He set the pieces in what seemed to Liang like a random order. As each connected, it lit from within. He moved faster and faster, setting them end to end and then stacking some, building in three dimensions.

"Yes, yes," Quinn encouraged him. "It's coming, snapper. Don't stop." He continued to caress the pieces, softly, their language becoming his, following after the boy around the edge of the workstation. "I can see it!"

Liang could feel an electric charge coming off the table. She held out a hand to experience the tingle. "Mr. Quinn? What is 'coming'?" *If something were to jump out of a newly opened interdimensional rift....*

Tasiq growled with an unpleasant twinge. His fur stood on end.

Liang's curious look drew a curt shake of the head and the felinoid moved back out of the way, tail twitching.

"The meaning. It's right. It's right." Quinn had his hands stretched over the table, like the boy. The movement had some effect on the pieces, the artifacts rattling against its surface like maracas. Quinn and the boys expressions were nearly identical, radiant and engaged.

"Benz, are you all right?" Dani's face reflected the same stunned concern that Liang felt at Quinn's odd behavior, as though he was possessed by the same spirit that motivated the boy.

Quinn did not respond. The charge in the room increased gradually until Liang could feel her scalp tingle, her hair standing on end.

Tasiq retreated from the table with a growl.

The odd feeling pushed the edges of Liang's personal comfort. They were dealing with an unknown force here, and she feared the situation was becoming dangerous. She activated her com-unit, paging Rogers and someone from medical to stand by, hardly able to transmit for the crackling of static.

"Mr. Quinn, please, perhaps we should wait for the—"

He shoved her violently aside. "No! No! He can't stop. Not now!" Quinn was mesmerized by the lights. "It's about to happen."

As Liang fastened her communications unit to her belt, a bright flash of amber light blinded them for a moment. They were all knocked back from the table into the wall. The deck rumbled under their feet. A sharp burnt odor was followed by the sweet smell of some warm climate flower. The smell and the light seemed diffused with joy.

Stumbling back to her feet, Liang watched in wonder as a holographic projection appeared in the center of the device, two meters high, able to be seen through the metals as though the device were transparent. The projected figure was humanoid, but asexual. It spoke in a warm baritone in a timbre which warmed Liang to her soul. The voice of Rodolphus, her dear teacher. But she could not understand his words.

Transfixed, the boy stared at the apparition. The projected golden light reflected off the faces watching, imparting a well being and harmony to them. Even the appearance a moment later of Okalani with her medical kit did not disturb the atmosphere around the device. Captain Rogers entered the main engineering room a few moments later, and stepped back, startled. "Liang? Report."

"The device is activated, sir." She knew it was an understatement. So much she did not know and was aching to learn from the voice, the dear voice. Then she noticed Quinn and she could not look away.

Benzi Quinn was standing before the midsection of the device, eyes fixated on the central figure, the amber light seeming to surround and embrace him. His lips moved, words which Liang could recognize, translating as the figure spoke. He understood. Quinn heard the words of the blessed forefathers. *We must have these words of wisdom.* She quickly reached for a recording device to capture the message.

Liang half listened to Quinn's recitation, absorbing the message. Quinn's lips moved softly, translating the story of the seeders of the galaxies, as they explained their hope for their descendants, the dream of peace. A life where each being could grow and live and love, relating to a larger family of others like themselves.

The words seemed to continue for many minutes, Quinn's voice underlying the tone of the speaker, and then the device suddenly went dark. When the amber light shut off, Quinn sank to his knees, exhausted.

"I know how to do it, Cap," he whispered. "I can save the day." The boy scrambled to support him as he collapsed.

CHAPTER 31

MYSTIFIED by Liang's frantic disrupted call, Rogers left Riviera Brown in command of the bridge and hurried down to engineering. Hardly stopping for the door to open, he stepped in and found the place transformed.

First, the eerie golden light that cast odd dark shadows on the walls. Half a dozen crew members stared, slack jawed, at a multilayered pile of rocks and metal on a worktable cobbled together by shoving several counters together. He recognized the parts as the collected artifacts, but he had never seen them in this configuration or condition before. The hieroglyphics on the sides of the relics were darkened, like charcoal outlines against the glowing mahogany of the artifact shells.

In the center of this pile stood a radiant figure, speaking to the boy, who stood directly in front.

No, not the boy. On closer observation, Quinn was closest, mesmerized, his lips moving in rhythm with the sound. Tas and Liang gaped, frozen, before the apparition. The captain approached the tables, and got a better look at the figure in the center of the relics. It was his Confederation school pilot's instructor, Captain Stuart Benjamin, his crisp tenor laying out what were obviously rules or terms, in some unintelligible gibberish.

"Liang, report!" Rogers barked, hoping to get some sense out of the one normally most sensible, but she just mumbled something about the device working and her attention faded back to the exhibition.

He was torn between shutting down the display, unsure if it might be hurting his people, and amazement that it was functioning. He did not even know where to find the controls. But the closer he got to the table his gaze was inexorably drawn to the mysterious figure, as Benjamin's voice continued to speak. Though he could not understand the words, he was convinced to the depths of his soul the speaker had only the best interests of everyone in mind.

Suddenly the projection grew fainter and disappeared. As the voice stopped, Rogers shook himself back to reality in time to hear Quinn mumble something about saving the day before his knees buckled, and he fell to the floor.

"Medic!" Rogers snapped. He turned to Liang as Okalani slipped past him to check Benzi Quinn. "So what's all this?"

"I recorded what I could," she explained, the peaceful expression not leaving her face. "I have never seen anything like this. It is not in Ramona's notes. Did this occur when you installed the device previously?"

Rogers shook his head, examining the structure more closely, now that it seemed safe, in its inactive state. The relics had returned to the inanimate brown and gray chunks and bits they had been previously. "Ramona had maybe a dozen pieces together in the console on the bridge. There were never any bells and whistles, not like this." He watched Okalani try to revive Quinn without success. The boy knelt beside them, his face a mask of dread as he hesitantly reached out to Quinn's unconscious body. "It had never functioned at all before that day, the day we crossed over. I had her load the final piece on a whim. We were desperate."

"This must be a complete device. Or at least complete enough to activate its primary programming." Liang walked closer to the table, holding a hand out near the metals. She explained what she had observed to the captain. "The lettering on the metal has faded now. Too, I can no longer detect the tingling electrical field. Apparently whatever message the device was meant to share has been delivered." She looked down at Quinn. "At significant cost."

The captain's face pulled into a scowl as he surveyed the damaged remnants of his crew. He had pushed them to make the artifacts function. *Maybe too hard.* His thoughts raced ahead as he watched Okalani work, with little success. "Review the recording to see what we can use." He dismissed Tasiq to return to the bridge, as Dani explained what had happened with Jerome.

"It was a good thing Tabio was here," she added.

"I was afraid he'd try something. I'd guessed this would be safer than the bridge, but I had no idea about this." He gestured at the tables. "Where's Hal?"

"He needed a rest. He should be back soon. Mr. Quinn was to rest as well, but he was otherwise distracted." She fiddled with the recorder, setting the time spot to play from the beginning.

Rogers rubbed his chin, thinking. "Now that Jerome's confined, Montgomery and Eddy may be suspicious when he doesn't come around or answer their hails." He frowned, considering what they could do to make sure Quinn got medical attention without alerting Montgomery to the new developments. "Aronka's watching them in medical. We can't very well send people there to become potential hostages or casualties. We can set up a makeshift medical facility."

"I volunteer my quarters," the navigator said quietly. "There would be little to disturb."

"I'm not sure that serves my purpose." Rogers walked around the device, studying its odd configuration as he waited for some word from Okalani about his engineer. "The boy did this? Unbelievable."

"Well?" he asked as Liang shut off the recorder.

"Nothing, Captain." Her face was puzzled. "I am sure I activated the machine correctly. It should have at least captured Mr. Quinn's spoken words, as he was next to the console. I understood what he was saying at the time, but the vision kept drawing my attention. But, listen." She pushed the button for playback and received only low grade static.

Curious. "Okalani?"

The resident looked over her shoulder, unsmiling. "His vitals are strong, and he seems physically sound. If I had to hazard a guess, I'd say he is suffering from information overload." She glanced at the device above her. "Whatever that was, it seems to have processed everything right through him at full speed."

"Do you think he'll remember what happened? At least what he said?"

"I have no idea. I can't even tell you when he'll wake up." She looked at the boy, clinging to Quinn's hand in desperation. "I think the boy's all right."

"Understood. If Quinn's the only source for the information, we need to keep him somewhere safe." He took his com-unit off his belt. "Aronka, report to engineering." *Quinn was going to hate this.*

When the Bellonan showed up a few moments later, he instructed her to take Quinn to the quarters she shared with Tabio, and ordered that either she or Tabio should be there with him at all times. He asked Okalani to stay as well, to monitor the unconscious engineer. "Take him, too," he snapped out when the boy protested the removal of Quinn.

"Yes, sir." Okalani called for a portamat. When the blue device, some two inches thick, was carried in by a corpsman, she laid it on the floor and she and Aronka loaded the unconscious Quinn on it. Activating the portamat, the control field formed into a hard surface, and she flipped the anti-grav control into life. The instant gurney rose to waist height, and she and Aronka guided the hovering device out into the hall and down to the Bellonans' quarters.

The captain turned to Liang, satisfied his orders were being carried out. "Time is short. I need you on the bridge."

She nodded and followed him, silent as space. On the bridge, a crisp tension resonated in the very muscles of each officer there, and was reflected on each face. Tasiq had taken his station again, and Riviera vacated the captain's chair as Rogers entered.

Rogers gave her a curt nod. "Thank you for minding the store. Current status?"

"Nothing new, Captain. Still at minimum orbit over the asteroid, no ships within one-hundred thousand kilometers."

He nodded. "You're relieved. Tas? Anything else?"

Tasiq shook his head. "Radio silence. Almost too quiet."

"Acknowledged." The captain sat down as Brown took an auxiliary tactical position. He had asked for her opinion of the Confederation. She made it clear it was Rogers to whom she gave her loyalty, not the fleet. He had chosen her, put faith in her, and she would stand by him, she stated. As a result, he asked her to sit on the bridge. *Another broken one saved,* he thought. *I need all the trustworthy officers I can get up front.*

Everything was ready, but their partner had not yet shown up for that final dance. So now they waited.

* * *

ONE issue still troubled Rogers: what to do with those crew members who maintained their loyalty to the Confederation?

He thought about it all that night, unable to sleep while he waited for the other shoe to drop. He would have to take action. At this point in time, execution of the three he knew, Heath Montgomery, Jerry Jerome and Parnell Eddy, and what others there would be, would be nothing less than cold blooded murder. He was not willing to consider such an alternative. Nor would he delegate that duty to others, though his new security officers would certainly be up to the task.

This mess is my fault. I'll handle the fallout.

He could abandon them on one of the planets, let them make their way as best they could. The men had skills that were marketable, they would survive. That was more appealing than killing them, but still stung his conscience. They were part of his crew, a crew that had counted on him to care for them and bring them home safely. Instead, he had brought them here, however unintentional it might have been. It was not their desire to remain. If he could bring them home, did he not owe it to them?

But how could he take them back without risking the possibility of being captured and court martialed? And it was not only him. The other rebels would hang with him. He owed it to those who had followed him not to endanger their lives, if it was not necessary.

The quandary kept him tossing on his hard bunk.

Shortly before dawn, he found a solution that would cost the *Doubtful,* but save his ethics. When they found Burko, he would load those who wished to leave in one of the slipcraft. Without weapons, the small vessel could not turn on the *Doubtful* in any way, but would support their needs until Burko could pick them up. They could return to Gilada with Burko and resume their lives. The rest could remain here, cutting all ties with their former existence. They would have to replace the slipcraft, but that was a small price to pay to retain their humanity.

Satisfied with that at least, there was no point in pretending to sleep any longer. He left his bunk and made a cup of the stimulant beverage to jolt his nerves into cooperation and readiness. He dressed in comfortable clothes, a bright shirt with blue flowers and dancing girls depicted on it, and well worn pants. No uniform today. He needed to be his own man.

When he finished, he took his cup to the observation deck. There he stood, as he so often did, before the glass and surveyed the stars. They were different stars than those he had grown up under, to be sure. But he knew they held the promise of a bright future. *If only....*

If only he had chosen a strong and good crew.

If only he could make Tommy see the truth about the Commander and the Confederation.

If only they could survive the inevitable encounter with Burko.

He had not yet puzzled out the correct approach to the battle. Every avenue he worked out to conclusion ended with the defeat of the *Doubtful,* baring some enormous mistake on Burko's part. He had known all along his ship could not defeat the *Talon,* even if it had been whole. Burko had the flagship of the fleet for a reason. And now he apparently had the support of the Agency.

Rogers had run some simulations that involved tricking themselves into an escape. But without damaging Burko's ship so they could not follow, it did not ring true. Burko would be determined, especially since the encounter on the planet. That had been a slap in the face, a challenge that would spur Burko on. Rogers pursued that thought to its extreme. Burko's ego might generate a mistake of such magnitude to allow defeat, but it was not likely.

Rogers also curiously awaited Benzi Quinn's return to consciousness. While Quinn's earlier words were normal for his boasting attitude, there was a different quality to them this time. The artifact device had made a profound impact on the crew who had been present. The same could certainly be true of Benzi Quinn.

He called Okalani for an update on her patient. She answered several minutes later, on her way to Tabio's quarters. "I'm sorry, Captain, I stayed as long as I could, but someone from medical was needed in the galley, and Dr. Montgomery was not available."

Rogers sighed. "I'm sorry you've had to be put in this position. But we've spoken about the doctor. I'm sure you understand."

"I understand just fine, Captain. I just can't be two places at the same time. Not yet, anyway. That's on next month's list of things to do. Take up cloning." A hint of amusement in her voice. "I'll update you in a few minutes after I see Quinn."

"Standing by."

Rogers looked out over the crystal towers of ice. It was a beautiful landscape, though unwelcoming. Other places they had been since crossing over were more suited for a place to call home. Marriel, for one. Rogers could not see himself as a farmer, but coming through on a business run, stopping for a drink with someone like Runyon from time to time, trading what they could, *that* he could envision. Even the city at Roandock with its traffic and mad fashions would be tolerable for a time. Any of it would be bearable, if he could spend most of his time here, on his ship. It was the one place he truly felt 'at home'.

His com-unit beeped. He answered. "Rogers."

"Captain, it's Okalani. Quinn seems to have slipped into a more normal state of sleep. He should wake within the hour. Otherwise he seems to have suffered no ill effects." She paused a moment. "The boy seems to be well, though he will not leave Quinn's side, even to get food. Nothing Aronka or I can say seems to get through to him."

"Then get him some kashi there. Alert me immediately when Quinn wakes. Whatever information he's got, I need it ASAP."

"Yes, Captain."

Rogers considered the possibilities Quinn might offer him. What could the aliens' words possibly teach of relevance to their current predicament? Granted, just hearing them had been soothing. But how could someone from that culture have anticipated a hundred years ago, a thousand, or more, that a ship using their technology would fall through into another universe? And that they would be in battle for their lives?

He could hardly believe that would be the case.

No point in speculating. Patience, Temms, patience.

Putting that decision aside until Benzi was awake, he walked onto the bridge for his morning update. Liang nodded in greeting and activated his monitor, which held the highest priority reports in order. Pleased and grateful, he seriously had to consider making her his first officer. Blending the command staff, some from this universe, some from the other, would shift the *Doubtful* further into unity.

Top of his list was a suspicious sighting of an unidentified ship on the very edge of their scanner limits, near Marriel. The ship hung in space, powered up but unmoving as if waiting.

Ah, Jal, could this be you, my never friend?

Rogers studied the data, wondering. The ID and registry markers were hidden from their scanners, but it was large enough to be the *Talon*. The captain felt his adrenaline start to rise.

Would this be the day?

His crew was brave and up to the fight. Without warning, his mind's eye skipped over the last six months in a horrifying flashback, saw the bridge again as it was on the day of crossover, the bodies lying in their own blood, the torn metal, the destruction. That crew had been ready for the fight as well, but he had nearly lost them all.

With a shudder, he covered his eyes, rubbing the image from his mind. He could not let the past cloud his preparation for the *Doubtful*'s next encounter with Jal Burko. Each moment had its related circumstances in time and space. That was then. Now there was a new horizon, a new crew. He had to hope for a new result?

"You need to sleep, sir," Liang said softly at his elbow. Her dark eyes were respectful, holding warmth he had not often seen there.

"I will, I will," Rogers replied in the same tone. "After we're settled. Still working things out, Liang."

She smiled. "We follow the path of reason. Trust in those who guide our feet."

"You mean I don't need that coney's foot any more?" He grinned, thinking again of the difference between Liang and his daughter Linz, who would have disintegrated under the kind of pressure they faced. *Although she did all right at organizing that whole wedding for 350 guests with a 12,000-credit wedding budget. Bet Liang would have some trouble with that one.*

Before he felt compelled to share the comparison with his navigator, he switched off his monitor and rose from his chair. "Keep an eye on that Bogey at vector 4G, I'm going down to rouse up Quinn. Maybe he really is the new Messiah."

Liang raised an eyebrow. "Messiah, Captain?"

"Messiah. An Ancients' word meaning savior."

"Even if Mr. Quinn has been given information that contributes to our survival, you will not tell him he is this…Messiah, will you, sir?" She paused, looking a little sheepishly. "There would be no living with him after."

Rogers laughed. He caught several other grins around the bridge, and a welcome loosening of the tension. "I'll keep that in mind, Liang."

Rogers surveyed the bridge once more, the view shaking his flashbacks, and left, stopping in engineering to order Halian to prepare the designated slipcraft for launch at ten minutes' notice with two days' supplies and a first aid kit. That done, he continued along the corridor until he announced himself outside the Bellonan's quarters.

CHAPTER 32

WHEN the door slid open, Quinn's raised voice, slightly hysterical, echoed in the background. Aronka smiled and stepped aside. "Your timing is impeccable, captain. Mr. Quinn has just joined us."

Rogers followed the noise. Quinn, seated on the edge of the bed, clutching at a gray blanket, was protesting that he did not want to be in the 'lizard's nest' under any circumstances. His strident tones were soothed by Okalani as she tried to convince Quinn that it had been Captain Rogers' orders to move him here for his own good.

The boy cowered under a small table, hands over his ears. Remembering Quinn's response to the boy in the medical office, he snapped his fingers. "Knock it off, Quinn. Look what you're doing." He pointed to the cringing child. "They were my orders. After all, you told me you had the answer for Everything. Would you have preferred I leave you at the mercy of any assassin who might be roaming the corridors?"

"I did?" Quinn looked confused, but did take in the boy's condition and calmed down.

"You said you knew how to save the day." Trying to curb his annoyance, Rogers sat on the bed next to the engineer. "I don't have time to play, Quinn. Something happened yesterday with that device. Hell, I experienced it myself. Captain Benjamin talking about something, some foreign language I couldn't decipher."

"Who's Captain Benjamin?" Quinn asked.

"My old flight instructor." Rogers shook his head. "Doesn't matter. That's not what you heard?"

"No, it wasn't a man. Couldn't really see the face through the mist, but I know it was my mother talking to me. She was tellin' me how the founders of the human race had traveled through many universes, leaving behind the seeds of what each race would become and clues for them to follow." He warmed to the subject. "They've watched the races come along, grow up, through pestilence and violence. They were so sad to see what all's become of their children. They wanted so much to see them succeed and be safe and at peace."

As the engineer spoke, his eyes watered, tears running down his cheeks, but he hardly seemed to notice. The boy inched closer, seeming to be drawn by the depth of Quinn's emotion. "But their children aren't at peace. They're fighting over inches of ground and religious beliefs and limited supplies. The Ancients have waited for millennia for us to show them we were ready to learn their ways, to evolve into a better race."

Rogers listened, but shook his head. "You know, philosophy is well and good, but I need some concrete answers. Liang tried to record what was said but the device apparently jammed the recorder. I have to know if it can help at all with our situation. Burko's out there, somewhere close, waiting to hunt us down. I don't think we can destroy him. That means he'll destroy us unless you can tell me something different."

Quinn seemed to be less belligerent, less defensive, but Rogers could not help feeling that pursuing help down this avenue was throwing his fate into a bitter wind. The man had not done a kind helpful thing without some guarantee of personal gain since they day they had met. "What can you tell me? You're the one who said you can save the day."

The engineer wiped his damp face with the edge of the gray blanket. "We've started the process somehow, Cap, by building the thing."

"Activating the machine notified them somehow? So now they're here?" The captain involuntarily glanced to his right and left, wondering if Benjamin would suddenly appear.

Quinn shook his head, beckoning the anxious boy to come sit next to him. He slipped an arm around the child in reassurance. Rogers was a little surprised to see Quinn show affection to anyone, but it was a pleasant surprise. "They're not *here*, not like that. Physically, they've moved on to other universes."

He eyed the captain. "But they know what you've done, how you've used their programming to punch through a rift. They know what you left and what's happened to the people on your side. The futile killing murders their sensibilities as the people you left behind have been murdered."

Rogers raised an eyebrow. "Quinn, are you saying these aliens are no longer here, yet they can interact with us as if they were?"

"Yes, Cap. I never run across anything like this, not even in my mother's church. They're, well, everywhere. Like God of the church, but not divine. Just human somehow, but good. Like all the bad qualities been washed from 'em." The engineer looked down at the boy and smiled. The boy returned the smile with shining eyes. "They want the killing to end."

"I'm all for that. Do they have any particular suggestions about how to stop the Confederation? Or even just get through this combat with Burko?" Rogers wondered if he was crazy to listen to the babbling of a man who had been unconscious after touching an alien device. *What next? Visit a psychic at Roandock? Have someone cast the runes or fortune sticks?*

But what choice do you have, Temms? It's not like you have a better idea at the moment.

"Give me a datapad. Quick!" Frenzied, Quinn searched for something to mark with, some compulsion bubbling up inside him. The boy moved closer as Okalani handed the engineer a datapad from her medical kit.

"It's not blank, but I think there's plenty of room on the disk," she said. She moved back, taking a chair near the door, standing by in case Quinn had another attack. Aronka moved in too, her posture guarded as she watched the engineer.

Oblivious to the attention, Benzi grabbed the small device and started typing into it, fingers flying. He went on for some time, the sound of the tapping of the keys the only sound in the room as the others nearly held their collective breaths in awe.

Several minutes later, he held the device out to Rogers. "There." The captain took the device. Quinn collapsed back onto the pillows. Okalani crossed the room in two steps to check him and bring him a glass of water.

Rogers looked over the information, but it meant nothing to him. There were scientific formulae and words in other languages and squiggles, diagrams he did not understand. "Will this disarm Burko's ship before he can attack? What does this do?"

Exhausted, Quinn leaned back onto his pillows and looked up at the captain. "It will stop the killing. It will disarm all the ships. It will bring peace."

"But what do we *do* with it?" Rogers asked.

"You'll know when. All you gotta do is plug the data into the ship's computer." Quinn stated, as if that was all the explanation needed.

Raising an eyebrow, Rogers looked back at the datapad. "We just enter this into the computer on *faith* that it won't destroy us? Do you know what this means?"

The engineer shook his head as though it weighed a hundred kilograms. "It was given to me, Cap. And now I've given it to you."

Rogers frowned, trying to make some sense of the gibberish as he dialed through what Quinn had entered. "I'm no engineer, damn my soul. Get me someone who—"

Quinn's gaze faded a moment. His body jerked upright, awkward. He spoke, but the voice was Benjamin's, as it had been in the engineering room the day before. The man's face seemed to reflect a soft amber glow, a warmth from deep inside. *Definitely not Quinn.*

"You were willing to take a chance once, even sacrifice yourself, to save an entire race, Captain Rogers. We see we have left our children far too long on their own. We cannot repair what damage has already been done by your people, but we can save others in the future. Your conscience is clear. Let your instinct guide you to wait until you have no other choice. Then activate this code and you will see the results."

Was this still Quinn? Or was he possessed? Just as it had the day before, the message coming to him in Benjamin's voice sounded right and reasonable as long as it continued. "Will it stop Burko? Will it protect others from the Confederation?"

"In ways you never dreamed." Quinn's face smiled with a relaxed confidence Rogers had never seen in his engineer. The voice started to fade. "Be well, Captain Rogers. You have been blessed." Quinn seemed to reflect the amber light for just a moment, then he slumped back onto the bed, eyes closed.

Okalani knelt next to the bed, scanning him, blonde hair hiding her face from the captain.

"Is he all right?"

"He needs rest. Did you get what you wanted, Captain?"

Rogers stared down at the datapad, oddly shaken the speaker had addressed him directly. "I believe so. I'll get this to Li—"

Before he could finish, he received an urgent hail from Windthorp on the bridge. The red alert signal blared out in the corridor simultaneously as the ship rocked. "Captain to the bridge immediately! We're under attack!"

CHAPTER 33

ROGERS clung to the walls on his way to the bridge, the shock of torpedoes connecting with the *Doubtful* nearly knocking him from his feet.

When he stepped out onto his command deck, he saw what he hoped never to see again: the *Talon* on the tactical viewing screen, its weapon ports glowing with heat. "Report!" Rogers snapped, taking his seat.

"Returning fire, sir! We've scored several hits, but our shields are weakening, Captain," Windthorp said, hands moving over his console board, making momentary adjustments as the readings fluctuated. "We've never—"

Rogers cut him off. "Hail them. Now."

Tasiq activated his communications board. "Standing by for response, sir."

"Hold them until I say so." The captain punched the intercom, formulating his words on the fly. "This is the captain speaking. We have a brief opportunity to reconnect with our fleet flagship, the *Talon*. Any crew members who wish to transfer onto the *Talon* with a better chance to return to our universe, meet at the hangar deck immediately."

He muted the broadcast for a moment, thinking, and then called engineering. "Hal, find Tabio. The two of you get the doctor, Parnell, Jerome, and whoever else wants that chance, into the slipcraft and get it launched. Now."

Holding his breath for a moment, he surveyed the bridge to see if anyone left. He had to give them the chance. Gratified to see that none of them even so much as looked up, he tossed the datapad Quinn had given him to Liang. "I want *that* ready to execute at my command."

The navigator nodded with a slightly puzzled look as she glanced over the images on the datapad. "This is what Mr. Quinn produced?" She dug in a drawer in her console until she found a cable to connect the datapad to her entry port.

"Yes. I just wish I knew more about what it does. He seemed convinced, or at least those speaking through him did, that this will solve our problem." He nodded to Tasiq. "All right, let's get this over with. Let me know when that slipcraft's clear."

Rogers watched the image on the central tactical screen take on the likeness of Jal Burko, seated, straight backed, in the raised command chair that disguised the fact his height fell short of average. His sallow jowls were well padded, though he was not obese, and his graying hair was shaved nearly level with his scalp. Burko wore the dark maroon Confederation dress uniform, his left shoulder spattered with ribbons and commendations. *Pretentious bastard. He's got to know that doesn't impress me. He must be trying to buck up his own courage.*

Burko's eyes widened just a bit as he recognized Rogers. "Well, well. Face to face at last with the traitor. You're looking shabby, Temms. I hate to see a Confederation officer looking shabby."

"Then put your mind at ease, Jal. I'm not a Confederation officer any more."

Rogers studied his opponent, stared into that hard emerald gaze, knowing this man had sent so many others to their deaths on missions Burko himself would never have taken. He preferred the glory to the action. All those commendations were bought with someone else's blood.

"You certainly haven't behaved like one, I'll give you that. Shameful what you did at Persios. Shameful." Burko clicked his tongue in disappointment and checked a black jacketed monitor beside him. "Your little rebellion caused a great deal of damage, did you know?" He looked up, his smile without warmth. "Six major ships of the Fleet destroyed, including the *Whirlwind* and the *Victory*." He shrugged. "Of course the *Victory* had gone renegade too, like you. Not a great loss to our fleet."

Rogers carefully controlled his face. All this time he had wondered if the *Victory* had escaped through the rift with them, and it had never left Persion space. He gave a silent prayer for the forty four souls on board, including his long time friend and captain Darien Pomeroy. *Sleep well. I'll have your revenge.*

"Is that it?" Rogers asked.

"Isn't that enough?" Burko let outrage fill in the corners of his voice. "Over two hundred killed. Twice that injured. Worst, you pulled us along with you into this primitive and hollow star system! One hundred more left homeless by your treason." Burko's voice took on a deliberate calmness. "But you, Temms… you managed to escape. Your kind Doctor has been quite generous with information about exactly how much damage you've suffered."

His eyes glittered. "And how considerate you were to provide your officers with purely factual information about how that damage occurred. Did you really think that men trained by the Confederation would believe such lies?" Burko's hand tightened on the arm of his chair until his knuckles were white.

"I'm not going to debate my command decisions with you." Rogers glanced at the small monitor mounted to his chair and saw updated readiness reports flashing across the screen as the minutes went by. The ship was as prepared as it was going to be.

"You always were an arrogant degenerate."

"Me!" Rogers was up out of his seat before he could stop himself. *Calm down, you need a clear head, damn him.* Making a show of walking forward to examine Windthorp's readings, he counted to a hundred, and then to a hundred again, not trusting himself to speak until he could swallow his hate.

Nodding to Kai, he returned to his seat, tapping into the teachings he had received from Liang. *Mind controls breathing, breathing controls the body. The mind is the wind, free to fly over the water. The breath is water, which ebbs and flows. The body is the rock, the solid, that which ties us to earth. The wind blows the water, making currents which move the rock. Breathe in, breathe out, let my mind be the wind.*

When he looked up at the screen again, he had regained his dignity. "So go home."

Burko growled. "Not before we repay you for what you've done." He looked around Rogers' bridge. "I see you've taken on new crew. I hope they're prepared to die with you today."

"The only one who'll die—"

A confident smirk grew on Burko's face. "We have friends here, Temms. Powerful friends. They've agreed to help us, for a price." He tapped agitated fingers on the arm of his command chair. "I just haven't decided whether they can have your ship before or after I wipe the rest of the traitors from it."

Rogers cleared his throat, determined not to allow himself to crawl down to Burko's level. "So you've struck up ties with the Agency. Like attracts like." He looked at the screen, finding no trace of the black ships. "Aren't they coming to help you?"

"I wanted to finish you off myself. I don't need help to dispatch one damaged ship of traitors." He lounged even farther back in the chair, the epitome of condescension.

Rogers was interrupted as Halian signaled his task was completed, the small ship launched. *One more task to pay the debt he owed to those who had served him well.* "About that, Jal. I've sent several loyal officers out on a slipcraft, including Heath Montgomery. They want to return to Gilada. None of them were aware of or participated in any rebellion activities, and they should not be punished for what I've done. They're on their way to you now. I will hold hostilities until you can retrieve the craft safely."

Burko looked over his shoulder as someone spoke to him. The sound was cut off for a moment, and Rogers took the opportunity to glance over to Liang. Her slender fingers tapped the keys of her console, processing the data from the datapad Quinn had filled.

"Does that make any sense to you?" Rogers asked softly.

"The data has been accepted by the computer." She indicated the button that would put the program into play.

"Stand by." Rogers turned to look at the screen again. He directed his own small monitor to find a shot of the slipcraft easing away from the *Doubtful* into the open space between the two ships. *Best wishes for your future, my former comrades.* He wondered how many of those below had joined Montgomery. Drenching emotion cold as ice sloshed over him as he realized Tommy would be among them. He had not even been able to say goodbye. Rogers fought a flashback to their last conversation, but still heard the disappointment and hatred in his son's voice. *He'll be better off at home. He can hate me from there and maybe, just maybe, I can forget how much it hurts.*

Confident he had done the best he could by those in the slipcraft as they reached the halfway mark, he turned his attention back to Burko, who had added an overconfident smirk to his unpleasant expression.

"Temms, I'm surprised at you. Do you really think I would welcome aboard an officer who has been disloyal to his captain? One who would divulge secrets? How would I know whether I could trust him with my own back, hmm?" Burko lifted his hand, glancing to his right to catch someone's eye.

"What do you mean? The slipcraft's not armed. This isn't a trick!"

"I can't be sure, can I? Remember we thought *you* were our friend at Persios," Burko said darkly and gestured to his gunner.

Rogers jumped to his feet. "Burko! Don't!" His words choked his throat as an orange light sliced out from the *Talon* to cut the slipcraft in half. The atmosphere inside the small ship leaked out as white vapor. Flames quickly snuffed out as they were exposed to the vacuum. "Tommy," he groaned. A gasp of horror went around the bridge, those closest to the captain overhearing him. Rogers doubled over, feeling this new loss like he had been punched in the gut.

He was not even prepared to send Tommy back across the rift, but in a split second to see his life just over, wasted by this insufferable sociopath of a captain? Rogers' heart pounded so hard he felt the pressure in his ears, and he wondered if he would blow a blood vessel.

"You bastard!" Rogers turned away from the tactical screen. "Shut that monitor off!" he snapped. From the corner of his eye he could still see the smoking slipcraft fade from view as the secondary screen went black.

He needed a minute. Hells, he needed a whole lot of minutes, but he doubted he had more than a handful.

Think, damn it, think.

He was furious. He had tried to do the right thing. *The right thing.* And Burko turned the kind gesture to ash, just like he did everything, just like he had intended to do to the Persions. Surely this last act had earned him whatever the ancients had in store.

"Scan for survivors," he said over a voice so thick with emotion he could hardly speak.

Tasiq cleared his throat. "Captain, the Commander on the com."

Did he care? Not very much. He would not give the man the satisfaction of seeing Rogers' grief. "Audio only."

"Yes, sir." He punched in commands, and a moment later, Burko's voice came over the unit.

"Having disposed of your peace offering, I now proceed to finish you. I hope the Jeffin hounds are waiting for you when you arrive in the third hell, Temms. I pray they rend your traitorous flesh for eternity!"

Enough.

He turned to Liang. "Survivors?" he asked again.

Her eyes held tears. "I'm sorry, Captain. Nothing."

He nodded once, sharply. *So be it.* "Gentlemen, it's time. Fire!"

Rogers returned to his chair, activating his small monitor. As the weapons launched, he both heard and felt their power as the *Doubtful* trembled. Trembling with righteousness, he watched as streaks of laser fire and several torpedoes lanced toward the *Talon.* Most were repelled by the *Talon*'s shields. The *Talon* returned fire, easily twice what Rogers' ship could send back. Their lives were probably saved by Windthorp's evasive maneuvers. He kept the ship moving in an effort to conserve what shielding they still had, rolling the shields forward as the *Talon*'s attack took its toll, its weapons fresh, its personnel not stretched so thin they were nearly opaque.

"Captain, I don't know how long I can hold out. We're at thirty five percent—"

"Keep firing!" Rogers grabbed his keyboard, and typed quickly, pulling up a few of the scenarios he had simulated on the computer, finding nothing that matched current circumstances.

Windthorp never looked up from his console, his voice weary. "Yes, sir."

The captain sensed the unity around him, the bridge crew prepared to follow him to the end, now that they had seen evidence of the icy blood of the man commanding the other ship, the meaningless death of the doctor and the others. He could push them until they destroyed Burko. Until they were destroyed themselves.

But is that our goal now?

He had lost his colleague, the doctor he shipped out with ten years ago. He lost those young men, their fresh young faces that once looked at him with such hope. And most of all, he lost Tom.

When is the loss enough?

This isn't about Burko any more, Temms. This is about your crew, the ones who have survived. You have a duty not to waste their lives just to satisfy your ego. The remembered rational tones of Captain Benjamin resonated along his emotional thermometer.

We have a choice.

Barely reining in the boiling anger urging him to revenge, he closed his eyes as the ship rocked with a torp hit. "Liang, I think we've reached the point the aliens meant. Execute." He opened his eyes in time to see Liang push the button. Then everything slowed to a crawl.

Burko's image vanished from the tactical screen, replaced, in default, by the outside view of space. A wormhole similar to the one they had seen at Persios appeared near the *Talon*, a seething tunnel of red gas and swirling flame.

The audio link to Burko's ship remained open, so they heard the *Talon*'s bridge crew's panicked yells.

We've lost the main drive!

Weapons are off line!

Weapons don't even register!

Helm is not responding!

We're being pulled in, Commander!

Screams followed the sound of lasergun fire. Burko bellowed orders to stabilize the vessel, to return fire, to do anything at all, at his hapless crew, but it seemed to be in vain.

Nothing's responding! Commander, what do we do?

Burko had to be in a state of panic. Rogers could imagine his frantic effort to regain control of his ship, his situation slipping through his fingers.

When you've lost control of the ship you're in command of, and you are under attack but have not weapons to fire back, when you're staring at your own death and destruction, do you signal for surrender?Doubtful, and this is why....

Rogers could not speak for Jal Burko, but he knew the other man would never surrender, even to save the lives of his crew. He would rather go down in flames. *And it looked as if he would.*

The *Talon* yawed violently, lurching toward the bright red, spinning hole in space. Rogers looked at Liang with a raised eyebrow. "Are we catching any of that?"

She shook her head. "No effect on the *Doubtful*, Captain. We appear to be out of range."

Rogers nodded. His gaze returned to the main screen. His body, his heart, his soul faded to a numbed state as the *Talon* was sucked into the wormhole, which exploded into a hail of stars.

CHAPTER 34

AFTER the screaming from the *Talon* ended in that blaze of color and light, silence settled in on the bridge of the *Doubtful*. Rogers let that silence settle into him as well, filling the emptiness. He was alone again, yet not alone. He had this crew.

Gradually the sounds kicked in again, the constant rumble of the engines, the beep of the communication console, the quiet voices of Brown and Tas and Liang and Windthorp, the normal sounds of a world that seemed increasingly far from normal. He could not just stay there, inside his head, as much as he wanted to. *I've got to face them.*

He stood up, feeling more capable on his feet. "What damage did we take?" he asked.

"Some structural damage to the hull, but nothing breached. Looks like the starboard weapons array took a hit," Windthorp said.

Rogers took in the words, considered them. "Injured?"

Liang tapped on her board a moment. "Okalani reports she's seen eight crew members for minor injuries."

Okalani. Because Montgomery isn't there any more. A stab of guilt. *Get a grip on yourself.*

"I want an accurate count on the number of crew that were on that slipcraft," he said.

A moment of silence. "Captain, your son?" Liang asked.

He fought the nausea down. "Liang. You have your orders."

"Yes, sir, I'll contact Halian," Liang promised.

Rogers took a deep breath, let it out slowly. *Not now. Keep your mind off it.* "Do we have any idea what the alien tech did? Besides open the rift again?"

Liang studied a printout from her console, her head cocked as she read. "When activated, the transmission altered the *Talon*'s power feed in some way. But it did not just cut the power. Somehow it sent a command into the *Talon*'s computer to deactivate all knowledge of weaponry and set a course for the ship. The ship was on remote control, presumably that of the Ancients."

The captain tried to wrap his mind around that concept. "They sent it across the rift?"

"The machine constructed from the artifacts commandeered control of their ship. They were unable to stop themselves from being returned to their own space." She frowned. "But it's gone now. I cannot locate the rift or even find a trace that it was here."

Riviera Brown stretched her shoulders, pointing a finger. "That bein't all, Captain. Whatever the Ancients did to the Talon was in nature of a virus It will spread. Any Confederation ships that come in contact with the Talon and share a computer interface will be affected as well."

Windthorp eyed them over his shoulder. "But that will be all of them."

Rogers nodded. It would be all of them. The entire Confederation would be effectively shut down. No planet would be in danger from them again.

"We've saved the Persions, once and for all," he said, the irony of his inadvertent success eclipsed by his loss. "I'm going below to see who else we lost." He felt their regard heavy on his shoulders as he walked off the bridge. Halian had loaded and sent the slipcraft into space. He would know who Rogers would have to replace.

He stopped at his office to compose himself. Concentrating on business gave him something to hold on to, a focus. He made a ship wide announcement that Jal Burko and the rest of his fleet were gone, and he broadcast the section of the ship's records that showed what Burko had done to the innocents on the slipcraft. *Let everyone see just what they had escaped.*

Then he went in search of Hal.

The closer he got to engineering, his mere footsteps seemed to drag. Somehow, the difference between knowing and *knowing* became almost a physical pain. *Hiding from the truth won't serve you or the rest of the ship, Temms. One surgical strike and this will be over.*

He entered engineering, no one even noticing at first. Dani pored over something on her desk on the level above. The wild boy was studying the artifacts, still in their constructed combination, though now in their natural, plain state. Why had not Benzi given the kid a name, anyway? Where was Benzi? The captain cleared his throat.

In a moment, Dani left what she was doing to hurry down the metal steps to the main level. "Everyone all right on the bridge?" she asked.

"Everyone on the bridge is fine." He stumbled over what else to say, and finally just asked for Hal.

"He's down on the lower level supervising some repairs."

"I need to see him."

She studied him a moment, then laid a hand on his arm. "I'm sorry about Dr. Montgomery," she said. "He was a good man."

"They all were good men," he said, a knot pulling together in the center of his chest. *Some of them were hardly men at all....*

Excusing himself, he took the shortcut through the engineering corridor to the lower level. The sound of metal clanging on metal and the smell of burning solder led him to the starboard section. In light of the turmoil that the ship had been through, he announced his approach, figuring it might save Hal and his team from taking a shot at him if they were surprised.

"Working over here, Captain."

Rogers continued around the corner, the sight that greeted him, vaporizing the air in his lungs. It was not the size of the patch the team of four had placed on the wall, or the pile of debris they had discarded on the floor that stole his breath, but the members of the repair team. *One in particular.* Staring at him, balancing the hind end of a drill on his shoulder, was his son Tommy.

The shock actually sent Rogers back a few steps, into the wall.

"Captain?" Halian's rough face displayed concern, and he came closer to catch the captain's elbow in his thick hand. "You're hurt?"

Rogers could not take his eyes off Tommy, whole, unharmed, *here.* "H-How? "I thought...I thought...." His throat closed with tears that also blurred his vision. He could not stop their flow.

"Thought what, Dad...Captain?" The young man's face reflected uncertainty that increased as his father's emotion boiled over, beyond control.

Leaning against the corridor wall, Rogers fought to remain upright while his knees threatened to give out. "Thought you were...the Confederation loyalists, I thought they went on the ship, and Burko...." Confused, he looked to Halian. "Who did you put on the ship?"

"Doc went, and two ensigns. Security man and science woman." He snapped chunky fingers. "Cannot think of name, but chaplain trainee."

"Sampson," Rogers said, almost idly. "But Tom made it clear he intended to follow the Confederation line." He glanced at his son, who hung his head. "Why didn't you go?"

"I was going to. I went to the hangar with Jerry and the others, but...I don't know. I couldn't leave the ship. The time I spent alone locked up, gave me time to think about what you said, what you had done."

Halian let go of Rogers' arm as he seemed to get a little steadier on his feet. "Maybe should leave you to talk."

"No, Hal, it's all right," Tommy said. "I can say what I have to say in front of you."

There it was, the edge in his voice. Tommy might not be angry, but he had not let go of the fight. Remembering their last conversation, the captain considered what it would be like to live on this ship, his son's hate and disappointment a daily steeping brew he would have to soak in.

It's all right. No matter what he does, what horrible accusations, or condemnation, I can take it. Any punishment he can hand out, I'll accept it. He's standing here in front of me. That's all I care about.

"Whatever it is, Tom, we're here as father and son, not captain and crew. Say it."

The others looked away, scuffing their feet against the deck, in varying states of embarrassed discomfort. Tommy sat down the drill, a heavy clunk against the deck, and stood tall, his feet slightly apart, somewhere between attention and parade rest.

"When you took that last assignment before you and Mom split, the one that lasted three years, I knew you'd gone on purpose." He paused, took a breath in, let it out, glancing at the ceiling a moment. "I thought you'd thrown yourself into your work. Mom thought you'd gone after Ramona. I—I didn't believe Mom. I knew you were a good officer. I knew you believed in what you did. In what the Confederation did. You brought order to the universe."

He took a step closer, but hung back out of reach. "I imagined you on the bridge of this ship, setting life right for peoples everywhere, making important decisions that changed the worlds, meeting new races to be gathered in to join the Confederation. I was so proud."

His right hand closed into a fist, before relaxing. "That's why I applied to the Confederation school, even when Mom said she'd disown me if I did. I wanted to belong, too."

"Even you weren't happy that I joined up. What was it you said? That I shouldn't 'waste my time' on the military. You wanted me to go into industry. Thought I'd make a lot of money there and establish roots, the kind that tied your feet to a planet so you'd never leave."

Tom's lips curved into a sad smile. "You know what they say about the Confederation school, that it empties you out and fills you up again. I wasn't the same person when I got out, but neither of you saw it."

Having invited his son to speak his heart, Rogers heard the pain and rejection his son shared, feeling his feet sinking in emotional quicksand.

True, he had not been happy with Tommy's choice. But by then he had started to become disillusioned about the Confederation and its 'goodwill mission'. He started to speak, but Tommy cut him off.

"Let me talk this out. I need to say this. I came here, like I told you, to see what kind of man you were. I wanted to know that you lived up to that ideal I had of you, that perfect leader and inspired commander. And I thought you were. Until I found out about the lie. The big lie."

Tommy looked away then, chewing his lip. His eyes blinked rapidly, chasing away tears. "I thought you were the worst kind of traitor." He shook his head. "I couldn't believe you'd fire on your own fleet, killing men you'd served with for all these years. I even tried to look it up in the computer records to see if I'd heard wrong, or if Eddy was lying to me. But there weren't records. Damaged in the fight…maybe." He cocked a brow in his father's direction. "Or hidden by a guilty party."

Halian shifted his bulk, moving closer to the repaired wall. "Tom, you not understanding—"

"No, that's where you're wrong. I'm understanding very well." Tommy walked up to face his father. "Once I cooled down enough to think, in the cargo bay, I thought about what you said. How you told me the truth. I know I didn't like it, and I sure didn't want to hear it. But you know, it fit with my picture of you on your bridge, doing what was right."

"After I saw what Burko did, blowing up the ship with the others on it, I knew your assessment of him was right, too." His voice caught, and he looked into his father's eyes. "If you hadn't stopped me, given me that time to think, I would have been on that ship. I wouldn't have been able to say that I was sorry I didn't trust you. Or that you're exactly the kind of captain I'd want to follow. Exactly the kind of father I thought you were and I always wanted you to be."

His heart breaking and rebuilding itself all in the same moment, Rogers did not need to hear anything more. He crossed the short distance between the two of them and pulled his son into his arms. His whole world became the touch of his son's body, alive and whole, something Burko and his like had not been able to take from him. He was hardly aware as Halian took the others and their tools and slipped away. He had his son, and his son had him, and they had a new life to face together. Nothing doubtful about that, in anyone's scenario.

CHAPTER 35

"LIANG! Are you ready to go down yet?"

Rogers, comfortable in a well worn and beloved tropical print shirt in shades of blue, checked over the several bottles and a wrapped gift he needed Liang to carry. His hands were full with the box of fresh meat steaks he had bought from Oke Runyon that morning. Time to relax.

Six months after their Ancients inspired battle with Jal Burko, the *Doubtful* had set down at Marriel for a very special occasion. Rogers had bought seven day rights to the property where they had first landed, the day he found Liang. It was high summer, the fields were lush and green, and Marriel was reasonably safe. The captain wanted his people to have some fresh air, enjoy the sun and forget their duties for a few days. They had earned it. To Temms it seemed right to return where they had begun.

Life is better played in full circle.

He checked the time. The others would be gathering outside, and he wanted to get to the party. "Liang! Have you lost your way?"

The slim girl hurried in from the bridge, walking a little taller now that Rogers had named her first officer. "I wanted to set the watch," she chided. "What shall I take?"

He indicated the stack, balancing the box in his arms. "Let's go! The ale will be gone!"

She smiled. "Yes, sir."

"No 'sir' today. Call me Temms." Pleased, he led the way down through the empty halls to the rear hatch. "We must be the last ones aboard!" Stepping out into the sun, he looked up in the sky, seeing it clear and free of enemies. There would be no more threat from the Confederation. The Agency ships, deprived of their ally and his promises of technology, had moved on without further contact, well aware that, even damaged, the *Doubtful* outgunned them on every level.

Though somehow I don't think we've seen the last of them.

Quinn's analysis of the data and subsequent attempts to restart the artifact creation had been fruitless. The true purpose of the Ancients, now that they had intervened in Rogers' life, remained a mystery. Rogers did not understand the scientific and religious implications, and he was not sure he needed to. What he did understand was that his people were safe, and they were happy. Especially today.

"The captain's here!"

Rogers heard Okalani's voice over the general hubbub. She came running toward him, huge smile on her face indicative of the personal interest she had showed since taking over medical. At first, she had couched her demands on his time in purely professional mode, but lately, she made it clear her intentions were much more personal. He gestured with the box, showing his hands were full and he did not need her hanging on his arm. She was pleasant enough, but he still had not fully grieved for Ramona.

I don't need that sort of complication. Not just yet.

From the hatch, he could see the entire crew camped out in their green field, tables and chairs all around. At the head of one table were Tabio and Aronka, in their human form, standing before a large wicker basket. He made his way there, directing Liang to hand out the celebratory bottles to various crew as he went. The gift, a set of polished warriors' swords, he presented to Tabio.

"Now you'll be able to play fair in the ship's fencing competition." With a grin, Rogers looked into the basket, seeing a writhing dark skinned lizard about half a meter long. There was no soft baby blanket, but a piece of leather about a meter square and several bits of what appeared to be animal skin that looked well chewed. "Congratulations! You've done it. It's a...." He stared at the growling infant for a few moments, puzzled.

How do you tell, exactly?

"A female, Captain." Tabio smiled. "And now the ceremony."

The olive skinned man slapped his hand on the table. When all had quieted down, he lifted the small lizard from the basket and held her up for all to see. He spoke in a tongue they did not understand for several minutes as the little one twisted and yowled. He finished with a bone-chilling cry that made Rogers glad he was not holding anything metal, for he might have been shocked.

"Child, wear thy name well!" Tabio cried. "Your name is Chandi."

The *child* did not appear very impressed at the announcement, as is true of most infants at such ceremonies. The others raised their glasses in a toast, and Tabio bowed his thanks at the applause and well wishes, before they returned to what they were doing. Rogers stayed a moment longer, gratified by the success of this small family.

"Thanks to your kindness, Captain," Aronka said, "a dream we've long held has come true." She smiled and caressed the squirming baby. "This offspring will grow up free, not bound in slavery to the Consortium or anyone else. She will choose her own life."

"A noble plan. I'm pleased to have had a part in it. Well done." Rogers smiled again and clapped Tabio on the shoulder, moving on as Liang quietly murmured good wishes behind him, leaving the box on the table with the other gifts.

Rogers' gaze scanned the area. Riviera Brown dealt cards on a round table in the shade, taunting Dani, Halian and several others as they laid out ante for a game of abril. Rebuffed by the captain, Okalani had retreated to the shade of a large deciduous tree to join Kai Windthorp and Rogers' son Tommy, who whispered something that made her smile. Tasiq lay curled up on a blanket in the sun, sleeping like any cat.

Finally, the captain grinned as he saw Benzi Quinn and the boy he had named Monty, slightly apart from the group, kicking an oval ball back and forth. Quinn shouted encouragement as the boy scored and laughed. The change in his engineer, began after his communion with the Ancients' machine, and had continued. Rogers had seen him blossom, his demeanor less abrasive and paranoid. The boy, too, had healed greatly in the intervening months with proper nutrition and the keen interest of the other members of the crew. Though he had not yet recovered speech, he had developed a sort of sign language to express his needs. His bond with Benzi Quinn had grown thick as an Old Country accent.

None of them remained untouched by the events of the day the machine had come to life. The Ancients had blessed them. Temms and Tommy had released their quarrel, sending it with Burko back across the rift, leaving that life behind forever. The crew had built connections, making it a family. Even Liang.

He looked across at his new first officer standing near the table where the rest were playing cards, offering advice. Where once she had been afraid and misused, now she had grown, secure because her valued place in their small universe was defined.

Pride glowed in him. He well knew his own part in the growth of each of his crew, so many, like himself, not simple cogs in a machine, but complex beings with motivations or circumstances they had to work a little harder to overcome. He had chosen well.

We all do our parts. Whatever sun is overhead, whatever sky we sail, it's why we survive.

Thankful for his life, Temms Rogers started for the main table. "All right, my friends! It's a celebration! Who's hiding the ale?"

THE END

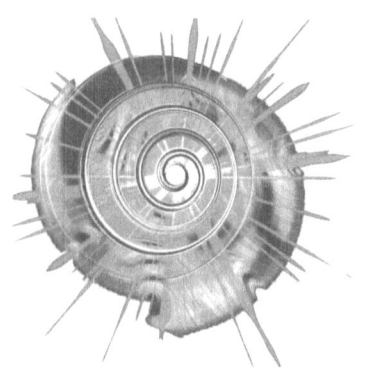

About the Author

Lyndi Alexander dreamed for many years of being a spaceship captain, but settled instead for inspired excursions into fictional places with fascinating companions from her imagination that she likes to share with others. She has been a published writer for over thirty years, including seven years as a reporter and editor at a newspaper in Homestead, Florida. Her list of publications is eclectic, from science fiction to romance to horror, from tech reporting to television reviews. Lyndi is married to an absent-minded computer geek. Together, they have a dozen computers, seven children, and a full house in northwestern Pennsylvania.

Publications include:

Clan Elves of the Bitterroot
(Fantasy series in order):
THE ELF QUEEN (Book 1)
THE ELF CHILD (Book 2)
THE ELF MAGE (Book 3)
THE ELF GUARDIAN (Book 4)

Horizon Crossover Series
(Science Fiction series in order):
HORIZON SHIFT (Book 1)
HORIZON STRIFE (Book 2)
HORIZON DYNASTY (Book 3)

Science Fiction Novels (single titles):
TRIAD